SHADOW & STORMS

HELEN SCHEUERER

SHADOW & STORMS

AN EPIC ROMANTIC FANTASY

THE LEGENDS OF THEZMARR
BOOK IV

For my readers...
Don't let the world – don't let <u>anyone</u> convince you that you're not
enough.
Only you define your story.

Dorinth

Delmira

Thezmarr

The Mourner's Trail

The Bloodwoods

Hailford

The Chained Islands

Darenth

The Broken Isles

Ciraun

Naarva

The Scarlet
Tower

The Veil

The Veil

N
W ⊕ E
S

Notos

Tver

Aveum

Vios

THE MIDREALMS

PROPHECY OF THE MIDREALMS

In the shadow of a fallen kingdom, in the eye of the storm
A daughter of darkness will wield a blade in one hand
And rule death with the other

When the skies are blackened, in the end of days
The Veil will fall.
The tide will turn when her blade is drawn.

A dawn of fire and blood.

CHAPTER ONE

WILDER

When Wilder Hawthorne came to in the cold, damp cell of the Scarlet Tower, his first thought was of Thea: fierce. Unflinching. *His.*

'We don't say those words again until we're on the other side. Until we can say them Warsword to Warsword,' he had told her, the warrior who had stolen his heart and soul, who had walked into the swirling mist of the Great Rite to face her fate and the Furies themselves.

She would light up the midrealms with her storms, and the thought comforted him as he rolled onto all fours and dry retched over the wet stones. The oppressive magic of the Scarlet Tower pressed down on him, making him dizzy and nauseous. The proximity to the sea and the Veil left everything wet. The cell stank of rot. There was no window to hear the crash of waves beyond, or taste the briny air.

The sounds of the prison changed with each passing moment. Sometimes there were a thousand prisoners just outside his cell, desperately clamouring for something, the noise overpowering. The next moment it was as silent as a graveyard. Worst of all, there was no way to tell what was real and what was a figment of his imagination, or some illusion woven beyond the confines of this wretched place.

Goosebumps rushed across his skin as he realised he'd observed the same thing before. How long had he been in this cell? How many times had he woken with the same thoughts, the same physical reactions? There was an eerie familiarity to it.

Manacles rubbed his wrists and ankles raw, treated with a recognisable form of alchemy; a more potent rendition of what Wren had concocted. Once, he'd been able to break iron chains with a simple brace of his body. But not here. Not now.

The restraints rattled as Wilder shifted stiffly to a sitting position, resting his bare back against the sodden wall, the sensation cold and shocking against his fevered flesh. He had been stripped of everything but his undershorts, including his shitty armour, though he couldn't remember when he'd been relieved of his weapons and clothes. He couldn't remember the journey here at all, only that he'd been so crazed with the effects of the arachne venom that he'd almost prayed for death. He shuddered at the memory of the monsters creeping towards him and Thea, a grotesque fusion of spider and human and darkness. One had sliced his forearm open with its pincers, leaving a translucent film of poison behind, burning him from the inside out.

The only thing that had stopped him wishing for his end was Thea, and the longing to see her again, as the Warsword she was always meant to be. For he knew in his bones that she would emerge victorious, Naarvian steel in hand, vows of vengeance on her tongue.

And that she would come for him.

The thought dragged a hoarse laugh from his chapped lips, the slight motion causing his body to seize in several places. The arachne venom hadn't killed him, but the acute pain in his kidneys and ribs told him that he'd been handled roughly on the way here.

Bruised, but not broken, he mused bitterly, for he knew they wanted him whole to experience the nightmares of this gods-forsaken place. And there would be many.

A sour taste lingered on his tongue and his gut was tight with hunger pains. He couldn't recall the last time he'd had food or water, not that he was sure he'd be able to stomach them now.

The bars of his cell were made of jagged rock, and beyond them, he could see the shadows of guards moving closer...

'Get up,' spat a poisonous voice.

Wilder did no such thing.

The door to his cell swung inward and two enormous howlers clamped their meaty hands around him, hauling him to his feet. They were bigger than the cursed men that roamed the midrealms, their voices stolen and replaced by blood-curdling howls, their forms mutilated by shadow magic. He lashed out, but his blows met only air – another horror of the tower: no matter how hard an inmate tried, there was nothing they could do to defend themselves against their keepers.

As Wilder was dragged from his cell, fighting with all his might against his chains and captors, he wondered if he'd been drugged. He'd surely been through this before. In a daze, he recognised the twists and turns of the thick stone walls, and the links of iron that wrapped around the structure, shifting and clicking as though they had minds of their own. He glimpsed the rows of cells; some empty, some filled with humans and monsters alike. Every pair of eyes he met was deadened, as though whatever had existed inside was long gone and all that remained was a husk. Wilder himself had put some of these creatures here. Now he was just another inmate alongside them.

He grunted, his already aching body barking in protest as he was thrown into another cold, dark cell, utterly indiscernible from the last, save for the bolts of lightning scratched into the wall. He'd been here before.

They liked to do this, he recalled. Move the prisoners from cesspit to cesspit, with no rhyme nor reason.

'Give him another dose,' that same poisonous voice said.

Definitely drugged, then. Wilder staggered to his bare feet, his palms and knees stinging where they'd scraped against the rough stone. He peered through the darkness, spotting a familiar gemstone nasal piercing. The inquisitor from Harenth's dungeons.

'Got a promotion, did you?' Wilder taunted thickly.

Bronze bangles chimed as the man in question gestured to someone Wilder couldn't see. 'Make it a double,' he ordered.

Wilder tensed, waiting for the impact of a dart, the slash of a poison-laced knife, to have his head forced into a barrel of liquid and held under – all things that seemed distantly familiar. What he was not expecting was the whisper of sickly-sweet breath washing over him like a wave.

It threw him bodily into an onslaught of nightmares and memories entwined, so visceral that he could taste the metallic tang of blood on his tongue, could smell the burnt-hair scent of the reapers, could feel the weight of his swords in his hands once more.

4

Wilder didn't know where one horror ended and another began, only that he knew every moment intimately. Slowly, agonisingly, he lost track of how many times he watched Malik break across the white rock at Islaton, or how many times he heard Talemir's scream as the reaper's black talons pierced his heart.

At least a hundred times he cradled Thea in his arms, begging her to drink his Aveum springwater, to heal the claw marks in her chest as shadows coiled around her body, draining the life from her.

A hundred times more he walked through his hometown of Kilgrave, or the burnt remains of it, tasting ash in his mouth. Horses screaming in the blazing stables. His parents lifeless and charred beyond recognition in the dirt.

A myriad of images plagued him with no reprieve. He saw the pleading eyes of the shadow-touched before he plunged his blade into them, over and over, until it wasn't the gaze of strangers he met, but Talemir's hazel stare, going wide beneath the carving motion of his swords.

Wilder watched as healers peeled away the bloodied bandages from Malik's swollen face as he thrashed beneath their hold, upsetting tables and trays, knocking assistants off their feet, bellowing in pain.

Wilder's memory took him to his own Great Rite – the red-hot slash of blades through his own flesh, the snap of bones and the blunt impact of trauma to vital organs. He couldn't breathe. There was no air to be had, no fight left in his ragged lungs. He felt every blow again and again, each more vividly than the last.

He cried out as the pain and images compounded. A broken body and a broken mind – that was their intent: torture at its finest.

And just when he could take no more, just as he considered cracking his own head upon the stone to make it stop, he was shown something else. Something good.

His cabin.

Home.

And Thea waiting for him inside, a simple band of fine silver on her fourth finger, a smile on her full lips.

'There you are,' she said.

He wanted to acknowledge that he knew this wasn't real, but couldn't bring himself to speak, to break the reverie. For any moment with her was a blessing, real or not. He fought the lump in his throat, wanting to say those words they'd denied themselves before she entered the Great Rite. What if it was now or never? What if he never saw her again? As the Warsword he knew she'd become?

He clawed at his neck, a ragged gasp escaping him as he realised that these moments of reprieve from the violence and memories were designed to break him just as much as any pain.

Icy water rained down on him, his chains rattling again as thick hands clamped around his arms once more.

Everything was distant – the flickering torchlight, the terrified screams, the fetid smells, the rough handling – as though it were happening to someone else far away. This time, when Wilder was dragged from one cell to the next, he understood the husks staring back out at him from behind the stone bars, for they looked how he felt: hollowed out, a fragile shell of what had come before.

When he was thrown into a new cell, as dank and wet as the last, he didn't fight, didn't get back up. He sprawled there across the stone, rebelling against the voice in his head that told him to stand —

Until he saw a pair of eyes blinking at him from the darkness.

Still strung out and disoriented, Wilder scrambled to his feet, raising his fists, meaning to use the manacles as a weapon.

But his cellmate made no move to attack. Instead, he moved into the dying torchlight and said, 'You don't remember me, do you?'

CHAPTER TWO

THEA

Through ribbons of darkness and bursts of lightning, Althea Embervale glimpsed the vast tempestuous sea and the forlorn island emerging from the mist below. It was no ordinary isle, no common landmass, but rather a place that existed on the fringes of the Veil, where the Scarlet Tower protruded like a shard of bone through flesh.

Wilder. Wilder was somewhere in there.

She was going to get him out, and then unleash a reckoning upon those who'd held him captive.

Thea's boots hit the black sand with a soft thud. A great pair of wings beat once, twice, before dematerialising behind the famous Warsword at her side.

'This is probably a trap,' Talemir Starling offered, scanning the jagged shore around them.

'Probably.' Thea didn't take her eyes off the dark tower in the distance, resting her hand on the hilt of her sword as she absorbed the uncanny energy toying with her power, hinting at an otherworldly force. 'Does it make a difference?'

There hadn't been much opportunity for strategising as

they travelled, nor had Thea had the chance to test her newly won Warsword strength and agility. They had flown through clouds and walked through shadows, but it hadn't been fast enough. Every second Wilder spent in that place was a knife to her heart.

Talemir's dark power flickered, as though he sensed Thea's impatience, and felt the strange presence permeating the island. 'Fuck no.'

'Good.'

They left the shore behind and made their way through the dunes, waist-high grass brushing against them as they moved. The screams and shrieks of howlers and wraiths echoed across the foul place.

Wilder's former mentor, and the man known as the Shadow Prince, turned to Thea, shadows swirling at his fingertips. 'Shall I?'

Without a second thought, she nodded. 'I think that would be wise.'

Darkness bloomed around them and a cloak fell in place. It matched the lay of the land, but offered something warmer, kinder: protection. Hope.

'Stay close,' the shadow-touched Warsword told her. 'They can't tell the difference between our brands of darkness. We should be able to walk right up to the perimeter undetected.'

Thea simply nodded and matched Talemir stride for stride. It was still surreal to think that the man who walked beside her was the dual wielding champion of Thezmarr, the warrior whose records she'd revered in the trophy room of the fortress all her life.

You're truly here to help me break Wilder out of the Scarlet Tower?' she had asked him on Aveum soil two weeks before.

9

'I can't do it alone. And nor can you,' he had replied.

And so here they were together, ready to take on the Scarlet Tower, and all the monsters within it. Warsword strength itched at her fingertips. With the way she was feeling, she could crush a wraith skull with her bare hands. The thought was bittersweet, for she'd won the Great Rite and achieved what she'd always wanted, only to have lost something more precious when she emerged.

As they trudged through the dunes and beyond, that Furies-given strength flowed through her freely, dancing with her magic that was *begging* to be unleashed upon the festering spit of land and the tower on the horizon. The weight of her Naarvian steel sword at her belt was profound, which was just as well, because she was going to use it to cut through every fucking creature who stood between her and Wilder. Man or monster, they would find no mercy at the tip of her blade, not this time, not ever.

'It's darker here...' she murmured. 'Because of the proximity to the Veil?'

It was the closest she'd ever been to the towering wall of mist that surrounded the midrealms, the barrier that had once supposedly kept the monsters *out*, but now seemed to be their gateway *in*. She could feel its otherworldly power, and the call of the realms beyond it.

'The whole world is this dark now,' Talemir told her. 'For a time it happened bit by bit, day by day, but now? It's been like this for a long time. And it will be forever, unless we do something about it.'

Thea gave a nod. The Shadow Prince was an expert in the darkness that plagued the midrealms. As a part-wraith – or *shadow-touched*, as they liked to be called – he'd somehow managed to master it, to cloak not only spies and rescue missions, but an entire part of Naarva, hiding it away from the reapers and their ilk.

Around them, the grass thinned out, revealing a swampland ahead. Thea covered her nose and mouth with her hand, her face wrinkling with disgust. It was a wretched expanse of rancid waters and twisted vegetation. The air hung heavy with the stench of decay and death, an eerie fog shrouding the landscape in an ominous grey haze. A boardwalk carved through it all, winding around the reeds and boulders.

'Think we can trust it?' Thea asked.

Talemir scoffed. 'No. But cloaked in shadow? Perhaps.'

'I'm game if you are…'

'I don't think we have another choice.'

'You could fly us closer to the gates?'

Talemir shook his head. 'I have zero information on what types of wards are set up around that thing. Matching shadows with shadows is one thing, but I won't risk us and our mission against defences I know nothing about.'

More ear-piercing shrieks sounded from the monsters beyond, echoing across the murky waters.

'Fair enough,' Thea said. 'Through the swamp we go.'

Cloaked in darkness, they started over the boardwalk trail. Thea's eyes fell to the marker in the near distance: a sinister monolith, a single spire, hewn from the rotten heart of the island itself – the Scarlet Tower.

'It looks like a lone turret.' Talemir's voice was low. 'But from what we've learnt over the years, there's a sprawling underground network of dungeons and chambers as well… There's no knowing where they're keeping him.'

Thea's strength radiated from her, and despite the strange ache that plagued the ragged scar at her wrist, she felt stronger than ever, ready to take on whoever she damn well needed to. No one, not a reaper, not the King of Harenth, not the biggest fucking monster in the midrealms, was going to stop her. But as much as she wanted to storm the place, she knew they had to be strategic.

'I couldn't bring reinforcements,' Talemir murmured. 'The rest of our forces are gathering to fight, and with the war ahead, we had no one else to spare.'

'Save for you...'

'They weren't exactly happy with me leaving when I did. But I'd never leave Wilder to this fate.'

'He should never have been here in the first place,' Thea replied, her breath catching as she spotted specks of light dancing among the reeds. She felt a sudden longing to follow them off the boarded path. The beautiful specks of light pulsed, beckoning her, promising something wonderful ahead —

A muscled arm linked through hers. 'Don't even think about it,' Talemir warned.

The sound of his voice snapped Thea right out of her trance. 'What the fuck...?' she muttered, staring after the lights that bobbed away from them.

'Might not have fangs and claws, but those things are just as deadly as any monster,' Talemir said. 'Will-o'-the-wisps, folk beyond the Veil call them. They're known for leading travellers astray with false promises of sanctuary.'

'What do the travellers get instead?'

'Nothing good.'

Thea watched with a shudder as they disappeared into the tall fronds of grass. 'I'll bet.'

She and Talemir continued through the marshland, arms linked beneath his cloak of shadow. When she wasn't focused on the steady rhythm of their boots hitting the boardwalk, Thea could hear the murmurs of long-lost souls echoing through the fog – perhaps those poor folk who'd followed the will-o'-the-wisps. Their voices created a haunting symphony as the pair crossed the swamp, one that chilled the very marrow in Thea's bones.

Talemir flinched, and she knew he was hearing them too. 'The closer we get, the more they sound like people we love,' he told her quietly. 'Don't let them fool you.'

Sure enough, the voices started to sound familiar. Wren. Cal. Kipp... All of them calling out to her, beckoning her towards the dark.

'Thea...' came the voice she longed for the most. Deep and melodic, the call of home.

Wilder.

'Thea,' he called again.

She tightened her grip on her sword and forced one foot in front of the other, ignoring the chorus of suffering that echoed across the marsh, the water rippling in its wake. It was a nexus of pain and darkness, a glimpse of what the world would be like under the rule of King Artos and his reapers. Here, the boundaries of reality were blurred, and the very air was tainted with the sorrow of those imprisoned in the tower beyond.

It only made her more determined. She would do everything in her power to stop this from becoming the fate of the midrealms, but she refused to do it without Wilder.

For him, the world would wait. And when he was safe at her side, they could watch the whole fucking thing go up in flames to be reborn anew.

What was it the prophecy said?

A dawn of fire and blood.

At last, Thea and Talemir reached the spiked iron gates of the tower. The space beyond was swarming with howlers, wraiths and arachnes.

They crouched in the brush on the edge of the marshland, watching, waiting. Thea could feel the wrongness of the place crawling under her skin, and upon closer inspection, she could see the shimmering telltale sign of wards blanketing the tower.

'You were right not to fly straight in,' she said.

'Don't tell my wife,' he replied. 'That was her warning.'

Thea raised a brow. 'Maybe you should have sent her instead.'

Talemir snorted. 'Don't tell her that either. She'd wholeheartedly agree.' He turned his gaze to the fortifications of the tower. Not only was it swarming with monsters, it was surrounded by a moat, its entrances guarded by iron-clad sentries bigger than Malik.

'Any ideas?' Talemir asked.

'One,' Thea replied, and she launched into outlining her plan.

When she was done, Talemir stared at her for a moment before finally saying, 'He taught you well.'

'He did.'

'He got that from me, so really, *I'm* the one we should be crediting,' he added.

'Or blaming, when it all goes to shit,' Thea retorted.

'Or that...'

Undetected beneath the shadows, both Warswords studied the tower, and the wraiths circling its peak. They watched the guards change shifts, once, then twice, tracking the rise and fall of the weakened sun beyond the dark clouds, and the rotation of the rest of the monstrous crew.

'Not many people trying to break in, I'll wager,' Talemir said quietly, as the guard changed for the third time.

'I've always revelled in going against the grain,' Thea told him, palming Malik's dagger with a twirl of her scarred wrist.

'That from the Rite?' Talemir asked, nodding to the marred flesh there.

'Yes.' Her response didn't welcome further questions.

Instead, Talemir handed her something round and compact, covered in a scrap of cloth. 'Don't let this touch me,' he said. 'But it might come in handy once you're inside.'

Thea turned it over, struggling to see any discernible markers in the dim light. 'What is it?'

'An explosive of sorts... Made with the substance we're protecting in Naarva.'

'Oh?'

'It will only affect those with darkness in their veins, so you and Wilder won't feel anything, but anyone touched by a reaper or its curse... They'll be disarmed at the very least. Better still if they disintegrate upon impact.'

'But *what* is it?' Thea insisted. If she was going to be throwing around something that did that kind of damage, she needed to know.

'It's made of sun orchid essence,' he explained. 'It's the natural repellent to the reapers' darkness. My wife, Drue, discovered it years ago. We'll tell you everything else you need to know when we're back on Naarvian soil.'

Thea nodded. That would have to do. And she'd take anything that gave her an edge against the wretched monsters ahead. 'Thanks.'

'Just don't fling it at me,' the Shadow Prince quipped.

'Noted.'

Thea let her gaze fall back to the tower of horrors before them, and the swarm of creatures around it. Wilder was somewhere in there. Her heart ached at the thought.

Talemir nudged her. 'He's going to be alright, you know,' he said. 'He's got the strength and courage of a thousand men.'

Thea didn't need Talemir to tell her that. She knew exactly the kind of man Wilder Hawthorne was. She let her increased strength surge through her, awakening her storm magic. 'You know what else he's got?'

Talemir waited.

'Me.' Thea didn't tear her eyes from the lone tower. 'We're coming for you, Wilder.'

CHAPTER THREE

WILDER

W hoever's voice he'd heard in the dark, it didn't matter, because suddenly all the cell gates opened, and barbaric pandemonium ensued.

In the centre of all the cells was a pit, designed for one thing and one thing only: carnage. Wilder found himself thrust into a violent free-for-all, mostly naked bodies clawing and punching at one another, teeth sinking into flesh, screams echoing up what seemed to be a miniature amphitheatre where gore spilt across stone like waves breaking upon sand.

And Wilder lost himself in it. Fists swinging, he broke jaws and ribs and arms, blood splattering hot and metallic across his bare skin, across the other prisoners. His opponents were barely human now, if they ever had been, and that only made it easier to rain blow after blow down upon them in the haze of madness. He relished every impact, every split of his own knuckles.

Screams for mercy didn't register. Cries for help fell on deaf ears.

Wilder half expected that when he closed and reopened his eyes, the swarm of bodies would be gone and he'd be alone in his cell once more. Only that didn't happen. Husks of prisoners poured from dungeons and chambers he couldn't see, and he kept swinging, tasting blood as he ripped people apart with his bare hands. He devolved, became his baser self, an animal, a killing machine.

The Hand of Death, they had once called him.

And he was here to deliver.

It went on for hours, or so it seemed. He welcomed it, welcomed the kiss of violence, the song of endings. Whether it was real or not, he didn't know, only that he was at the heart of the bloodshed, and that was where he belonged. Countless bodies, man and monster alike, were piled up around him, their blood slippery underfoot. By the end he was bathed in it, his skin slick with black and red warpaint.

Panting, he realised that the amphitheatre had grown quiet.

There was not a sound in the whole Scarlet Tower but for the blood dripping onto the stone from his clenched fists.

Wilder staggered. The wave of violence, *his* wave of violence was over, and it settled around him like a heavy weight. He collapsed against a column, sliding to the blood-soaked floor. As the shock ebbed away, he felt the keen pulse of pain in his chest and the sting of the cuts across his knuckles, noted the blurred vision of his left eye as it started to swell shut.

He gasped through the sharp stabbing sensation across his ribs. He couldn't put a face to the blow that had potentially cracked a bone. In fact, he couldn't recall a single face from the brawl at all.

With his one good eye, he stared out at the pit.

It was empty.

Though the bloodstains remained.

Wilder rested his head back against the column, breathing through the fire in his chest and cursing the manacles at his wrists and ankles, his skin shredded beneath the iron there.

That voice from his cell came back. 'You don't remember me,' it repeated.

Wilder peeled open his good eye. The man before him was practically a skeleton in rags.

'Should I?' he rasped. Gods, what he would give for some water, mind-altering substances within it or not.

As if reading his mind, the man pressed a tattered waterskin into his bloodied hand and helped him lift it to his lips. Cool water cascaded onto Wilder's cracked lips and parched tongue. He nearly moaned as it soothed his throat.

'Perhaps not,' the man said. 'I didn't look like this when you put your spear through my cloak and detained me in the Great Hall of Hailford...'

Frowning hurt Wilder's face, but his brow creased anyway. 'Who are you?'

His new companion gave a hollow laugh. 'I'm the man who tried to poison King Artos... The man you and the would-be shieldbearer condemned to this place.'

Somewhere in the back of Wilder's mind, realisation dawned. *Crushed Naarvian nightshade,* Thea had said in that hall, pointing at the blue stains on a nobleman's fingers.

The man now watched him intensely. 'The name is Aemund.'

Artos' voice came back to Wilder. *'Well, Aemund... You*

19

have a choice... You can choose death... Or you can choose the Scarlet Tower.'

'Death,' Aemund had choked out. *'I choose death.'*

Wilder remembered how King Artos had studied the man, a predator sizing up its prey.

'Take him to the dungeons. Interrogate him. We need to know who he is working with. Then, he goes to the Scarlet Tower.'

'No! Your Majesty, I beg you —'

'The time for begging has long passed, Aemund.'

That had been over two years ago. Wilder focused his blurred vision on the figure before him. Aemund looked utterly ravaged, thin skin hanging off his bones, deep purple circles beneath his eyes. His hands shook at his sides and his knees knocked together, but he seemed alert – haunted, but not quite a husk of his former self, not like the other prisoners.

'You've been here all this time?' Wilder managed.

Aemund nodded. 'I'm the last new prisoner who has survived what they do here.'

Wilder blinked, his swollen eye throbbing. 'How?' From what he remembered, the man before him had been an oily-haired nobleman, not a stoic warrior.

Aemund didn't answer. Instead, he stared at Wilder. 'My guess is that if you're in here, you couldn't beat him either.'

'Who?'

'Artos. Had you and your shieldbearer not interfered, neither of us would be here now.'

Wilder spat blood on the stone, thinking back to that time at Harenth. The irony was not lost on him that he'd lectured Thea about actions having consequences. Here they were. He had helped detain this man, and now they were cellmates in the Scarlet fucking Tower.

'They say this is where they send the monsters of the midrealms, but it is their birthplace,' Aemund told him.

'Is that so?' Wilder wiped the blood from his beard with the back of his hand. 'I'd say monsters are born everywhere nowadays, wouldn't you?'

'Not like this.'

'No?'

'I'll show you, Warsword. Then you can see how far wrong you've been led your whole fucking life. Are you coming?'

Strangely, there were no guards patrolling the pit, no reapers or wraiths or howlers lashing out with their shadows. The prison was quiet, disturbingly so.

Grunting in pain, Wilder got to his feet, disoriented and suspicious. 'Apparently I've got nothing better to do. Lead the way.'

Wilder limped after the nobleman, waiting to be wrenched from some kind of illusion, expecting to wake, curled up and shivering, on the cold stone floor of his cell. But no such thing happened as he followed Aemund across the red-and-black-splattered floor of the amphitheatre. Dazed, he stayed close behind the strange man, trailing behind as Aemund made his way deeper into the tower, which now seemed barren of all life.

Did I kill them all? Wilder wondered abstractly as they passed empty cell after empty cell. Or was it another mind game? Another trick to make him think he was going mad? Blood still coated his fists, his body, but whose?

'This way,' Aemund called, taking an iron spiral staircase, down, down, down.

'Why should I trust you?' Wilder paused on the threshold of another level. 'I'm the one who put you in here...'

'There's nothing I can do to you that they can't do worse, Warsword.'

'Even so... If I hadn't interfered in the palace —'

'I'd have ended up here anyway. I wasn't cut out for espionage.' He motioned for Wilder to follow.

Seeing no other option but to be forced back into a cell, Wilder did, grimacing with each step as his injuries flared to life with new pain.

Aemund led them to a laboratory. There, they lingered in the unguarded doorway. Torchlight illuminated the horrors within: twisted instruments and arcane contraptions gleaming in their silver trays. More than anywhere else in the prison, the air here reeked of iron, sweat and piss, and Wilder saw why. Prisoners were chained in the corners, huddled together, their gazes hollow, their bodies emaciated, their whimpers drowned out by the screams from distant chambers. There were bodies strapped to tables as well, and the intention became crystal clear: experimentation.

Wilder didn't dare breathe. He saw several alchemists at work, dressed in masks and leather aprons, injecting writhing bodies with shadow magic. Before his very eyes, ordinary men became howlers, their screeches echoing off the prison walls as they thrashed against their restraints.

'The birthplace of monsters,' Aemund said without feeling. 'This is just the beginning.' He gestured to the corridors leading away from the laboratory, where within the grim confines of twisted iron bars and moss-covered walls were more poor souls awaiting horrific fates.

Wilder stared. The Scarlet Tower was full. Once, it had been reserved for the vilest of criminals from across the midrealms, but looking at its numbers now, that was certainly not how it had been utilised of late.

Ignoring the throbbing pain in his ribs, he started forward. 'We have to —'

'Help them?' Aemund scoffed, grabbing his arm. 'There is nothing left of them to save, Warsword.'

He led them to another chamber where, to Wilder's shock, he spotted his own Naarvian steel swords on display in a glass case. He moved towards them, but Aemund gripped his arm again, his grasp slipping over Wilder's blood-slicked skin.

'Another stupid decision. They are trophies of war. Just as you are, for now.'

Wilder swallowed, watching the figures he'd originally thought to be alchemists at work on tables and benches. They were no such things. They were creatures of darkness – not howlers, not quite, but they too had once been men and women, and now their eyes matched the clouded blue of the reapers.

'Why are we here?' he said, his skin prickling. 'How are we here? Why are they letting us see all of this...?'

'Men become monsters in this place.'

Aemund's voice sounded distant as every pair of clouded blue eyes snapped up and latched onto Wilder.

His blood ran ice-cold. There was a gleam in those gazes, brimming with a sense of foreboding, of hunger.

But even in his current state, shying from a fight had never been who he was. He dug deep. Despite the magic of the tower suppressing his Warsword power, despite the injuries already covering his body and the heavy manacles at his wrists and ankles, he let out a roar of rage and charged at the creatures.

Tables and instruments went flying, as did their attendants. With his bare hands, he vowed to do as much damage as humanly possible, to dismantle every contraption, every vile apparatus. Unlike in the pit, he did not lose himself; every strike resonated with his own fury, his own desperation for the destruction of the torture chamber. He pummelled them with fists and with the irons clamped around him. He was a whirlwind of rage, leaving a trail of carnage in his wake. He would destroy every inch of this festering place from within, so the bastards couldn't inflict their curse on anyone else. He would ruin them all, then he'd escape – he'd get to Thea, to the rebel forces, and tell them of all that was happening here, that it needed to be burned to the fucking ground.

Aemund forgotten, Wilder didn't stop. With a primal cry, he crushed skulls, strangled creatures with his chains, slit throats with discarded scalpels. Darkness leaked from broken vials and tanks, but he didn't care. He had faced worse, and would do so again before his time was done. More trays and glass bottles went flying across the room, shattering into a million shards —

A single person's applause rang out across the space.

Wilder whirled on his feet, not feeling the broken glass beneath his soles, or the wounds from the previous brawl that had worsened. Panting, he spied the jewellery-clad inquisitor of Harenth's dungeons in the furthest doorway, and beside him a robed man he didn't recognise, whose face was contorted in a smug smile.

Wilder heard Aemund's intake of breath. 'That's the Archmage of Chains,' he whispered, cowering as the man in question came forward, his eyes not leaving Wilder's heaving form.

'Aren't you something?' the Archmage said, an eager lilt to his voice.

Wilder took a step towards him, ready to wrap his hands around his throat —

'I like your tattoo,' the man said unexpectedly, that oily smile still on his lips. 'It's not often I see scripture of the ancient tongue of the Furies...'

'What do you know about it?' Wilder growled.

'*Glory in death, immortality in legend,*' the Archmage of Chains recited, his eyes sparkling in the torchlight.

An icy talon raked down Wilder's spine, exactly where those words had been inked: a vow and a motto he and Malik had lived by, now sullied by the vermin before him.

'I'm glad you've shown us what you're capable of, Warsword,' the man taunted. 'You'll become a legend among monsters.'

Several powerful, invisible hands grabbed Wilder, and he struggled against their grip, horror dawning.

They had meant for him to see every nightmare imaginable within this place. They had wanted to witness his strength against all odds.

The Archmage of Chains smiled as he revelled in Wilder's realisation. 'You will be our best creation yet... A general of darkness in Artos' growing forces. A weapon of our own making...'

Wilder thrashed against his manacles and his captors, against the horrific fate that awaited him as they forced him down onto a table.

Darkness swallowed him whole.

CHAPTER FOUR

THEA

Thea was restless, but she didn't take her eyes off the
towering monolith casting long shadows across the
desolate landscape. Day and night were barely discernible; it
was the guard change that marked the passage of time, and
Thea was more than ready to spring into action. They had
waited and watched long enough. Somewhere in there,
Wilder was suffering, and she wouldn't stand for it a
moment more.

'You ready?' Talemir asked, shadows dancing in his
palms.

'I was born ready,' Thea replied, faint sparks of lightning
crackling at her fingertips in kind.

'You need to be careful with how much magic you use...'
the older warrior warned.

Thea nodded. 'I'll only use a little,' she reassured him. 'It
knows him, so will be able to scope out where he is and alert
him that I'm coming.'

Talemir frowned, gauging the distance between their
hiding spot and the gates of the tower for the hundredth

time. 'If they discover who you're after, they'll know it was you. No doubt Artos already suspects your loyalty lies elsewhere. And if you use too much storm magic, any remaining cover you have will be blown. They'll know that the heir of Delmira and Althea Zoltaire are one and the same. The world will know exactly who you are, and who's important to you.'

Thea centred herself, letting her Furies-given strength interlock with her power, fuelling her from within.

Strong of mind, strong of body, strong of heart, she reminded herself.

'Then the world will know that if they hurt him, I'll burn them all to the ground.'

Talemir nodded. 'So be it.'

Wrapped in his shadows, they passed through the gates, past the trio of wraith guards undetected. Talemir's power was born of this place, and like recognised like amid the darkness.

But his disguise couldn't cloak lightning, and so when the pair reached the drawbridge that lay across the moat to the tower, Talemir turned to her.

'Don't get yourself killed,' he told her, his wings flaring at his back.

'Likewise.'

With that, the shadows vanished, and Talemir Starling launched himself skyward, the ultimate distraction for the wraiths circling the peak of the tower.

Thea had never seen anything like it – a shadow-touched Warsword battling monsters *in midair*. He was cloaked in midnight, his membranous wings unfurling with each mighty beat, carrying him effortlessly through the swarm of wraiths. He brandished twin blades of Naarvian steel, twirling them amid the shadows, cleaving like a comet through the night. Talemir's movements in the sky were a symphony of precision and predatory prowess that she recognised in her own style. With a roar, he spun, bringing both blades together, and a series of wraith heads and hearts fell from above, splattering to a bloody pulp on the stone.

The chaos overhead brought many wraiths from the tower, each one shooting into the sky with a screech, their shadows surging for Talemir.

But the older Warsword didn't fight with steel alone.

His own shadows lashed out at the enemy. He became a whirlwind of onyx power and deadly blades, his dual wielding mastery blurring the lines between sword and shadow.

As another wave of wraiths stalked from the tower, their attention latching onto the pandemonium that ensued above, the diversion offered Thea a window of opportunity. She slipped across the drawbridge, over the moat's murky waters. Ripples marred the surface below and she felt the same strange luring sensation from the bog: another enchantment, another illusion to pull her off course and to her demise.

Shadows roiled overhead as Talemir kept his battle airborne, but Thea's focus was singular: *get Wilder out.*

When she reached the end of the drawbridge and approached the entrance to the tower itself, she faced three howlers with a sinister smile of her own. For the first attack, she didn't bother to unsheathe her Furies-gifted blade. Instead, she marvelled at her newfound abilities, finally able to test their limits.

There were none. Not yet, anyway. It had never been so easy to move like a warrior, to inflict damage. With her fist clenched, she punched through the rotten flesh of a monster's throat and ripped its spine out of its front in a shower of blood. Gore dripped from the vertebrae dangling in her hand before she cast it aside.

For a moment, she stared. This was strength. This was power. This was… *disgusting*. Grimacing, she wiped her hands on her already filthy pants, deciding she very much preferred using her sword.

From there, Thea relished the song of her Naarvian steel as she unsheathed it from its scabbard and palmed Malik's dagger in her other hand.

She took a step towards the howlers, savouring the tremor of fear in their gaits after witnessing the decimation of their kin. Then, she swung her blade. Every movement was a testament to the skills she had honed, a flurry of silver as she struck, sparks flying as her steel clashed with the howlers' inferior weapons. She gave herself over to the dance of precision and power she knew so well now, carving through cursed flesh and bone with her newfound strength that made every motion as easy as a hot blade through butter.

It was over in mere moments, in a handful of swift and lethal blows. She dispatched them one after the other without so much as breaking a sweat, finding the gaps in their piss-poor defences with deadly accuracy, ignoring their garbled shrieks of pain. She was almost disappointed they hadn't put up more of a fight; she could have ended them with or without her Furies-given gifts. But time was of the essence. She glanced up to see Talemir still airborne, his great membranous wings beating in the pale moonlight, wielding his swords against a swarm of wraiths. He had it handled.

Thea made for the entrance, only for the pungent scent of burnt hair to fill her nostrils. She found herself face to face not with a howler or wraith, but a *rheguld reaper*.

Heart pounding, she twirled her blade in invitation, sizing it up as it stalked towards her. Thea knew the reapers had once been men, but this monster... It was a corrupted vessel of nightmares, consumed by the very essence of evil long ago. Its sinewy form stretched grotesquely, towering over her at nearly ten feet tall. Horns curled from its head, leaking shadow, and its clouded blue eyes latched onto her hungrily.

It struck first, with a swipe of its wicked talons.

Thea's blades became an extension of her, and she blocked the blow, delivering one of her own with unnatural speed. Steel met flesh, black blood pouring from the laceration instantly.

As the creature staggered, Thea squared her shoulders and attacked, her blade and dagger slashing through the air with strong, calculated strikes. The reaper's flesh was tough, but it was no match for her Warsword blade. She spun and dodged, slicing the reaper apart cut by cut until it was roaring in pain, claws slashing down at her, obsidian power lashing for her like whips.

'Is that all you've got?' she taunted, blades gleaming black with its blood now.

Darkness billowed around them. It charged her with its antler-like horns and cords of shadows, a harbinger of doom, reaching for her in the hopes of wrapping its talons around her heart and bringing her nightmares down around her.

Thea leapt, dragging her sword across its throat and plunging her dagger into its chest as she landed on top of it, already carving through its flesh and bone. The monster thrashed, its shriek nearly deafening as it collapsed beneath her.

There, she reached into its vile chest cavity and wrenched out its heart.

The only sound that followed was that of its bloody organ hitting the stone floor with a wet thud.

Leaping once more to her feet, Thea didn't hesitate. She entered the Scarlet Tower, blades at the ready, and headed straight for a winding iron staircase at the end of the antechamber. The stairs spiralled both up and down. The air tasted sour with blood and fear.

Sheathing her dagger, Thea cupped her hand in front of her, conjuring the first whisper of power to life at her fingertips.

Fine bolts of brilliant white light sparked there, and with a single command, she sent a quiet pulse outward, to search. She watched as it forked off, disappearing to explore the paths both up and down the tower.

Moments later, it sang to her, and she made for the staircase.

Realising that the true entrance to the Scarlet Tower was below, yawning like the maw of a great beast, Thea started down the steps, blade in hand, trailing the whisper of lightning she'd sent into the dark.

She was ready to shed blood. Ready to take back what was hers.

CHAPTER FIVE

WILDER

A flash of light penetrated Wilder's dreams, enough to wrench him back into consciousness. He woke in chains. The manacles were gone, but thick, heavy links bit into his bare chest and wrapped around his limbs, numbing him with their bone-chilling coldness, securing him to a hard metal table. His senses were assaulted by the now familiar acrid tang of the prison – blood and suffering and death. In the distance, he could hear the tortured moans and cries of the other prisoners, a symphony of despair that seemed to feed the tower itself. He didn't know if this was another nightmare, another vision born of the drugs they administered —

The chains were *moving*, slithering across his torso like snakes, matching those he'd seen shifting across the stone walls of the prison when he'd been dragged from his cell. Suddenly he was sure they were altering the fabric of his mind.

Real or not, he twisted in the irons, scanning the space

around him. A map of the midrealms was pinned to one of the far walls, dark shading denoting the sheer size of Artos' forces, heavy ink outlining which territories the King of Harenth had seized. How long had the empath been building these forces?

Craning his neck, Wilder could still see his swords in the glass case nearby – if only he could get to them... He had to get out of here, to warn Thea and the others of what Artos had concocted in the shadows.

As though they could hear his thoughts, the chains tightened around him, to the point where Wilder's eyes nearly bulged out of his head with the pressure and pain. If his ribs hadn't been broken before, they were now. He rasped for air, sharp bursts of agony lancing through his chest as he did.

For the first time in a long while, cold, hard panic set in. Dread hung heavy in the sour air, clinging to his skin like a shroud.

Here in the underbelly of the Scarlet Tower, the Archmage of Chains meant to make him a monster.

The man in question came to stand at his side. 'You are right to fear,' he said coolly, eyeing the cursed creatures at work around them. 'For it's not just one of them I mean to turn you into, but something more... A true embodiment of the power that plagues the lands. Not just a soldier in an army, but a general. One who adheres to every despicable command I give.'

'Fuck you,' Wilder spat, ignoring the pain and rallying his remaining strength against the bonds.

The jewelled inquisitor appeared at the Archmage's side. 'Shall we gag him?'

'Gag him? Whatever for? The shadows will enjoy his screams.'

Another flicker of brilliant white light sparked in the distance, but then it was gone. Another trick of his mind. What had he realised before? That on the brink of insanity, the tormentors liked to show their captors something good, something to save them from total destruction, so they could suffer anew.

'Begin,' the Archmage instructed.

Wilder's whole body seized as the shadows came for him like vipers in the night, ready to strike, coiling around him, cold and relentless. He fought and fought hard. He'd sooner die than become a pawn in their war games against everything he held dear.

And then came the blinding pain.

Wilder bit down. He wouldn't give those bastards the satisfaction of his screams, he wouldn't let them —

In the distance, something shuddered, a faraway rumble that reverberated through the stone walls. The ground trembled beneath them. For a fleeting moment, there was a reprieve from the pain. Sweat, mingled with dirt and blood, trickled from his brow, stinging his eyes before carving through the grime on his face. Wilder panted, his chest straining against the chains, watching as the inquisitor rushed to a barred window on the far side of the laboratory and peered out to the corridors beyond.

'What is it?' the Archmage demanded, his voice cleaving through the room, sharp as any blade.

The inquisitor craned his neck and replied unsteadily, 'I don't know, sir.'

'Find out.'

In a blur of fabric, the spineless jewelled bastard vanished from sight.

The Archmage's eyes bored into Wilder's, filled with contempt. 'Is this your doing?' he sneered. 'It won't save you.'

The darkness began anew, swirling in thick obsidian masses around them, taking shape as cords of sheer pain. Each movement sent more white-hot agony through Wilder, his senses heightened to feel every second.

On the verge of passing out, light flickered in his peripheral vision. Not the orange glow of a flame, but something else entirely. Something brilliant and blinding, something familiar…

The Archmage of Chains stumbled back from the torture table. 'What in the midrealms —'

But he was cut off.

Gold exploded all around them.

Screams and shrieks filled the air as the gilded dust filled the space, settling on everyone and everything, including Wilder's chains.

He watched in awe as they sizzled across his skin, and fell away like ash.

The pain faded from his body as he threw himself from that gods-forsaken table. With the movement, his Warsword strength returned to his limbs, a warmth washing through him like a powerful wave. He felt nothing but energy as he found his feet and locked eyes with the Archmage.

Wilder offered a savage smile.

He grabbed the man by the back of the neck and, with a single downward motion, used his head to smash the glass case surrounding his twin swords.

Blood splattered, screams sounded, and this time, it was nothing but music as Wilder's fingers wrapped around the

HELEN SCHEUERER

grips of his blades. With their weight in his hands, he came
back to himself: the Warsword, the Hand of Death.

Monsters' throats opened beneath the edges of those
blades, spilling gore across the ruined laboratory.

As blood dripped from Wilder's swords, that brilliant
white light flared again.

At last, he tasted the storm on his lips, and looked up.

CHAPTER SIX

THEA

A whimper escaped Thea as she took in the mighty sight of him. Wearing only a pair of tattered undershorts, Wilder Hawthorne was a blaze of bare-chested bloodshed and glory. Though his body was bruised and brutalised beneath the gore, he moved like a god of war, becoming a savage blur of steel as he carved through the remaining monsters to get to her.

Thea held her breath, her lightning dancing at her fingertips as he reached her.

When he met her gaze, she exhaled. For his silver eyes were *his*. He was whole.

Wilder's stare widened at the sight of her. Despite the carnage around them, he took in the Warsword totem at her arm, the strength that radiated from her and the power thrumming between them.

He staggered towards her, lips parted in awe. 'Thea —'

But she lunged for him, gripping the back of his neck and silencing him amid the madness with a deep, searing kiss. She didn't care that he tasted of iron and sweat, only that he was *hers*. His lips met hers in a fierce claiming, his mouth opening for her and her tongue brushing against his as she pressed her armour-clad body to his bare torso.

She broke away, panting. 'I love you,' she gasped, refusing to tear her eyes away from him. 'I love you so much I can hardly breathe. I've wanted to say it for so long —'

Wilder gave a hoarse, broken laugh. 'Tell me again later. Tell me when we're safe.'

Thea kissed him again, desperate to show him that tempest he'd brought to life within her from the moment they'd met. 'I'll tell you every day until my last,' she murmured.

Outside, beyond the blanket of darkness, something exploded, ripping through the air.

Thea and Wilder broke apart, rigid with tension as they listened.

It started as a distant, muffled sound, akin to the low rumbling of thunder echoing across the marshland, only to crescendo into a near-deafening blast that shook the very foundations of the Scarlet Tower.

Thea grabbed Wilder's hand and pulled him towards the exit. 'Come on, let's get the fuck out of here.'

'What is that out there?' he asked, following, his hand not leaving hers.

'Our back-up,' she replied, kicking debris from their path. The laboratory was ruined, empty but for the rivers of black blood at their feet.

When they reached the corridor beyond, she halted them, crouching by a body on the floor and wrenching its boots from its lifeless feet.

'Here.' She held them out to Wilder. 'They'll be a snug fit, but your feet —'

Wilder was already hauling the pants off the corpse and tugging them on before stuffing his feet into the too-small boots. 'They'll do,' he said, his gaze flicking to the darkened hallway. 'How —'

'A story for another time,' Thea said, snatching his hand back in hers, dragging him down the passageway towards the spiral stairs. Spotting a unit of howlers coming towards them, she took the lead. Though he was keeping up, she knew Wilder wasn't at his full strength and she wasn't about to let him take the brunt of their violence.

'Thea,' Wilder objected, but she simply gave him a wicked grin and flung herself into the heart of the fray, cleaving through one howler after the next, spraying blood on the stone walls and letting her steel sing. In the frenzy and rhythm of the rampage, she was dying to use her magic, to unleash that powerful storm magic like a wave upon them all, but with Talemir's warning fresh in her mind, she reined that part of herself in. If she couldn't kill them with lightning, she'd cut them down the Warsword way.

Wilder was far from passive in her wake. His twin swords glinted in the torchlight as he parried and struck with the same mesmerising dance of strength and precision he'd taught her, a force to be reckoned with, death's own calling card.

He didn't question why she wasn't using magic. He simply let her take the lead, an equal, a fellow Warsword in command.

When the way was clear, they scrambled up the staircase, towards the open gates of the tower. More howlers, and wraiths too, were spilling across the drawbridge in swarms.

Closing in, a wraith aimed a lash of darkness at Wilder, who stumbled slightly before righting himself, his silver gaze molten with determination, still gripping his swords menacingly.

But Thea's rage surged within, like a flood breaking through the walls of a dam, nearly blinding her with its force. She stared the wraith down, swinging her sword as she closed the gap across the bridge, her stormy gaze meeting its clouded blue eyes.

'You're dead anyway,' she promised. 'But touch him again, I *dare* you.'

A whip of darkness came for the Warswords, but it never landed.

Thea cleaved it and its master in two with one slash of her blade, leaving its heart to simply fall out of its chest with a grotesque slap against the bridge.

Behind her, Wilder gave another hoarse laugh. 'Furies save us all,' he murmured with a savage grin.

Together, Thea and Wilder fought the howlers and wraiths back across the drawbridge, discarding their corpses into the murky waters either side. Bodies piled up high, and the Warswords clambered over them, slaying every vile creature in their path.

Overhead, membranous wings blocked out the yellow sliver of moon, arrows raining down on the enemy from above and striking wraiths from the sky.

Thea didn't know how Wilder was still standing, but they ran, crossing the outer grounds of the tower, monsters still falling from the sky thanks to the Warsword defending them from above —

But when they reached the iron gates, three enormous figures blocked their path.

Rheguld reapers.

The largest Thea had ever seen, easily fifteen feet tall.

They were beyond grotesque, their sinewy frames pulsating with that nightmarish quality, their talons gleaming in the pale moonlight and their horns foul and twisted atop their heads. But it was their eyes that were the most unsettling feature of all; she had always thought so. Round and unblinking, clouded with a hazy blue hue, they pierced the world around them, reflecting the void of evil within.

A bleat of fear sounded. At their feet cowered an emaciated man. He was clad in rags and covered in all manner of filth.

'Aemund?' Wilder breathed beside her, staring at their prisoner.

Thea's stomach bottomed out. 'You know him?' she murmured, training her gaze on the wretched soul between the reapers.

'*We* know him. He's the man we put here... The one who tried to poison Artos in Harenth,' Wilder told her, his expression pained. 'He... he was in there with me.'

Thea surveyed the reapers. One of them had a taloned hand resting atop Aemund's head, the way a master might comfort a pet. 'I don't think he's with you anymore —'

A shout sounded from above – a warning from Talemir. Thea's gaze snapped up, but it was too late.

Darkness billowed from all three reapers in thick, rolling masses, a swell of power expanding around them. Thea had never seen reapers join forces like that before, a solid wall of obsidian taking shape before it came crashing down upon them.

Thea lunged forward, blades raised, but was knocked back by a powerful, invisible force. She went sprawling across the dirt, but was on her feet again in an instant, only

41

more determined to end the monsters before them. They had taken enough from her, enough from the midrealms —

But the darkness grew stronger still, taking form around them, around the tower – a shimmering shield of shadow, trapping Thea and Wilder within and blocking Talemir outside. The sliver of moon beyond disappeared, leaving them in pitch-black. The only sounds were the beating of wings beyond the barrier, and Aemund's short, shallow breaths. The reapers made no noise, but she felt them moving closer; could sense their malevolence, their thirst for power and pain, as though it were tangible, a hand reaching out to coax their nightmares from their minds.

The stench of them became overpowering, rancid enough to make Thea gag. But she held her ground, Wilder's presence stoic at her side.

Thea closed her eyes and felt the first whip of obsidian lash out.

It came for Wilder, not her, as though it knew where to strike to hurt her the most.

With a precise slash, she severed it from its host.

A shriek pierced the air.

Rage dripped through the silence that followed, and she felt the reapers close the space between them, the air shifting.

'Thea...' Wilder warned. 'We need to run.'

'I'm done running,' she replied.

And the storm-wielding Warsword, Althea Embervale, summoned her lightning.

Forks of white light kissed her fingertips and illuminated the dark.

Wilder grabbed her arm. 'You saw what they planned on

doing to me in there.' His voice was rough. 'If they capture a storm wielder, this war is over before it starts.'

Thea's power swelled. 'I have no intention of being their captive.'

'Then the whole world will know who you are.'

He'd echoed Talemir's concerns. But Thea had made up her mind. A tempest roared within her, demanding to be unleashed upon the evil in their midst.

'It's about time that they did.'

The reapers hissed. The lightning at her fingertips illuminated their forms stalking towards them, their clouded eyes drinking her in, hungry for a taste of her power.

Beside her, Wilder gave her a nod and twirled his blades, and that told her all she needed to know. It was her choice, and he would stand by her until the end.

Thea felt the storm rise in her blood instantly. It had been simmering just beneath the surface, waiting to be released.

She set it free.

Overhead, thunder rumbled, thick grey clouds swallowing the wall of darkness created by the reapers, and Thea reached inward, to the ancient power that resided deep in her bloodline, and the core of the very world she stood upon.

Whips of darkness came for her, but Wilder slashed through them with his twin swords, clearing a path for her and her magic, allowing her the time to draw it out. The thunder roared this time, vibrating through the ground, reverberating in her chest and echoing her heartbeat.

Thea tipped her head to the sky and stretched out her hands. She tasted the rain on the wind, and lightning crackled from her fingertips – not in fine forks, but in mighty bolts. She felt the intensity of their charge in her palms before she unleashed them on the reapers, throwing them like spears at the monsters.

The creatures shrieked as each bolt landed, sinewy flesh burning in their wake.

Thea summoned rain as sharp as daggers, and with a shower of lightning breaking through the shield of shadow above, both pelted down on their already writhing enemies. With a swirling motion of her hands, Thea conjured a vortex of wind. The scent of burnt hair tangled with that of wet soil, and she deflected another attack of shadow before aiming the tunnelling gale right for the reapers, charging the very air with the promise of their demise.

She advanced, the three monsters trapped in the clutches of her storm. But she was far from done. At her command, the energy intensified, and she sent more bolts of lightning surging for the reapers, electric tendrils of power striking them over and over again, illuminating their leathery forms in a surreal blue light.

They screamed in earnest now, and it was a melody she relished. Around her, the wind howled and rain poured, drenching the grounds of the Scarlet Tower, turning it into a muddy field. She let her storm rage, her senses heightened to a blade's edge, becoming one with the tempest as it shattered the barrier of darkness around the tower and shadow wraiths beyond it fell from the sky.

'Thea...'

Wilder's voice brought her back from the lure of the storm, her gaze snapping to his.

Silver eyes met hers. 'Let's finish this,' he said, starting towards the twitching reapers, their power now nothing but dissipating wisps of dying shadow.

Palming her dagger, Thea followed.

But there was no need to carve out the monsters' hearts.

For she had burned them right out of their chests.

Panting, she and Wilder stood amongst the remnants of battle, the ground around them scorched, craters scattered far and wide across its surface.

Thea's heart ached with regret as Wilder stared at the tower, his body tense. Amid the smoke and carnage, it still stood, tall and foreboding: a symbol of the darkness that threatened their world, a grim sentinel, a bleak silhouette against the smouldering battlefield.

Thea knew no words would comfort her Warsword in that moment, and so she said nothing. Instead, she summoned another charge of lightning, and held it in her palm: an offer.

A muscle twitched in Wilder's jaw as he looked from her magic to the question in her eyes.

'Bring it down,' he said at last. 'Bring the whole fucking thing down.'

He didn't need to ask her twice.

Thea rallied her strength, her power, and threw everything she had at the Scarlet Tower. The place that had held her love captive, that had hurt him, that had seen monsters created and thrust upon the midrealms...

'I am the storm,' she told herself.

She let her lightning rage, right alongside her heart, and she split the gods-damned tower in two.

CHAPTER SEVEN

WILDER

S till clutching his swords, Wilder watched in awe and reverence as his love took on the world for him. A deafening crack echoed through the night as a white bolt struck the spire in a blinding flash. The entire tower groaned, its ancient stones falling away with the force of the impact – impact that vibrated through the earth, through Wilder's bones.

Time seemed to slow, caught in the breathless moment between disbelief and inevitability. With a cataclysmic crescendo of lightning, Thea shattered the Scarlet Tower into two halves, its black heart exposed to the realms as it broke apart. For a second the pieces teetered on the brink of ruin, before succumbing to the unforgiving embrace of gravity. The horrific interior of cells and torture chambers was wrenched apart, destroyed in thick clouds of dust and flame as whatever concoctions stored there were detonated. The remains were sent hurtling towards the ground below.

Together, Wilder and Thea watched the tower collapse,

chains and charred stone cascading in a dance of total decimation, laying bare the underbelly of the prison.

Only when the Scarlet Tower lay in ruins upon the storm-and battle-scarred land did Thea stop. Her hands fell to her sides, tendrils of smoke drifting from her fingers.

Wilder wanted nothing more than to gather her in his arms, to breathe in her sea-salt-and-bergamot scent and hold her close, but something snagged his attention —

Movement on the ground.

As more smoke and shadows dissipated, he saw Aemund.

The man's lower half was crushed beneath a pile of debris, blood pouring from the wound. His eyes were wide, his face pale and sweaty, but he made no sound despite his clear agony. Instead, his gaze seemed to implore Wilder.

Thea seemed to understand before he did, handing him her dagger wordlessly.

Inhaling deeply, trying to steady himself, Wilder crouched at Aemund's side, resting a hand on his shoulder.

'I'm glad you destroyed it,' Aemund rasped. 'Glad it's been wiped from the world.'

Wilder didn't have the energy to mask his pity. He had only spent two weeks inside the tower, but Aemund... Aemund had been subject to its torture for years.

'Please,' Aemund said. 'End it.'

Wilder lowered his voice. 'We can try to get you out of here.'

Aemund attempted to shake his head. 'I thought for a time that perhaps I could have a life beyond this place, but... No. I don't want it.' He took another rattling gasp. 'The darkness will follow me always. Please, do me this kindness.'

A lump forming in his throat, Wilder nodded. 'Go in

peace, my friend,' he told him. And then he slipped Malik's dagger between Aemund's ribs, right into his heart.

Aemund's eyes went wide, his expression morphing into one of pure relief before he took his final breath. Wilder's body sagged as he removed the blade, and he felt Thea beside him.

'It was what he wanted,' she said quietly.

'I know,' he croaked.

For a moment he stayed like that, on his knees in the dirt by the corpse of a man he hardly knew, as fragments of shadow fell around them like ash in the wind. He barely registered Thea looping his arm around her shoulders and hauling him to his feet.

'I've got you,' she murmured.

He leant into her. Beneath the sweat, grime and blood, she smelt of home. He paused, drawing her face to his so that he could kiss her —

Power surged around them; strangely familiar, but not belonging to Thea.

The earth shuddered beneath them as something – *someone* – landed in front of them.

With his arm still slung around Thea, Wilder could only stare at the winged figure before him.

The man hadn't changed, not in all the years that had passed, but for the dusting of silver through the dark golden-brown hair that was swept back in the same knot he'd always worn. He was as broad and tall as ever as he tucked his wings behind his back and sheathed his swords at his hips, his plain black armour shining with wraith blood.

'Hello, Apprentice,' said the familiar rich, warm voice.

Wilder blinked, not quite believing it, his knees threatening to buckle. 'Tal…?'

Talemir Starling smiled broadly, his hazel eyes bright as his shadows danced around them. 'Told you there'd come a day when you'd need us...'

He came forward, and were it not for the hand that grasped Wilder's shoulder, he would have sworn the winged Warsword was a figment of his imagination, a ghost from a distant past.

But Talemir's grip was firm and solid. 'It's good to see you, Wilder,' he said earnestly, his gaze brimming with emotion.

At Wilder's side, Thea made a noise of frustration. 'You took your time.'

Talemir's hand dropped from Wilder's shoulder and he gave her a grin. 'Seemed like you wanted to make a statement.'

Wilder knew he was gawking as he watched the surreal exchange unfold. Thea was here, with Talemir... They had worked *together* to save him from the Scarlet Tower and the terrible fate that had awaited him there. *How?* It was taking every ounce of his willpower to remain upright, to hide the tremor in his hands.

'We should get out of here,' Talemir said, gesturing to the smouldering ruins. 'It won't be long until word spreads of this. They'll send more —'

'Can you carry us both?' Thea asked.

'Not all the way to headquarters.' Talemir stretched his wings with a grimace, his shadows unfurling around him. 'But I wouldn't take you there straight away even if I could. There's a chance there'll be wraiths on our tail, and I don't want to lead them to our doorstep. But I know a place I can leave you while I check for breaches and get help.'

Wilder was rigid beside Thea. He felt untethered from

himself, from the situation unfolding before him. He had kept the feeling at bay for weeks in the cells and violent pits of the tower, but here, surrounded by people he knew, and loved, his armour was starting to crack.

'Preferably somewhere with liquor,' he heard himself say hoarsely.

Talemir barked a laugh. 'I'll see what I can do.'

Then, without warning, shadows swept in. Not the shadows of evil and tyranny, but another kind: warmer, protective. Shadows that Wilder himself knew from long ago. Talemir's power.

He heard the beat of Tal's wings, and felt the pull of his magic, wrapping around him and Thea and launching them skyward.

Wilder had only experienced it a handful of times before, once with Talemir himself, the other times with Anya and Dratos. He would never get used to it – a surreal backward freefall, wind whipping all around him.

Thea's hand in his anchored him as space and time seemed to warp around them, toying with each of his senses. He knew they weren't simply flying, that Talemir was transporting them with shadow magic. Wilder didn't care, so long as it stopped soon. He'd never liked the sensation —

Solid ground met his ill-fitting boots and he staggered forward. Only when he was steady on his feet did Talemir's shadows retreat, revealing a familiar place.

A pale stream of moonlight illuminated the white stones and wooden beams of a large building. A rustic sign swung outside the door.

Wilder stared. 'You've got to be joking.'

Talemir gave a roguish grin and reached for the heavy wooden door. 'You said somewhere with liquor, Apprentice.'

Wilder glanced at Thea, who was staring at the sign, shaking her head in disbelief. 'Kipp is going to have a fit.'

The door creaked loudly as Talemir pushed it open and waited for Wilder. 'Welcome back to the Dancing Badger.'

Dazed, Wilder stepped inside, Thea close behind. Talemir lit several candles before he disappeared behind the bar, giving them a moment to look around the tavern.

It was as though no time had passed. Dark timber beams adorned the ceilings, along with iron chandeliers that hung low over the long tables. A great hearth lay at the centre, cold and unused, the corners of the space furnished with generous cushioned booths. Someone had cleared away the discarded plates, cups and empty bottles that had been strewn about the last time he was here, but other than that...

The portraits lining the walls were the same, even including the face of Albert, the owner of the Laughing Fox in Harenth, and the man he now recognised as Everard, the owner of the Singing Hare in Aveum. He could only imagine how irritated Marise would be to learn his likeness wasn't included in the drinkers and thinkers' hall of fame...

Wilder hesitated. It was too good to be true, too real.

Feeling a tremor take hold in his little finger, he backed away, his heart in his throat. It was the tower's most visceral illusion yet, and he'd fallen for it. He'd wanted so desperately to believe that it was over, that they had triumphed over the dark, that he'd let his mind be taken. This was a warped fragment of memory, of two parts of his life colliding, and they were using it against him with elaborate cruelty —

Thea squeezed his hand firmly, hard enough to force his gaze to hers.

'It's real,' she told him, seemingly understanding where his mind had gone. '*I'm* real. You're here. With us.'

Talemir appeared again and pressed a glass bottle into his hand. 'Drink that,' his former mentor told him. 'If you're in some sort of dream, it'll taste like that fine wine you love so much.'

Wilder pulled the cork out with his teeth and put the bottle to his lips, taking a generous swig. The liquor washed over his tongue and burned down his throat with a familiar ferocity.

Wilder coughed, eyes streaming. 'Fucking fire extract,' he rasped. 'Still tastes like death —'

'Guess you're not dreaming, then,' Tal said, clapping him on the shoulder.

Wilder took another, deeper drink this time before passing the bottle to Thea. 'Guess not.'

He watched as Thea took a swig without so much as a grimace, her eyes never leaving him.

'I'm alright,' he murmured, pulling her closer to his side before he looked back to Talemir.

It had been a long time since he'd stood on Naarvian soil, and suddenly, the most vivid memory came crashing back into him.

'Not all is as it seems at Thezmarr. You know this in your bones...' Talemir had told him. 'Keep the current state of this kingdom a secret. To the outside world, Naarva should appear as it has for the last year or so: an overgrown ghost kingdom but for its forge.'

'I take no orders from you. You're no longer a Warsword, no longer a brother of mine.'

'Your anger with me will fade in time, Wilder. But for now, you need to go on. You need to hunt the reapers...'

'Fuck you, Tal.'

Wilder came back to himself, watching as his former

mentor spoke in hushed tones with Thea. It was as though they had only seen each other yesterday. Tal moved with the same commanding grace as he always had, and gestured with the same ease, as though he'd known Thea his whole life, as though they were *friends*.

Wilder sucked in a breath. There was so much he wanted to say. He opened his mouth to do so, only for Tal to wave him off.

'There'll be enough time for that later,' he said. 'I have to return to headquarters and brief the others, secure the perimeter before we come back and get you.' He made for the door. 'The tavern is safe, as are the grounds with the well out back. But don't stray far. I won't be long.'

'Thank you,' Thea said, seeing him out.

Talemir nodded. 'Rest. Recover. You'll need all your strength for what's ahead.'

Wilder knew he wasn't talking to Thea, but she nodded all the same.

The door clicked closed behind him, and suddenly, Wilder found himself alone with Thea.

At long last, he allowed himself to look at her, not in the blaze of battle or in the eye of one of her storms, but properly. She stood before him, covered in grime and blood, but proud, and he drank in the sight of her like a parched man in a desert. Her bronze-and-gold-streaked hair was matted, but braided down the side as it always was, some tendrils loose and framing her dirt-smudged face. She wore fitted leather pants and a shirt that might have once been white, the sleeves rolled to the elbow.

He took a step towards her, his breath catching at the Furies-gifted totem around her right arm. It was just like the one he had once possessed, its steel shining in the glow of the candlelight: two crossed swords, a third cutting down the middle, only... behind the three blades were streaks of lightning.

Pride swelled in his chest. The Furies had marked Thea's totem differently, for the exception that she was.

Next, Wilder looked to the blade of Naarvian steel at her belt. He had seen her wield it at the tower, but to see it here, as a permanent part of her...

'You're a Warsword,' he murmured at last, his voice thick with emotion.

'I am,' she said softly, letting him observe her without a word as his gaze fell to the mangled scar around her left wrist. He froze. When he'd emerged from the Rite, all the scars he'd earnt had vanished, but this scar seemed different – more vicious, as though her whole hand had been severed at the joint —

He didn't even realise he was reaching for it until Thea flinched.

She pulled her sleeve down, covering the ragged skin there, but the hurt must have shown in his face because she said, 'I'm sorry. I'm just... I'm not used to it yet.'

'You have nothing to be sorry for,' Wilder told her. Instead, he reached for those loose strands of hair in her eyes and tucked them gently behind her ears, relieved to find her leaning into his touch.

'Did you go to Tver to get your stallion?' he asked, closing the little distance between them, wondering once more if this was a trick of his mind, if the Archmage of Chains had broken into his dreams again.

Thea raised her brows. 'There was something a little more pressing to attend to first, Warsword.'

'I can't imagine what...' Wilder's gaze dropped to her lips.

'Besides, I thought you might want to be there with me. You did threaten to name my stallion Pancake, after all...' Thea's warm hands trailed up his torso, and he was surprised to find that he was still bare-chested. *One less thing to remove*, he thought distantly, leaning in.

Thea threaded her fingers through his hair, a sigh escaping her, as though she'd been holding it in all this time. But there was something he had to know, something that would define them from here on.

'Did they grant it to you?' he whispered, as his mouth almost brushed hers. 'Immortality?'

Thea drew back, only slightly, and shook her head. 'No,' she answered, briefly hesitating. 'You never told me what you asked... What you asked instead?'

Tension rolled through Wilder as he pressed his brow to hers, trying to contain the ache in his chest. The grains in the hourglass moved against them at breakneck speed now. Less than a year... That was what they had left together, and that was *if* they survived the war to come.

'Wilder?' Thea pressed.

'I asked them if I'd regret it... not seeking immortal life.' He met her celadon gaze, memorising every one of her features anew. 'They told me that I'd never regret it. That while my life would hold much pain, it would also hold more love than I could ever imagine.'

Thea's stormy eyes lined with tears. 'Fuck,' she muttered, looking down. 'I told myself I wouldn't —'

But Wilder gripped her chin between his thumb and forefinger, bringing her face up to his once more. 'You never have to hide your tears from me.'

Thea's hand slipped from his hair and cupped the side of

his face, her expression softening. 'I love you,' she said, her voice cracking.

Wilder's legs threatened to give way beneath him. She had spoken those words amid the carnage of the Scarlet Tower, and they had uttered them to one another before in Tver... In the hot springs, on the eve of battle, afterwards as well... But Thea had never been the one to say it first, and he'd told himself he understood, that it didn't matter. He would take whatever she gave him and be fucking grateful. And then everything had changed. The Great Rite had called her and he'd stopped her from saying it. In the dank cells of the prison, it *had* mattered, and in his darkest moments, he'd feared he might never again hear those words from her lips.

'Say it again,' he murmured, his heart racing, his grip tightening on her chin.

Thea traced the lines of his face with reverence. 'I love you.'

A shuddering breath escaped Wilder. He didn't trust himself to speak.

Thea peered into his eyes. 'I have never been so scared in my life, never —'

'I know.' His voice threatened to falter. 'Me either.'

'There is so much I want to tell you, so much I want to —'

'Later,' Wilder said, and kissed her.

He kissed her to close the distance he felt between them, the distance created not by time and space, but by each not knowing what the other had been through. His lips ghosted over Thea's and her mouth opened for him, his tongue brushing hers.

She drew him tighter to her and moaned, the sound vibrating down into his chest, into his soul.

'I love you,' he whispered, breaking away for just a

moment. 'I love you so fucking much.' And then he deepened the kiss, claiming her fiercely, dragging his hands over her body as though he could imprint the shape of her onto his palms.

As her mouth moved over his and her hand rested against his heart, he wondered abstractly if it was another dream.

If it is, he thought, his blood heating as he pushed Thea against a table and she wrapped her legs around him, *I'll stay here forever.*

CHAPTER EIGHT

THEA

Wilder kissed her like a man possessed, and Thea whimpered, giving everything she had right back and refusing to let go as he laid her down on the table, covering her body with his powerful frame. They were a clash of tongues and teeth and pawing hands; that familiar dark frenzy that had always been between them threatened to take hold. He gripped her hard enough to bruise and she bit his lip hard enough to draw blood. A low rumble of desire escaped him, the sound sending a bolt of longing straight to her core.

Thea hadn't let herself feel it at the tower, but now, the terror she'd held at bay came bubbling over. They had hurt him. One ruined building was not nearly payment enough for that crime.

She traced the rippling planes of his abdomen, his sculpted chest and his broad, round shoulders, wanting to memorise every inch of him, careful of any wounds he might have suffered. But Wilder leant into her caress with a ferocity that told her he wanted to feel every inch of contact between them, no matter the pain. His fingers mapped her in the same way. As she writhed beneath him, her blood coursed with lightning and longing entwined, and the urgency to feel him inside her amplified almost unbearably.

'I love you,' she whispered against his lips. 'Gods, I love you.' Her hands moved to his hair, grabbing it by the roots, holding him in place against her, where he belonged. And then Wilder's mouth was on hers again, heated and desperate, as though he meant to devour her over and over, a man starved. He squeezed her breasts roughly, her nipples hardening, and she arched into his touch, demanding more.

Even with leather and fabric between them, when he ground his cock against her, she felt how hard he was. He angled himself right where she wanted him and she cried out, drawing him close. She needed him, needed to feel him inside her. Together, they could overcome anything. Together, they were strongest —

But when she reached for his buttons, she saw his expression turn distant.

'Wilder?' she said, sitting up. 'What is it?'

He broke away, panting. His silver eyes were molten with lust, his need just as potent as hers, evident in the massive bulge in his pants. But there was something...

'You can tell me anything,' she told him, bringing his hand to rest against the drumming of her heart.

He didn't pull away, but gazed upon her as though he couldn't quite believe she was there.

'Wilder?'

His hand covered hers, and he stared at their scarred and dirt-lined fingers. 'I told myself I didn't care if this was real or not. That if I woke up in that rotten cell again, at least I'd have had this with you, for a moment...'

Thea felt the wind knocked out of her, her heart fracturing for him. 'It's real,' she whispered. 'I'm real. You're here with me. You're safe. This is real.'

Wilder's powerful shoulders caved inward and he gave a sad smile. 'It seemed real enough then, too.'

Tears burned, but Thea refused to let them fall, not now. Now, she had to be strong for him.

She got down from the table and led him to a chair, gently pushing him onto the cushioned seat and kneeling before him. There, she took his chin between her fingers and forced his silver gaze to hers, as he had done with her so many times before. 'You and I? We're forever. We have been since I spied on you atop the cliffs at Thezmarr, since you shot that arrow at me in the Bloodwoods, and every moment since. We will find a way through this,' she vowed. 'Together.'

A hint of that dimple she loved followed. 'I have no doubt, Princess.'

Ignoring the ache in her chest, Thea pressed a gentle kiss to his mouth. 'Still not a princess,' she said.

He shifted, his discomfort suddenly obvious. 'There's a well out back,' he told her, getting to his feet. 'I'm going to clean up as best I can.'

'Do you need help?' She didn't want to push him, but he'd been through a lot. She could see the bruises across his body as he moved, could see the uncertainty in his silver gaze.

'I've got it covered,' he replied gently.

Thea nodded. Her Warsword needed a moment to himself, to sort through the mess in his head. She let understanding soften her features. 'I'll be here,' she said.

A short time later, Wilder returned to her, his skin damp, some parts red where he'd clearly scrubbed hard at himself. He all but collapsed back into the chair, but he seemed calmer, more grounded.

'Now, let me look at you,' Thea said, feeling protective.

Wilder raised a brow and leant back, giving her a full view of his battered but sculpted torso. 'Who am I to deny you?'

Thea nodded to an open wound at his side. 'You might feel differently once I start stitching you up.'

'Good thing I taught you well.'

Thea forced a smile. 'Good thing Talemir left the liquor.'

Conflict warred across Wilder's face at the mention of his former mentor, but she didn't press. Instead, she went to the counter and picked up the medical kit Talemir had placed on the bar beside the bottle of fire extract.

When she returned to Wilder, he was frowning at the offending wound in the candlelight. It was a long gash along his ribs on his left side, streams of blood trailing from its ragged edges. 'Another scar to impress the ladies with,' he said roughly.

Thea scoffed. 'Ladies? Plural?'

'Just the one.' He winked.

That small gesture alone lightened the weight pressing down on Thea's heart. Her Warsword was still in there, and he'd find his way back to her.

She poured fire extract over a scrap of cloth from the medical kit and waited. 'I'd be more impressed if you let me clean it.'

Wilder bared his side to her. 'I can't even feel it —' His body stiffened and he hissed through his teeth as she pressed the alcohol-soaked fabric to his wound. '*Fuck.*'

Thea focused on the task at hand, gently wiping as much blood away from the cut as she could before she prepared the needle and thread, just as he'd taught her. 'Tell me about this tavern,' she asked. 'What were you doing here last time?'

Wilder grunted as she made the first suture, but then he looked around the tavern, his expression distant. 'It was... about eight years ago now. We didn't stay here long...'

'Who's we?'

'Me, Tal, Drue, Adrienne and their force of Naarvian rangers. Some of their people had been kidnapped by wraiths – Dratos and Gus were among them. You remember them?'

Thea laughed, but kept her hands steady as she worked. 'They're hard to forget.'

'Don't tell Dratos that,' Wilder replied, taking a swig from the fire extract with a grimace. The shadow-touched warrior's head was already big enough. 'We planned our assault from here. Only stayed one night, if I remember rightly. Definitely didn't make the most of its secret stores...'

Thea didn't look up from her sutures, trying not to wince as she threaded the needle through Wilder's flesh. 'Kipp would call that a disgrace. To stay at the Dancing Badger and not indulge.'

'The Son of the Fox does enough indulging for everyone.'

'He'd disagree,' Thea retorted, finishing her last stitch and tying off the thread. 'Done. Any other injuries I should know about?'

Wilder surveyed her handiwork. 'Not bad, Apprentice.'

'I think we're well past "apprentice" now, don't you?' Thea quipped, rummaging through the medical kit. 'Let me bandage it.'

Wilder leant forward in the chair, making room for her

to wrap the bandage around his middle. As she worked, her fingers brushed over his heated skin and she saw goosebumps rush across his torso, his nipples hardening and his gaze darkening.

'Don't get any ideas, Warsword...' she murmured as she finished.

But his eyes fell to where her sleeve had slipped up, her scarred wrist revealed once more. This time, she offered it to him. Ever so gently, he took her hand in his and studied her marred flesh. With a featherlight touch, he traced the jagged line of it around the circumference of her wrist. His head bowed and he pressed his lips to the mottled markings.

Thea didn't move as he kissed every inch of it, a ring of reverence.

'All my other Rite scars disappeared,' she said. 'But this one... This one was different. I wondered if it was because it was done with Naarvian steel, by my own hand... I guess I'll never know. They said I would always feel it.'

Understanding gleamed in Wilder's gaze. 'You did it to yourself?'

Thea nodded.

'I'm sorry you went through that.'

Thea cupped his face, fighting back tears again. One day, they might find a way to share their experiences, to lay it all out for one another, but not today. She wasn't sure she could handle hearing what they'd done to him, not yet. First, she would piece them physically back together. The rest would come.

'I'm sorry you went through what you went through,' she told him.

Wilder leant into her touch with a shudder, his hand covering hers, as though he still didn't quite believe she was

63

there. 'When we rejoin the others… we have to look unshakeable. We have to be strong for everyone.'

'I know,' she said. She hadn't seen their friends since she'd left for the Great Rite, their party not exactly the unified front they needed to end a war. But darkness was coming for them all.

'I don't feel strong,' Wilder admitted quietly. 'I don't —'

Thea silenced him with a hard kiss. 'You are the strongest person I know,' she told him as she withdrew breathlessly. 'For the longest time I have lived upon the frayed edges of memory, of life. But with you by my side, I feel… reborn. Like you've answered the restlessness within me with power of your own. Power that fits together like pieces of a puzzle.' She traced the line of his jaw, hoping he saw everything she felt for him shining in her stare. 'Tell me what you need and it's yours.'

Wilder's throat bobbed before he spoke. 'Do you remember the balcony in Notos? Before the battle began?'

Thea nodded. Those moments would be forever etched into her mind.

'Do you remember what you said to me?' he asked softly. 'You said, *I need to do something that makes me feel alive. I need you.*'

Thea threaded her fingers through his hair once more and hauled his mouth to hers. 'You have me,' she murmured against his lips. 'All of me. Mind, body and heart.'

Wilder groaned, his mouth parting beneath hers as she claimed him. This kiss was more frantic, more determined than the ones that had come before, as though it could anchor them to one another. Thea straddled Wilder on the chair and ground herself against the hard length of him. He was like granite, and the pressure of him made her heart stutter. She guided his hands beneath her shirt, his calloused palms grazing her bare skin.

'This is real,' she told him firmly as she worked herself over him, feeling her undergarments dampen with need, revelling in how his body responded to hers instantly. 'It's real.'

He pinched her nipples through the band around her breasts and she moaned, aching to feel him bare against her. Wilder's hands shot to her hips, where he gripped her hard, rocking her back and forth over his cock. Pressure was already building from the base of her spine, and she braced herself over him.

'Thea...' He said her name like a prayer, his voice thick. 'I —'

Three obnoxiously loud knocks sounded at the door.

They sprang apart. Wilder adjusted the bulge in his pants just in time as Talemir and Dratos the Dawnless strode into the Dancing Badger.

With a regretful glance at Wilder's glorious form, Thea cursed the shadow-touched and their terrible timing, but Dratos simply grinned, his shadows dancing around them, wings tucked neatly behind his back. 'Time to go, lovebirds,' he drawled.

'Where?' Wilder asked, taking another swig of fire extract, as though he needed it to deal with Dratos.

But it was Talemir who answered, his own shadows rippling. 'To the University of Naarva.'

CHAPTER NINE

WILDER

As they travelled with shadow magic for the second time in as many hours, Wilder realised he liked it less each time. He'd take a month-long journey by horse any day. Cloaked in darkness with the wind rushing around him, he felt nauseous, his eyes streaming and his stomach plummeting. Nor did he enjoy such close proximity to Dratos, not when he'd been just about to slide into Thea.

'Prick,' he muttered.

He heard Dratos' chuckle echo in the wind.

Wilder didn't know how long they flew, but he soon felt his ears pop, as though he'd dived too far below water. They'd passed through some sort of magical shield – Tal's magic, he realised, not for the first time. How powerful had his former mentor become over the years? How deep did that well of shadow magic run?

At last, his boots hit solid ground and the shadows dissipated. Wilder shielded his eyes against the unexpected light, golden like the sun, a foreign entity in these parts. When his vision adjusted, he stared.

They had landed in a majestic quadrangle, its sandstone pillars illuminating the structure in all its glory. With its rib vaults, painted walkways and flying buttresses, it was reminiscent of the citadel in Ciraun, Naarva's capital – or at least, what it had been like before it fell.

'Welcome to the University of Naarva,' Talemir said with a sweep of his hand, his own shadows ebbing away.

'This didn't fall with the capital?' Thea asked, eyes wide as she took in the rectangular building and the towering spires, adorned with intricate carvings and arched windows.

'It did,' Talemir told her. 'We've worked hard to restore it over the years. It's obviously not a working university, but it has all the foundations. There's a library, residential halls, lecture halls, a theatre, a dining hall and a scholar's lounge, and further out are the greenhouses.'

Thea beamed. 'My sister would love those. My younger sister, Wren, I mean,' she corrected herself.

'You said she's an alchemist?' Talemir asked thoughtfully.

'One of the best.'

'Then she'll have an even deeper appreciation for this place. Not far from here used to be the midrealms' most prestigious academy for alchemy. Farissa herself trained there, if I'm not mistaken.'

Thea's brows shot up. 'Truly?'

Any recollection Wilder had of an alchemy academy in Naarva was vague, but he knew the art hadn't always been taught at Thezmarr.

A flurry of movement unfolded on the other side of the courtyard, with a procession of shadow-touched folk carrying armfuls upon armfuls of vibrant yellow flowers across the way.

'When's the wedding?' Thea asked with a laugh.

67

Talemir's gaze slid to Wilder. 'Eight years ago.' There was no note of malice in his tone, but the comment cut deep all the same.

Wilder shifted on his feet and looked from his former mentor to Thea and Dratos. 'Can you give us a minute?'

Thea didn't hesitate to elbow Dratos. 'Come on, you can show me where we're staying. I need a fucking bath.'

'No arguments from me,' Dratos retorted, stretching his wings leisurely before tucking them behind his back. The shadow-touched ranger led Thea away, leaving Wilder to face Talemir alone for the first time in almost a decade.

Time had etched lines on both their faces, but something softened the edge of their previous conflict. Tal met Wilder's gaze with understanding in his hazel eyes. 'I hope you're not going to challenge me to another brawl,' he said with a faint note of amusement.

A pang of regret pulsed through Wilder as he recalled one of their last conversations, in which he'd attempted to pummel the older Warsword into the ground for keeping his wraith side a secret.

'You're not exactly in fighting shape,' Talemir continued, his stoic facade breaking into a genuine grin. 'And I bet that left hook still needs work, Apprentice.'

Once, the term would have sparked irritation in Wilder – anger, even. But now relief and gratitude swept through him. And guilt.

'I'll never forgive you for this,' he had ground out long ago. *'You're no longer a Warsword, no longer a brother of mine...'*

'Tal...' he croaked, emotion threatening to bubble over.

Strong hands gripped his shoulders, steadying him.

Wilder hung his head. 'I'm sorry. I'm so sorry —'

The weight of those years apart seemed to dissolve in the

charged atmosphere, in the unspoken language of brotherhood. At last, the armour cracked, and Talemir's heartfelt embrace bridged the gap of hurt and pride.

For a moment Wilder froze, his apologies numb on his lips.

'It's alright,' Talemir said, holding him firmly. 'It's not your fault.'

A ragged breath escaped Wilder. 'I'm sorry. I didn't —'

'It's not your fault,' Tal repeated. The shadow-touched Warsword didn't let go. He held Wilder upright, until Wilder lifted his own arms and returned the embrace. The camaraderie he'd missed for all those years surged to the surface, and he clapped Talemir on the back.

Returning the gesture, Talemir released him at last, his eyes lined with tears. 'Gods, it's good to see you.'

'And you,' Wilder replied hoarsely.

Talemir gave him a roguish grin and squeezed his shoulder. 'There's someone I want you to meet —'

But the Shadow Prince was interrupted by the return of Thea and Dratos, who were squabbling.

'Just think,' Dratos was saying. 'Now the whole of the midrealms knows you're *Princess* Althea Embervale.'

'For fuck's sake, shut up,' Thea replied. 'You're worse than Kipp and Cal.'

He observed her with mock scrutiny. 'You don't seem particularly fond of the whole *royal* thing.'

Thea clicked her tongue in annoyance and gave Dratos a playful shove. Only she clearly wasn't used to her Warsword strength yet – to Wilder's delight, the shadow-touched rebel went flying into one of the stone archways, fragments of stone crumbling around him.

Thea clapped a hand over her mouth. 'Gods, I'm so sorry, I didn't mean to —'

Talemir laughed as Dratos dusted himself off with a scowl. 'He'll survive. When we were fighting, I didn't think to caution you about your strength, but now... you might want to exercise more care.'

Thea raised a brow. 'He started it.'

Dratos scoffed. 'I merely pointed out the obvious —'

'I *did* warn you there would be no going back, no hiding,' Talemir interjected with a sympathetic glance in Thea's direction, followed by a sigh. 'I already briefed the others on Wilder's rescue while you were at the tavern, but we need to gather together to make our plans for the war ahead.'

With a glance at Wilder, Thea waved him off. 'First, the *Princess* of Delmira would like a bath and a hot meal.'

Tal snorted at that. 'Drue's going to like you.'

Wilder swayed on his feet. Willpower alone had kept him upright since he'd escaped the tower, but now... it was all catching up with him. He staggered forward, praying to the Furies that he wouldn't eat stone in front of —

'What's not to like?' Thea quipped, squeezing her small frame in at Wilder's side and casually draping his arm over her shoulder. Gratefully, he leant against her. 'I'm exhausted,' she declared.

'You remember where to go?' Dratos asked her.

Thea gave a mock salute, already pulling Wilder away. 'Scholars' quarters, off from the library.'

Without another word, Thea laced her fingers through his and led him from the university quadrangle into the surrounding building. Wilder was too exhausted to notice the details: the twists and turns of the corridors, the people they passed. How he was still on his feet at all, he didn't know.

At last, Thea pulled him through a library, the air thick with the scent of parchment and leatherbound books, then into a private chamber at the far end.

'Apparently this was the headmaster's residence at some point,' Thea said quietly, kicking the door closed behind them.

Wilder lurched away from her, bracing himself against the nearest piece of furniture as a wave of exhaustion and pain hit. He sucked in great lungfuls of air, trying to push past whatever threatened to overcome him. All he knew was that suddenly, it was all too much, too fast, that he had been chained up in the dark for so long that now everything was too bright, too loud —

'I need a moment,' he rasped, as Thea hovered close by.

She moved away, letting him breathe.

He stayed there, leaning on the chest of drawers, inhaling and exhaling, trying not to collapse as his knees trembled under his weight.

Thea was there again.

He made to pull away. 'I said —'

'You said a moment, and I gave you one,' she told him firmly. She pointed to the door. 'Out there, you can have your armour on as much as you need, but in here with me? We are equals. It was you who told me, *what hurts you, hurts me*. You told me we'll take it on together.'

He remembered the words well. He'd spoken them to her in Harenth, just before they'd been shot full of drugged darts and carted off in chains to a warehouse full of mercenaries.

'Do you understand?' she echoed him again.

He said nothing, still braced on the drawers, still overwhelmed.

Thea pulled him towards a tub of steaming water at the far end of the room. 'Right now, I need to care for you, and you're going to let me.'

Wilder drew a trembling breath and stood beside the bath as she slowly removed his filthy pants and ill-fitting boots. He stilled as she gently unwrapped the bandage she'd tied around him earlier, careful of his wound. He let her guide him into the water, where at last, his weight was off his aching feet and his tremors subsided.

In the fractured amber light streaming through the stained-glass windows, Thea washed the blood from his hands, and the pain from his heart.

CHAPTER TEN

THEA

Thea woke with a strangled scream, agony blazing at her wrist, a ring of fire around her ragged scar. She had been sawing through her flesh and bone all over again, her friends at the mercy of the reapers all around her, talons piercing their hearts. Next, she'd been standing before the Furies themselves, chanting their names: Iseldra, Morwynn, Valdara…

Panting and slick with sweat, Thea looked around frantically, slowly recognising her surroundings as the headmaster's quarters Dratos had shown her to yesterday. She was in Naarva, at the university there…

'I couldn't wake you,' Wilder's voice sounded from nearby, laced with apology. He stood at the window in nothing but a pair of loose-fitting pants slung low around his hips, looking out onto the quadrangle. He was gilded by the early morning light, so at odds with the darkness they had faced the day before. A golden warrior, a golden king.

She met his gaze, ignoring the shiver that tracked down her spine. 'I wouldn't snap out of it?'

'No. And your lightning... It wouldn't let me get close, not this time.'

Only at the mention of her magic did she register the charred scent in the air, and the scorch marks on the sheets clenched in her fist.

Thea fought her heart rate down. 'Did I wake you? Hurt you?'

Wilder shook his head. 'I never slept.'

Still trembling, Thea slipped from the bed, wearing only a thin nightshirt. The evening before had been a blur. She hardly remembered washing herself and putting it on; she only remembered Wilder – caring for him into the late hours of the night, bathing him, making sure he ate, combing her fingers through his hair until his tremors subsided.

When she reached him now, she wrapped her arms around his waist from behind, mindful of his stitches. She rested her cheek on his bare back, inhaling the leather-and-rosewood scent of him, grounding herself.

'Maybe we should just stay in bed today,' she said quietly. 'We've earnt it...'

He laughed roughly, his hands trailing her arms before interlocking his fingers with hers across his middle, holding her in place. 'I wish. But I think there's a war to plan... An enemy or two to defeat.'

'That list grows longer by the day,' she muttered, listening to the steady drum of his heart.

'Such is the life of a Warsword, Princess,' he replied.

Thea hummed against his warm skin and pressed her lips to the ink that followed his spine. *Glory in death, immortality in legend.* She didn't realise she'd said it aloud until Wilder tensed beneath her touch.

'The Archmage of Chains...' He shuddered, releasing her hands to grip the windowsill hard enough that his knuckles paled. 'He could read the script. He said they would make me a *legend among monsters*.'

Thea didn't move, knowing how hard it must be for him to share that fear, that pain, even with her.

'They meant to turn me into an abomination, to unleash me upon the midrealms.' Wilder turned to face her, uncertainty in those silver eyes.

'And yet here you stand,' Thea said, lifting her chin in defiance. 'And them? They're nothing but fucking dust in the wind.'

'I... No matter how much I wash, I can still feel the tower on my skin,' he told her. 'Crawling beneath it.'

His admission broke her heart and sent rage surging through her like a current of flames, but she listened.

'I don't feel like myself, not yet. I can't...' With a noise of frustration, Wilder encircled her waist with his large hands and hauled her body to his, kissing her. 'I need to touch you.' His voice was hoarse.

Thea understood what he was asking. He needed to feel her, needed to know that she was real. And he needed to be in control.

She unlaced the front of her nightshirt and let it fall from her shoulders, the fabric cascading down her body and pooling at her feet.

'I'm yours.'

Hunger clouded his gaze, and without another word, he hoisted her up, muscles bunching at his forearms as he seated her bare backside on the windowsill. For a moment, he didn't touch her, but his eyes mapped every inch of her naked skin, following the flush down her neck and across the tops of her breasts, to her nipples hardening in anticipation.

Thea spread her legs for him, letting him see what his stare alone could do to her. Her whole body thrummed with want for him, craving his fingers, his mouth, his cock.

Wilder groaned at the sight of her, spread and bare just for him, before he closed the gap between them, pressing her back against the window and kissing her fiercely. She opened her mouth to him, letting his tongue sweep in and tease hers, his calloused hands tracing the curve of her neck, the dip of her shoulder, before cupping her breasts.

Thea bowed off the sill, but he held her in place as white-hot need blazed through her, centring between her legs. She moaned as he circled one nipple, then the other, teasing her.

Wilder's erection strained against the loose fabric of his pants, but she didn't reach for him, no matter how badly she wanted to. He had asked to touch her. He needed the control, at least this time, and so she opened her legs for him wider still, in invitation, revealing the slickness he'd created there.

'You wanted to touch me,' she breathed. 'So touch me, Warsword.'

A low, rumbling growl escaped him and one of his hands moved lower, trailing her sternum, her navel, lower... Until his fingers slid down the centre of her.

Thea moaned, arching into his taunting touch as he spread her wetness in slow, luxurious circles around her clit.

'Is this all for me?' he said, his voice vibrating in the shell of her ear.

'Yes,' she gasped as he increased his pace. 'It's all for you. Only you.'

'Good.' And then he slid a finger inside her.

Thea cried out, her nails digging into the hard muscle of his shoulders. 'Wilder —'

He answered by adding another finger, slowly moving inside her, drawing out delicate coils of pleasure. She turned molten, desperately rocking her hips against his hand as he worked her, seeking more, already aching for release.

'I'm not done with you yet.' Wilder fell to his knees before her, his mouth descending, painting her with tongue and teeth, blending rapture and pain in a way that had her panting, in the way only he knew how.

He kissed her inner thighs, his beard scraping lightly before he sank his teeth into her skin, hard enough to leave marks. She watched the tapered muscles of his tattooed back shift as he moved between her legs, draping them over his broad shoulders.

Thea trembled and whimpered in need as he slipped his fingers from her, only to replace them with his tongue a moment later.

The back of her head hit the window and she cried out again as he licked her with the flat of his tongue, right up her centre, a long, lavish stroke that would be enough to send the sanest woman mad. She squeezed her breasts and pinched her nipples to the point of pain, trying to alleviate some of the pent-up tension.

Wilder moaned against her and she looked down to find him watching her, his gaze hooded with lust.

'You're a masterpiece,' he murmured against her, brazenly surveying her hands on her heaving breasts before his attention snapped back to her core, wet and wanting.

'Wilder...' she panted.

His silver eyes gleamed with feral desire. 'Is there something you want, Princess?'

'Please.'

'Say it,' he commanded. 'I want you to say it.'

'Make me come, Wilder. Please make me come.'

He put his mouth on her again. This time, he lavished her clit with attention, circling it with his tongue, sucking until she saw stars. All notion of restraint vanished and she rode his face with complete abandon, relishing every sweep of that talented tongue. She lost herself in him completely. Tighter and tighter she wound, ready to combust —

He pushed two fingers inside her and that was it.

'Gods, *Wilder* —' She unravelled in a tidal wave, her climax hitting her with such force that she went taut and limp all at once, shuddering around him with a sob. He didn't stop until he'd wrung every last ounce of satisfaction from her, until she couldn't hold herself up on the sill any longer.

Wilder scooped her up and took her to the bed, still surveying her with those molten silver eyes.

'I'm real,' she murmured, waiting for the uncertainty to hit.

But his handsome face broke into a grin, his gaze lingering on her naked body, still slick with her climax. 'Oh, that I know.'

'Is that so?'

'No dream or spell can replicate that taste, those sounds...'

Thea flushed.

Wilder leant down and kissed her. 'Thank you.'

'I feel like I should be thanking you...'

Wilder smiled and tucked her hair behind her ear. 'You can thank me later,' he said, before disappearing into the bathing chamber.

Thea stared after him, still breathless, in awe of the Warsword, *her* Warsword. He was in her blood, as much a part of her as the lightning and thunder coursing through her.

And in that moment, her fate hit her like a blow to the chest. Were she not already on the bed, her knees would have buckled beneath her.

Time.

They had so little of it now.

And when her time was done, he would still be here. Alone. She imagined how she would feel if their places were reversed, what she would do. Oblivion. That was all she could picture. A void of nothingness without him. Any ounce of fire within snuffed out.

Thea made a decision then, scrambling off the bed to the desk by the hearth. She had to leave something behind, something to ease those first few weeks without her.

And so she snatched up a piece of parchment, an inkpot and quill, and began to write.

CHAPTER ELEVEN

THEA

F reshly bathed and dressed, Thea went to find the others ahead of Wilder, leaving him with a pile of food and strict orders to eat his greens.

'Not sure I like how the tables have turned, Princess,' he'd laughed.

Thea had savoured the sound. *If I can keep him laughing, everything will be alright,* she told herself as she made her way through the strange university building.

She had never been in a place like it before. Wooden beams graced the ceilings in nearly every room, along with stained glass in the windows and pointed arches. The walls and even the tapestries adorning them were intense and dark, which should have made the place seem cold, only it didn't. There was a rich warmth to the halls that Thea appreciated, and she could see why Talemir had worked so hard to restore it.

The entire university and its grounds were encompassed by a film of darkness, a great dome of protection, shielding it and its people from the monsters crawling across Naarva's lands. Thea marvelled at the ingenuity of it, somehow allowing light to filter through – from where, she didn't know; she'd seen no buttery rays of sunlight in the fallen kingdom beyond.

'I was about to send Dratos up to get you,' the Shadow Prince himself said by way of greeting, leaning against one of the sandstone pillars, a steaming mug cupped between his hands.

'I don't think Wilder would have appreciated that,' Thea replied.

Talemir smiled. 'That's half of Dratos' appeal.' He took a sip from his drink before eyeing her with a more serious expression. 'How is he?'

'He's managing.'

Talemir gave a stiff nod. 'That's more than we can hope for. That place...'

'I know.' Thea rested her hand on the pommel of her sword and looked out onto the grounds, noticing the ivy and the midnight blooms for the first time. 'It's beautiful here.'

Talemir made a noise of agreement. 'Drue and I worked hard to make it so.'

'When do I get to meet her?'

'Soon enough. She's dying to meet the woman who "tamed Wilder's moody arse" – her words, not mine.'

Thea laughed. 'I like her already.'

Returning her smile, Talemir tossed the dregs of his tea into a nearby bush. 'In the meantime, there's one or two people who want to see you.'

He motioned for her to walk with him. Slightly bewildered, Thea followed the Shadow Prince from the courtyard and away from the university buildings entirely. They walked in comfortable silence across the sprawling green lawns and stone pathways that wound through clusters of towering oak and willow trees. Not for the first time, Thea marvelled at the life here, at how, behind a shield of darkness, vibrant wildflowers bloomed and soft grass cushioned her steps. It was a far cry from the barren marshland they'd just come from, and before that, the dying winter forests of Aveum.

'How?' she said, her fingertips brushing the waist-high lavender that lined the walkway.

'The shield is my doing,' Talemir replied. 'It took a long while after I was turned for me to realise I was capable of more than flying and wielding darkness as a weapon.' He motioned to the shimmering dome around them. 'I and others like me maintain this shield around the clock, protecting our people, and protecting the sun orchids from discovery.'

'Sun orchids?' Thea asked.

'We'll get to that. But first...' Talemir pointed to a lone figure sitting on a stone wall in the near distance, wings tucked in at her back.

Anya.

'I'll catch up with you later.' Talemir gave her an encouraging smile before heading back to the main university grounds.

Thea started towards Anya, who turned at her approach. Her sister's head was freshly shaved close to her skull, making the scar through her eye seem all the more brutal, but she gave Thea a wolfish grin and lifted three fingers to her shoulder in the midrealms' respectful salute.

'Well, well, well,' she said. 'Althea Embervale, the Warsword and tower destroyer, is in our midst.' She let out a low, appreciative whistle at the sight of the Naarvian steel at Thea's belt. 'Nice blade.'

Thea couldn't help returning the grin as she unsheathed it and held it out to Anya. 'It certainly does the job.'

'I'll say.' Anya weighed the sword, testing the balance in her hands before handing it back with a nod of approval. 'Knew you'd have one of your own the next time I saw you. I heard you carved them up good at the Scarlet Tower...'

'Did a little more than that,' Thea ventured.

Anya barked a laugh. 'Heard that too. No putting the lightning back in the bottle, huh?'

'Not this time.' Thea sheathed her sword. 'Did I fuck everything up? By announcing our existence to the world?'

Anya hopped down from the wall and started down the crest in the land. 'Guess we'll find out soon enough.'

'That's not exactly reassuring.'

'I've never been in the business of reassuring.'

'Isn't that what big sisters are for?' Thea asked, falling in step beside her.

Anya snorted. 'I'm a bit out of practice.'

'No shit.'

Thea followed her gaze to a field of golden flowers at the foot of the hill, where several workers were among the rows, harvesting.

'You going to tell me where everyone is? What the plan is now that we're here?'

'There's an official meeting of allies due to take place here in two days' time,' Anya replied. 'We'll make all our plans for the war to come then.'

'And who are these allies? What happened while I was in the Great Rite and dealing with the tower?'

'We strategised at the Singing Hare for another day after

you left, then we went about carrying out those duties – rallying more shadow-touched to our cause, trying to get word of Artos' treachery to the remaining rulers...'

'And?'

Anya shook her head. 'No luck with the rulers. They're convinced that the Daughter of Darkness is behind all of this, and Queen Reyna hasn't left her chambers since the death of her husband. They're saying she's in no right mind to ally with anyone. Meanwhile, Artos spreads his poison across the lands like a fucking swarm of locusts.'

'What of Princess Jasira?' Thea asked, realising with a start that she hadn't spared her friend a second thought amid the rest of the realm's horrors.

'We think she escaped in Vios,' Anya said. 'She's not been seen with Artos, or anyone else, for that matter.'

'I should have —'

'You can't watch everyone, Thea,' Anya told her. 'If she's in danger, it's because her own father put her there.'

It didn't stop Thea recalling Jasira's scream of terror as wraiths had descended on her carriage on the way to the eclipse. She hoped the princess had someone looking out for her now, but Thea knew the best thing she could do was fight – fight for a world in which shadow didn't swallow all that was good.

Thea glanced at Anya, the note of vulnerability in her voice nearly palpable as she said, 'Do you think we can win?'

Anya's jaw worked before she answered. 'We can win.'

Thea raised a brow. 'This is where practising your reassurances might come in handy.'

'I'll keep that in mind,' Anya replied. 'Come. I want to show you what that cloak of darkness has allowed us to do here in Naarva...'

Beneath it, the rebel territory had thrived, not least of which in the breathtaking field of golden blooms before her now. The same flowers she'd seen being carried across the quadrangle the day before.

'What is all this?' Thea asked Anya, watching as workers cut blooms from their stems and deposited them in baskets.

'Our greatest weapon,' Anya replied. 'Sun orchids... The natural adversary of anything shadow-touched, myself and Talemir included. Drue and her family discovered them years ago and have been working to grow and harvest them ever since.'

Thea gaped. 'How has Artos not found out? Even with the shield? Have there been breaches?'

'In eight years? A handful,' Anya replied. 'But we're careful, as careful as we can be. That's why we let the majority of the midrealms think the worst of us. It stops anyone looking at this patch of darkness too closely. No one suspects that the University of Naarva and its surrounding grounds holds a rebel force.'

'And what do you do with a bunch of flowers against wraiths and reapers?'

'We extract the essence, treat our weapons with it. Over the years we've perfected the formula so that a blade imbued with sun orchid extract can be as powerful against a reaper as a Naarvian steel sword.'

Thea blinked. 'You didn't want to tell me that before I went through three deadly trials to obtain one?'

Anya laughed. 'We needed a lightning-wielding Warsword in the mix regardless.'

Thea thought back to the strange sphere Talemir had handed her, the exploding device she'd used in the prison. 'You're not just treating blades with the stuff, are you?'

Anya shook her head. 'Why do you think we wanted Thezmarr's alchemists on hand?' She spoke the words with a playful glint in her eyes.

Movement blurred in Thea's peripheral vision. 'Althea Nine Lives!' cried a familiar voice.

Thea barely had time to brace herself as Wren tore away from the flowerbed and crashed into her, almost crushing her in a bear hug.

'What in the realms...' Thea muttered, squeezing her back once the shock had ebbed away.

'Told you we needed them,' Anya shrugged.

Thea looked over Wren's shoulder. 'Are Samra and Ida —'

Wren shook her head. 'We couldn't take *every* alchemist from Thezmarr. They volunteered to remain at the fortress, though they're working for us. The sun orchids have advanced some of our developments drastically.'

The realisation dawned on Thea instantly. She turned her attention back to Wren. 'You designed that thing,' she said. 'The ball that exploded with gold and turned all the wraiths to ash?'

Wren broke away and sketched a bow. 'Obviously. That kind of genius doesn't grow on trees, Thee.'

'How long have you been here?' Thea asked, looking from Anya to Wren in disbelief. The last time she'd seen them together, Wren had been far from friendly, but now... There seemed to be an ease between the two, a familiarity that sparked a pang of envy in Thea.

'I didn't return to Thezmarr after we all met in Aveum,' Wren explained. 'And thank the Furies I didn't —' A quiet gasp sounded from Wren as her gaze fell to the scar on Thea's wrist. 'Thee...' she murmured, her voice strained. 'What did they do to you?'

But unlike with Wilder, Thea found she couldn't talk of it. Instead, she said, 'It aches. All the time.'

Wren hesitated, just for a moment, before nodding to herself. 'I'll make you a salve when we get back. I have just the thing.'

'Thank you.'

Thea could feel Anya's eyes on them, could feel the distance that a lifetime apart had created. Wren seemed to sense it too.

'Can we show her, then?' she asked, turning to Anya. 'She'll love it.'

Anya shrugged. 'Why not?'

Bewildered, Thea followed her sisters from the field of sun orchids. As they walked, Wren eagerly built upon what Talemir had told her about the nearby alchemy academy.

'Before the fall of Naarva, it was the most highly regarded institution for alchemy novices. People came from all over the midrealms to attend,' she told them. 'It was known for producing the most elite master alchemists in history, Farissa included.'

'Has she told you much about it?' Thea asked.

Wren shook her head. 'It disbanded when the kingdom fell to the shadow wraiths. Its scholars and masters were swallowed up by the world... But its archives were touted as the most extensive on record.' Her voice was wistful. 'What I would have given to see it.'

'Maybe after...?' Thea ventured.

Wren gave a sad smile. 'It's nothing but a shell now, Thee.'

Anya's gaze slid to Wren with a knowing glint. "So they say..."

After a while, they reached an outer building on the

grounds. Smoke drifted from the chimney in great, thick plumes.

Wren elbowed Thea. 'We wanted to show you... They rebuilt the Naarvian forge, right here.'

Even Anya was smiling as she pushed the door open. 'Fendran? You up for some company?'

Someone grunted within, but that seemed good enough for Anya, who motioned for Wren and Thea to enter.

The heat hit Thea first, a wave of it, blazing from the furnace at the centre of the forge, which cast flickering shadows on the soot-stained stone walls. The air was thick with the scent of burning coal and hot iron, as well as the earthy leather aroma of the heavy aprons the workers within wore. Inside was a symphony of hammers striking anvils, sending sparks flying like molten stars. Thea drank in the sight of the tongs, hammers and mallets, the chisels and rasps bearing the marks of countless meticulous carvings – the tools that had shaped all the Warsword weapons before hers.

'This might not be the original forge,' Anya said. 'But it's one of the original blacksmiths...' She pointed to the far corner where the worker in question toiled, his brow glistening with sweat, his hands crafting legendary weapons from fire and iron.

The blacksmith lowered a red-hot sword into a trough of water, the metal hissing and steaming upon contact. When he was satisfied, the man motioned to an assistant to take over, and he approached Anya with a wide smile.

'I see you and Drue have recruited more women warriors, Anya,' he said fondly, his kind eyes scanning over Wren and Thea with a glint of amusement.

'Oh,' Wren said. 'I'm not a —'

But Anya waved her off. 'We're all warriors here, Wren,' she said. 'Fendran, these are my sisters, Elwren and Althea, from Thezmarr.'

Fendran's eyes widened.

'Wren, Thea... This is Fendran, Drue's father and our chief blacksmith.'

'Pleasure.' The older man shook both their hands eagerly. 'Welcome to Naarva, ladies.'

'Thank you,' Wren replied warmly.

As Thea shook Fendran's thickly gloved hand, an idea sparked. 'Fendran,' she said. 'Do you, by chance, make armour?'

CHAPTER TWELVE

WILDER

Wilder was beyond grateful to find Biscuit, his Tverrian stallion, in the university stables. The hand told him it was the 'Bear Slayer behemoth' who had managed to swindle the horse from King Artos' possession and send him Anya's way.

Breathing in the scent of fresh hay in the stall, Wilder brushed Biscuit's black coat into a shine, making a mental note to thank his brother in arms. As a Warsword, he'd never gone into battle without Biscuit, and he didn't plan on starting anytime soon, not with the war ahead looking so grim.

The thought lanced him with another pang of regret. There were many these days. Because of his capture, Thea hadn't gone to Tver to capture her own stallion. Because of him, Thea wouldn't be riding into battle with a horse that was Furies-made for her.

There was something a little more pressing to attend to first, Warsword,' she had said.

'Beautiful, stubborn woman,' he muttered, shaking his

head and taking a comb to Biscuit's mane. Thea's stubborn streak had infuriated and fascinated him from the very beginning.

'It's a nice change when you're agreeable,' he'd told her on the road to Delmira.

'Don't expect it to last.'

'Wouldn't dream of it, Princess.'

When she swore at him, he warned, *'Be cordial. Or when you become a Warsword I'll be there to name your Tverrian stallion "Pancake", or something worse.'*

Those earlier days of travelling together as master and apprentice seemed so long ago, and yet he looked back on them fondly. The memories were full of colour, rather than the stifling darkness of so many others.

The tower had left him scrambling for reality and control, and it was manifesting in ways he hadn't expected. He was holding back with Thea. He was questioning the world before him, and he couldn't seem to let go.

Desperate to ground himself, Wilder continued combing Biscuit's mane. The repetitive motion of teasing out the knots soothed him, stilled the tremor in his right little finger that still plagued him. With a shudder, he wondered if it was a withdrawal symptom from whatever drugs they'd forced into him, before he instantly shut the thought down, boxed it up and shoved it deep in the recesses of his mind.

But the damage was done. The thought took root and the tremor returned. Suddenly, he was back in that dark cell, the weight of the tower's magic pressing down on him, his own abilities muted, his body slick with sweat as the onslaught of nightmares flashed before him.

Biscuit whinnied, shifting beneath Wilder's touch, sensing his unease, his fear.

'You'll become a legend among monsters.' The Archmage of Chains' voice came back to him in a poisoned whisper, making his skin crawl, a shiver racing down his spine. He had been moments away from becoming a weapon in their army, a tool to be used against everyone he held dear, his free will stripped away entirely.

Cursing silently, Wilder tossed the comb back into the grooming kit and searched for the farrier's rasp —

Only to find it clutched in a large, outstretched hand.

He knew those hands. Had seen them braid countless belts. He didn't dare believe it, not until he looked up and saw his brother's face, and even then, he wasn't sure if he was dreaming again.

'Malik?' he managed.

His huge frame took up the entire entrance to the stall, even with his shoulders slightly caved in as he handed Wilder the tool.

'This isn't real,' Wilder muttered, as he took the rasp. 'This is what they do...'

It followed the same pattern as it had in the cell. A myriad of horrific memories and imaginings, and only at the point of the mind breaking would they show something good... Only to start the torture all over again.

Malik's huge hand came down on Wilder's shoulder, a gentle but firm weight, his fingers digging in just enough to give Wilder pause —

A soft bark sounded from his brother's side.

'Dax?' Wilder stared at the mongrel. His ears were pricked up, as Wilder had seen countless times before when Malik had been in a trance of sorts.

Wilder's gaze slid back to his brother. 'You're really here...'

Malik's eyes crinkled as he grinned and pulled Wilder into a near-suffocating hug. Wilder let him. And a moment later, he squeezed Malik back, taking solace in his brother's presence like he had when they were younger.

At last he broke away, emotion welling in his throat. Malik simply smiled and motioned for Wilder to continue with Biscuit's grooming. Wilder shook his head in disbelief, a smile tugging at the corner of his mouth.

'You certainly get around nowadays,' he told his brother, picking up Biscuit's front leg and tending to his shoe.

Malik made a noise of amusement, reaching for Biscuit's mane and dividing it up into sections.

'You're not seriously about to braid my warhorse's mane?' Wilder said.

Malik ignored him and went about doing exactly that.

With another shake of his head, Wilder continued cleaning and shaping Biscuit's shoes. Someone had been taking decent care of them in his absence. It was surreal, to be working quietly in the stall with his brother at his side, Dax sprawled in the hay by the door. He could feel Malik watching him, just as he was stealing glimpses at Malik, as though neither of them quite believed the other was there. It had been a long time since they'd been alone together.

When Wilder returned the tools to the kit, he found himself staring at the faint scars that littered Mal's face. The memory of him being attacked at Islaton felt more fresh than it had the day after it had happened, thanks to the Scarlet Tower.

'I told you before,' a rich voice sounded from the door. 'None of it was ever your fault, Wilder.'

Talemir was there, leaning against the frame, his hazel

eyes brimming with more understanding than Wilder felt he deserved.

'I didn't say —' he started.

'You didn't need to say. You've been carrying that burden since the day it happened.' He strode forward and slung an arm around Malik's enormous shoulders. 'We're safe. We're whole,' he said. 'Wouldn't you agree, Mal?'

Malik covered Talemir's face with his gigantic palm and gave him a gentle push with a grin.

Talemir laughed and raised a brow at Wilder. 'See? Same old shit.'

Wilder forced himself to take a deep breath, to process the sight of his brother and his former mentor before him, something he'd thought he would never see again.

Dax gave another bark and Biscuit snorted in protest at the mongrel's presence, but Wilder still stared, stuck. Here were the men who had suffered because of him, the men he had cared for his whole life, whom he'd been unable to save from their fates —

Talemir's expression softened. 'It's time to let go.'

Wilder's whole body sagged. 'But I —'

'No.' Talemir shook his head. 'No buts. What happened at Islaton was never your fault. We were never your responsibility. Our own choices led to the events of that day, not yours.'

Malik made a sound of agreement.

'We won't be your excuse any longer,' Talemir said firmly.

Wilder baulked. 'Excuse?'

'To not live your life fully, to hold back —'

'What do you know about it?' Wilder asked quietly. 'I haven't seen you in over eight years. You don't know anything about my life.'

'Is that what you think?' Talemir scoffed. 'You think that I haven't checked in over the years?'

Wilder stared at him, the stall suddenly seeming far too small with Biscuit, Malik and Talemir all crowding the space around him.

'It's time to let that day go,' Talemir said again.

'You could have died. Both of you.'

'Such is life.' Talemir exchanged a knowing look with Malik. 'And yet here we stand.'

For a second, Wilder felt like a young Guardian again, standing in the presence of far greater men than he. He and Torj had followed them around like puppies, in awe of how the Shieldbreaker and Prince of Hearts moved through the world. Despite everything that had happened, they stood just as tall now, just as unyielding.

'What do you say, Apprentice? Will you put all this shit behind you?' Talemir prompted, hazel eyes gleaming with mischief.

'I'm not your fucking apprentice,' Wilder muttered, unable to stop the tug of a smile.

'Well?'

Wilder grunted. 'I'll try.'

'Good enough, for now.' Tal started towards the door. He paused on the threshold of the stables, surveying the lush grounds before them and letting out a small sigh with a glance at Wilder. 'Every now and then, just for a moment, I forget the horrors outside these walls. The war brewing so close by. For a fraction of a second, I can breathe in the peace —'

Something collided with Talemir's torso, sending him staggering sideways.

HELEN SCHEUERER

Wilder jumped back, his dagger half-drawn, before he saw the source of the mayhem.

'Boo!' A little boy had flung himself onto Talemir. A pair of tiny wings flapped at his back and a slouchy knitted cap fell about his eyes as he laughed with glee.

'You...' Talemir's eyes crinkled in amusement as he peeled the child from his torso and held him at arm's length, the boy's legs kicking joyfully in the air. 'Are not meant to be here.'

The child only grinned wider.

Wilder could only stare at the wriggling bundle of mischief in Talemir's arms. With the same nose, the same chin and even the same wave in his dark golden-brown hair, the boy was almost a mirror image of the Shadow Prince, except for the ice-blue shade of his bright eyes.

A garbled noise escaped Talemir as a small foot hit a soft spot, and he snatched the child around the waist and hung him upside down, the boy's tiny wings flapping. 'What have I told you about doing that?' Talemir said, though there was no missing the note of amusement in his tone. 'Your mother —'

'Thought it was high time his father experienced some of the insanity this morning,' came a voice from nearby.

Wilder turned to see a beautiful woman watching them from the stable fence line, her arms folded over her chest, a sword and cutlass hanging at her hips. She stood as elegantly as a dancer, burnt-umber hair threaded with streaks of red falling loosely to her mid-back. Perched on her shoulder was a familiar hawk.

'Drue?' Wilder gaped at her. Terrence flapped his wings and launched from the ranger's shoulder.

'I haven't aged a day, Hawthorne,' she quipped. 'So quit your gawking and give me a hug.'

He hadn't seen her since he'd left on such bad terms all those years ago, but Drue greeted him with a wide smile, her piercing blue eyes bright as they settled on him.

She didn't hesitate, striding forward and throwing her arms around his neck. 'Good to have you back.'

After the shock ebbed away, Wilder returned her embrace. 'I'm sorry,' he told her. 'I'm sorry for how I behaved.'

Drue clapped him on the back and held him at arm's length to peer into his face. 'You were young and stupid.'

Wilder gave a hoarse laugh. 'As opposed to now?'

'Now you're just stupid,' she said with a grin.

'You haven't changed.'

'Why would she?' Talemir interjected, striding forward and dropping a kiss to his wife's temple. 'There's no improving perfection.'

A blush stained Drue's cheeks, but she looked pleased.

Wilder glanced back at Talemir, who had his hands full with his spitting image.

'This was who I wanted you to meet yesterday,' Talemir explained, throwing the boy over his shoulder. 'This is our son, Ryland.'

Breaking away from their embrace, Drue huffed a laugh. 'Son. Menace. Harbinger of destruction. Whatever you want to call him.'

For a moment, Wilder stared, suddenly hit with the gravity of all he had missed over the years. Talemir had a son. And he hadn't been here, hadn't even known —

'I'm happy for you,' he managed somewhat awkwardly.

Talemir chuckled good-naturedly. 'Didn't think you'd see the day, did you?'

That, at least, put Wilder at ease, a genuine smile spreading across his face as his friend wrestled with the unruly child. 'Fatherhood looks good on you, Tal.'

'Everything looks good on me,' the Shadow Prince replied.

Drue rolled her eyes. 'We're late for lunch.' She motioned towards the main grounds.

Ryland threw his hand to his brow in salute. 'Captain!'

Talemir laughed deeply. 'You've got that right, Trouble.'

But Wilder blinked, still in shock. 'Lunch?'

'It's a meal you have around midday,' Drue quipped. 'And we're late.'

Wilder's side warmed as Malik stood at his left, Dax's tail beating against his right leg, as though they could sense him on the verge of overwhelm.

'Sounds good,' he managed, shooting his brother a grateful look.

As they walked through the university, Wilder was torn between marvelling at the lush grounds and the startling fact that he was here with his brother and Talemir after all this time, with Talemir's *son* darting about their feet with Dax. There was no missing the pride in Tal's gaze as he watched the little boy make a nuisance of himself. It was surreal, to say the least. So much had changed.

When they reached the quadrangle, Wilder spotted Thea in one of the alcoves. She was hunched over a notebook, scribbling away, looking deep in thought, far away from here.

What's she writing? Wilder wondered.

He realised he'd stopped walking, and that Talemir had

halted beside him, while Drue, Malik, Dax and Ryland had gone ahead. Tal followed his gaze to Thea.

'Thank you,' Wilder said quietly. 'Thank you for going with her to the tower.'

'Nothing would have stopped her,' Talemir replied.

Wilder smiled, warmth blooming in his chest. 'I know.'

Talemir gave him a broad grin. 'I'm happy for you, my old friend.'

'As I am for you.'

'Took you long enough,' Tal quipped.

Sensing their attention, Thea looked up from her writing, her eyes finding Wilder's across the quadrangle instantly.

But Talemir made a pained noise as he spotted something soaring towards them.

'What?' Wilder said, making out Terrence's form as the hawk made a beeline for them.

'If Drue's sending Terrence back, we're in trouble.' Talemir started towards the entrance of the main building.

'I'll catch up,' Wilder called after him.

'It'd be in your best interests if you do.' Talemir winced as Terrence landed hard on his shoulder. Knowing the hawk, he'd done so on purpose, Wilder mused as the pair disappeared inside.

Thea's voice sounded beside him. 'You two talked?'

Wilder turned to her, the sight of her stealing the air from his lungs. The light filtering through Tal's shadow shield caught the gold in her braid. Her eyes were bright and alert as she studied him in turn, her luscious lips slightly parted.

'We did.'

He leant down to kiss her, marvelling at how he was able

to do so freely now. Her mouth met his eagerly, opening for him, allowing his tongue to sweep in. He moaned at the taste of her. Would it ever end? The insatiable need for her? The feral desire to possess her mind, body and soul? He wanted to have her against one of the stone pillars, not caring who saw him claim her —

Thea broke away. 'Don't start what you can't finish, Warsword,' she warned.

'Who said anything about not finishing?' he growled.

'We've got to meet the others.'

'Fuck the others.'

Thea laughed and tugged on his hand. 'I didn't think you'd be up for sharing.'

A startled noise escaped him at her filthy words. 'Never.'

'That's what I thought,' Thea replied smugly. She led him into the main university building. She seemed to have gotten acquainted with the place far more quickly than he had.

'Where are you taking us?' Wilder asked as they entered an area that looked more residential than formal.

'The Scholar's Lounge,' Thea replied.

'I think we're meant to go to some sort of meal...?'

'We are.' She pushed open a pair of double doors and entered the room, leaving Wilder with no choice but to follow.

He didn't know what he was expecting, but it wasn't the warm and inviting space beyond. Not a dining room, but cosy and comfortable living quarters. Floor-to-ceiling windows graced the far walls, light filtering through the glass and the leaves of the trees outside.

Malik was already there, looking out onto the grounds. Thea gasped, lurching forward.

'Mal!' she cried, pure joy brightening her whole face. As

she greeted the former Warsword, Dax jumped up to lick her cheek and she laughed, the sound lighting up the entire room.

Wilder watched for a moment, the sight warming his fragile heart. They had been friends long before Wilder had ever laid eyes on Thea, and the pairing somehow worked: the Shieldbreaker and the lost heir of Delmira. Malik beamed at her and tugged on the end of her braid before tapping the pommel of her Naarvian steel blade, as if to say, *I always knew you could do it.*

Thea's answering grin was bold and bright.

Leaving them to their reunion, Wilder turned to the rest of the room. The furniture was all mismatched, as though it had been taken from all over the university and mashed together. Somehow, it suited the place. It was carpeted with thick rugs, with several lounges and armchairs framing the edges. Adrienne, Dratos and Anya sat with plates balanced on their laps, talking quietly among themselves, each of them giving him a nod or a wave of acknowledgement. He was glad Adrienne and Anya didn't leap to their feet to make a fuss, though he saw the relief in both their eyes at the sight of him whole and unharmed.

Dratos' cousin, Gus, was cross-legged on the floor with Ryland, who was stealing grapes from his plate with a gleeful laugh. A long table was pushed up against another wall, plates stacked on one end with a variety of steaming dishes waiting.

Drue approached, linking her arm through his. 'Are you going to introduce me to your lady Warsword or what, Hawthorne?'

A chuckle escaped Wilder at that, and he led Drue over to where Thea was still talking with Malik.

'Thea,' he said. 'I want you to meet Drue Emmerson, Talemir's wife.'

Drue thrust a hand out to Thea, who shook it firmly.

'That's not my only claim to fame, I assure you,' Drue said with a grin. 'But thank you for keeping my husband in one piece. Though I'm yet to hear the story of how you won Hawthorne's moody heart.'

'He's still as moody as ever,' Dratos offered from nearby, flexing his wings.

Wilder rolled his eyes. 'Always a pleasure, Dratos.'

But Drue was pushing him towards the table with the food. 'Get a plate. You too, Thea,' she called.

It wasn't long before Wilder found himself in an armchair, a plate piled high with food on his knees and a tankard of ale at his feet as the chaos of family unfolded around him. Thea had pulled up a seat beside him and was fighting back tears of laughter as, against his parents' protests, Ryland proceeded to strip off his pants and dart around the room wearing not a stitch of clothing but for the ugly knitted hat that kept falling over his eyes.

Talemir sighed, rubbing the back of his neck. 'It's a phase he's going through,' he said. 'Hates wearing clothes. Wants to be naked all the time...'

'I remember you going through a similar phase,' Drue retorted.

'Oh, that wasn't a phase, Wildfire,' Talemir replied with a wink.

Dratos made a noise of disgust. 'Will you two cut it out? Some of us are trying to eat.'

A tiny hand reached for his food.

'Put some pants on, you terror,' Dratos barked, but

Ryland only laughed and snagged a chicken leg from his plate.

Drue shook her head and took a long drink from her tankard. 'It's a lost cause.'

Wilder watched it all unfold, realising his cheeks were aching from smiling as Talemir scooped up Ryland and tried to wrangle him back into his clothes. Talemir's joy was contagious, and for the first time in years, Wilder understood. He saw it for himself: even amid the pending war and the encroaching darkness, Talemir was more than whole, more than happy. Wilder hadn't robbed him of anything.

'Definitely your son,' Drue called, her voice light with amusement as Ryland kicked and squealed against his father's efforts.

Wilder's throat bobbed as he tried to swallow the lump forming there. He caught Thea watching him in his peripheral vision.

'You're alright?' she asked, quietly enough that only he could hear.

He covered her hand with his and stroked the scar-littered skin there with his thumb. 'Yes,' he told her, and for the first time since leaving that tower, he meant it.

Drue hit her fork against the side of her tankard, commanding their attention.

'I had planned on a grand welcome speech,' she said after clearing her throat. 'But truth be told, I just wanted us to have a meal, have a moment together, before...'

Drue trailed off. She didn't need to finish her sentence. They all knew what she meant: before the war. Before everything changed. For they all knew it was coming, knew there was no stopping it now.

'Tomorrow, we start planning. The training begins, the strategising starts in earnest, but today... today, we eat.'

Wilder raised his own tankard, gratitude swelling in his chest. 'To good food,' he toasted.

'And even better company,' Dratos drawled, tipping his own tankard back and draining it.

'And —'

But Adrienne was cut off by one of the doors flying open. A dishevelled Wren entered, wearing an apron, her face smudged with dirt. 'Sorry, sorry!' She wiped her hands on a clean patch of her apron and reached for a plate as she scanned the room. 'Did I miss anything? Did anyone else arrive —'

'Like who?' Anya said, a coy smile on her lips.

Wren pinned her with a challenging glare. 'Like Cal, and Kipp...?'

'No one else?' Anya pressed, her eyes bright. 'Not a golden-haired Warsword, perhaps?'

Beside Wilder, Thea glanced between her two sisters and bit her lip, fighting a smile of her own. Wilder waited for her to explain, but she just shook her head. *Later,* she mouthed.

Wren was still glaring at their shadow-touched sister.

'Cal and Kipp are on their way,' Anya replied, still grinning.

Wren's eyes narrowed and she looked as though she wanted to ask something more, but instead she turned back to the food and scooped an enormous serving of salad onto her plate. 'Good.'

A huff of amusement sounded, and Wilder looked across the room to see Talemir cradling Ryland in his arms. The little boy looked so small sagging against his father's broad chest, his tiny wings drooping at his back, his cheeks flushed with sleep.

'Thank the gods for that,' Drue muttered from her armchair, downing the rest of her drink. But she looked at the pair with utter adoration in her eyes.

'Turned out pretty well for them, don't you think?' Thea said quietly, following Wilder's gaze.

'I wouldn't have believed it yesterday,' Wilder admitted. 'But... yes, I think it did.'

He didn't want what Tal and Drue had, not exactly. He only wanted Thea. A future with her. And for a moment, he allowed himself to dream that fate would allow them to have it.

CHAPTER THIRTEEN

THEA

The festivities lasted well into the evening, and Thea found herself enjoying the odd company. It was a combination mad enough that it might just make their alliances work.

For a time, she sat between Wren and Anya, trading stories about their worst name days. Both Thea's and her older sister's were on the horizon, just two months apart.

'I spent my last freezing my arse off in the hinterlands, hunting down Wilder,' Thea offered, glancing at her Warsword across the room. Warmth bloomed in her cheeks as she took in his handsome form, his smile soft as he watched Talemir conjure shadow birds for Dax to chase around the room.

Wren scoffed. 'That's nothing. What about my fourteenth name day? When that tonic exploded all over me and I had to stay wrapped in those smelly leaves for three days to treat my burns?'

'That was gross,' Thea admitted.

'I see your smelly leaves and raise you a bog,' Anya declared, leaning back and resting her boots on the table.

'A bog? You spent a name day in a bog?' Thea asked, barely keeping the laughter at bay.

'It had been a while since I'd had a hot dinner, and there was this chicken...' Anya began.

Wren blinked. 'A chicken?'

Anya nodded solemnly. 'A chicken —'

'Gods, not the chicken story,' Dratos moaned from nearby.

'It's my *name day* story,' Anya objected.

'It's your *everything* story. Chicken. Name day. Bog. Last I heard there was a rogue artist involved too —'

Anya gave a dramatic sigh. 'You've built it up now. It was my name day. I followed a chicken into a bog and got stuck. Mud up to my tits. Couldn't move a muscle. For the entire day. The end.'

'But what of the rogue artist?' Thea pressed, her cheeks aching.

'That's Dratos' description of himself, because he hid in the grass, trying to draw the whole thing. Bastard waited hours to help me out.'

Thea and Wren exchanged a glance and burst into hysterics.

Anya was shaking her head, her eyes gleaming. 'I never did get that chicken, either.'

That only made Thea laugh harder. 'You win,' she conceded. 'Worst name day ever.'

Wren smiled widely at both of them. 'Perhaps one of these days we'll be able to celebrate one together. As a family.'

'Perhaps,' Thea said at the same time as Anya. Though

Thea didn't remind Wren that she only had one more name day up her sleeve.

As the wee hours of the morning approached, slowly but surely, different groups retired, while others cleaned up the leftovers in a comfortable quiet. Dratos and Gus had fallen asleep on twin lounges, their arms flung over their heads in exactly the same way, their wings draped carelessly beneath them.

Wilder came to Thea's side and pressed a firm kiss to her lips. 'I'm going to the aviary with Talemir to send word to Torj. I'll be back in a little while. According to Wren, Audra is somewhere around here, if you wanted to see her?'

'Audra's here?' Thea gaped. How had it taken so long for someone to mention it? 'Why didn't she join —'

'You'll have to ask her, Princess,' Wilder murmured against her mouth before departing with Talemir.

Thea didn't have to guess where Audra was; she knew on instinct. She headed to the library, the one just outside her and Wilder's quarters.

Thea had never been overly bookish, having always preferred the outdoors and the weight of a blade in her hand, but even she could appreciate the sheer vastness of the shelves. She hadn't had the chance to take it in the night before, but now, with all the torches lit, she let out an appreciative whistle. Soft golden light flickered from glass lanterns and the hearth at the far end of the room, casting a warm, ethereal glow upon the countless rows of shelves. They stretched tall and wide, laden with leatherbound tomes and yellowed scrolls.

Thea spotted the Thezmarrian librarian perusing the stacks by the fire, murmuring softly – not to herself, Thea realised, but to Malik, who sat in one of the armchairs before the flames as he did back at the fortress, Dax sleeping soundly at his feet.

At Thea's approach, Audra looked up, and though the stern-faced older woman didn't smile openly, there was a spark of joy behind her spectacles.

'So you became a storm-wielding Warsword after all, Althea…' she said by way of greeting.

'You told me I had to choose,' Thea replied, raising a brow.

'And so you did… You chose to be exactly what you are, nothing less.'

Thea stared at her former warden. 'Did you know? What would happen in the Rite? What would be asked of me?'

'How could I? Not even *I'm* that knowledgeable.'

Thea reached for the jewelled dagger at her belt and held it out to the older woman. 'Thank you for this.'

Audra didn't take it. 'Did it make a difference?'

'I think it might have made all the difference,' Thea said.

Audra didn't flinch at the sight of her scar, nor did she question Thea about the Great Rite at all. Instead, she simply pushed the dagger back to her. 'I'll have it back when the war is won. I have a feeling you'll need it again before long.'

Thea knew better than to argue with the librarian, so she sheathed the tiny blade at her waist again and turned her attention to the rows of shelves around them.

'I suppose this is far more impressive than Thezmarr's library,' she ventured, running her fingers along several spines. 'Even for a fallen kingdom…'

Audra scoffed, moving towards the shelves. 'Half the

books here are love stories,' she retorted. 'I don't know what Starling has done with the academic texts, but there are more romances here than history books. He always was a dreamer.'

Thea's brows shot up in surprise, but she didn't comment further. Instead, she peered around the library. 'You can't find what you're looking for, then?'

'I'm not even sure what I'm looking for yet. I'll know it when I see it.'

Audra's attention lingered on Malik by the fire. His huge frame took up the entirety of the armchair as he stared into the flames.

'I asked if he needed anything,' Audra said quietly.

Thea shook her head. 'Sometimes he just needs to decompress. I imagine being here, as much as he loves everyone, is a lot for him to take in.'

'It's a lot for everyone to take in,' Audra admitted before glancing at Thea, her brows knitting together. 'Something on your mind?'

'These days? Always.'

Audra simply waited.

'I was wondering… What happens to a person's magic when they die?'

Audra pinned her with a sharp stare. 'Why?'

Untucking her fate stone from her shirt, Thea sighed. 'You know what this is,' she said. 'You always have. You know what's coming for me.'

'I have never pretended to know what the Furies have in store for any of us,' Audra replied tersely.

'Their names are Iseldra, Morwynn and Valdara,' Thea heard herself say before she came back to the moment, rubbing her fate stone with her thumb. The numeral it bore was darker than it had ever been before. 'Does the magic die with its wielder? Or is there a way to… pass it on?'

Audra was quiet for a moment before she spoke again. 'Pass it on?'

'I'm just trying to be prepared,' Thea told her. 'If there's a way I can pass it on to Wren and Anya, if I'm not here for… for the end… If there's a chance I can do that, then I want to. I want to give them every advantage imaginable. I want —'

'I'll look into it,' Audra said.

'Thank you.'

Audra nodded stiffly. 'Althea?'

'Hmm?'

'Might I make a suggestion?' When Thea didn't protest, Audra gripped her shoulder, her long fingers surprisingly strong. 'Get some sleep. Tomorrow is a big day.'

Thea nodded. 'In a little while. For now, I'd like to catch up with my friend.' She glanced to Malik and Dax by the fire.

'Very well.' Audra took several books in hand and left.

Thea sank into the vacant armchair and turned to her companion with a smile. 'How are you, my friend?'

Malik's eyes sparkled, his fingers working on a leather belt.

'I'm glad,' she said. 'Glad you have had Talemir and Drue all this time.'

Malik continued braiding.

With a contented sigh, Thea watched the fire for a moment before she turned to the stack of scrolls and volumes Audra had left on the side table. She slid a hefty tome from the top of the pile and glanced at Malik. 'Should I read to you? That used to be our thing, didn't it?'

Malik gave a slight dip of his head, but his eyes didn't focus, and she saw a slight tremor in one of his fingers.

'Reading it is.' Thea turned the book over in her hands before she groaned at the title. *'Tethers and Magical Bonds Throughout History...* Furies save us, not exactly what I'd call a scintillating read, Mal.' She hauled herself out of the armchair. 'A library full of love stories and that's what Audra picks? I'll find us something that won't bore us to tears.'

Thea soon found a sweeping tale of adventure and read to Malik for the next two hours, until he'd nodded off in the armchair.

When she had stoked the fire and draped a blanket across her giant friend, she murmured her goodnights to him and Dax, and returned to the old headmaster's chambers. They felt cold without Wilder, and the bed seemed far less appealing without his powerful build taking up the bulk of the space.

Instead, Thea lit all the candles and got a small fire crackling in the hearth. Before the flames, she sat writing.

Wilder, every entry began. And then whatever was in her heart poured onto the page, raw and unfiltered. She wrote to him until the candles burned low – wrote of her fears, her dreams, everything that might offer him some semblance of comfort when she was gone. Instead of her name, she signed off with a small bolt of lightning, the little gesture only they had shared since she'd started training as his apprentice.

'What are you doing?' Wilder's voice sounded as the door clicked closed behind him.

'Nothing important,' Thea replied, snapping her notebook shut and wincing at the thought of the wet ink bleeding into the pages.

'I thought you'd be dead to the world by now.'

Interesting choice of words, Thea mused. 'Not without you,' she said instead. 'You sent word to Torj?'

Wilder nodded, shucking off his outer layers and hanging them on the stand by the door. 'Hopefully it reaches him soon. We want him here for when Tal's forces arrive. We'll need to train them as a single unit. We need to be able to fight as one.'

Thea ran her fingers over the scar on her wrist. 'I can't believe it's come to this. All that training at Thezmarr, all the things I went through during the Rite... I guess a part of me still didn't believe...'

'I've been watching the midrealms disintegrate for years, and even I'm having trouble believing we're facing its reckoning,' Wilder admitted, pulling off his shirt. 'Come to bed.'

'To bed, or to sleep?'

Wilder grinned. 'What do you think, Princess?'

CHAPTER FOURTEEN

THEA

Wilder ravished her body with his wicked fingers and talented mouth. Stars burst across her vision, the pleasure he wrought upon her so utterly unrelenting that she thought she might combust. He wrung climax after climax from her with barely a moment's pause, until she was a trembling, half-sobbing mess, and yet he wouldn't let her touch him. Thea didn't press the issue, not when she saw just how deeply she affected him by the bulge in his pants. She just gave herself to him, over and over, hoping that by mapping her body with his teeth and tongue, he would find his way back to her.

In the early hours of the morning, the nightmares descended, and Thea woke to Wilder thrashing in the sheets. He wouldn't wake, no matter how hard she shook him by the shoulders, no matter how many times she called his name. And so she held him through the night, wrapping herself around him, trying to shield him from the pain.

When the morning light filtered through the stained-glass windows, Thea reached for him, only to find his side of the bed cold. Sitting up, she found the fire crackling away and a tray of food left out for her, but otherwise there was no sign of him. The realisation that she was alone made her chest ache.

Violently cursing the Scarlet Tower and King Artos, Thea dragged herself from the bed and bathed quickly in the washroom. As much as she would have loved to take a long soak in the tub, she knew that the time for rest was over, that war awaited her on the other side of the door. And so she dressed for battle.

With her damp hair braided down one side, Thea dressed in light leathers, fastening her Warsword totem where it belonged around her arm, buckling her sword at her waist and sheathing Audra's jewelled dagger in her boot. Just as she reached for the door handle, it swung inward.

'Hooooly shit.' Kipp stood in the doorway, openly gawking at her.

'For fuck's sake, Kristopher, *move*,' Cal complained from somewhere behind him before he, too, clapped eyes on Thea. 'Whoa...'

After a beat, both young men surged forward and lifted Thea up in the air, jumping up and down with unabashed joy, cheering. Thea couldn't understand a word they were saying, but her face broke into a grin as they bounced her on their shoulders, carting her around the room like she'd won a damn jousting tournament.

'Fucking knew you could do it,' Kipp declared when they at last set her back down on her feet. 'Let's see the sword.'

'I want to see the totem.'

Laughing, Thea tossed her totem to Cal and unsheathed her sword, offering it to Kipp. Neither friend made any mention of the mangled scar at her wrist, both too caught up in the spoils of her Great Rite triumph. Kipp marvelled at her blade, while Cal blinked at her totem.

'Yours is different,' he said, unable to tear his eyes from the palm-sized symbol.

Kipp's gaze snapped up. 'Different how?' He snatched the totem from Cal and blinked at the design.

Cal glared at him. 'I was still looking at it.'

'You snooze, you lose, Callahan,' Kipp said with a wave of dismissal, studying the totem. True enough, Thea's Furies-gifted armband differed from those that had come before with the lightning detail that encased the three swords.

'We should have met you at the Dancing Badger for a proper celebration,' Kipp said, finally handing it back to her.

'Wilder and I stopped there before we came here,' Thea said, before instantly regretting it.

Kipp's eyes nearly bulged out of his head and he clutched his chest in shock. 'You *what?* Without *me?* How could you, Althea Embervale?'

'Sorry, sorry,' she said, sheathing her sword once more and fixing her totem back around her arm. 'It wasn't the same without you.'

'Of course it wasn't.' Her friend flung himself down into one of the armchairs by the hearth.

'Don't we need to get going?' she asked with a frown.

'Allies aren't meeting until noon,' Cal explained, helping himself to the pot of tea on the table. 'We've got the morning.'

'Well then,' Thea said, sitting down as well. 'You'd best tell me what the fuck you've been up to all this time.'

Kipp's answering grin told her there were many stories to be shared.

'Don't you dare,' Cal cautioned him.

'I would never. That tale is a main course, not a starter.'
Kipp wiggled his brows at Thea, and she laughed. She would
never tire of time with them, and here in their presence now,
she realised how much she'd missed being with them on the
road. The journey had been long and hard, with little
amusement along the way. Cal and Kipp were a gift in that
respect.

'So where *have* you been, then?' she asked, settling in.

Cursing the empty teapot, Cal set the kettle above the fire
to boil before answering. 'Well, after you left for the Rite, we
travelled to the Guardian barracks around Aveum.'

'Just you two?' she asked.

Cal nodded. 'Torj wanted to stay close to Artos, so he
sent me as his apprentice under his banner.'

'He has his own banner?'

Kipp produced an embroidered patch from his pocket,
offering it to Thea. A bear surrounded by flames was
stitched there.

'Is that a…'

'Cursed bear? Yep,' Kipp replied, tucking the fabric
away once more. 'Anyway, the barracks were as you'd
expect. No one really knows what's going on, but with
Artos still acting the role of the benevolent king, there's
little we can say in broad daylight that doesn't fall under
treason.'

'And when it's not daylight?' Thea prompted.

'Where we could, we started telling the truth – about
Artos, about the Daughter of Darkness and what he did.
What Osiris did…'

Thea could only imagine what her fellow Thezmarrians
would think of King Artos being in league with the reapers,
of him framing a little girl for his own attack on the fortress

and the longstanding Guild Master of Thezmarr, Osiris, helping him cover it up.

Kipp seemed to read her thoughts. 'Reactions were mixed. Got ourselves into our fair share of trouble.'

'You do that no matter what tale you're telling.'

'I resent that.'

'That's generally how you feel about the truth,' Cal retorted.

Kipp waved him off. 'No one has seen poor Princess Jasira, though most hope that she was taken into hiding by those loyal to her mother. The most pressing worry for our cause, though, is that no one has heard from Esyllt in weeks.'

Thea faltered. 'No one? But he's the weapons master! First port of call for all our resources, for all Guardian strategy. How can no one have —'

Kipp shrugged, though the bounce in his knee belied his concern. Esyllt was his would-be mentor, his fellow strategist. 'Word is that the shieldbearers' training has been downright dangerous back at Thezmarr in his absence —'

'It was plenty dangerous when we were doing it,' Thea interjected, picturing Kipp's swollen face and her own knife wound courtesy of Seb Barlowe.

Kipp grimaced with her. 'It's worse. Osiris is using his power as Guild Master to force people to take the initiation test early. He's bowing to pressure from the rulers that we need more Guardians.'

'They won't be Guardians if they're dead,' Cal muttered.

Thea had to agree, recalling the dangers of their own initiation trials. They had risked their lives several times, and had they not had adequate training... She shuddered at the thought.

'Where's Torj?'

'Last we heard he was still playing the role of loyal Warsword at King Artos' side,' Cal told her. 'But with Esyllt nowhere to be found, it's only a matter of time before those associated with him are picked off.'

'Have you told —'

'Talemir, Anya? Yes,' Kipp replied. 'We got in last night and made our report. Speaking of which... *Talemir fucking Starling*, Thea? You fought with him? You destroyed the Scarlet Tower with him?'

'Something like that...' Thea said with a smile, watching the awe spread on both her friends' faces.

'I can't believe he's here,' Cal breathed. 'That we *met* him. One of the great legends of Thezmarr right in our midst...'

'I think someone has a crush,' Kipp said sweetly.

'Oh, fuck off, you were just as starstruck.'

'I was nothing but professional.'

Cal snorted. 'Horseshit. You were on about how many trophies and banners feature his name back at the fortress. You were gushing about all the reasons he was called the Prince of Hearts.'

'I don't know what you're talking about.'

Thea couldn't help but laugh, savouring their company, their banter. For a brief pocket of time, it was as though there wasn't a war on their doorstep. They could have been anywhere in the midrealms, joking around.

'Have we got to the main course story yet?' Thea prompted, almost pitying Cal as the tips of his ears went bright red.

Kipp's face lit up. 'Well, it happened shortly after you left for the Rite,' he began eagerly.

Cal groaned. 'Please, Kipp... Can't I just have this one thing?'

Kipp made a show of looking appalled. 'You want to keep secrets from our best friend? A Warsword of the midrealms, a *princess* of Delmira?'

Cal buried his face in his hands.

That was all the permission Kipp needed. He turned to Thea, beaming. 'Naturally, we were all concerned about your safety and wellbeing,' he assured her. 'And in times of need —'

'You got roaring drunk?' she guessed, unable to keep the smile from her voice.

'Me?' Kipp blinked. 'Never. But you know Callahan the Flaming Arrow can't handle his liquor on the best of days. And my dear Thea… This was not the best of days. Not for Cal, anyway.'

'Furies save me,' Cal muttered, his face matching his ears now.

Thea was already shaking her head, imagining all sorts of trouble the pair could have found themselves in. 'What happened?'

'We were at the Singing Hare, and someone mentioned that a few doors down was a man who was something of an artist… A tattoo artist.'

Thea's gaze shot to Cal, but her friend refused to look at her.

'Someone,' Kipp said pointedly, 'got it in their head that they'd very much like a tattoo… Something like the Warswords have, wasn't that what you said?'

'Fuck off, Kipp.'

Thea laughed. 'I didn't know Torj had tattoos…'

Kipp nodded sagely. 'Oh yes, very impressive, very masculine pieces… Cal described them in titillating detail to the artist.'

'Well, come on,' Thea urged. 'Show me what you got.'

'No,' Cal ground out.

'Where did you get it?' Thea pressed.

'An excellent question,' Kipp declared. 'As is: *what* did he get?'

'Kipp,' Cal warned, his voice low.

But Kipp darted forward, wrestling Cal to the ground with surprising strength and, to Thea's horror, dragging the back of Cal's pants down, enough to expose a pale cheek.

A small shape marred the skin there, and upon closer inspection, Thea tipped her head back, suddenly unable to breathe for the hilarity of it. She clutched her stomach, tears streaming down her face as she wheezed.

'Tell me that's not a —'

'Laughing Fox?' Kipp finished for her, grinning. 'I'm afraid so.'

'Fuck you, Kipp,' Cal growled, trying to wriggle away from their friend, who still had him pinned to the floor. 'I know you're to blame for it. You were there, whispering in —'

'I had nothing to do with it!' Kipp said, but the gleam in his eyes said otherwise.

'Thea —' Wren's voice sounded from the door, before she stopped in her tracks, her eyes going straight to Cal's bare backside. 'What in the midrealms are you doing?' she gaped.

Kipp shoved Cal away. 'Put your arse away, Callahan, there's a princess present,' he said, turning to Thea's sister. 'Elwren, you look as lovely as ever.'

Wren glanced at Thea with a look of disbelief.

'Don't ask,' Thea told her, getting to her feet. 'What is it?'

'They asked me to come get you,' Wren replied, still looking baffled at the Guardians who were straightening their clothes and expressions. 'The allies' meeting is starting early.' She slid a small silver tin onto the chest of drawers. 'And this is the salve I promised. Use it twice a day for a week and the pain should subside.'

Thea ignored her friends' questioning looks and pocketed the tin, her scarred wrist aching at the mention. 'Thank you.'

Instead of taking them to the Scholar's Lounge like Thea expected, Wren took them to a formal dining room. A long mahogany table ran the length of the space, lined with high-backed chairs. Talemir sat at the head, with Drue on his left and Malik on his right. Mal was braiding a strip of leather between his huge fingers, with Dax curled up a few feet away. Dratos, Anya and Adrienne lined Drue's other side, while Audra sat next to Malik and Farissa, Thezmarr's alchemy master, took the place at her right.

Wren strode forward and sat beside her mentor, and Cal and Kipp followed her, taking their places as well.

Where's Wilder? Thea wondered, scanning the room for his handsome face. Where had he gone so early in the morning without so much as a word to her? Was he alright? It had only been a few nights since his rescue from the Scarlet Tower, and she knew his sleep had been fractured, plagued by nightmares —

A scraping noise sounded as Adrienne pushed back the empty chair beside her. 'Here, Thea,' she offered.

Thea took a breath, grounding herself in the here and now before she went to Adrienne, accepting the seat. As she looked around, goosebumps rushed across her skin at the familiar faces that met her gaze. Friends and family, new and old – each and every one of them meant something to her now. They had all come together again, but it was a far cry from the drunken, crowded room at the Singing Hare. This was so much more formal, more sombre... It suddenly felt so real. They were here in Naarva to plan battles. The decisions they made here would impact countless lives, would end just as many...

A steaming mug was placed in front of her, tendrils of peppermint wafting up to her nose, as Wilder took up the empty chair beside her.

'Shall we begin?' he said, placing his scabbards on the table and leaning back in his seat.

At the head of the table, Talemir bowed his head. 'The first order of business is the consequences of what Thea and I did to the Scarlet Tower,' he said, with an apologetic glance in Thea's direction.

'I knew there would be consequences,' she replied. 'Do you know what they are yet?'

Talemir nodded gravely. 'King Artos declared that you're not only a fallen Warsword, but the lost heir of Delmira, come to finish what your parents started all those years ago...' He looked to Wren, who dug through her pockets and produced two crumpled pieces of parchment.

'After your little lightning display at the tower, they put a price on both our heads.' She passed Thea the yellowed flyers.

Wanted. Elwren Embervale (previously known as Zoltaire). Alleged storm wielder and heir of Delmira. Wanted dead or alive, in association with the Daughter of Darkness.

'Where did you get these?' Thea turned to the second sketch, where her own likeness stared back at her, a similar message scrawled beneath it:

Wanted. Althea Embervale (previously known as Zoltaire). Fallen Warsword. Alleged storm wielder and firstborn heir of

Delmira. Wanted dead or alive for: treason, the destruction of the Scarlet Tower, aiding and abetting a known criminal, murder, unnamed crimes against the midrealms, association with the Daughter of Darkness.

'That's quite a list,' Wilder murmured beside her.

'Don't be put out,' Dratos interjected, sliding another poster across the table. 'There's one for the Hand of Death, too.'

Thea turned the parchment over and met the vicious gaze of Wilder Hawthorne, his features drawn far sharper and more unforgiving than the true lines of his face.

'They were a tad unkind about his nose,' Wren pointed out helpfully.

Thea held out the drawing for Wilder to see and a laugh bubbled from his lips. 'Only a tad?'

Shaking her head, Thea turned back to Talemir. 'What does this mean?'

'Thezmarr's resources are dead to you,' he replied. 'The remaining rulers won't ally with you. You're a known heir of a kingdom that fell to darkness. Your word means nothing.'

'Wonderful,' Thea muttered.

'But there are fewer rulers than there were yesterday,' Talemir continued. 'King Leiko of Tver has bent the knee to Artos.'

Thea's gaze shot up. 'What?'

She wasn't the only one shocked. Several gasps sounded from around the table.

'Has Artos declared himself for the reapers, then?' Wilder asked.

Talemir shook his head. 'Not yet. The official word is that after the battle of Notos, Tver was weakened, to the point where Artos has been carrying the kingdom with his own resources and rebuilding efforts. Leiko's statement outlined all this, and how Tver would prosper under Artos' rule, as Harenth has.'

'The fool,' Audra scoffed. 'Aveum will be next... It's already teetering on the edge of collapse, with Queen Reyna confined to her rooms, bereft with grief. We must convince her to fight. Artos will be on her doorstep before long.'

'Can we assassinate Artos?' Drue asked. 'Cut off the head of the snake before the war begins?' She looked around. 'Have we tried?'

'Countless times,' Adrienne replied, cracking her knuckles. 'He's guarded too closely. His empath magic seems to sense anyone with ill will towards him. He's rooted out several of our best spies, and spiked their heads to his gates.'

Thea shuddered. Harenth had seemed so beautiful when she'd visited. It was hard to imagine severed heads adorning its walls.

'So it will definitely come to open battle,' Wilder said.

'Unfortunately,' Talemir conceded.

'How firm is Artos' hold over Thezmarr?' Audra asked. 'Will the Guardians rally to defend the midrealms?'

'It depends who makes the call,' Kipp said thoughtfully. 'Thea and Wilder are fugitives. No one will answer to a shadow-touched Warsword.' He gave Talemir an apologetic glance. 'Vernich is widely hated across the lands... It would have to be Torj the Golden Bear Slayer, and Esyllt the loyal weapons master, if we can find him. If they can convince the shieldbearers and Guardians of Thezmarr to fight against Artos, we might have a chance.'

A beat of silence followed as the company read between the lines of their strategist's words. Their chances were slim. They always had been. They needed to unite people from all walks of life, all different backgrounds, with all the prejudices that came with them, in order to defeat their common enemy. An enemy that most of the common folk didn't even know of yet.

It was Wilder who spoke next. 'We need to be mindful of where we place Warswords on the chessboard,' he said slowly, clenching his fists before him. 'Including Tal and Thea, there are five of us now, and whether we're declared fallen or not is irrelevant to Artos and the reapers' plans. In the tower...'

He trailed off for a moment, and quiet settled over the room.

Thea slid her hand beneath the table, resting her palm on his thigh, feeling the muscles tense there. She heard him exhale before he spoke again.

'In the tower, they had plans to make a monster out of me. Something beyond shadow-touched, something to wield against the world... "A general of darkness in Artos' growing forces", the Archmage there said. Though the tower is gone, it won't have been their only site for such experiments. We need to be prepared that they'll want to capture some of us alive. That they'll sacrifice a good many of their own forces to do so.'

'What are you saying, Hawthorne?' Dratos demanded.

'Well, for one, that we need a measure in place so that if we're taken, we can ensure we're not taken alive.' He gave Wren a pointed glance. 'I'm sure you and Farissa can come up with something for us?'

A bitter taste filled Thea's mouth as she realised what Wilder was asking of her sister, of all of them.

But Talemir gave a stiff nod. 'A precaution,' he added.

'We need to alert Torj and the Bloodletter,' Anya cut in. 'If there's a hunt for Warswords, they need to be on their guard.'

'A Warsword is always on their guard,' Wilder said gruffly.

'And yet you wound up in chains in that tower all the same,' Anya replied.

Wilder's leg jolted beneath Thea's touch, but he fixed her older sister with a flat stare. 'It was the best of a bunch of bad options. Which brings me to my next point... They made their intentions for Warswords clear enough, but I imagine they have a similar stance on magic wielders. If they get their talons in you, Wren or Thea, we're equally as fucked.'

'That's not going to happen.'

Wilder folded his arms over his broad chest. 'Saying it doesn't make it so.'

Thea didn't miss the muscle twitching in Anya's jaw.

'Do we know Vernich's position in all this?' Talemir asked.

'He helped us defeat the arachne in Aveum,' Cal replied.

'That means fuck all,' Dratos growled.

Talemir looked to Wilder and Thea. 'What do you think?'

'I suspected he was a fallen Warsword for the better part of a year,' Thea admitted. 'But now... I don't know.'

Wilder's hand found hers beneath the table and he squeezed her fingers gently. 'My gut tells me that if Artos openly aligns himself with the reapers, Vernich will fall to our side. He's a bastard through and through, always has been. But he takes his Warsword vows as seriously as any one of us. He'd defend the midrealms to his death. I've seen it.'

Thea's stomach bottomed out as she recalled fighting at

the Bloodletter's side in Notos, how he'd had her back when they'd thought Wilder had betrayed them all...

'Perhaps you're right,' she murmured.

'Then we send word with Terrence,' Talemir declared. 'To both Torj and Vernich.'

'Tal,' Drue said. 'Terrence isn't enough. Someone will have to go.'

The shadow-touched Warsword nodded. 'I'll go —'

'We'll send someone else. You're needed here,' Drue objected. 'You need to get the forces in shape, introduce them to the others. They'll need to know who commands them before long —'

A loud crash sounded and every warrior in the room was on their feet in an instant, swords unsheathed – but it was little Ryland who charged into the room with a wide grin on his face, his grandfather Fendran racing after him.

'For fuck's sake,' Drue muttered, pinching the bridge of her nose as Ryland successfully dodged his grandfather's attempts at capture and knocked over several empty chairs in the process.

'Draw!' the boy shouted excitedly, waving a piece of crumpled parchment. 'Ry draw!'

'You drew something?' Talemir asked, watching with amusement as his son made a beeline not for him, but for Wilder.

Thea couldn't help the laugh that bubbled from her lips as the adorable little boy climbed up Wilder's legs as though he were a tree and waved a piece of parchment in his face.

Baffled, Wilder took the outstretched artwork. Thea smiled. Ryland had drawn three rudimentary figures. It was easy enough to identify Malik – the giant stick figure with what she assumed was a dog at his feet. Next to him was

Talemir, his misshapen wings extended across the width of the page.

The Shadow Prince rose from his chair and peered over Wilder's shoulder, pointing to the third figure. 'I believe that's you.'

'Me?' Wilder frowned, but Thea could see the emotion lining his silver eyes.

'We've told him stories about you his whole life,' Talemir explained. 'He's always known who you are.'

With a huff of amusement, Wilder studied the drawing. 'What sort of stories have you been telling him? He seems to think very... highly... of me.'

Thea leant across and followed his gaze to the enormous appendage attached to Wilder's supposed likeness.

Behind them, Talemir barked a laugh. 'That's your *sword*.'

Thea gave Wilder a wink. 'I'll say.'

'Didn't need to know that,' Talemir said with a snort before hauling his son off Wilder, perching him on his hip.

'Are we done here?' Audra said sharply.

The lighthearted moment passed all too quickly, and Thea suddenly felt restless herself. 'What now, then?' she asked.

Drue rose from her chair. 'Now, we introduce you to our armies.'

CHAPTER FIFTEEN

WILDER

Wilder had vastly underestimated Talemir and Drue's preparations. It was hard to believe that just outside the main university walls lay a camp like this: an army of shadow-touched folk who bore the evidence of Talemir's discipline in the neat lines of their tents and the condition of their weapons. Judging by the ruts in the earth and the rhythm of the place, Talemir's men – and women, Wilder noted – had been here for some time.

'How's that armour feel?' Tal asked, with a nod at the boiled leather breastplate he'd given Wilder that morning.

'Fine,' Wilder replied. 'Better than my last set.'

Talemir baulked. 'You were still wearing that? It was a pile of shit to begin with.'

'I know. Managed to slay as many monsters as you though,' Wilder quipped.

Tal snorted. 'If you say so, Apprentice.'

Wilder felt Thea's eyes on him during this exchange, as though she were drinking in their camaraderie, her expression subtly pleased.

It made him smile, for a time.

As Talemir led Wilder and Thea between the tents, there was no missing the suspicious glances shot their way. Wilder wondered how many knew or recognised him as the wayward apprentice who had abandoned their Shadow Prince long ago.

'Don't take it personally,' Talemir said, spotting where Wilder's attention had strayed. 'They don't trust outsiders – usually with good reason. It's why I wanted everyone gathered here first, to build some semblance of trust between our leaders and units.'

'Seems like a tall order,' Thea ventured, with a sceptical scan of the campground. All around, shadow-touched folk were watching their every move, some making a point to grasp their weapons, their bodies poised in readiness, as though Wilder and Thea meant to attack their beloved leader right in front of them.

'We're all going to lead units of our own,' Talemir continued, as though they weren't facing a significant hurdle. 'I can't lead them from every flank. Thea, Drue reserved a special unit for you. On the north-east side of camp, you'll find them waiting for you.'

Thea raised a brow. 'Consider me intrigued, Shadow Prince.'

Wilder watched her go with a pang of regret. It had only been a matter of days since their reunion, and already this war was robbing them of their limited time together. He felt the urgency in the very marrow of his bones, and could almost hear the grains of sand falling through the hourglass. Fate. Destiny. Despair. All entwined.

'Wilder?' Talemir's voice wrenched him back into the present.

'What?'

'I was saying that we'll need to take the new recruits through the basic drills, the same as the ones we did in Naarva all those years ago.'

'Are any of them born fighters?' he asked, scanning those who were bold enough to meet his gaze.

Talemir sighed. 'Some. We've got civilians who heard about Drue and Adrienne and became rangers after Ciraun fell. There are a handful who were once soldiers. But most were commoners who fell victim to the wraiths in the same way I did, same as Dratos and Gus... Their advantage is their magic. We just need to give them an edge with a blade.'

'I've made warriors out of less,' Wilder said.

Talemir scoffed. 'Recently? Because to me it looks like the Furies gifted you a ready-made storm-wielding Warsword.'

Wilder followed his former mentor's gaze across the sea of canvas tents to the north-east corner, where Thea stood at the head of an all-women force with Drue. She was magnificent. Her braid caught in the wind, dancing behind her as she held out her blade and demonstrated a number of manoeuvres he'd taught her. Only she'd tweaked them. They were no longer just his techniques, but moves she had perfected to suit her own unique fighting style and her own strengths. She whirled and parried against an imaginary opponent, thrusting her sword, blocking would-be blows and delivering swift justice with a precise slash of her steel.

A round of applause echoed across the camp as she finished her demonstration with a flourish.

'I'm not sure you'll win as many hearts so easily,' Talemir said with a note of amusement.

'We'll get there,' Wilder replied. 'I managed to win her heart, after all.'

'Beats me how,' Talemir quipped, his gaze trained on Drue, who was handing out practice blades to the women warriors.

Wilder realised that he and Talemir had stopped completely in their tracks to watch, and they weren't the only ones. Plenty of shadow-touched soldiers from all over the camp had paused whatever menial task they were carrying out, elbowing each other as Drue invited Thea to spar.

'They don't waste time, do they?' Talemir mused, his voice rich with pride.

Around them, banners fluttered like restless spirits and the scent of burning wood hung heavy in the air as the two women circled each other amid the gathering crowd of eager onlookers.

Thea flicked her braid over her shoulder and gave Drue a wolfish grin before raising her blade in salute. Drue answered with a grin of her own, and lunged.

The clash of steel rang out, a familiar song of battle, as Drue's blade, swift as the wind, met Thea's with a resounding clang. The metallic ring of swords permeated the air, mingling with the camp scent of sweat and ash from the fires.

Wilder's chest swelled as he watched Thea. Her movements were a fluid poetry, her blade an extension of herself, striking with precision and grace... and yet he could tell she was holding back. There was no storm magic in the air, nor even a hint of that Furies-given power he knew flowed through Thea now. No, she was fighting with the abilities she'd honed over the years and nothing more.

Drue countered with significant strength, her strikes a testament to her own years of training and extra tutelage under Talemir, but she was no match for Thea, not truly. The gathered throng held its breath, seeming to revel in the rush of wind as swords sliced through the air, the tang of anticipation heavy around them. Sparks flew like fiery stars, and Wilder watched as the women in the audience became rapt, mesmerised by the warriors in their midst who looked like them, who had become legends in their own right.

'You taught her well,' Talemir said.

'It's all her,' Wilder replied without hesitation. He might have helped shape the Warsword before them, but she'd been a warrior all along.

'Well then, your work is cut out for you with your unit...' Talemir nudged him. 'We can't let the women have all the glory. Follow me.'

Talemir led him to a unit of thirty shadow-touched men of varying ages. Some were teenagers like Gus, others older than Drue's father Fendran. It didn't bode well.

Talemir put his fingers between his teeth and whistled to get their attention. 'Everyone, this is your commander for the battles ahead, Wilder Hawthorne.'

Wilder heard the intake of breath, noted several men shifting uncomfortably from foot to foot, and even a sneer or two in the back. He clenched his jaw. Once, the mere mention of his name demanded respect, had men clamouring to be taught a single manoeuvre by him. But now...

'Isn't he the fallen Warsword?' said a nasal voice from the group. 'The one who killed a bunch of shadow-touched —'

Talemir silenced him with a single look. 'Wilder Hawthorne is one of the most formidable warriors in the history of the midrealms,' he said coolly. 'He's here to make men out of you, if you've got the stomach for it.' He glanced at Wilder. 'They're all yours until sundown.'

'I'm not making any promises,' Wilder grunted, surveying what he had to work with.

Talemir moved on to another unit, leaving Wilder with the unruly crew of shadow-touched. He turned to them, giving them a cold, hard look he usually reserved for the most hopeless shieldbearers.

'We're doing laps,' he said. 'Let's find out what you're made of.'

Wilder drilled his shadow-touched unit all afternoon. They were unfit and undisciplined, but not completely beyond help, though he was no more popular by the end of the day than he had been at the start. Which was fine with him; he wasn't there to make friends. He was there to make soldiers.

What he didn't admit was how he himself felt the burn of the exercises more keenly after his stint in the Scarlet Tower, how his brow broke into a sweat far sooner than it should have. When the day was done, he felt wrung out, but he hid it well – or so he thought, until Thea took one look at him in the quadrangle and grimaced.

'That bad, huh?' he asked casually, walking over to her and trying not to limp as the stiffness took hold of his muscles.

Thea was sprawled on a bench beneath an ivy-covered archway, wearing a loose shirt and pants, her armour stacked beside her, her feet bare. A notebook was clutched tightly between her hands, as though it were something precious.

Making room for him, she tucked her feet up beneath her and kissed him as he sat down, hiding his wince.

'You're exactly how I like you,' she said with a mischievous grin. 'Rugged and dirty.'

'Is that right?'

'Absolutely,' she said with another kiss.

Wilder tried to take the notebook from her hands. 'What have you been scribbling away at?'

Her grip tightened on the pages. 'Nothing,' she replied, tucking the notebook under her pile of armour and rummaging through the rest of her things. 'Anya gave me my pack back and I realised I've got something of yours...'

To his surprise, Thea produced the sapphire necklace he'd kept stuffed away in his cabin since his last visit to Naarva. Slightly bewildered, he took it from her and stared at the blue gem as it twinkled in the sunlight.

'Thought you might want it back, or that maybe you should give it back to Adrienne...'

The furrow in Wilder's brow deepened. 'Adrienne?'

'Oh.' Thea flushed. 'I just assumed it was hers... From before. It's fine, I just —'

Wilder couldn't help the broad grin that broke across his face. 'You mean all this time you thought I was carrying around a jewel that belonged to a former —'

'I didn't know what to think!'

Wilder laughed. 'Thea, this belonged to Talemir's mother.'

Thea's blush deepened further. 'Oh.'

Shaking his head and still chuckling, Wilder pocketed the sapphire. 'Apparently she gave it to him when they had to part, and told him that "*Sometimes, to love someone, we have to let them go*". He then gave it to me when I left him in

Naarva, angry at him and raging at the world. Suppose I'd better give it back after all these years. Unless you'd like to keep it?'

'Not really my style, Warsword.'

'I didn't think so.'

'You probably *should* give it back,' Thea said, her cheeks still tipped pink.

Wilder loved her even more in that moment, and moved to wrap his arm around her, but this time, he couldn't hide his grimace of pain.

Thea perched herself behind him on the back of the bench, hands finding his shoulders and beginning to knead the tense muscles there. Wilder moaned, the sensation of instant relaxation sweeping over him as she worked through his knotted upper back.

'I do like coaxing those noises out of you,' Thea murmured in his ear, digging her thumbs right into a tender spot that needed loosening.

Wilder closed his eyes, savouring the relief her touch offered. She seemed to know exactly from where each hurt stemmed, her strong fingers rubbing firm circles through all of his aches.

As a good kind of pain bloomed through his shoulders and down his spine, he started to decompress from the day, from the pressure he'd forced onto himself as he'd trained his unit into a similar state of exhaustion. He knew it wasn't just the lack of movement in the tower's cells that had him struggling – it was the drugs they'd misted over him time and time again; it was the lack of nourishment and water. It was everything.

'Fuck,' he muttered, raking his fingers through his hair as Thea continued the massage. Her hands moved over his back expertly, like she knew every dip and hollow, every tightly coiled cluster of muscles.

'It's going to be alright,' she said quietly.

How can it be? Wilder wanted to ask her, so badly that the words were burning on the tip of his tongue. But he bit them back. She had rescued him from those horrors, mere days after facing her own nightmares in the Rite – things that still plagued her dreams now – and yet here she was, comforting him. How had he faced so much in his life, only to come undone now?

Wilder didn't reply. Instead, he looped his arms behind him, wrapping them around the backs of her legs, pulling her close to him. All the while, her fingers worked the tension from his muscles as they looked out onto the quiet courtyard, where ivy and midnight roses rustled in the cool breeze.

Moments later, Dratos came jogging towards them from the main building, his wings tucked tightly behind him. 'You seen Ry?' he called.

'Not since this morning,' Thea replied.

Wilder shook his head when the shadow-touched ranger reached them.

'Shit,' Dratos replied. 'Tal and Drue can't find him. No one's seen him…' There was no mistaking the note of panic in his voice.

Thea gave Wilder's shoulders a firm squeeze before reaching for her boots. 'We'll help you look.'

Wilder launched himself onto his feet. 'Where have you looked so far? Does he have any favourite hiding spots?' He could only imagine the sheer terror gripping Talemir and Drue. They were both seasoned warriors, but a missing child was a different kind of fear altogether.

'All checked,' Dratos told them with a grimace.

Thea finished with her laces and faced Dratos, a determined gleam in her eyes. 'We'll find him.'

Dratos nodded stiffly. 'We've searched the entire building from top to bottom,' he said. 'Though a fresh set of eyes might be all we —'

A bone-rattling explosion sounded, shattering the tranquillity of the quadrangle in one fell swoop. It seemed to emerge from the very depths of the underworld, a thunderous blast that echoed through the air.

Wilder had his swords unsheathed in seconds as a deep, resonant tremor coursed through the ground beneath their feet, reverberating in the sandstone all around them, shaking the very foundations of the university.

'What the fuck...?' he muttered, glancing at Dratos. The air around them pulsed with the aftershocks, and the leaves of the nearby oak tree shivered.

Thea was already slipping her armour back on, tightening its ties with steady, efficient fingers. Then her blades were out as well, and she was scanning the skies. Wilder followed her gaze and cursed under his breath as he saw what she'd already spotted.

Fault lines now appeared in Talemir's shadow shield around the university. Its protection was straining against whatever impact lay beyond it. A barrier forged with darkness now fought against its like. Dread bloomed in Wilder's gut as flakes of shadow fell from the sky towards them.

'We're under attack,' he said, turning to Dratos. 'What's the protocol?'

All three of them recoiled as another rumbling barrage of sound clapped overhead, and a quake gripped the earth beneath their boots. Loose stone fell from the walls around them and the telltale scent of burnt hair filled the air.

The wraiths were coming.

'To the fields,' Dratos shouted, bursting into a run. 'We have to protect them at all costs.'

Wilder sprang into action, his pain and exhaustion long forgotten in the face of such peril. If the fields of sun orchids were compromised, the war would be lost before it truly began.

Thea sprinted at his side, her blades swinging in her hands as they cut through the university grounds and made straight for the crops. 'Do you think they have Ryland?' she asked.

'Furies save us all if they do,' Dratos replied.

Heart pounding, Wilder crested a ridge and reached the field of sun orchids first – just in time to see onyx power exploding as three shadow wraiths breached Talemir's shield.

CHAPTER SIXTEEN

THEA

A dark chaos bloomed before them, a shocking contrast to the golden glow of the sun orchids and their delicate petals. Soaring through the air, the trio of wraiths unleashed vicious tendrils of shadow, lashing at the figures defending the crops below. The crops that were vital to the defence of the midrealms, that gave their allies an edge against the darkness.

Thea surged forward, instantly spotting Drue and Talemir at the heart of the madness. Talemir was wielding his own blasts of obsidian power, while Drue cleaved through any whips of shadow that came for her husband. Talemir wasn't attacking the wraiths, Thea realised; he was trying to patch the fractures in the shield.

'He needs help!' Thea shouted. 'Someone get Anya, and the other shadow-touched!'

'She's leading the defence for the northern perimeter. It's under attack too,' Cal called, making for the high ground. 'It's just us!'

'Then we have to bring down these wraiths so Tal can

mend the tears.' Thea threw herself into the fray, severing those dark arms of power that threatened to stir nightmares into reality before them. Wilder and Dratos joined her, their great swords carving through any pulse of magic that came for them.

'Cal!' Thea yelled. 'Hurry!'

The creak of a bow answered, and a flaming arrow speared through the sky, right through the skull of one of the wraiths. The creature screamed, the noise high-pitched enough to shatter the glass of a nearby greenhouse.

Its grotesque form fell from the clouds, limbs and wings flailing, its sinewy frame convulsing. Bone cracked as it hit the ground hard, and Thea leapt upon it in an instant, her dagger at the ready, Cal's arrow still protruding from its monstrous face. She had lost count of how many wraiths she'd killed, but each time her Naarvian steel pierced one of their chest cavities, she relished the screams as though it were her first. As the others fought around her, she sawed through flesh and bone, reaching into the monster's torso with her bare hand, her fist closing around its still-beating heart, warm and wet. With a few flicks of her dagger, the final tendons and arteries were severed, and she tore the organ from the wraith's body, casting it onto the scorched earth beside them.

With the creature's foul scent in her nose, she was on her feet again, her steel dripping with black blood, scanning the mayhem for her next victim. She had energy to burn, debts to repay. She'd slay wraiths all fucking night if she had to.

An eye-watering screech sounded and the second wraith fell through the air in Thea's peripheral vision, but Drue was there in an instant, delivering the same justice. Her blades deflected clumsy slashes from the wraith's talons as two more arrows shot through the creature's wings, pinning it to the ground while Drue leapt upon its torso and carved out its heart.

All the while, Talemir stood in the centre of the orchids, defending everything they had fought so hard to protect over the years. His large hands moved skilfully before him as he wove an intricate pattern of shadow and sent it skyward, attempting to mend the tears in his shield. Beads of sweat trickled down his furrowed brow as he braced himself against the relentless assault of the third wraith. Wilder and Dratos guarded him against the onslaught of shadow magic as he worked, the pair of warriors slicing through every strike of shadow, the wraith above hissing and shrieking with every blow.

Thea whirled around, trying to spot Cal once more amid the surge of black tendrils as she fought back the lashes of power that came for her. They struck like vipers from a nest, vicious and determined to inflict as much pain as possible. But her steel cut clean through them, like severing a head from a snake's body.

There! She spotted Cal on the next ridge over, his chest expanding as he took aim, his eyes narrowed in concentration. With a swift release of the bowstring, another flaming arrow streaked through the shadow-filled air. It found its mark, engulfing the leathery flesh in flames. Like its brethren, the monster fell from the sky with an agonised shriek, smoke trailing in its wake as it hurtled towards the earth.

'This one's mine,' Wilder's voice boomed across the field.

He has debts to repay too. Thea watched him move with predatory grace. Before the wraith hit the ground, Wilder's bare knuckles punched through its chest, tearing its heart from its flaming body. The rest of its corpse collided against the dirt with a crash, splattering black blood all over Wilder and the sun orchids at his feet.

Thea watched in fascination as the flowers shifted, seeming to recoil at the contact, before burning the blood from their petals.

'Is it over?' Cal called from the ridge, shouldering his quiver and bow, making his way down to them to retrieve his arrows from the wraith corpses.

'For now,' Dratos replied, surveying the largely untouched crops.

'Those were some fine shots,' Talemir told Cal hoarsely, shifting the last piece of shadow patchwork into place in the shield.

Cal flushed. 'Thank you, sir.'

'Just Talemir,' Tal replied, wiping the perspiration from his brow. 'Has anyone found Ryland yet?'

Thea turned on her heel to see Drue already running back towards the main building. She didn't hesitate to follow.

The quadrangle was packed with shadow-touched folk, some from the war camp, others from elsewhere in the stronghold. All of them had come together to defend the university, and now, to find Ryland.

'Is the perimeter secure?' Dratos demanded, scanning the crowd.

Anya pushed her way towards him. 'Yes. We slayed four wraiths on the outer grounds. No damage to the crops.'

'How'd they breach the shield?' Thea asked.

'An accident. They didn't know we were here —'

'We can deal with that later,' Talemir's voice cut in. 'We need to find Ryland. Now.'

The dread was palpable. For even if the wraith attack had been won, what would happen to the rebellion's fearless leaders if their son wasn't found?

Drue's face was a mask of cold calm as she scoured the grounds, but Talemir... Thea had seen Talemir take on the brunt of an entire airborne wraith force at the Scarlet Tower, had seen him patch a magical shield that covered an entire territory. He was unshakeable, a force of his own to be reckoned with. Only now, he wasn't a Warsword or a Shadow Prince. Now, he was a father. A father who was panicking.

'Have you checked the kitchens?' he was saying. 'What about under the —'

Drue silenced him with a squeeze of his hand and continued to search. Wraiths momentarily forgotten, the university bustled with movement, punctuated by shouts of Ryland's name.

Kipp, ever the strategist, organised everyone into teams, each assigned to comb through a specific area – old lecture halls, the libraries and greenhouses, the outer grounds. Every search party was on high alert, more concerned with every passing moment. Time was of the essence.

After giving out his instructions, Kipp appeared at Thea's side, looking pale. 'What if they've taken him? What if the attack just now was a diversion so they could snatch him —'

'Keep that thought to yourself,' Thea warned. 'At least for now.'

Still shaken from the attack, they combed the grounds together, working to find any sign of the little winged boy who'd stolen all their hearts.

As the hours passed and the light filtering through Talemir's shield took on the orange glow of dusk, the sense of panic reached new heights. The exhaustive search bled out into the surrounding fields once more. Quiet conversations ground to a halt and Thea found herself retracing her previous steps to no avail —

A shout sounded. Thea and Kipp rushed towards it.

Talemir was kneeling in the dirt, clutching the lumpy knitted hat Ryland had been wearing since their arrival.

Drue fell to her knees beside him. 'Where is he, Tal?' she whispered, her voice breaking. 'What are we going to do?'

Talemir simply stared at the woollen cap. 'I…'

Thea's heart broke for them. She could only imagine what might be going through their heads, and the longer Ryland was gone, the worse the potential outcomes became. Both parents were hunched over the cap together, Drue's shoulders shaking with silent sobs, Talemir's arm wrapped around her back.

A flurry of movement across the grass caught her eye and Wilder appeared, cresting a ridge in the land, something bundled in his arms.

'He's here!' Wilder called. 'I've got him.'

He strode across the grounds, the little boy safe in his arms, Dratos' cousin Gus at his side.

'Oh, thank the Furies,' Drue cried, leaping to her feet and surging towards them.

Wilder dropped Ryland in her arms and stepped back as Talemir engulfed his wife and son in a powerful embrace, his wings closing around them.

'He's alright,' Wilder told them. 'He's safe.'

A unified sigh of relief sounded, matching the rush of lightness that flooded through Thea at the sight of the reunited family. She passed a hand over her face, shaking her head. 'Thank fuck for that,' she muttered.

Kipp made a noise of agreement beside her, making to follow the rest of the search party heading back to the main building. Thea remained, waiting for Wilder, who in turn watched as Talemir's wings finally unfolded, revealing the trio within.

'He and Gus were playing in the western field when the wraiths attacked,' Wilder explained. 'Gus kept them out there until they knew it was safe to return.'

'He was crying at first, but I thought... I thought it might be safer to distract him, to play a game, so he wouldn't draw attention...' Gus' cheeks flushed.

Talemir at last released his wife and son, turning to face the shadow-touched teenager. 'Thank you,' he croaked. 'You did the right thing.'

'Sorry to have scared you,' Gus replied.

But Talemir shook his head. 'You protected my son,' he told him. 'Never apologise for that.' Then he glanced at Wilder. 'Thank you for finding them.'

'Always,' Wilder said.

Visibly uncomfortable in the swell of emotion surrounding him, Gus bolted towards the quadrangle. Thea laced her fingers through her Warsword's and tugged him in the same direction, trying to give the family some privacy.

But they weren't out of earshot when Talemir spoke to Drue, his voice still laced with panic. 'You need to take him to safety. That place beyond the Veil. I couldn't... I couldn't handle it if something happened to him, to you —'

'I don't fucking think so,' came Drue's sharp reply.

'Please, Wildfire —'

Thea didn't like to eavesdrop, but Drue's words carried in the wind. 'I told you who I was before we had him. I will change for no man, no child. He's the son of a shadow-touched Warsword and a law-breaking Naarvian ranger. He will know this world for what it is, and he'll be stronger for it. We've been through this, Tal – we know that Ry will be safe with Gus and Malik. There is no one I trust more. You know that Malik will protect him with his life. The war efforts need us, and we need to end the war for him, so he has a future. I will fight at your side, as always.' There was not a hint of compromise in Drue's voice, only pure steel.

Thea glanced at Wilder, who grimaced as they heard Talemir's stammering apologies.

'You're right,' he said. 'I know. I'm not going back on our agreement. I was – I was terrified, Drue.'

'As was I,' Drue replied. 'But we cannot fall apart in the face of adversity.'

'I'm sorry,' the Shadow Prince said.

Drue huffed a tired laugh. 'You'll make it up to me later.'

Thea hid her own smile at that.

The attack and the search for Ryland had rattled the Naarvian forces to the core. According to Dratos, there had never been a full breach of the shield before, not to that extent. As night fell, he set out with several other prominent shadow-touched leaders to reinforce Talemir's magic with their own.

Thea turned to Anya. 'How does it work? The shield? The protection?'

Anya gave a heavy sigh. 'In a similar way to the wraiths' shadows. But instead of using our power to maim and hurt, we weave it together like a net, to cast outward, over the university and its grounds. Over the years we worked out that because it's the same essence as their own magic, the wraiths don't question it, don't try to push past it. They assume it's just the territory of other wraiths and move on.'

'So how did the breach happen?' Thea asked.

'On occasion, it happens by mistake. A squabble breaks out among one of their units and one gets thrown through our defences.'

'But not today?' Thea couldn't help but press. 'There were too many for it to have been an accident.'

Anya shrugged. 'We suspect they believed a wraith swarm was here and they wanted to assert their dominance. They don't know we're here. And we mean to keep it that way.'

Thea and Wilder returned to the Scholar's Lounge for the evening meal, finding the atmosphere within sombre and strained. Nearly everyone was there: Malik by the fire, as usual; Wren and Farissa, mixing potions on a table in the far corner; Anya in an armchair, her legs dangling over the side; Adrienne cleaning her fingernails with a dagger by the window; and Gus sitting on the floor, his knitting needles clicking between his hands as he crafted something that looked like it would match Ryland's slouchy hat.

Audra pulled Thea aside and spoke in a low voice. 'That thing you asked me to look into. About transferring magic.'

'Did you find something?' Thea asked eagerly, glancing around the room to make sure no one was listening.

Audra shook her head. 'It can't be done. Thought you should know that it's impossible, so don't go doing anything stupid.'

Thea's heart sank, but she plastered on an offended expression. 'When do I ever —'

Audra was already walking away, making a beeline for Cal.

'You killed them all, correct?' the former librarian demanded bluntly, seating herself at the Guardian's table by the hearth.

'Yes, ma'am,' he replied. 'Well, not me, *exactly*. But they're dead all the same.'

'Nothing escaped? That's good.' Audra nodded to herself. 'Let us hope this means we can keep our secrets a while longer,' she said, with a meaningful glance at Talemir.

Talemir dipped his head in acknowledgement, but returned his attention to Drue, who was tucked tightly under his arm, and Ryland, who was sleeping soundly against her chest. Thea watched them a little more closely than before, her heart aching for the shadow-touched Warsword who was clearly still reeling from the events of the day.

It was Kipp who came forward and pressed a large glass of amber liquid into the Shadow Prince's hands. 'You look like you could use this.'

An exhausted laugh broke from Talemir's lips. 'Forever the Son of the Fox, eh?'

Kipp sketched a bow. 'At your service,' he quipped, raising his own glass.

'If you're handing them out, Fox Boy, I wouldn't say no,' Anya declared.

'Make it two more,' Adrienne chimed in.

'Three,' Thea said, sinking into one of the worn lounges, the cushion beside her dipping beneath Wilder's weight as he joined her.

'Four,' he added gruffly.

Kipp shook his head in disbelief. 'If everyone wants a drink, why didn't you just say so?'

'We're saying so now,' Thea told him. She smiled to herself as he went about fixing everyone's drinks without further complaint. Kipp was always happiest when everyone had a beverage in hand.

Just as he handed Wilder a goblet of wine and offered Thea a tankard of ale, Wren stood up so suddenly that she knocked over the concoction she was mixing.

Farissa leapt back. 'Elwren, what's got into you —'

A second later, the doors to the lounge flew open, and the Bear Slayer, Torj Elderbrock, strode inside, his mighty war hammer resting on his broad shoulder.

'Esyllt's been taken prisoner,' he declared to the room as soon as the doors clicked closed behind him. 'Osiris has him confined to Thezmarr's dungeons, where he's awaiting execution.'

Kipp dropped the drink he was holding, the glass shattering across the wooden floor. 'On what charges?' he exclaimed loudly, not even glancing at the shards by his feet.

Ryland stirred against Drue's chest with a whimper, but miraculously did not wake. The rest of the company fixed their eyes on the Bear Slayer.

'Treason,' Torj replied, sweeping the loose golden hair from his eyes. Thea didn't fail to notice how his ice-blue gaze lingered on her younger sister at the back of the room.

'We have to get him out,' Kipp said at once. He was unofficially apprenticed to the weapons master, and Thea knew he held Esyllt in high regard.

Torj grimaced. 'We'll get to that. But there's more you should hear first.' He lowered his hammer and rested it against the wall. 'King Artos' army has grown – man and monster alike fill his ranks. He's using his empath powers to take what little free will is left and bend it to his cause. At his bidding, Tver has declared war on Aveum. Its army marches on the winter kingdom as we speak.'

Thea's blood went cold.

'War on Aveum?' Wilder slid his goblet of wine onto the side table and stood. Talemir was on his feet as well, fists clenched at his sides.

Torj gave them a grave nod. 'All of Artos' chess pieces are moving into place. Our time of plotting in the shadows is at an end.' He stepped forward then, allowing a grin to spread across his face as he offered Talemir a hand. 'It's good to see you, Prince of Hearts.'

Talemir gripped his arm and then pulled him into a hard embrace. 'You too, Bear Slayer.'

It was Anya who spoke next, reluctantly rising. 'I think it's time we took this to the war room.'

CHAPTER SEVENTEEN

WILDER

Since their meeting that morning, someone had transformed the formal dining space into exactly that: a war room. Maps covered one end of the table, while an enormous model of the midrealms covered the other, complete with mountainous terrain and colour-coded climates. Markers had been positioned all over the model to indicate the various forces throughout the kingdoms: from units of Guardians stationed in outer villages to King Artos' considerable armies.

Wilder noted the thick black Xs that had been marked in the far reaches of the model. 'What are those?'

'Suspected reaper lairs,' Anya answered, folding her arms over her chest and surveying the replica before them with a critical eye. 'Ideally, if Artos wasn't forcing our hand, we would have opted for a three-pronged attack. One to the lairs, one to Artos' main army, and one to the Heart of Harenth.'

Wilder raised a brow. 'His palace?'

'It's a symbol of his strength,' Adrienne said from across

the table. 'To bring it down would weaken not only his position, but his image.'

'But he *is* forcing our hand, by marching on Aveum,' Thea countered. 'We're compelled to address that attack first, lest he defeat Queen Reyna's armies and bring them to heel. If he manages to swallow her forces, we don't stand a chance.' She pointed to the markers stationed in the winter kingdom, signifying the main army there. 'If he takes those numbers and turns them into howlers or worse, we may as well pack up now.'

Wilder looked to Torj. 'How long until the army reaches Aveum?'

'From what I learnt, they're advancing on foot, with a small unit of cavalry. No shadow wraiths in the mix yet. If it remains that way, I'd wager it'll be no more than two weeks until they reach the foothills of the mountains.' Torj pointed to the spot on the replica where the terrain became uneven.

Cal let out a low whistle. 'This takes apprentice training to a whole new level.'

'Hate to break it to you, Callahan,' Kipp retorted, 'but I think we're well past training now.'

Torj gave a rough laugh. 'He's not wrong, Apprentice... Consider this graduation.'

'Focus,' Anya cut in. 'So, what I'm hearing is that we need to go to Aveum. We need to convince Reyna to take up arms against Artos, not roll over for him.'

'How do you propose we do that?' Wilder asked. 'Between the Daughter of Darkness and her Delmirian heir accomplices? Not to mention a company of supposed fallen Warswords and an army of shadow-touched that the world will only see as half-wraiths?'

Thea squeezed his arm. 'Do we have any proof that the

arachne attack on Aveum during the eclipse was by Artos' hand?' she asked the others, scanning the strained faces around the war table.

'Actually, yes,' Wren replied, stepping forward, a small, familiar vial in her hands.

Seeing it, Wilder remembered that Torj had given it to her in the Singing Hare. It was the gift of Harenth to a newly forged Warsword, a poison none of them had ever used. Torj had landed himself in hot water by declaring it a 'woman's weapon'.

The alchemist glanced at the Bear Slayer before she spoke again. 'Farissa and I made a study of this after we left Aveum,' she told them. 'It's not poison, not in the way that you mean. It can't be used to kill or incapacitate, not directly. But because of that, most Warswords have deemed it useless in the past.'

'What is it, then?' Thea pressed. Wilder was keenly aware that it was another one of the Warsword gifts she was yet to obtain because of him.

'Simply put, it's bottled empath magic,' Wren told them. 'And its properties match those that were used to meddle with the Pools of Purity in Aveum after the arachne attack. This little vial here directly links Artos to the horrific consequences of that attack, including King Elkan's death.'

'How does it do that?' Anya asked, brow furrowed.

'Farissa reached out to the Master Alchemist at Vios. Empath magic was found in King Elkan's system post-mortem... Artos told Reyna he'd done it to ease the king's suffering in his final moments, but with the link to the pools as well, there's no denying that Artos was responsible for the attack.'

Torj let out a whistle. 'So in other words, his handprints are all over this?'

'Exactly,' Farissa concluded at Wren's side. 'We discovered that for a brief time, a few drops of this elixir will give the user control over their target's emotions. Not quite poisonous, but just as powerful, just as dangerous in the wrong hands.'

'How did you uncover that?'

Farissa gave Wren a sideways glance. 'We experimented.'

'On each other?' Audra gaped. 'Farissa, you're telling me you experimented with a drug you know nothing about, on a princess of Delmira?'

'It was my idea!' Wren interjected.

Audra shook her head.

'You didn't care so much when it was your ward flinging herself off cliffs in initiation tests,' Farissa said defensively. 'Or pitting herself against wraiths in the midst of battle. Or are you forgetting that Althea is also a princess of Delmira?'

'There's plenty of us to go round,' Anya said, silencing them both.

'For now,' Thea muttered beside Wilder, only loud enough for him to hear. He nudged her with his elbow, hating how quickly those words left her lips.

Kipp cleared his throat from where he surveyed the model at the end of the table. 'And what of Esyllt?'

'What do you suggest?' Torj asked him. 'As the weapons master, he's under substantial guard in the dungeons.'

'We need him,' Kipp argued, bracing his weight on the table's edge, clearly agitated. 'Not only as another strategic mind to plan the battles to come. Without him, we won't have the loyalty of the Guardians stationed throughout the realms. Regardless of Artos and Osiris, our warriors will answer to him. Without the Guardians rallying to his call, we'll be vastly outnumbered.' He glanced around the room. 'If you want the military term, it's: *fucked.*'

'I'm still waiting for your suggestion,' Torj replied. 'Something tells me you know the underbelly of Thezmarr better than anyone. Can he be rescued?'

'We broke Wilder out of the Scarlet Tower,' Thea declared. 'Thezmarr's dungeons should be child's play.'

Kipp nodded. 'I'll go,' he said. 'I'll get Esyllt out, and take any willing shieldbearers with us.'

'I'll go with you,' Cal declared.

'I'll take one of the shadow-touched with me,' Kipp told him. 'Your archery skills serve our cause better here – not just in the territory's defence like today, but in training anyone who shows a lick of promise with long-range weaponry.'

Wilder was impressed. With the life of his mentor on the line, Kipp had dropped the joker act and descended into full-blown strategy mode. No one argued with him.

'Who goes to parley with Queen Reyna?' Wilder asked, searching the group for the best option, each seeming more unlikely than the last.

'We do,' Anya said, thrusting her chin towards her sisters. 'All three of us together. A united front of Delmirians, taking a stand against the darkness that claimed our family, our kingdom.'

'Agreed,' Wren said firmly.

'Also agreed,' Thea added from Wilder's side.

He suppressed the urge to pull her close. It was selfish, but his first response was regret. Regret that in the face of that hourglass that ticked against them, they would be pulled apart yet again. But the Embervale sisters were right. No one else could make a stronger case. No one else had lost more in the face of Artos' corruption, and it was something the widow queen needed to see for herself.

'So be it,' Talemir said. 'Kipp will return to Thezmarr for Esyllt and any willing fighters remaining in the fortress. Anya, Wren and Thea will go to Aveum to secure Queen Reyna's alliance.'

'Who will escort them?' Torj asked, not taking his eyes off the youngest sister.

Anya made a derisive noise in her throat. 'We're three storm wielders. A warrior, a Warsword and an alchemist.'

'If you're attacked, Wren can't just throw potions at the enemy,' the Warsword argued, his face lined with concern.

Wren's nostrils flared. 'Care to bet?'

Anya's expression contorted as she fought to hide her amusement and resume her hardened countenance. 'We need no escort to the winter lands, Bear Slayer. I'll take us there myself.'

'And I'll pretend not to be insulted that you're dismissing my Warsword prowess,' Thea added.

'But —'

'No buts,' Talemir said in agreement with the sisters. 'The Embervales are more than capable of defending themselves. You're needed here. I'll send for more shadow-touched units to arrive by the end of the week. They'll need training, as much as we can give them if we mean to take a stand against Artos on the field.'

Torj fell quiet.

'So while Kipp rescues Esyllt, and the Embervales go to Aveum, the rest of us are to make something of your forces?' Wilder sought Talemir for confirmation. 'And we have two weeks, likely less, to do so?'

'Pretty much.'

Anya cleared her throat, running a hand over her shaved skull as she addressed Thezmarr's former librarian. 'Audra, any development on what we discussed in Aveum?'

Wilder wracked his mind for what Anya was talking about. What had she asked of Audra at the Singing Hare?

The older woman scowled, pushing her spectacles to the bridge of her nose. 'My answer remains unchanged.'

'That you know nothing?' Anya said, deadpan.

'Not a clue,' Audra replied.

Thea leant in. 'Anya thinks Audra's holding out on the whereabouts of the former women warriors of Thezmarr,' she whispered.

That rang a bell in Wilder's head. But Audra was being cagey, as always.

'If that's all for tonight...' Audra gave the midrealms model a final fleeting glance before she headed for the door.

Anya caught Thea and Wren's attention. 'We leave at dawn tomorrow, yes? I'll meet you in the quadrangle.'

There was no room for negotiation in her tone, and so Thea and Wren simply nodded.

Slowly, the chamber began to empty out, and Thea let out a long sigh, resting her weight on the edge of the table, closing her eyes as she tipped her head back to the ceiling. 'Long day,' she murmured.

'I'll say,' Kipp called out from the door with a farewell wave.

Wilder gave a tired laugh, and Thea made to go after Kipp, no doubt realising that she wouldn't see her friend for some time if she was off to Aveum in the morning, and he was travelling back to Thezmarr. As Thea pushed off from the table and jogged out of the room, something fell from her pocket.

Wilder stared at the thing that had hit the maps with a soft thud, falling open on the table.

A notebook. The very one she'd been scribbling in since they'd arrived.

Wilder meant to close it and pocket it to return to her later, but his gaze caught on a detail scrawled at the top of the page.

His name.

Dear Wilder, it began.

How could he not read it when it was addressed to him?

He glanced at the door, where he could hear Thea talking with Kipp and Cal just beyond. Wilder's stomach lurched as his eyes returned to Thea's messy handwriting. He knew he wasn't meant to read it, but he also knew there was no way he could stop himself now.

Dear Wilder,

I didn't want to leave you, ever. If I had it my way I'd be by your side, always. But Fate had other plans for me, for us, it seems...

Wilder's shoulders caved with the weight of her words, the first few lines alone causing his eyes to burn with tears. He flicked through the notebook, finding countless entries, some only a few sentences long, others spanning several pages.

Wilder,

I'm so sorry. I'm so sorry I'm no longer there with you. I wanted to travel the midrealms with you. I wanted to capture my stallion with you riding alongside me. I wanted so many things for us...

Thea's innermost thoughts, her regrets and her unrelenting declaration of love, all written down for him.

She had signed every entry with a lightning bolt, as she'd done with the notes she'd left for him in his cabin, a lifetime ago.

'What the fuck is this, Thea?' he demanded when she returned to the war room.

The remaining stragglers left in a hurry. Wren shot Thea a grimace before closing the door behind her, leaving Wilder and Thea alone, to deal with... whatever the fuck this was.

He gestured to the open notebook, anger and hurt entwining into something that was bubbling over, something he couldn't control. 'Well?'

Thea's eyes were lined with sorrow. 'It's for you... For after.'

'After what?' he growled.

'You know what.' Thea's lower lip trembled, but she met his gaze with a determined look. 'After I'm gone.'

Wilder raked his fingers through his hair, fighting to get enough air into his lungs as he snatched up the offending item and held it out to her, hopeless. 'You've left me a death book, is that it?'

'Not a name I would have chosen, but... in a way, yes...?'

Wilder was trembling, fury gripping his bones and sending fire to his heart. 'You've been writing me death letters? Since when?'

'Since we got here.'

He flipped through the countless pages. 'If you had this much to say, why not say it to me? I'm here. I'm with you now.' He could hear the pain straining his voice, but he didn't care. Didn't she know that she was breaking him apart? Didn't she know that he wouldn't let her go anywhere without him?

'It's just in case,' she whispered, her eyes wide.

Wilder cast the notebook aside and grabbed her, hoisting her up onto the war table, sending maps and markers scattering. He shoved her thighs apart and seated himself between them. He hadn't allowed himself this, hadn't allowed himself to be touched by her since before the Scarlet Tower. But now? Now he needed her hands on him. He needed to bury his cock deep inside her, needed the sanctuary of her body.

'We're not doing anything *just in case*,' he growled, before ripping her shirt in two and tearing it from her body.

She gasped, but he didn't stop there.

Instantly hard and aching for her, he tore the band around her chest down the middle, exposing her full, round breasts to him in the flickering candlelight.

'Wilder,' she murmured. 'Anyone could come in.'

'I don't give a fuck,' he told her, and closed his mouth around one of her nipples.

Thea's head tipped back as she moaned, her body bowing beneath him as his teeth scraped the hardened peak, teasing the sensitive spot. Her legs widened, wrapping around his lower back and drawing him close so that he could grind his rock-hard erection against her core. The friction sent stars into his vision.

Thea seemed to understand the shift in him, because her hands were at the buttons of his shirt. He couldn't wait; he tore straight through that fabric as well, letting the tatters fall from his arms to the floor. Thea's hands were on him in an instant, tracing the lines of his chest, the plane of his abdomen and the dip of sinew that pointed right to the bulge in his pants.

'You're everything,' she whispered, but he silenced her with a savage kiss.

Wilder claimed her brutally, and she welcomed his exploration of her mouth with frenzied strokes of her own tongue. All the while her nails marked his skin, heating his blood to boiling point.

He caught her lower lip between his teeth and bit down hard, pinching her nipple at the same time, eliciting a sharp cry from her before he kissed over each small pulse of pain.

Thea's hands went to his belt, and he helped her with the buckle and then the buttons of his pants. He shoved them down his muscular thighs, letting his thick length spring free, kicking his pants aside.

Thea's mouth fell open at the sight of him and he let a sly smile grace his lips. 'See something you like, Princess?' he said, his voice rough with desire.

'Yes,' she breathed, reaching for him. 'Something I've missed...'

Wilder didn't give a fuck who heard them as her hand closed around his shaft and he let out a carnal moan. Her thumb swiped across the broad, leaking head of him, teasing his tip with decadent circles before she stroked him in earnest.

'*Fuck.*' Wilder braced himself against the power of that single touch. She worked him in gloriously long, unhurried caresses, coaxing waves of desire to unfurl from the base of his spine, tightening in his balls. He thrust into her hand, savouring each pass over his cock as he popped open the buttons of her pants.

He wrenched them down to her knees, along with her

undergarments, her breasts bouncing with the movement. Thea's grip left him as she wriggled out of her pants completely. More army pieces fell from the table, maps tearing beneath Thea's shifting body. Wilder grabbed his cock and dragged it through the slickness between her legs.

They both moaned at the sensation.

'Gods,' Wilder murmured. 'How is it that you feel so good and I'm not even inside you yet?'

Thea ground against him, edging him closer to her entrance. 'Wilder...'

His name was a curse and a plea, and the sound of it on her lips nearly had him throwing all notion of restraint to the wind. Furies save him, he'd never been so fucking hard in all his life. White-hot need blazed through him like wildfire and it was all he could do not to sheathe himself inside her in one powerful thrust.

'Do it,' Thea challenged, staring up at him with hooded eyes while she parted her legs even further for emphasis.

Smiling darkly, Wilder notched his cock to her entrance and slid in just a fraction, his control nearly slipping at that first hint of tight heat around him. But he paused, teasing her clit with his thumb and revelling in the way her body opened for him.

'Wilder...' she warned.

It was the most delicious form of torture, for the both of them, but he couldn't stand it a moment longer.

'Pinch those nipples for me, Princess,' he commanded.

As Thea's fingers clamped around her hardened peaks, Wilder shifted his hips and thrust inside her with one powerful stroke. His vision blurred and Thea moaned loudly beneath him, her whole body welcoming him inside, clenching around his cock like he belonged there.

'*Holy fuck*,' he muttered, enveloping her with his torso as he sank even deeper into the wet heat of her. A low, rumbling sound of need escaped him and he gripped her hard enough to bruise, his thrusts brutal, unapologetic, uninhibited.

Thea met him stroke for stroke with a tilt of her hips, allowing him deeper still. The noises that left her had Wilder's body turning molten, his balls tightening, begging to empty into her.

'Harder,' Thea panted. 'Faster.'

Wilder was only too happy to oblige, adjusting his grip on her, dragging her across the war table so that her lower half hung off the edge, so he could drive himself into her with even more fury. For that rage was still simmering below the surface. At everything that had happened to lead them here, every injustice, every stolen moment – even at Thea herself, for having accepted the fate carved for her in that gods-damned stone.

And so he fucked her hard and fast, just as she asked.

'I don't want your death notes,' he managed between thrusts, applying pressure to her clit, causing her to jerk beneath him. 'Do you hear me?'

'Yes...' she cried, her naked body flushed with desire.

He closed one hand around her throat. 'Never again.'

Thea's eyes flew open, her pupils dilated, her muscles clenching around him. She licked her lips. 'Are you going to punish me?'

Wilder's thrusts slowed and he blinked at her. 'Do you *want* to be punished, Princess?' he asked.

Slowly, Thea nodded, once, then twice. 'I deserve it...'

A new rush of longing swept through Wilder and he ground into her. 'You do.'

In that moment, he came back to himself in full force, his strength, his rage, his power all coursing through him alongside his insatiable desire for the woman writhing beneath him. He flipped her onto her front and bent her over the edge of the war table, baring her backside to him.

As he buried his cock deep inside her from behind, his open palm came down hard on her pale flesh with a crack.

Thea moaned, spreading her legs beneath her and pushing back onto his length. He could feel her wetness dripping down her thighs. 'Again.'

Wilder spanked her other cheek, feeling the sting through his fingers as he slammed into her again and again, wringing frenzied cries from her. He was barely holding on.

'Thea...' he panted against her sweat-slicked spine, wrapping the tail of her messy braid around his knuckles and pulling her back onto him. 'I want you to come. Come all over my cock.'

'Wilder...' Her breath caught in ecstasy.

'*Now*,' he commanded.

Thea's whole body tensed and she cried out, shuddering around him.

Wilder arced his hips, restraint a distant memory as he fucked her on the precipice of climax. She pushed back on him and he passed the point of no return, sheer pleasure flooding his veins.

Wilder erupted with a roar, trembling as he spilt himself inside her.

He jerked as Thea coaxed the last waves of his orgasm from him, rocking against him slowly.

He kissed the base of her spine, breathless and in awe of what they'd just done. Leaning back as he pulled his cock from her, he surveyed the bright pink handprints on each pale cheek of her backside. He pressed a kiss to the first, then the second, before turning her over beneath him.

Thea's face was flushed, a smile tugging at her lips. 'Was that...'

'Mind-blowing?' he asked without hesitation. 'Yes.'

On the table, Thea propped herself up on her elbows and surveyed their flushed, sticky bodies, her gaze lingering on Wilder's cock, already halfway back to attention, heavy between his legs. 'Welcome back, Warsword,' she said with a devious grin.

Wilder cupped her chin and brought his mouth to hers, kissing her deeply before breaking away. 'Next time you need punishment... It won't just be here,' he murmured, shifting his hand beneath her to squeeze her backside. With his other hand he swiped through her wetness before giving her clit a light slap.

A gasp escaped Thea, and then she laughed. 'Don't tempt me with a good time.'

CHAPTER EIGHTEEN

THEA

They tidied the war table as best they could before clutching their torn clothes to their chests and darting through the university halls like rebellious teenagers. Thea couldn't stop the laughter bursting from her lips as they sprinted through the empty library to their quarters.

Gods, she could only imagine who'd heard them. But she didn't care.

Wilder's silver gaze was bright and trained on her, his full lips curved into a disbelieving smile as she flung their door open and tossed her clothes aside.

'I hope you brought your sewing kit,' she said as he followed suit, their shirts in complete tatters thanks to his impatience.

He chuckled, the sound making her toes curl as he faced her.

She drank in the sight of him. He was even more perfect than when she'd first laid eyes on him. *Carved by the Furies themselves* had been her first thought back then, and she stood by it now. He'd recovered from his time in the tower spectacularly. His whole body was chiselled and corded with muscle, and he seemed to drip with strength and power. Her mouth went dry as her brazen study trailed to his cock, hard and ready for her once more. A fresh wave of desire pulsed through her.

Wilder appraised her hungrily.

Thea gave him a lazy smile, and let her hands start to explore her own body, his silver eyes tracking every movement as she cupped her breasts and let her fingers drift south, sliding through the evidence of what they'd already done.

'Ready again so soon, Princess?' His voice was low and husky.

Thea smirked. 'Warsword stamina,' she said, echoing words he'd spoken to her a lifetime ago.

Amusement gleamed in his eyes at that. He wrapped a hand around his cock, stroking it leisurely as though he had all the time in the world. Longing coursed through Thea as she watched the up-and-down motion over that glorious length.

Wilder Hawthorne was a god, and she would gladly worship at his altar.

And so she did. She went to him and dropped to her knees, her hand replacing his, guiding his cock to her mouth.

'Thea...' he moaned as her lips closed over the tip.

She nearly laughed, revelling in the instant power she held over him, in the fact that even on her knees, she held his pleasure in the palm of her hand. Circling the broad head of him with her tongue, she hummed around him, realising that he tasted of them both.

'Stop toying with me,' Wilder pleaded above her, jerking his hips.

That only made her want to tease him more. Thea tongued the crown of him and felt his muscular legs tremble beneath him, saw the thick tendons flex in his thighs. Smiling to herself, she licked the sensitive underside of his head, featherlight strokes of her tongue taunting him with what was to come.

He groaned, grabbing a fistful of her hair, his whole body shaking with restraint.

Cupping his balls, Thea licked the length of him, from base to tip, before she glided her mouth over him and swallowed him down without warning.

'*Fuck,*' he barked, bucking beneath her.

Thea sucked his cock, moving up and down over his shaft, letting him hit the back of her throat as she worked him. Wilder moved with her now, gripping her hair by the roots and thrusting into her mouth, muttering curses to the Furies as he stared down at her through a haze of lust.

'Play with yourself while you suck my cock, Thea,' he ordered.

He didn't need to tell her twice; her own arousal was dripping down her thighs. She parted her knees on the ground and slid her free hand to that sensitive spot that ached for contact.

Wilder's eyes widened at the sight of her and the carnal noise that vibrated down his body and into her mouth was nearly her undoing.

Thea rubbed her clit, moaning around Wilder's cock as fire unfurled within. Holding his hungry gaze, she slid a finger inside herself, heat swelling between her legs, begging for release.

'That's it, Thea... Eyes on me,' he murmured, watching where she fucked herself with her fingers. She added another and he groaned, as though he couldn't handle the sight. Candlelight gilded him above her, illuminating that powerful body, how it shifted with every thrust into her mouth.

'Show me,' he growled. 'Show me you're ready for me.'

Toes curling at his filthy words, Thea removed her fingers and showed him the glistening wetness coating them.

Whatever leash Wilder had been holding over his control snapped, and he pulled himself away and hoisted her up, carrying her to the armchair before the fire.

He sat down, pulling her on top so she was straddling him. His hard cock, still wet from her mouth, pressed against her core and she whimpered, sliding over the length of him.

Wilder traced her curves, his expression one of sheer awe. 'There's no counting the ways I love you, Thea,' he murmured, cupping her breasts in his calloused palms. 'There's no counting the ways I want to take you...' He circled a nipple with his thumb, eliciting a soft cry from her.

He kissed her, long and hard, deeply and passionately, his tongue exploring her mouth, his lips coasting over hers again and again as his hands mapped every inch of her skin.

Thea shifted on his lap so that his cock pressed against her entrance. 'I love you,' she said against his lips.

'I love you, too,' he told her, and sheathed himself inside her to the hilt.

Thea cried out, spots marring her vision as he filled her, stretched her so thoroughly she felt as though she might burst. A raging need blazed inside her, and suddenly she was wound so tightly that every breath sent a frisson of longing straight to her core.

'Ride me,' Wilder told her, gripping her hips and grinding her back and forth, his cock buried deep inside her still.

Thea's whole body tightened at the instruction, and her head tipped back in ecstasy as she slid up the length of him, only to slam back down.

'Fuck...' Wilder gasped. 'Do that again.'

She obliged him, revelling in the carnal moans that escaped him, her own cries mingling with his as he hit that spot deep inside her.

Though they'd been rough in the war room, a different kind of frenzy took hold of them now. She rode him with the abandon of someone who was leaving in the morning, with the desperation of someone who wanted to leave her mark on the love of her life, so he'd feel her even in her absence. The brutal way Wilder fucked her in turn told her he felt the same way. He thrust into her from beneath, coaxing waves of desire from deep within, building that pressure to the cusp of its breaking point.

Then, he reached between them and circled her clit with his thumb.

Thea cried out, only to be silenced by his fierce kiss as he increased his pace, strumming where she was most sensitive, driving into her from below.

She gasped against his lips. 'Wilder... you're going to make me —'

He broke away to watch her come undone, and she did.

Her climax barrelled into her like a tidal wave, sweeping her up in its path and crashing spectacularly all around her. She was half sobbing with the force of it, her whole body a shuddering mess atop her Warsword.

'You can give me another,' he said.

Her eyes widened as she panted through the aftershocks of her orgasm. 'I can't – I —'

'You can.' Wilder switched the rhythm on her clit with long, luxurious strokes over the sensitive bud, all the while still thrusting inside her, drawing out his own pleasure. His mouth closed over her nipple, sucking gently before biting down.

The flash of pain sparked something anew inside her, and Thea's body turned molten once more.

'There she is,' Wilder murmured as she moved with him, picking up her pace again, matching him.

Fused together, they were one. There was nothing more perfect, nothing that made more sense than this.

Thea was trembling uncontrollably now, shaking with the force of it all, of *him*, fucking her into utter oblivion.

'Come with me, Thea,' Wilder rasped, sliding into her again and again, pushing her over the edge —

She came apart, her third climax ripping through her like a savage tempest, blurring all her senses. Chaotic sparks shot through every inch of her body, so intense that she blinked back tears, unable to fathom putting herself back together.

And beneath her, Wilder came undone with a hoarse shout. His body shuddered beneath hers, his release spilling inside her.

As they both rode the aftershocks, Wilder kissed her soundly and breathed her in as though she were something to be savoured, cherished.

Thea's heart nearly burst as he gazed upon her with nothing but love – pure, adoring love in his silver eyes.

'No man could have you and not be consumed,' he murmured.

CHAPTER NINETEEN

THEA

Wilder's words stayed with Thea well into the next day. She clung to them when the brutal cold of Aveum's hinterlands bit into her bones as she, Wren and Anya landed atop the snow in the icy woodlands. Anya's ribbons of power dissipated and her wings dematerialised at her back, all evidence of her shadow-touched magic gone in the blink of an eye.

The sisters had decided that arriving on Queen Reyna's doorstep swathed in darkness would likely set the wrong tone for their meeting, and so Anya had brought them to the outskirts of Vios, where they would make their way on foot to the floating domes at the heart of the capital.

Thea had forgotten how much she detested the cold. Even with Furies-given power thrumming inside her, the grip of Aveum's winter was unrelenting, pain already blooming at her extremities and her scarred wrist aching like a bitch. In the chaos, she'd forgotten all about the salve Wren had made for her, and she made a mental note to use it as soon as they were somewhere her fingers wouldn't snap off.

'Where exactly are we?' she muttered, burying the lower half of her face in the woollen scarf she'd looped around her neck. Barren trees surrounded them, evergreens that should have borne leaves even in the frost. But there was no sign of life in sight, only the trickle of the half-frozen stream nearby. Thea already longed for the warmth of Wilder and their bed.

'The woods just outside of Silverbrook village. Kipp said you rode through it before – it's just beyond the treeline,' Wren replied. 'We should get moving before we freeze to death.'

Anya cupped her hands to her face, blowing hot breath over her fingers. 'Sounds like a solid plan to me. Of all the ways to die after everything I've been through, turning to a block of ice in some dead forest would be rather underwhelming.'

Thea snorted at that and trudged after her through the snow.

Together, the sisters wove through the skeletal trees and navigated the icy terrain without much complaint, though Thea could hear their teeth chattering. She found it increasingly surreal to be walking at their sides – the heirs of Delmira, united after all this time. Most of the midrealms knew it now, and they were on their way to declare it to another ruler, in the hopes of securing her alliance. Life had changed a lot since she'd been forced to mix potions as a would-be alchemist at the fortress.

'I think we need to train together,' Anya declared as they crested a ridge and spotted the outer buildings of Frostvale.

'Wren's got basic defence training, same as all Thezmarrians,' Thea replied. Their younger sister had never shown much inclination towards fighting beyond the basics, insisting that her alchemy skills were just as dangerous as fists and blades.

Anya laughed. 'That's not what I meant. Though...' She turned to Wren. 'It might be time to brush up on some of those basics.'

Thea suppressed a chuckle at Wren's answering scowl. 'What did you mean, then?' she prompted.

'Magic,' Anya said. 'We need to train our magic together, so we can work as a unit, when the time comes.'

'I thought the same thing,' Wren admitted. 'We're strongest together. Though I haven't the faintest idea how it might work...'

Anya tucked her gloved hands under her arms, cursing the cold. 'I spoke with Audra. She showed me a few things we might try, but she wasn't sure those techniques would help us so late in the game.'

'Not exactly encouraging, as always,' Thea retorted.

Wren silenced her with a well-placed elbow to the ribs, finding her mark even beneath all the layers. 'What did she suggest, then?'

Anya forged on. 'Her main point was that joint magic is all about connection.'

'We're connected by blood. Doesn't get more solid than that, surely,' Thea said, training her gaze on the nearing village.

'Audra seemed to think otherwise.'

'Audra going against the grain?' Thea mocked. 'Never.'

'Shut up, Thee,' Wren snapped.

Anya gave her a grateful look, a silent exchange that would never have happened a matter of months ago. Thea reeled back a little. She had clearly underestimated how much her older and younger sister had bonded in her absence. A twinge of jealousy bloomed in the wake of the realisation.

'Audra said that in order to create a powerful link between the three of us, we have to know one another, deeply. That our shared blood is only the beginning of a meaningful connection.'

'That would have been great advice years ago, but how are we meant to build decades' worth of sibling dynamics in a matter of weeks? Should I just hand over my fucking diary?' Thea clicked her tongue in frustration, still bitter about the fact that Audra had been unable to find a way to transfer her power to her sisters when the time came.

Anya levelled her with a stare, her scar never failing to elevate her fierceness. 'You could start with telling us about these supposed death notes.'

Thea stared at her. 'How the fuck do you know about those?'

Anya and Wren exchanged another look, which only served to agitate Thea further.

'Half the building heard you and Wilder yelling about them last night,' Wren supplied with a shrug. 'If you don't want everyone in your business, maybe take it somewhere else next time. In fact, *please* take it somewhere else next time. The aftermath of that row is seared in my brain forever. I'm scarred for life.'

Anya made a garbled noise as she tried not to laugh.

'You're just jealous,' Thea quipped. 'Everyone wants a Warsword of their own.'

177

Anya did laugh that time. 'Oh, I think Wren could have a Warsword if she wanted one.'

'We're not having this conversation,' Wren said firmly.

'But we can talk about *my* private matters as much as you want?' Thea countered.

'You forfeit the right to privacy the moment you fuck on the rebellion's war table.' Anya folded her arms over her chest and waited for Thea's argument.

But Thea shrugged. 'Fine.'

'Tell us about the notes, then,' Wren said, more gently this time.

Thea tugged her cloak tighter around her, feeling the press of her fate stone against her naked skin beneath all her layers. 'I…'

To her surprise, her sisters waited patiently for her to form the words, somehow recognising that this wasn't the moment to push, but the moment to let her speak at her own pace.

'I wanted to leave him something for when I'm gone,' she heard herself say. 'We can pretend it doesn't exist all we want —' She motioned to the stone under her clothes. 'But it doesn't change the reality. Fate will come to claim me soon enough, and when it does, I wanted to leave something of me behind. I —' Her voice cracked, but she forged on. 'I wanted to say all the things I won't get time to say. I wanted him to know…'

Mortified, Thea found tears tracking down her cheeks. She hadn't spoken to anyone about this, not even Wilder himself, and she didn't realise how much it had been eating away at her.

Wren's arm came around her shoulders. 'He knows, Thee. Believe me, that man knows.'

Clearly not one for offering physical comfort, Anya nodded at her side. 'Fate is nothing to fear,' she said quietly. 'It comes for us all in the end.'

'Doesn't make it easier,' Thea muttered.

'No,' Anya replied. 'It doesn't.'

Thea cleared her throat and shrugged Wren's arm off her. 'Well, that was me. Who's next?'

'Didn't realise this was a tit-for-tat sort of situation.' Anya pointed ahead. 'Plus, we're here.'

'You're not getting away with it that easily,' Thea replied.

But sure enough, familiar buildings made of stone and timber stood before the trio, roofs heavy with snow. The streets beyond were narrow and winding. Wren was right: Thea had ridden through these parts with Wilder, Cal and Kipp on their way to the floating domes, wherein she'd given Wilder over as a prisoner to the rulers of the midrealms. The memory tasted bitter on her tongue now.

On foot, the sisters made their way into the village, and Thea realised how much it had changed since she'd last passed through. The shops and stalls spilling out into the streets were gone or boarded up. The aroma of meat roasting on spits, the laughter and music from the taverns – all gone. How long had it been since she'd watched that quartet of performers juggling flaming torches?

'What happened to this place?' she breathed.

'Is it so different to what it was?' Wren asked.

'Yes,' Anya and Thea replied in unison.

Anya grimaced. 'I had heard that after the arachne attack, Aveum sort of fell apart at the seams... But I didn't want to believe it. I thought Queen Reyna was stronger than that.'

'She lost her husband,' Thea pointed out.

179

'She has a kingdom to run,' Anya countered. 'Life does not stop after the death of a single person.'

Her sister's words cut deeper than any blade.

Thea knew that when her existence was wiped from the world, everything else would remain. She knew and hoped that everyone would move forward, her ashes fading in their wake, but it didn't make it hurt any less that she wouldn't be there, that life wasn't hers for the taking.

'Sorry,' Anya muttered, giving her a nudge.

'It's fine,' Thea replied, quickening her pace. The sooner they got through the village, the sooner they'd get to Vios, and the sooner they could rally Reyna to their cause and get the fuck out of here.

Anya matched her strides. 'I'm not... I'm not the most sensitive person,' she admitted, her breath clouding before her face. 'The result of spending the majority of my developing years in a cave, I'm afraid.'

'No one ever accused Thea of being overly sensitive, anyway,' Wren interjected. 'Maybe it's an Embervale trait?'

'I wouldn't know the first thing about Embervale traits,' Thea said.

Anya nodded to Thea. 'I brought those letters I told you about. When we were at the shadow-touched camp before the Singing Hare? I thought you both might like to read them.'

'What letters?' Wren asked.

'The ones our mother wrote to the Queen of Naarva before the kingdoms fell.'

Thea had never seen Wren look so hopeful. 'You have letters from our mother?'

'Here.' Anya dug through her pockets and offered Wren a small bundle of envelopes tied together with twine.

But to Thea's surprise, Wren pushed them back. 'Let's read them together.'

The only outward sign that this had moved Anya was the fresh flush of pink at the tips of her cheeks, but she simply nodded and stashed the letters away once more.

Soon, they were on the main road to Aveum, the floating domes of Vios hovering in the near distance. Thea wished she had a horse; she could no longer feel her toes.

'While it's just the three of us,' Wren ventured, with a tentative glance at both Thea and Anya, 'we should talk about our plans for Delmira.'

'It's rubble and rot,' Thea replied.

'But it's ours, by birthright,' Wren argued.

'It's Anya's by birthright,' Thea corrected. 'So by all means, have it. Be queen of the ruins.'

Anya snorted. 'I'm already the supposed Daughter of Darkness – I don't think I can take another title. How about we give it to you, Wren?'

Wren crossed her arms. 'This isn't a joke.'

'Who said I was joking?' Anya said.

Wren shook her head. 'I won't be the only one to ask this question. I thought it might be prudent to have some semblance of an answer before standing in front of the Queen of Aveum.'

Anya sighed. 'She's right. When the fighting is done, the people will want to know who rules what kingdom.'

'And they'll rally to their homeland,' Wren added.

'Let them rally to whichever one of you wants to rule over the ashes,' Thea said. 'I'm not long for this world anyway.'

'Thea,' Wren chastised. 'Don't think like that —'

It was Thea's turn to sigh. 'We have to win the fucking

war first. Then we can argue over what to do with the fallen kingdom. A pile of ashes isn't going anywhere, Wren.'

'No,' Anya agreed. 'But what rises from the ashes, Thea? A phoenix, that's what.'

Thea shrugged. 'In that case, Wren looks like a great phoenix to me.'

As they trekked towards the capital, bracing themselves against the wretched winds and flurries of snow, they spoke of how their lives might have been as princesses of the midrealms. The juxtaposition of their current status was not lost on any of them, and Thea found it almost laughable as she surveyed the three of them. Anya with her shaved head and scarred eye, not to mention her wings and shadows when she called on them; Wren with her potions and experiments; and Thea the Warsword. It was hard to picture them dolled up in ballgowns and tiaras, meeting Queen Reyna as near-equals. They would have grown up with royal feasts and dances, surrounded by riches and people of noble stock.

'We could have been married off to princes,' Wren mused.

'What princes?' Thea scoffed. 'None of the royals have male heirs.'

'Perhaps a prince from the realms beyond the Veil,' Wren replied. 'A marriage of alliance.'

'I think Thea might be off the marriage market,' Anya quipped.

Wren made a noise of agreement before she turned to Thea, her brow furrowed. 'I thought Warswords didn't take wives? Isn't it part of their vows?'

Thea shrugged. 'I took no such vow. And nor would I take a wife.'

'Have you and Wilder talked —'

'There hasn't been much time for talking,' Thea cut her off.

'Don't we know it,' Wren muttered.

'Oh, piss off.' Thea gave her a gentle shove.

But Wren simply grinned. 'Wasn't I right, all those years ago? When you were heartbroken over that stupid stable master's apprentice? What was his name? Evander?'

Thea knew exactly what Wren was talking about. 'I've no idea what you mean.'

'You do so.'

'Do not.'

'What were you right about?' Anya asked, her gaze flitting between the two.

'Evander had a problem with Thea's ambition to become a warrior, a Warsword... He was threatened by her. I told her: a true man won't cut you down as you fight your battles... A true man helps sharpen your sword, guards your back and fights at your side.'

Anya's brows shot up, impressed. 'That was very wise.'

Wren looked pleased. 'I know.'

Mischief lit up their older sister's eyes. 'Tell us, Wren... Anyone in particular you want fighting at your side these days?'

'No.'

'You sure about that?'

Wren shot her a warning look. '*Yes.*'

Thea's cheeks ached from grinning at this exchange, only to be robbed of the joy as she realised that she wouldn't get this time with her sisters for long. She had already wasted years of bickering with Wren, when they could have had friendship. Now they'd only just found Anya, and she was almost out of time.

Thankfully, neither Wren nor Anya noticed her mood souring as they reached the city of Vios. The floating domes and surrounding residences were nestled in the heart of a deep valley, on the banks of a glacier-fed river – an impressive sight, framed by snow-capped mountains.

As they drew closer, Thea saw that the floating domes were adorned with black flags for mourning, and the official gates to the inner city were flanked by more guards than last time. *Aveum guards, at least,* Thea thought, recalling how it had been Artos' men on the perimeter last time. Hope was not lost – not yet.

Two burly soldiers barred the way into the keep, staring down at all three sisters suspiciously. Thea cursed Artos and his damn wanted posters. The men here had no doubt seen their likenesses plastered all over the city.

'We're here to see Queen Reyna,' Thea declared.

'The queen is not entertaining visitors. She is in mourning,' one of the guards told her coldly.

'We're aware,' Anya said with equal iciness. 'We're not here to be *entertained.*'

The guard's eyes narrowed. 'What are you here for, then?'

'To plan for the war ahead,' Anya told him without hesitation.

The guard blinked at her. 'War?'

'Did I stammer?'

'Take your attitude somewhere else, girl. Before we sound the alarm and have you thrown in the ice dungeons.'

But Anya stood firm, resting a hand on the handle of her scythe. 'We're not leaving until we see the queen.'

The guard's eyes widened as he noted the gesture, and the weapon itself. 'I know you! You're the —'

Thea glanced at Wren, who gave her a subtle nod. Thea pulled Anya back before she started a brawl, and addressed the guard herself.

'Tell Queen Reyna that the heirs of Delmira beg an audience.'

CHAPTER TWENTY

WILDER

Talemir's call to arms had been heard all over Naarva, and the shadow-touched forces grew by the day, the camp now spilling out into surrounding fields. Wilder had had no idea there were so many in hiding, certainly not this many willing to fight.

He stood by a fire pit now with the Shadow Prince himself, along with Torj, Dratos, Drue and Adrienne, trying to pull together some semblance of a plan. It was official: Tver was marching on Aveum with King Artos' forces at its back, and the rebellion was to meet the attack on the open battlefield. If they could unite their men.

'We have to expect discord between the different units,' Wilder said to the others. 'Both among the shadow-touched themselves, and between them and the allies when we join forces.'

'He's right,' Tal agreed. 'Just like the rest of the midrealms, Aveum has been told the narrative that we're of the same ilk as the wraiths. Even if the Embervales secure the alliance with Queen Reyna, we can't expect things to go smoothly.

We have to prepare to combat the prejudices from and within both sides.'

'How do you propose we do that, Tal?' Dratos drawled. 'Our people have lived in secret for years for fear of what common folk do to our kind. We've all heard about Artos' experiments —'

'We need to get our people to accept Wilder and Torj as leaders in our army.'

Dratos shook his head in disbelief. 'Good luck with that.'

Wilder was inclined to agree with him. Though he'd been training his own unit to the point of exhaustion, they still whispered about his execution of their kind, and those whispers echoed through the camp. 'Torj will have better luck,' he said.

'Luck or no, we need you both. There's no winning this war without the right commanders at the helm.' There was no compromise in Talemir's voice, and it reminded Wilder of his earlier days as the apprentice of the legendary Warsword, when he'd demanded complete obedience and nothing less.

'First order of business,' Drue cut in. 'Every weapon-wielding soldier in our ranks is to report to the forge to have their blades imbued with the orchid essence. Then they'll be able to carve out wraith hearts just as well as if they hold Naarvian steel. Fendran said to send them in groups of twenty. The forge and its surrounds can't hold many more than that.'

Drue's command was law in this place, perhaps even more so than Talemir's, and her orders quickly filtered down the ranks before Wilder's eyes. He wished Thea was here to see it.

When their strategising was done for the evening, the

group of commanders broke up, leaving Torj at Wilder's side by the fire. There was no point in returning to the main building when they had to be up at dawn for training, so they had pitched tents alongside the rest of the army. Wilder didn't miss the soft mattress of his bed so much as he missed Thea in it with him.

'You're thinking of her, aren't you?' Torj ventured, staring into the campfire flames.

'Always,' Wilder replied without hesitation. He'd once been stupid enough to deny all he felt for Thea, but those days were long behind him now.

His blunt reply didn't seem to faze the Bear Slayer. 'Do you think they're alright?'

Wilder heaved a sigh and raked his fingers through his hair. 'Do I like the idea of Thea out there without me? No. Do I think she's alright? She's a storm-wielding Warsword... The safest place is at her side. Which is exactly where Wren is.'

Torj didn't respond.

'Not going to deny it?' Wilder pressed, hoping to rile up his brother in arms just a little.

But Torj shook his head. 'Why should I? Why shouldn't I want what you have?'

That took Wilder aback. Despite all the wisdom Torj had dispensed over the years, he still hadn't expected the Bear Slayer to be so open.

'You shouldn't deny it,' Wilder said honestly. 'You deserve what you want, brother.'

Torj's expression grew distant as the flames cast shadows across his face. 'If only wanting made it so, eh?'

Wilder thought of the piece of jade that was nestled

between Thea's breasts. He wanted for it not to matter, for their fates not to be ruled by a gods-damned stone.

'If only.'

The next morning, the training began in earnest. Wilder left the endurance and fitness drills for the captains to oversee while he took charge of the battle tactics and formations they needed to master before they'd hold their own on the field. He found an empty paddock by the perimeter of Talemir's shield, and there he led a cavalry unit of fifty men and women with varying riding and fighting experience.

In simple terms, he swiftly explained some of the more basic military formations they would need to understand before he moved them into position himself.

'Not there,' he called to one man who seemed intent on ignoring him. 'In line with the rest. You need to form a wall.'

Not for the first time, he found himself deflated by the quality of the soldiers in their midst. He was used to training shieldbearers and Guardians of Thezmarr – those who wished to be shaped into warriors, true defenders of the midrealms. He said as much to Talemir when he joined Wilder to assess their progress. The older Warsword fixed him with a long, hard stare.

'Being shadow-touched doesn't make you a natural fighter. A lot of these men and women were civilians,' Talemir told him. 'I've been visiting them in their hideouts throughout Naarva over the years to oversee their basic training, to convince them to join our ranks for this war... But they didn't sign up for this, Wilder, not truly. Fighting wasn't a choice for them.'

'Are you saying I should cut them some slack?' Wilder asked as they watched his unit march their horses across the field, their lines messy and unevenly spaced.

'No,' Talemir replied. 'Train them hard, harder than you would at Thezmarr. This is our survival we're talking about.'

The mood was tense when Talemir left. Wilder could feel how on edge every single one of his soldiers was. And he understood; he truly did. It felt like the task ahead of them was impossible: to become a united and formidable unit in a matter of weeks, possibly even just days. If they wanted to survive the fight ahead, they needed a fucking miracle.

As if that wasn't enough, Wilder could still feel their resentment rolling in waves towards him, and he found himself empathising even now. The shadow-touched, who had fought their own battles within a wraith-infested kingdom for all these years, now had to yield to his command. Wilder knew how dangerous that resentment was. Orders were for nothing if no one respected him enough to carry them out.

'Take five minutes. Drink some water,' he told them. 'Then we go again.'

No one openly rejected his instruction, but he'd have wagered it was only because they were all actually parched. No one spoke to him either, so he watched them talk quietly among themselves, drinking from their canteens and mopping the perspiration from their brows with their sleeves.

Wilder let his mind wander to what Talemir had told him earlier. They had sent scouts to assess the terrain between Tver and Aveum for the strategic advantage, and to clap eyes on the forces that marched across the border. No word yet as to how many men, how many monsters graced King Leiko and King Artos' ranks.

Wilder took a sip from his own flask, letting the cool water wash down his throat, which was hoarse from shouting. He needed to do better. He needed to make *them* better. When there were no heroes among them, it would come down to their formations, their lines. They had to hold their own, and break the enemy's, if there was to be any hope of winning the battle —

'— giving the Delmirian bitches too much say in the matter —'

The voice cut through Wilder's thoughts, his gaze snapping to his unit as a deadly calm slid into place. All notions of empathy vanished.

'They come from a family of traitors. Just look at their kingdom. It's been in ruins for decades. Now they expect us to follow them? I'd sooner —'

'Sooner what?' Wilder bit out, closing the distance between them on horseback and towering over the spineless bastard.

'Nothing,' the man replied sullenly, his knuckles turning white around his reins.

Wilder stared him down. 'By all means, tell me what you'd rather do than follow lightning-wielding warriors into battle.'

'I meant nothing by it.'

'Then don't say it,' Wilder snapped. 'There is enough discord in our ranks as it is. And you would do well to remember that the Delmirians might be all that stand between you and those monsters out there.'

The man hung his head. 'As you say, sir.'

Wilder clenched his jaw to stop himself from delivering

another verbal lashing. Instead, he beat down his anger and turned to the unit as a whole.

'Time's up,' he barked. 'Form up.'

They manoeuvred their horses into a crooked line, and it was all Wilder could do not to drop his head into his hands in defeat. He guided Biscuit to the front of the unit and made a point of meeting every gaze that stared back at him.

'You *must* hold the line.' He ensured that his deep voice projected to the far reaches of the group. 'It's easy enough here in these fields, but when a charge is hurtling towards you, it's another story entirely. I want your reins held short.' He demonstrated with his own. 'I want you to keep pace with the man or woman on either side of you. The horses will want to gallop – *do not let them*. If one breaks formation, they all will. We *cannot* have that.'

Silence followed.

'Like getting blood from a fucking stone,' he muttered before addressing them at full volume again. 'You *must* hold the line,' he repeated. 'Do you understand?'

Still nothing.

Hanging on to his patience by a tattered thread, Wilder rose to his full height in the saddle, let his Furies-given strength emanate from his body, and unsheathed his blades from their scabbards. 'I said, *do you understand?*'

A chorus of *yes* filtered through the ranks.

'Good. Then we go again. Form the fuck up.'

They did as he asked, albeit messily. He rode through the whole unit, positioning each person exactly where they needed to be, pointing out markers for them to remember, so they could line themselves up properly next time.

He had them canter across the paddock, wincing as he saw the weak links in the armour he was working so hard to forge. Wilder was watching his unit so intently that he barely registered Torj's approach until the Warsword's Tverrian stallion brushed up along Biscuit's side.

The Bear Slayer grimaced at the state of his unit.

'This is going to be a problem,' Wilder muttered.

'No shit,' was Torj's only reply.

CHAPTER TWENTY-ONE

THEA

To Thea's great relief, she and her sisters weren't thrown into Aveum's ice dungeons, but nor were they taken straight to the queen. They had been escorted to the royal guest quarters, which Thea found laughable considering the heirs of Delmira were still considered threats to the realm. But threat or not, apparently there was no greater danger than to offend a visiting royal. The quarters they'd been given were the most lavish Thea had ever seen. It was a suite of adjoining rooms, each housing a four-poster bed draped in silks, each with its own hearth, bathing chamber and balcony that overlooked the great frozen lake below.

The rooms opened out into a formal lounge and dining area, as though Thea, Wren and Anya might feel the need to entertain their own guests in the floating domes. Another laughable consideration. The only person they wanted to see was Queen Reyna, and she hadn't deigned to answer their request for an audience, not since they'd arrived three days ago.

Thea tried to keep at bay her growing sense of dread that Reyna might be colluding with King Artos, giving away their whereabouts and holding them here until he arrived. But they were not treated like prisoners. All three of them had left their suite and perused the domes as freely as they might have done in their own homes, but their patience was wearing thin.

In secret, they worked on their magic together, sharing the methods they'd used to control their own, trying to figure out how to forge a connection between the storm within each of them. But the confines of a palace were no place for summoning thunder and lightning, and so their practice was limited. When they weren't discussing magic, they talked of their family and what little they could remember of their parents.

On the third night of their stay, Anya showed Thea and Wren the letters she'd found, written in their mother's hand. The young women pored over the pieces of parchment before the fire, getting to know the former Queen of Delmira by her loopy scrawl and loving descriptions of her daughters to her friend, Queen Yolena of Naarva.

'It's so surreal,' Wren murmured, tracing over the cursive. 'She's talking about us... Anya had a dress she wouldn't change out of. Thea had a favourite stick she carried everywhere, and I... Apparently I had a tendency to eat grass.'

Thea laughed, but seeing Wren's expression taut with anguish, she went to her. 'It's not fair that this is how we meet her. That this is all we get.'

'No, it's not.'

Anya watched them closely. No doubt she had already gone through the same grief when she'd first discovered the letters, but judging from her watery gaze, she shared their pain anew.

'Yolena talks about her sons...' Thea ventured. 'It's strange to think that somewhere out there are lost heirs of Naarva.'

Anya nodded. 'Not that they'll be any help to us now... Where are you up to?'

Thea glanced down at the letters. 'Our mother is writing about... her sense of dread, for the days to come.'

'I think she might have suspected Artos all along,' Anya said. 'She doesn't name him, but there's a lot of references to feelings that seem unexplained, reactions that don't align with the situation. That sounds like empath magic to me. Like he was there, manipulating everything for a long time before the kingdom fell.'

'We could show these letters to Queen Reyna,' Wren suggested, looking up from the sheets of parchment surrounding her.

'We could,' Anya allowed. 'Though I don't know how much it would help. She could just as easily say we forged them.'

Wren sighed. 'I suppose she has to actually deign to see us first, anyway.'

'True.'

'Do you think she has seen something?' Thea asked, opening the tin of salve Wren had given her. She'd been applying it to her scarred wrist since they'd arrived, and of course, Wren was a genius; the balm soothed the ache there almost instantly.

Her sister's brow furrowed. 'What do you mean?'

'Like a vision,' Thea clarified. 'When I was here for the

eclipse, she mentioned a premonition she'd had. Only she didn't realise that it was about Artos, not Wilder...'

'Who knows,' Anya said. 'Seers are notoriously unreliable – not to mention Reyna is in the throes of grief for her husband. Even if she did have a vision, I wouldn't trust it for all the ale in the Singing Hare.'

'Speaking of that place,' Wren interjected, looking to Thea. 'Was that a *tattoo* I saw on Cal's arse the other day?'

Thea snorted. 'Yes, it was.'

Anya baulked. 'Why on earth are you seeing *Callahan's arse?*'

'Apparently while I was off doing the Great Rite, they saw fit to get blind drunk at the Singing Hare and Cal somehow wound up with a tattoo of a fox on his backside.'

Anya blinked, once, twice, and then tipped her head back and roared laughing. The sound came from deep in her belly, and she actually clutched her stomach with one hand, wiping the tears streaming from her eyes with the other.

Thea gaped. She'd never seen the fearless Daughter of Darkness laugh like that before. She found herself grinning, and then laughing with her.

Wren was shaking her head. 'There's never a dull moment with those two...'

'Kipp's apparently determined to make you fall in love with him,' Thea said.

'Kipp's an idiot and a flirt. I'd sooner pluck out my own eyes and eat them.'

'I told him as much.' Thea grinned before turning her attention on their older sister. 'And what about you?'

Anya raised a brow. 'What about me?'

'Anyone, uh... tickling your fancy?'

Anya scoffed. 'Who says that?'

'People.'

'I disagree.'

'There's a shock.' Thea smirked. 'But that doesn't answer the question.'

Anya looked amused. 'There's no one *tickling my fancy*,' she replied slowly. 'But...'

'But?' Wren leant in eagerly.

Anya sighed. 'But I fucked Dratos before we left.'

'What?' Thea and Wren cried in unison.

'Oh, don't make a big song and dance about it.' Anya waved them off. 'It was a one-time thing. A mistake. We were drunk and stupid.'

'And?' Thea pressed.

'And what?'

Thea exchanged a smirk with Wren. 'How was it?'

'You're not seriously asking me that.'

Thea shrugged. 'Isn't that what sisters do?'

'I wouldn't know,' Anya replied.

Wren got to her feet and pulled both Thea and Anya in for an embrace, during which Anya looked about as uncomfortable as Thea felt. The three of them had never embraced...

But Wren squeezed them together. 'We can make this sister thing whatever we want it to be,' she said quietly. 'I, for one, would like to be able to talk to you both, about anything and everything. We might have been robbed of our earlier years together...' She gave Anya a sad smile. 'But even Thea and I weren't as close as we could have been. I'd like to change that.'

Thea struggled to swallow the lump forming in her throat, and when she glanced at Anya, she saw tears tracking down her face.

'I'd like that,' the Daughter of Darkness croaked.

Wren smiled. 'Good.'

'Me too,' Thea said.

They stood there, their arms wrapped around one another before the fire, and despite the weight of her fate stone pressing against her sternum, Thea was glad. If this was sisterhood, she thought, it wasn't half bad.

A knock at the door interrupted the moment. It opened to reveal an Aveum guard. 'The queen will see you now,' he said with a sweep of his hand.

The sisters broke apart. Baffled, Thea looked to the clock above the mantle, noting how late the hour was. It didn't feel like a terribly good sign, to say the least. They followed the guard from the room all the same, exchanging suspicious glances.

To Thea's surprise, they were not taken to the throne room or any sort of formal receiving space, but to the queen's private residences. They were ushered inside, finding the rooms within dimly lit, the air stale. Thea had expected countless attendants and ladies in waiting, but as they moved through the suite, they found it empty.

At last, they were shown into a sitting room, smaller and less grand than the rest of the quarters. On a wooden chair by the fire sat Queen Reyna.

Thea tried to mask her shock. The last time she'd seen the winter queen, Reyna had been resplendent in a beautiful gown, glittering jewels atop her head. She'd commanded the attention of the entire throne room with a lift of her chin, the flick of a wrist, every bit the ruler of a kingdom. But now... now she was a husk of her former self.

Grief had aged her. She sat hunched over in a tattered robe, her hair dirty and unkempt, falling loose around her weary face. Her gaze was hollow when she looked upon the three sisters.

Together, they bowed, albeit awkwardly.

'So...' Queen Reyna said slowly, her voice hoarse from apparent disuse. 'The heirs of Delmira have come forward at last.' Her eyes fell to Thea, emotionless. 'You...'

'For what it's worth,' Thea told her, 'I didn't know until I became a Guardian, and even then, it has taken me until now to come to terms with it.'

'How could you not have known?'

Wren stepped forward. 'It was my doing, Your Majesty. I created something to suppress her power, so she wouldn't know. So she wouldn't be in danger.'

If this news surprised the queen, she didn't show it. Instead, she turned her attention to Anya. 'And you...' This time, there was an unmistakeable note of rage in her tone. 'My husband is dead because of you and your monsters.'

'Your husband is dead because of Artos and *his* monsters,' Anya said calmly.

'Artos?' Queen Reyna gave a dark laugh. 'You are the enemy. You have brought pain and suffering on the midrealms. You are the *Daughter of Darkness.*'

Anya took a breath, seeming to steel herself against the harsh words. 'I am the daughter of King Soren and Queen Brigh of Delmira,' she said. 'Rulers who were once your allies against all that poisons our lands now.'

'They were no allies to Aveum. To anyone. Because of their dark obsession with power, the midrealms are cloaked in shadow.'

Thea went to the queen and knelt at her side. 'Your Majesty,' she implored. 'You know me, have seen me fight for the good of the midrealms —'

'You are in league with her.' The queen pointed a shaking finger at Anya. 'You broke the fallen Warsword out of the Scarlet Tower and destroyed it. You —'

'All is not what it seems,' Thea said, her spine tingling with the realisation that once it had been Wilder trying to convince her of such things, and that she'd been determined not to believe him. 'Artos is behind all of this. We have proof.' She stood, motioning for Wren to come forward with the vial of empath magic.

Wren held out the tiny glass bottle. 'Do you know what this is?'

'The poison Harenth gifts to Warswords upon their completion of the Great Rite,' Queen Reyna replied. She glanced at Thea and added coldly, 'I haven't yet decided if I should award you your Aveum springwater.'

'I passed the Great Rite. I am a Warsword of the midrealms,' Thea replied bluntly. 'You forsake your own duties by refusing to do so.'

'Don't speak to me of duty.'

'I'll speak of whatever is necessary —'

'I'm glad you mentioned the springwater,' Wren cut in. 'It was at *King Artos'* command that your Pools of Purity were contaminated with shadow magic. It was *King Artos* who allowed that arachne to breach your domes on the night of the eclipse. The night your husband died, Your Majesty.'

'Surely you know by now that he marches on Aveum with Tver's forces?' Anya said. 'Your watchmen in the foothills must have reported this.'

Queen Reyna simply stared at them.

Desperation clawed at Thea's chest. The others were counting on them to secure this alliance, to rally the winter kingdom's numbers to their cause. Without Aveum, they wouldn't stand a chance. 'Artos *killed King Elkan*. He's the reason your husband is dead. He's the reason you sit before us wearing widow black right now!'

An exhale shuddered out of the queen, and when she looked up, her eyes were lined with tears.

'Your Majesty,' Thea implored again. 'You have a choice... Bend the knee to the man responsible for your husband's death, or fight.'

'Do I look like a fighter to you?' The queen's words were bitter.

'All women are fighters,' Anya said, small wisps of shadow appearing at her fingertips. 'Artos made me what I am. When I was just a child, he framed me for the attack on Thezmarr, the one that stoked the flames of the supposed prophecy – a daughter of darkness, a dawn of fire and blood... But it was him. He threw me to the wraiths, and this is what I became.'

Wings materialised at her back, and Queen Reyna's face paled.

'But I am no monster,' Anya continued. 'I fight against the evil that is knocking on your door. And you need to take a stand with us, with the rest of the midrealms. Without you, we are lost to the darkness.'

'Artos has already taken Tver,' Thea added. 'King Leiko is under his spell. Their forces march on you as we speak.'

'These matters are for warriors and Guardians of the midrealms.' A tremor laced the words as they left the queen's lips. 'Is the state of our world not proof enough that the prophecy was right about women wielding blades? You are making it worse.'

'That's not true,' Thea argued, something coming back to

her from long ago. 'In a book called *The Constitution of the Founding Furies*, there is a passage that reads: *In times of dire need, as declared by the Guild Master, all those capable may take up arms in the name of Thezmarr, as protectors of the midrealms…* Are these times not dire? Do the midrealms not need protecting?'

The queen's throat bobbed as she studied them, their desperation clearly etched on their faces. Her own expression grew suddenly distant as she reached into the folds of her robe. Meeting Thea's gaze, Queen Reyna offered her a vial.

'One of the last to be bottled before the Pools of Purity were contaminated,' the queen told her. 'I will not fail in my duties, nor break the vows I swore to the guild. There are too many oathbreakers in these realms.'

Thea blinked as the queen pressed the small glass ampoule into her hands.

Aveum springwater.

'I knew long before now that you would come for it.'

'You *saw* that I would become a Warsword?' Thea managed, carefully taking the vial and turning it over, watching the liquid swirl within.

'I saw many things. Sweeping darkness. An army of monsters. Pain and suffering.' The queen glanced at the scar on Thea's wrist before continuing. 'But that was not all I have seen.'

'What else?' Anya pressed. 'What else have your visions shown you?'

Reyna's eyes flicked to her. 'Shadow and storms. A reckoning. I have seen that gold will turn to silver in a blaze of iron and embers, giving rise to ancient power long forgotten. And I have seen your fates,' she told them. 'They are tangled. I cannot discern one from the next, only that they meet in a dawn of fire and blood.'

A shiver raked down Thea's spine. She could almost picture the carnage. She felt it in the marrow of her bones – a reckoning was coming, for all of them.

Silently, she pocketed her springwater, her chest tight. The fate of the midrealms did not rest on a single glass vial.

It was Wren who knelt at the queen's side this time, taking Reyna's hand in hers. 'Your Majesty,' she said softly. 'Regardless of what the gods have shown you, it is as my sisters say. You have a choice: bend the knee, or fight.'

Slowly, Queen Reyna's eyes slid to Wren, her expression unreadable. 'I will think on it,' she said.

CHAPTER TWENTY-TWO

WILDER

The undercurrent of resentment lingered among the shadow-touched, and Wilder could hardly blame them. They knew they wouldn't be so easily accepted by the midrealms' forces, if they allied with them at all, and yet here they were, training to come to their aid at the eleventh hour.

Wilder kept himself busy with drills for his unit, keeping them as simple as possible: how to form the lines, how to hold them, how to break the enemy's. Simple was best, for if they did unite with other midrealms forces, simple would be all they could manage to learn en route to the battle itself.

It had been a week and they had received no word from Thea about the queen's decision, no word from Kipp about Esyllt's rescue, which meant they were strategising blindfolded. All the meetings in the world wouldn't save them if they had no allies.

Exhausted to the bone, Wilder trudged back to the main university building to find Talemir; his mother's sapphire was still burning a hole in Wilder's pocket. He quietly hoped he'd be able to hand it back and then take advantage of the bar in the Scholar's Lounge in front of the fire, just for an hour or two before duty called again.

Talemir was doing exactly that, already reclining in an armchair, his boots on the low table before him, a glass in hand. 'Had the same idea?' he asked as Wilder shut the door behind him.

'Seems so.' Wilder went to the cart in the corner and poured himself a generous glass of garnet wine. 'Might be the last chance we get.'

'My thoughts exactly,' Talemir replied, draining his drink.

Rolling his aching shoulders, Wilder brought him a bottle and then sank into the chair beside his former mentor, his friend.

Tal took the bottle gratefully and topped up his glass with amber liquid. 'Don't let me have any more after this one.'

Wilder huffed a laugh. 'Like I've been able to stop you before.' He produced the sea-blue jewel from his pocket and held it out, watching the light of the fire dance across its facets.

Talemir stared. 'You still have it? I thought you'd have given it away by now.'

'Thea never needed to learn that lesson… And she told me point blank it wasn't exactly her style.'

Talemir laughed, taking the sapphire between his fingers thoughtfully. 'Guess she's like Drue in that respect. They'd prefer swords and monster hearts as gifts.'

'Without a doubt.'

'*Sometimes, to love someone, we have to let them go…*' Talemir repeated his mother's words and tossed the gem onto the table. 'I don't think either of us needs that anymore.'

Wilder made a noise of agreement. 'Never letting Thea go again, not for the world.'

His mentor offered a knowing smile. 'Glad to hear it. Lesson learnt —'

The doors swung inward and Torj stormed in, raking his fingers through his golden hair, a curse of frustration on his lips. 'Tal, I swear, these soldiers —' He paused, reading the room with a frown. 'What are you two talking about?'

'Oh, you know,' Talemir replied casually. 'Life and love.'

Torj swiped the liquor from him and threw himself down on one of the lounges, drinking straight from the bottle. 'If you've got any advice, I'm all fucking ears.'

Wilder bit back a laugh. 'It wasn't all that long ago that you were the one shoving your wisdom down my throat.'

'You were in dire need of it,' Torj replied.

'I believe you once said to me: *"Your bullshit is your bullshit, Hawthorne".*'

'You were being particularly thick-headed at the time. More than usual.' Torj sighed. 'I also said you had to let someone in. And if I recall correctly, you told me to fuck off.'

Wilder's mouth tugged into a smile, remembering the moment well before another sprang to mind. 'Some other words of wisdom you shared with me when I learnt of Thea's heritage seem incredibly fitting now... *"You're fucked, aren't you?"* That one's gotta hurt.'

'Fuck off,' Torj muttered. 'I gave you plenty of useful advice.'

'But it's more fun this way,' Wilder teased.

'You're no fucking help.'

'We might be more helpful if we knew what was going on,' Wilder told him.

The Bear Slayer sighed. 'If I knew, I'd tell you.'

Talemir was grinning. 'You're telling me that Torj Elderbrock, the Bear Slayer, whose charms are endless, is having trouble —'

'Don't even start, *Prince of Hearts.* I would have thought you'd be more supportive given your obsession with love stories.'

'My library is at your disposal,' Talemir quipped, leaning over to snatch the bottle back from Torj.

Wilder surveyed the anguish in Torj's blue gaze and felt a stab of pity for the Warsword. 'Someone wise once told me: *"If there's one thing that transcends time and distance and all else, it's love".*'

Torj made a disgruntled noise. 'Try telling her that,' he muttered.

Wilder's gaze slid to Talemir, who was watching on, a twinkle of amusement in his hazel eyes. He gave the sapphire on the table a pointed glance, and Wilder bit back a chuckle. Perhaps they'd just found its next owner after all.

What felt like only moments later, Wilder was standing in the training camp with his fellow Warswords, double-checking their numbers, when a young shadow-touched boy sprinted towards them, a scroll of parchment clutched in his hand. He came skidding to a stop by Biscuit's flank and stared up at Wilder with wide eyes.

'Warsword Hawthorne,' he panted, holding out the scroll. 'News from Aveum, sir. Queen Reyna —' He struggled to catch his breath. 'Queen Reyna has agreed to ally with us. We're to march against King Artos. We're going to fight!'

The camp fell silent.

Heart pounding, Wilder took the scroll and scanned its contents, anticipation building with every word. The message wasn't in Thea's hand, but in the bottom corner of the page was something drawn just for him.

A lightning bolt.

'Is it true?' someone called. 'Are we going to war?'

Wilder lowered the parchment to find his entire unit of shadow-touched watching him. Their expressions were mixed. Some seemed eager, eyes bright, fists clenched; others' faces were lined with fear and disbelief.

He addressed them all. 'It's true. We're going to war. Pack up your tents, your weapons and your supplies. We await orders from Talemir, but we need to be ready.'

No one argued.

Wilder met Tal, Drue, Adrienne, Cal, Audra, Farissa, Torj and Dratos back at the main university building. There, in the Scholar's Lounge, they let the news sink in. Queen Reyna had *agreed*. According to Anya's message, they would join forces in the foothills of the mountains bordering Vios, where they would set up camp and prepare for Artos' attack. They would transport the majority of their forces and supplies by shadow magic, and hope that there was enough time to regain their strength between then and the battle. It wasn't perfect, but no battle plan ever was. It was always about finding the best option among the bad.

The door to the lounge opened with a creak, revealing Fendran, Drue's father and the head Naarvian blacksmith, Ryland perched on his hip.

'Shouldn't you be asleep, Trouble?' Talemir got to his feet and took his son in his arms.

'I thought you might want to say goodbye,' Fendran said, tousling the boy's hair.

Drue went to her husband and child, dropping a gentle kiss on the latter's cheek. 'We'll put him to bed.'

Fendran hesitated.

'Something to say, Father?' Drue arched a brow.

Wilder recognised that tone – he'd heard it from Thea a thousand times before, not to mention Drue herself when they'd first met. It said, *Challenge me if you dare, but you'll leave this conversation in pieces, if you're lucky.*

But with a tender look at his grandson, Fendran squared his shoulders and faced his daughter. 'Are you sure you want to leave him?'

'*Want* has nothing to do with it,' Drue replied tersely.

Fendran faltered. 'I know. Poor choice of words —'

'It was.'

'But I can't say nothing —'

'I wish that you would, Fendran.' Drue stared him down.

The tension in the room grew taut, everyone wishing that they weren't witnessing this private family discussion.

His eyes taking an empathetic sweep of the lounge, the older man sighed. 'I just want what's best for my family. For you all.'

Drue reached out and rested her hands on her father's shoulders. 'I know you do. But what point is there in us being here with him when the world is on fire? What is the point when there is nothing left? Ryland needs a world to grow up in. We're going to give that to him. We have to.'

Fendran's expression caved with defeat and Drue squeezed his shoulders before taking Ryland from Talemir.

'Don't be long,' she told the winged Warsword, pulling him in for a kiss.

There was no missing the way Talemir dragged her body to his, deepening the kiss despite their son on Drue's hip, despite the audience around them, including her father.

Dratos cleared his throat pointedly. 'Alright, alright. Gods, you're as bad as you were when you met. Get a fucking room.'

Drue laughed. 'If the brink of war is no time for a kiss, I don't know when is.' With that, she left, taking a yawning Ryland with her.

Talemir stared after her for a moment, and Wilder recognised that expression. Disbelief at his own luck. Wilder had felt it many times himself.

'When do we leave?' Adrienne's voice cut through the silence.

Talemir rubbed the back of his neck and faced the group. 'Are all the units packed?'

There was a unified murmur of accord.

'Then we leave in two hours.'

Wilder went to find his brother. Malik was in the stables, Dax curled up in the hay by his feet as the gentle giant braided Biscuit's mane, the stallion already saddled.

'You didn't have to do that,' Wilder said by way of greeting.

Malik didn't turn around, but his fingers stilled mid-motion and Wilder knew his brother had heard him.

Leaning against the stall wall, Wilder raked his hair back from his face and sighed. 'I miss fighting with you,' he admitted. 'Sometimes it felt like it was just you and me against the entire world...'

Malik continued braiding.

'But right now,' Wilder continued, 'I'm grateful that you'll be here, not in the thick of the battle... I've got enough to worry about with Thea out there in the madness.'

At that, Malik turned to him and gave him a hard look as if to say, *She can handle herself just fine.*

'I know, I know,' Wilder said, shaking his head before surveying his brother. Malik hadn't changed in a long time. He was still the huge figure he'd always been, still that stoic, sturdy presence that put Wilder at ease.

Swallowing the lump forming in his throat, Wilder straightened. 'I just came to say...' *Goodbye* didn't sound right; it was too final, too heavy. 'I love you, brother,' he said instead.

Mal's face broke into a broad smile, and he offered Wilder Biscuit's reins.

Wilder smiled back, blinking back stinging tears. 'I'll be seeing you.'

As he led his stallion from the stables, Dax followed, as if instructed by the gentle giant within. *I guess part of Malik is coming with me,* he mused. And he found that the thought gave him a small sense of comfort.

Wilder swore that when the war was done, he'd never travel by shadow magic again. Nothing could quell the queasiness in his gut as wind and darkness swept in around him and lifted him from solid ground.

He never thought he'd be glad for the biting cold of

Aveum, but when he landed in the snow, he could have kissed the icy flakes in relief. Dratos left him there, shadows blooming in his wake as he spread his wings and headed back to Naarva to bring Torj next.

All around Wilder, shadow-touched folk were emerging from the darkness, hauling supplies, weaponry or other people with them. Others were meeting them via the network of tunnels beneath the midrealms, finding their way to the foothills by other means.

A crescent moon and starry night illuminated the wintry landscape, the dark forests at their back, and the seemingly endless plain stretching before them. They had positioned themselves on the north-western side of Vios, placing the mountains between them and the capital, and themselves between Artos' incoming forces and the kingdom of Aveum.

Wilder barked orders at his unit as soon as their boots hit the snow. They needed to pitch their tents and establish secure supply lines. There was no way of knowing how long they'd be camped there, and ensuring a steady flow of food, water, weapons and medical supplies for their troops was paramount. A starving army was as dangerous as an unskilled one. They would all be on rations, but Wilder realised that the shadow-touched folk were used to eating lean.

Before long, the campsite was bustling with activity, and even as the snow set in Wilder could see it taking shape far more quickly than he'd anticipated. Rows of tents were pitched, including their command centre; wood was chopped down for fires; the horses were tended to beneath the sparse shelter of the trees.

Wilder consulted his own instructions. Kipp had left them with a list of traders to negotiate with, and the positions of several local villages that would help them secure routes through the treacherous terrain, so he set about ensuring that everything was in place, sending messengers to their contacts so they knew the battle would soon be underway.

There was still no word from Kipp, no whisper of what had happened to Esyllt, whom they needed to rally the Thezmarrian Guardians. But they couldn't afford to wait any longer. This war was going to start with or without the strategists.

In the weak torchlight of his tent, Wilder penned several copies of the same letter, pleading for aid, and sent them in every direction to any Guardians stationed within a few days' ride of the foothills. They needed all the fucking help they could get.

He had no notion of the hour as clouds crept across the face of the moon and the campsite grew quiet. But he made no move to take shelter in his tent. Instead, he stood watch on the perimeter, willing Thea to hurry.

CHAPTER TWENTY-THREE

THEA

Thea didn't know how they'd done it, but she, Wren and Anya rode at the head of Queen Reyna's army, a host of Aveum soldiers at their backs.

Thea had been convinced of their failure, going so far as to pack her bag and demand that Anya use her shadow magic to take them back to Naarva. But not only had Queen Reyna surprised them all with her alliance, she had also offered Thea a vial of springwater.

Thea had attached it to the leather string she wore around her neck, and now it rested against her fate stone, knocking gently against her heart as they rode towards the war camp waiting for them. The irony wasn't lost on her: one object marked her death, while the other had the power to save a life – just not hers.

Even from the furthest perimeter, Thea understood why they'd chosen this position. The woodland areas, however barren, still provided cover for the troops. Across the way, the hillside at the base of the other mountains allowed for ambush tactics should they need them, and the terrain itself offered numerous strategic advantages. Spending so much time with Kipp made these things far easier to spot. She saw that commanders would be able to control the high ground and gain a vantage point, perhaps use the elevation for defensive positions or archers. Cal was likely scoping out the area already.

As they rode deeper into the camp, Thea grimaced at the patches of ice. They'd be an issue, causing additional hazards and making footing treacherous for both infantry and cavalry. She only hoped that on the actual battlefield they'd be few and far between.

The atmosphere shifted, both in the ranks behind them and in the camp beyond as they dismounted and asked after Talemir's whereabouts. Leaving the Aveum commanders to warm themselves by the fires, Thea and her sisters were directed to a tent at the centre of it all.

'You did it!' Adrienne shouted as they lifted the canvas and entered the makeshift war room. The ranger came forward and embraced Anya hard.

'I don't think the hard part's over,' Anya told her drily.

'Gotta celebrate the small wins,' Adrienne declared with a grin.

'She's right,' Talemir said from where he was braced over a table covered in maps. 'You did well. Thank you.'

Drue appeared at Thea's side. 'With the mood he's in, that's like getting a Warsword totem from a Fury.'

'Has something happened?' Thea asked, her heart rate spiking. 'Where's Wilder?'

'On sentry at the northern perimeter,' Drue replied. 'And nothing has happened, yet... but there's bad blood between some of our units, and the arrival of the midrealms' forces will only fuel the flames. We're going to keep the two camps separate at first, to avoid any skirmishes breaking out. The men are tired and weary. It wouldn't take much to trigger a brawl.'

Thea nodded. 'I'll tell the Aveum commanders.'

'Who do they take their orders from? I'm assuming the queen gave someone military power?'

'Commander Sylas Yarrow, but actually, she insisted that Torj Elderbrock lead them,' Thea explained, scanning the tent for the Bear Slayer. He wasn't there. 'Queen Reyna had a vision, not that we understood it. She said, *"I have seen that gold will turn to silver in a blaze of iron and embers, giving rise to ancient power long forgotten..."* What that has to do with Torj, we have no idea, but we assured her she'd have him.'

Drue's brow furrowed in apprehension, but she looked to Talemir, who simply shrugged. 'It's her army. If she wants Torj to lead it, and Torj is willing, then we'll make adjustments to our own ranks.'

Thea nodded. 'I'll let Yarrow know.'

Truth be told, she was eager to leave the tent, deliver her message, then find Wilder. She had been gone far longer than she'd anticipated and she missed her Warsword with a ferocity that scared her. They had already spent too much time apart in the face of her limited days; no more. She wouldn't stand for it.

As she made her way back towards the Aveum commanders, she knew Drue had made the right call by opting for separate camps among the allies. The animosity was rife, so thick in the air she could feel it pressing down on her shoulders. What she hadn't realised was that the sense of ill will wasn't just between the shadow-touched and the regular foot soldiers of the midrealms. It was directed at *her* as well.

Storm wielder. As she walked through the camp, the name was whispered behind her back, not with wonder or respect, but with contempt. Her skin crawled as she felt eyes boring holes in her, the pieces clicking into place. Storm wielders, the Delmirian royal family, were still widely blamed for the influx of darkness on the midrealms. According to most, *her parents* were responsible for the downfall of both Delmira and Naarva. Because of her family, the poison had never truly left the lands, and here they all were, suffering in the face of it once more, ready to fight it again.

Growing wearier by the second, Thea spotted Commander Yarrow, who'd been left in charge. She approached him – only to hear vicious words spilling from his mouth about her, about Wren, about Anya.

'Don't see why we should take orders from the Delmirian bitch, why she was riding ahead of us,' he spat. 'The girl is the offspring of traitors. She's no better than the fucking filth marching beside Artos as we speak —'

Thea stood at the fringe of the circle that had gathered around the man, exhaustion latching onto her bones. She had travelled far and wide to be here; she had overcome one obstacle after the next, all to fight against the looming darkness.

'Thinks she owns the damn place. You've seen how she talks to our queen and speaks to us. Maybe it's time we taught that bitch a lesson.'

Thea exhaled shakily, steeling herself against the bastard's tirade, her magic prickling at her fingertips, begging to deliver justice where justice was due. She should have expected some level of resistance. Be it because she was a woman, a Delmirian, a Warsword – it was always something. She didn't want to fight her own men, her own allies, not on the brink of battle. But she also wouldn't stand for disrespect. It created a weak link in their armour. If she had to reforge it with lightning and steel, so be it.

She took a step forward —

A gentle hand came down on her shoulder, and the scent of rosewood and leather quelled the fire within her.

'You have proven time and time again that you can fight your own battles,' Wilder murmured in her ear. 'But there are those you shouldn't have to. Let me fight this one for you. Let me carry this burden.'

Thea looked up, meeting those silver eyes she knew and loved so well. She nodded.

And with that confirmation, Wilder strode forward into the group and gripped the commander by the throat. He hoisted the man up into the air as though he weighed nothing, the commander's boots kicking beneath him desperately as he clawed at the Warsword's hand.

'You wouldn't kill me, not in cold blood,' Yarrow rasped.

'That's right. A Warsword is a moral man, a man with honour,' someone else chimed in, though they didn't have the balls to intervene beyond words.

Thea watched the offending commander's eyes bulge as Wilder applied more pressure to his windpipe.

Wilder's expression was cold, lethal. 'A Warsword is also a killer. A man – or woman – of violence and fury. Any good in me is because of that storm wielder you so vehemently insulted.'

Commander Yarrow gasped, his eyes turning bloodshot, his face beet-red as he fought against Wilder's hold. Wilder drove a fist into his gut and dropped him. Yarrow collapsed on all fours, dry retching. But Wilder wasn't done. He punched the commander in the face this time, bone cracking, blood spurting onto the pristine snow.

'This is a mercy compared to what she could have done to you,' Wilder spat. 'Consider my fists a kindness, and know that if one more of you shows disrespect, you're dead. Althea Embervale will turn the tide of this war. You owe her your allegiance.'

The Aveum forces gaped, first at Wilder, whose knuckles were painted with blood, and then at Thea, whose lightning was dancing along her skin.

She held her chin high and surveyed them without emotion. 'I only came to tell you that you're now under the command of Torj Elderbrock.'

The crowd parted and the Bear Slayer himself came forward, his expression venomous. 'Any midrealms warrior who lays a hand on a shadow-touched, or who murmurs a word of discontent against the Embervale family, will find themselves facing my wrath, to a similar effect to what my Warsword brother has demonstrated here.' He projected his voice to the far reaches of the force, and gave the crumpled commander a kick for good measure.

Talemir strode forward then, his wings tucked behind his back, his shadows dancing menacingly. 'The same goes for the shadow-touched. Any who harms or speaks ill of a midrealms soldier will deal with me. We are here to fight side by side, not tear each other's throats out. Tomorrow, we will train. We'll make allies of you yet.'

Thea felt Wilder return to her side, felt the brush of his lips against her temple, and it took every ounce of willpower not to melt right into his body. 'Thank you,' she said quietly.

'You never need to thank me,' Wilder told her. 'I will always fight for you. And it's my honour to do so.'

Thea swallowed, not allowing the tears stinging her eyes to fall.

For a moment, they just stood there, as though Wilder sensed she needed to gather herself. She did exactly that and at last met his gaze. 'Where to now?' she asked.

Wilder sighed and looked to the heart of the camp. Thea willed him to say *To bed*, so they could fuck the tension of this place away and hold each other through the night.

But her Warsword gave her a regretful look before lacing his fingers through hers. 'To the command tent,' he said. 'To start the war.'

CHAPTER TWENTY-FOUR

THEA

The command tent was crowded, but however exhausted Thea was, seeing Kipp in the centre lifted her spirits significantly. She threw her arms around him, squeezing until he gave a dramatic gasp for air and she released him.

'What took you so long?' she demanded, hitting him lightly on the chest. 'Did you find —'

'Esyllt is a free man once more,' Kipp told her. 'He'll be joining us soon enough, but for now...' He motioned to a detailed map spread out on the table before him. 'I've been a busy man.'

Thea found herself beside Cal and Wilder as they, along with everyone else at command level, looked at the plans Kipp had put into place. They were far more detailed than even the model they'd had back at Naarva, with every hill and crest marked diligently.

'I learnt a few things on my way here,' Kipp began, smoothing out the map with his palms. 'In the early morning there's more fog, low visibility. Artos may use it as cover to attack. We need to double the sentries where we can, station some further out, perhaps with Terrence, or a shadow-touched who can alert us.'

Talemir nodded. 'What else?'

'I spoke with our scouts and double-checked the numbers they reported. Right now, there's no sign of an aerial force, wraiths or otherwise. He's marching straight from Tver on foot and with several cavalry units. According to our spies, they're a few days out at most.'

'When can we expect Esyllt? And how many men will he have?' Wilder asked.

'Within the next day or two,' Kipp said with a wince. 'As for his numbers, I can't say. It was messy, getting out of Thezmarr. But judging by the reports, Artos will outnumber us, which is why we need to talk about this.' He pointed to a patch of land marked on the map. 'See the lay of the land here? How the main river runs alongside this empty ravine? It used to be another riverbed. It's a flood zone,' he told them. 'We can drive them back into that space.'

'And what? Hope that it rains?' someone called from the back.

'Exactly. If only we had a storm wielder in our midst,' he retorted sarcastically, with an incredulous shake of his head. 'We need to draw them into this area here, and when we do... We have one of the princesses flood the shit out of it.'

Thea huffed a laugh, watching Kipp's mind work at breakneck pace.

'Speaking of our beloved Delmirians...' He made a point of locking eyes with Anya, Wren and then Thea. 'I think it's wise if we keep the three of you separate over the course of the upcoming battle.'

'What?' Wren said. 'We can work as one, Kipp. We can —'

'I have no doubt,' he said, without his usual mockery. 'But you're an easier target altogether. If they get their hands on not one, but all three storm wielders, well —'

'We're fucked,' Dratos offered helpfully, then added, 'What? You did say that was the military term for it, if I recall correctly.'

'You're not wrong,' Kipp told him. 'And in saying that, I propose we do the same with the Warswords where we can. It may weaken us a little initially, but it's a better alternative than —'

'No fucking reaper's going to get its claws in me,' came a gravelly voice from the tent flap.

Along with the rest of the company, Thea turned to see Vernich the Bloodletter enter the command tent, dressed head to toe in Warsword armour, his hand on the pommel of his blade. He looked older, with more lines etched around his eyes, which scanned each and every one of them before his gaze landed on Talemir.

'So it's true. The Prince of Hearts is the Shadow Prince of the rebellion,' he said, approaching the table and surveying their plans.

Talemir gave a derisive laugh. 'Come to join our cause?'

'I'm sick of the stench of burnt hair,' Vernich replied gruffly, before his attention fell to Kipp at the head of the table. 'Who would have thought Thezmarr's most useless shieldbearer would be here planning our fights for us.'

'You were always slow off the mark,' Kipp said casually.

To everyone's shock, a deep chuckle burst from the Bloodletter. 'Never thought I'd say this, but... you're not half bad.'

Kipp looked at him, deadpan. 'Your vote of confidence is

heartwarming. You sure you don't want to have your apprentice beat me to a pulp again?'

As if in answer, movement at the entrance caught Thea's eye and she shuddered as Sebastos Barlow entered like a snake in the grass. He looked the same as he had the last time she'd seen him, his expression sour, his nose crooked from where she'd broken it with her fist.

Vernich made a noise of disgust. 'That spineless prick is no apprentice of mine.'

Seb's face went bright red, and Thea didn't think she'd ever felt so much glee as she had in that moment.

'Why the fuck is he here, then?' Wilder growled from behind her.

'I owe his uncle a favour,' Vernich replied without an ounce of shame.

But from Seb's expression, he felt enough shame for them both, until he looked up and saw Thea. She watched the realisation dawn on his ugly face as his eyes tracked from the Warsword totem on her arm to the Naarvian steel sword at her belt. His nostrils flared, and pure, unadulterated fury blazed across his expression.

'Keep looking at her like that,' Anya warned, stepping forward with her shadows spilling forth. 'Keep looking at her like that and see what happens.'

Seb had the good sense to blanch, and run from the tent.

Vernich made that same noise of disgust.

Torj shook his head as he stared after Seb. 'Must be one hell of a favour...'

CHAPTER TWENTY-FIVE

WILDER

'I hated being apart from you,' Wilder murmured into Thea's hair as he led her back to their tent.

'Me too.' She looped an arm around his waist and held him close as they walked.

'Will you promise me something?' he asked.

Thea raised a brow. 'Depends what it is.'

'Wise woman,' he chuckled.

'Promise you what?'

'Promise me never again. Whatever we do from here on out, we do together.'

'I don't think Kipp's battle plans —'

'Not on the battlefield. In life,' he said. 'Where you go, I go, from now on.'

Thea smiled, and Wilder didn't think he'd ever seen anything so beautiful. Her face was illuminated by the moon, fresh snowflakes flushing her cheeks pink.

She drew him to a halt and rose up on her tip-toes, brushing his lips with hers. 'I like the sound of that.'

'Promise me.'

'I promise, Wilder,' she said.

'Good.' And then he kissed her.

In the dark of their tent, he scorched her lips with his own, his tongue exploring her luscious mouth, her answering strokes fraying his ability to think beyond the primal desire to claim her, mind, body and soul.

His cock was already aching for her, desperate for her touch, but he wanted to savour this, savour *her*. He peeled away her clothes, layer by layer, tracing over her smooth skin and sinful curves, worshipping her body. Her breasts heaved under his stare, her nipples hard. He had to see more, had to see all of her. He stripped her bare, and when she was completely naked before him, he let out a groan.

'Look at you, Thea...' he rasped in reverence. She was a goddess. 'Just look at you...'

'We didn't come here to look,' she replied, and she reached for his hand, placing it between her legs.

Wilder groaned again at the wetness he found there, his hard cock twitching against his pants. 'Is this what I do to you, Princess?'

'Yes. Always.'

Wilder jerked Thea closer and slid his fingers through the slick heat, rubbing her clit and swallowing her moan with a rough kiss. Gods, she felt incredible. Not for the first time, he was hit with the surreal realisation that she was *his*, that this privilege belonged to him and him alone.

Thea's cheeks flushed as she rode his hand, breaking away to palm his heavy erection through his pants. 'I need you,' she said. 'Now.'

'I'm yours,' he told her.

Shoving his pants down his thick thighs, Thea freed his

cock and dragged the broad head through her arousal, a gasp escaping her.

They didn't make it to the cot on the far side of the tent. Wilder pulled her to the floor right there, kicking his pants off his ankles and bracing himself over her, covering her body with his. He felt more animal than man, the possessive urge to mark her, to claim her as his own rising to the surface as the uncertainty of tomorrow threatened to break the spell they'd cast over one another.

Thea's impatient hand came between them to his base, guiding him to her entrance with a sharp intake of breath. 'Wilder,' she demanded.

With a single shift of his hips, he sheathed himself inside her, her head tipping back as he slid in deep. Her muscles clenched around him and his vision blurred. He gritted his teeth, trying to claw back some semblance of control, the intensity almost too much.

'Yes...' Thea's fingernails dug into his back, her legs wrapping around him to pull him closer, deeper.

'You're my everything,' he told her, relishing the glorious, torturous slide of their bodies together. She was made for him. Having her in his arms was beyond perfect. It felt *right* in every sense.

Wilder fucked her slowly, intimately, rocking into her and drawing out their pleasure until he had to clap his hand over her mouth to muffle her cries of ecstasy. With each rolling thrust of his hips, his cock found that sensitive spot deep inside her and he worked it hard, so that she was a panting mess.

'That's it, Thea...'

When she tightened around him, he slid his hand

between their sweaty bodies and strummed her clit in rhythmic strokes. Thea bucked beneath him.

'Wilder, fuck – I'm there, come with me,' she gasped as her orgasm crested.

He followed her into oblivion, spilling his release inside her with a stifled moan.

And then he held her, all through the night.

Wilder left Thea sleeping in their tent to run dawn drills with his unit. There was plenty of grumbling, but they did as they were told, staring at his bruised and bloodied knuckles.

Let them see, he thought with satisfaction. *Let them see what I'd unleash on them all for her.*

Midmorning, Thea came to find him. 'Esyllt's here,' she told him, already starting towards the command tent.

Thezmarr's weapons master was indeed within, though that was where the good news ended.

'Myself and my unit of shieldbearers discovered a unit of Artos' men far closer than we anticipated,' Esyllt said. 'They'll be here by tomorrow morning.'

'You think they're here to batter our frontline before the main attack?' Kipp asked. 'That those soldiers are disposable to Artos?'

Esyllt nodded. 'I'd say so, yes.'

'Then I have another suggestion. We keep the storm wielders off the field —'

'What?' both Thea and Anya snapped, taking similar stances as they braced themselves against the table.

Wilder almost pitied Kipp. But he threw up his hands in surrender. 'Not off the battlefield, as such. Slice as many fucking wraiths in half as you like. But we keep your *magic* off the field, for now. We can be certain that Artos won't play all his cards at once, and we should keep something up our sleeve, too…'

'We can still fight?' Thea asked, eyes narrowed.

'Furies save me, *yes.* Just no lightning and thunder, except for Wren.'

The youngest Embervale stepped forward, brows knitted together. 'Why me?'

'I'll need you to flood that spit of land I mentioned last night,' Kipp told her. 'Out of the three of you, from what I've seen, you've got the most control.'

'Hey!' Thea protested.

Kipp scoffed. 'Please. Half the time your magic is as much a temper tantrum as it is a power.'

Wilder bit a knuckle to keep from laughing at that.

'Should we talk numbers?' Esyllt said, drawing them back to the maps and charts. 'I'm afraid there's no good news there either. I brought as many willing shieldbearers from Thezmarr as I could, but…'

Wilder's heart sank. 'We're still outnumbered.'

The weapons master nodded. 'Outnumbered and very unlikely to be able to match the dynamics his forces will oppose us with.'

Talemir came to stand at Wilder's side, his expression grave. 'What have you been training for?' he asked.

'To hold the lines,' Wilder replied. 'Our only choice is to hold our own, and break theirs. Continue to break them. And once we decimate their frontlines, we smash them open from within.'

There had been no reports of wraiths or reapers in the opposing forces, and Wilder was not alone in his concern over that fact. Thea could hardly stand still, flitting about the war camp like lightning that didn't know where to strike. Convinced that Artos was hiding the wraith forces, Talemir himself flew out to spy on the enemy's march from overhead. He returned to them shaking his head. He too reported that there wasn't a leathery creature in sight.

Hours later, as fresh snow fell around Wilder, settling in his hair and on his shoulders, he looked out onto the misty moors. *By this time tomorrow, they'll be stained red and black with blood.*

He knew the odds they were facing – forces with divided loyalty, the quality of soldiers varying from one person to the next. Orders meant nothing if one link in the chain faltered. They had Warswords and shadow-touched and storm wielders, but... none of them had fought together as a single unit. And their lower ranks were made up of opposed men. None were trained like Thezmarrians. None were capable of complicated fighting on the field.

Against an army of cursed men, monsters and evil tyrants, how could they win? Artos had been preparing for this for decades. His army had been specifically created for this purpose. The King of Harenth had chosen the playing field... Who knew how long he'd been lurking in the shadows, readying for this moment?

Wilder remained there until Thea found him, coming to stand at his side and survey tomorrow's battleground with him.

She drew a long, steadying breath, her gaze unflinching as she stared out onto the moors. 'We smash them open from within,' she said.

CHAPTER TWENTY-SIX

THEA

I t was the eve of battle, and Thea couldn't shake the nagging sensation that they were missing something. She had expected to smell the acrid scent of burnt hair drifting through the air at any moment, yet it didn't come. Why would Artos not use the wraiths at his disposal? Or the reapers? It didn't make any sense.

She said as much to Esyllt in the command tent while they forced down what would likely be their last meal for a long while. The weapons master nodded in understanding, a far cry from the prickly man who'd once barked orders at her and made her polish shields in the armoury.

'Artos likely needs the wraiths and reapers to hold Tver,' he explained. 'Some of his forces will have stayed behind to keep the castle protected.'

'From who?' Thea pressed. 'He must know that all our forces are here. No one can take Tver unawares from the north.'

Esyllt shrugged. 'He may be expecting some resistance from Thezmarr. He might not know I escaped with those who remained loyal. There are also Guardians still stationed throughout Harenth and Tver who could rally to our cause. They could attack Notos.'

Thea raised a brow. 'And how likely is that?'

'Not very,' Esyllt admitted. 'The fact remains, we can only approach this battle with what we know. And what we know right now is that the wraiths aren't in his forces. Howlers, yes, arachnes, also yes, but not wraiths, which at least keeps his attack grounded.'

Thea gave a frustrated sigh. 'This doesn't feel right.'

'Welcome to war, Zoltaire,' Esyllt told her. 'It never feels right.'

Those words made her blood run cold. Wishing he'd offered some notion of comfort instead, she bid him goodnight and went to find her sisters.

Anya and Wren were with Drue and Adrienne in the latter's tent. The women were perched on various objects around the cramped space, talking quietly. It was much smaller than the command tent, but cosier.

'Thea.' Wren smiled as the tent flap dropped behind her.

'I'm worried,' Thea said without preamble.

Anya nodded. 'As are we all. I'd be concerned if you weren't.'

Looking around, Thea observed a notable absence. 'Has anyone seen Audra?' she asked.

The women exchanged troubled glances.

'No,' Wren answered. 'She's probably with Farissa, checking our alchemical supplies on the eastern front.'

Drue offered Thea a flask, which she gratefully accepted. Taking a swig of fire extract, she sat herself on the end of Adrienne's cot. 'What are we talking about?'

Drue waved a hand in Wren's direction. 'We were just

discussing how we need to find Wren some armour. She might not be swinging a blade, but she'll be on the field wielding her potions and concoctions alongside us.'

'Good idea.'

'I should have thought of it earlier,' Drue muttered. 'Given the leather a chance to mould to her body.'

'You should see that it goes to someone who can actually fight,' Wren argued. 'I'm no warrior.'

Anya cut her a sharp look. 'What have I told you? All women are warriors, Elwren. And you deserve to wear armour as much as anyone else. You're putting your life at risk, same as the rest of us.'

Wren flushed. 'But...'

Thea's heart broke at her sister's protests. Was it her doing that Wren didn't feel worthy of armour? There had been a time when they were younger that Thea had not-so-subtly classed her own pursuits as worthier than the rest, believing physical fighting was a more noble undertaking than anything else. She knew better now – she had known better for a long time – and now she'd make sure Wren knew it too.

She strode forward and gripped her younger sister by the shoulders. 'For the longest time, women have been erased, little by little, or in the case of the Furies themselves, in one fell swoop. We have lived in the shadow of the rights and laws of men. But when the world is reborn, it will be of our own making. You're fighting for that world, and you have the same right to armour as the rest of us. You are surrounded by women who want to see you empowered, and that is stronger than any fucking army in these realms. Don't let the world – don't let *anyone* convince you that you're not enough. Only you define your story. You and you alone. When they tell you what you're not, when they tell you what you can't do, remember: *you are the storm*, Elwren. You split the skies and flood the plains. You make the ground tremble beneath their boots. No one can fucking stop you.'

Adrienne let out a low, appreciative whistle, but Thea kept her gaze trained on the celadon eyes that matched her own.

Wren's lower lip trembled, but she lifted her chin. 'I'll wear the armour.'

'Damn straight you will.'

The hour was late when Thea excused herself, needing a moment alone to clear her head as dawn approached all too quickly.

She went into the woods to relieve herself, hoping she'd get a few hours of sleep with Wilder's arms around her before she donned her armour and the clash of steel rang out across the icy field. When she had finished seeing to her needs, she started back towards camp, threading through the barren trees, marvelling at how the world seemed to be dying before their eyes. Evergreen pines bore no leaves, daggers of ice and flakes of frost the only things adorning their branches. Beyond the skeletal canopy, clouds gathered over the moon and stars, blanketing them in darkness as if in preparation for what was to come —

A stick snapped behind Thea.

She whirled around to see Sebastos Barlowe's contorted face as he lurched forward, the pommel of his sword raised to club her across the head.

Thea ducked, though her skin crawled at the sight of him. He'd been waiting for her.

'I knew you weren't really what they said,' he sneered, eyes catching on her Warsword totem. 'You didn't even hear me coming.'

'What do you want?' Disdain dripped from Thea's words.

Seb took a step towards her, resentment etched across his face as he spoke. 'You're the reason Vernich denounced me.'

Thea snorted. 'That was all you, Seb. Imagine, even Vernich the Bloodletter can't stand the sight of you.'

But Seb's gaze was locked on her Naarvian steel sword, a taunt lifting his lip. 'I can only imagine what you did to get that.'

'You mean pass the Great Rite like the Warsword I am?' she scoffed.

There was a glint in Seb's eye now that made her uneasy, but she refused to step back, to yield. She had more strength and power in her little finger than he had in his whole body, whether the bastard believed it or not.

His free hand moved, not to the second weapon at his hip, but to his belt. To Thea's horror, he started unbuckling it. 'I think it's time I saw what all the fuss was about when it comes to you. You must have a cunt made of gold if it got you this far.'

Thea unsheathed her blade, the steel singing as it left her scabbard. 'After everything, you still can't accept the fact that a woman beat you, can you?'

Seb laughed darkly, advancing. 'Beat me?'

'I am a Warsword of the midrealms.'

'You're a pretender. You always have been.'

'You truly mean to attack a Warsword, and an heir of these realms, in the dark here like a coward?'

'I don't give a fuck about your supposed titles. I'll show everyone what truly lies beneath that pretty face.'

Thea's skin crawled at his words, at the unhinged twist of his features. 'You're delusional,' she realised aloud. 'You really can't see that there's no outcome in which you walk away from this.'

Seb made a grab for her.

Thea sidestepped easily, twirling her blade, resignation settling heavy in her gut. 'I should have ended you years ago.'

And then, he attacked in earnest. With his belt buckle still undone, Seb raised his sword and lunged for her.

Thea barely needed to think as she deflected his blows with quick taps of her blade. She was stronger, faster, more agile than he would ever be. For all his parries and strikes, his sword got nowhere near her. Thea let him attack with everything he had, watching as his rage intensified with every unsuccessful blow, sweat beading at his brow.

As she deflected another jab, she realised that his fury wasn't for her alone, but for all women. That despite every ounce of evidence she'd shown him over the years that she was capable, that she was a true protector of the midrealms, he would never believe it. He didn't want to. And that meant there was no place for him in this world, the world they were trying to defend and rebuild anew.

Panting, Seb thrust his sword at her and Thea knocked it aside, wondering how long it would take him to realise that he was at her mercy, that he could never win against her.

Vile words spilt from his mouth along with flecks of spit. 'I'm surprised you can walk after taking so much cock for that totem. But at least you're broken in. When I'm through with you —'

Thea blocked another pitiful strike of his blade.

He snarled. 'I'll leave you bleeding in the dirt where you belong, *stray*.'

Stray... The name he'd called her since they were teenagers; the word he'd spat in her direction at every chance he got.

'Have you said everything you need to say?' Thea asked, her voice cool and steady.

He lashed out with his sword, swiping it through the air clumsily. 'Fuck you, whore. Drop the blade and it'll be over soon.'

Thea took a deep breath and poised herself to strike. 'You're right,' she said. 'It will be over soon.'

She knocked Seb's blade from his grasp without a thought, his eyes widening as it hit the snow. Her gaze didn't leave him as she sheathed her own sword, waiting.

Momentary confusion flashed across his face before he tried to take the advantage. Seb charged her.

And Thea's hand closed around his throat.

With her Furies-given strength, she lifted him up so his feet kicked the air beneath him and his nails clawed at her.

This time, she showed no mercy.

This time, he would not walk away.

His pulse raced beneath her palm and she stared into his bulging, bloodshot eyes, watching as a pitiful realisation dawned there.

But it was too late. There was no coming back from this now.

With a flick of her wrist, Seb's bones broke beneath her strength, and Thea snapped his neck.

He went limp instantly in her hold and she dropped his lifeless body in the snow.

A blur of black fur shot out from her side, a vicious growl echoing through the trees. A powerful canine jaw closed around Seb's neck —

Blood spurted.

And in one violent wrench, Dax ripped out Sebastos Barlowe's throat.

Though Seb was already dead, Malik's dog tore him to shreds, and Thea watched every gory moment of it. When his blood stained the snow in wide red pools and his face was an unrecognisable pulp, Thea stood over his body.

'It was everything he deserved,' she told Dax, who rubbed his bloodied snout through a patch of clean snow. 'Thank you, my friend.'

Thea had wanted to end Seb so badly herself that she'd forgotten there were others who were owed that taste of vengeance as much as she was – more so. Malik, Cal, Kipp… They had all suffered at Seb's hands, had all endured his malice and cruelty, but no more. Blood oozed from the corpse at Thea's feet and she felt no remorse, only relief, for there was one less monster in the midrealms now.

'Come on, Dax,' she said quietly. She didn't know what the consequences of Seb's death would be, for her or for her canine friend, but she wasn't going to risk Dax being discovered beside the mauled body.

With a soft bark, the mongrel followed her back to camp. But Thea didn't return to her tent, didn't seek out her friends to tell them of Seb's fitting demise. Instead, she sought out Fendran in the weapons stores. When she entered the tent, her eyes found the blacksmith immediately.

'Is it ready?' she asked.

CHAPTER TWENTY-SEVEN

WILDER

W ilder was sick of the inside of the command tent. They had gone over every possible enemy manoeuvre, every feasible counterattack with their limited numbers and capability. He seemed to be the only one who knew they'd done all they could do, and that only dawn would tell how they'd fare against Artos' monsters and men now. However, Esyllt and Kipp were strategists through and through, and they pored over their maps and inventory as if charts and drawings would reveal the answers at the eleventh hour.

Torj worked with them, pacing around the table and offering suggestions, pointing out hazards in the terrain. The golden-haired Warsword looked as restless as Wilder felt, as was always the way when battle loomed. There would be no sleep for them tonight, no rest until —

The tent flap shifted and in strode Wren, who was clutching a piece of parchment in her fist, and, to Wilder's surprise, wearing *armour*.

The Bear Slayer didn't take his eyes off the younger

Embervale sister, his gaze tracking the tight leathers that followed the curves of her body.

'What in the midrealms...' he murmured, his mouth still agape, taking a step towards her —

Wilder thrust out his hand. 'Watch out for the —'

A loud thud sounded as Torj walked right into the support pole of the tent.

Blushing furiously, he rubbed his forehead, where a red mark bloomed.

'It's called *armour*,' Wren said pointedly. 'I'd have thought a Warsword would be more than familiar with the concept.'

'You... you look...' Torj stammered.

Stifling his laughter, Wilder tried to save Torj from himself by addressing Wren. 'You look like a warrior,' he told her.

She lifted her chin. 'I am.' Approaching Kipp and Esyllt, her gaze bright with determination, Wren handed over the piece of parchment. 'Farissa asked me to give you this. It's all the alchemical weapons we have at our disposal, as well as where we think they might be deployed most effectively.'

'Excellent,' Esyllt said.

Kipp winked. 'You ever want to talk strategy, Wren, you always know where to find me.'

Wilder saw Torj tense.

But Wren laughed. 'At the nearest tavern, ten pints deep?'

'You know me so well.'

Wilder leant against the table, folding his arms over his chest and trying to hide his amusement as the alchemist and strategist chatted, and the Bear Slayer glowered in the background. He'd have to remember to tease Torj about it later. If there was a later.

The familiar scent of sea salt and bergamot wrapped

around him, and he turned to find Thea at his side. 'Do you have a moment?' she asked.

'For you? Always.'

Smiling, she laced her fingers through his and pulled him towards the tent flap. 'Come with me. There's something I want to show you.'

As they made their way through the camp towards their own tent, there was no mistaking the kiss of dawn on the horizon.

'As much as I'd like to fuck you senseless right now,' Wilder said, 'I think we'd best be getting ready —'

Thea gave a soft laugh and pulled him inside their tent. 'Here.'

Momentarily confused, Wilder looked at her. His storm-wielding Warsword, strength and power radiating from her. Strands of bronze-and-gold hair had come loose from her braid, framing her beautiful face. Emotion threatened to overwhelm him as he pictured her spying on him, Torj and Vernich on Thezmarr's clifftops, peering through the bramble with wide eyes. She'd been a girl fighting to become a shieldbearer then. Now she was a Warsword, the woman he loved with every fibre of his being.

'Maybe if we're quick,' he murmured, reaching for her.

Thea batted his hands away with another laugh. 'I didn't bring you here for that,' she told him, gripping him by the arms and turning him to face the back of the tent. 'I brought you here for *that*.'

Instantly, his gaze fell on the mannequin in the far corner.

Upon it was the finest suit of armour Wilder had ever seen. *Warsword armour.*

'How...?' he murmured, approaching the mannequin and studying the set, tracing the interlocking metal rings that covered the torso and arms – a chainmail hauberk. It was incredible, a seamless blend of the unyielding strength of iron and leather, offering both protection and mobility.

'I found the designs in the Dorinth armoury in Delmira, after we were attacked in the ruins,' Thea replied, watching him as he marvelled at the masterpiece. 'Are you going to stare at it all day or are you going to put it on?'

His hands shook as he pulled his shirt off and reached for the armour. Since passing the Great Rite, he'd worn imitation armour, which rubbed him raw and left him vulnerable – he had the scar through his shoulder to prove it. But this... He slipped the chainmail over his head, the mesh-like fabric fitting him like a glove and moving with him smoothly. This was everything he'd ever imagined his armour to be.

Warmth bloomed in his chest as he fitted the bracers to his forearms and the greaves to his legs. He secured each piece in place with the leather straps and buckles, feeling Thea's gaze on him with each added layer.

When at last he'd fastened his belt and scabbards in place, he looked up. 'It's perfect,' he told her.

'As it should be.' Thea began strapping on her own armour – the same set of boiled leather plates he'd had Audra alter for her back in Thezmarr. He'd had to help her into it the first time, lacing the pieces in place as he knelt before her. Now, she dressed for war herself, quickly and efficiently.

'What about yours?' he asked. 'You need Warsword armour too.'

243

'There were only enough materials for one set,' she said with a shrug. 'I figured you'd waited long enough.'

Wilder closed the gap between them, pulling her hard to his armoured chest. 'Thank you.' He kissed her, groaning with need as her mouth opened beneath his and allowed his tongue to sweep in.

For a moment, their kiss was all there was. Deeply passionate, a claiming of one another on the precipice of battle, a promise.

Reluctantly, Wilder broke away, breathless.

But Thea fixed him with a hard stare. 'When the battle is won, I'll be peeling this armour off piece by piece, and worshipping what I find beneath,' she told him.

His lips quirked into a smile. 'Is that a bribe to stay alive, Princess?'

'Yes.'

He laughed. 'Good. I think you'll find it very effective. Never underestimate how badly I want to bury my cock inside you.'

She strapped her sword in place and checked her daggers, and winked. 'Oh, I never do.'

Outside, a horn sounded.

Three short blasts.

A warning.

With a final lingering look at one another, Wilder and Thea left their tent, and went to face Artos on the battlefield.

CHAPTER TWENTY-EIGHT

THEA

As the sun crested the wintry horizon, Thea and Wilder rode out to meet Talemir and the others. From their vantage point on the field, with a spyglass pressed to her eye, Thea spotted Artos at the rear of his forces, clad in golden armour. If he were closer, she would have spat on him, for that gilded breastplate seemed like a further insult – a taunt after inviting darkness into the world, after breeding monsters in the shadows.

Those very monsters bolstered Artos' numbers and ranks before them: howlers, arachnes and all manner of filth in between, and then... a combination of Harenth and Tver men, no doubt manipulated by fear and empath magic. She had seen Artos' power back in Aveum, had seen how it could transform the very nature of people. Despite having heard Torj's report and Wilder's recount of the plans from the Scarlet Tower, Thea hadn't wanted to believe it. It was all so wrong.

She glanced back at their own forces. Aveum's winter

soldiers, the shadow-touched folk, shieldbearers not yet seasoned, Guardians from all over the midrealms, and the Warswords – old and new.

No matter what they did, many lives would be lost in the hours to come. The thought opened a chasm of dread low in Thea's gut.

She sat atop her mare at the head of the army, listening as Esyllt and Kipp gave final instructions.

'Find the leaders within and slaughter them,' Esyllt said, unsheathing his own sword. 'If we cut off the head of the snake, we may be able to avoid mass losses on our end.'

Thea scanned the company for her sisters, finding Anya at Dratos' side, staring out onto the battlefield as though she were about to start the charge herself. Wren was further back, and Thea knew she would be in the second wave, aiming straight for that patch of land earmarked by Kipp for flooding. There was no sign of Audra, or Farissa, but Thea imagined they were hanging back to oversee the deployment of Wren's alchemical weapons.

Drue and Adrienne arrived, both clad in black armour, riding straight to the frontlines. They grinned at one another.

'Luck be with you, sister,' Adrienne said, offering a hand.

Drue shook it, her expression fierce. 'Not if he's been with you first.'

They laughed roughly, as though they'd done this a thousand times before, and went to take their places in the ranks. Thea watched them in awe, pride blooming. She was glad to be fighting alongside them, honoured. She wished she'd told them that.

But there was no time left for sentiment. Talemir rode

his Tverrian stallion to the front of the army and turned to look upon them, unsheathing his twin blades and addressing them all.

'I won't tell you that glory awaits us beyond this field,' he called, pointing one of his swords towards Artos' forces marching on the horizon, the sky already stained blood-red in their wake. 'I won't tell you that we will overwhelm the enemy with our strength, and certainly not with our numbers. But what I will tell you is this: that bastard's forces aren't as unified as they appear. They are made up of monsters and beasts, with no rhyme nor reason to their actions, no loyalty to one another, or to him.'

Talemir surveyed their ranks, his shadows materialising around him, great wings spearing from his back and spreading impressively behind him.

'We may be divided in our own histories and prejudices, but one thing unites us. We stand against tyranny. We stand against the poison and curses swallowing our world. We will break their lines. We will shatter them from within. We've been forced into hiding, persecuted, kept down for far too long. This is our time to rise. So rise!'

A near-deafening roar sounded from their forces, along with the song of steel as it was unsheathed from scabbards all around.

Thea leant over in her saddle to whisper to Wilder. 'I see where you got your battle speech inspiration from.'

'Mine are better,' Wilder quipped with a wink.

'I don't know,' Thea teased, forcing lightness into her tone. 'Tal's efforts seem quite stirring...'

Wilder raised a brow. 'Maybe you'll make a speech of your own one day, Princess.'

247

'Here's hoping this is the last of our battles for a long while.'

'Here's hoping,' he agreed.

They could hear the march of Artos' army clearly now, along with the war drums beating in the near distance, a rhythm that seemed to match the pounding in Thea's chest. She studied the Warsword beside her: the straight set of his broad shoulders, the sharp line of his jaw, the molten silver of his eyes that promised violence and bloodshed. The only telltale sign of nerves was the way he kept adjusting his grip on his reins. He followed her gaze and smiled softly, acknowledging that only someone who knew him deeply, intimately, would notice such a thing.

'Will you hold it against me if I tell you I love you?' he said quietly, so only she could hear.

Her breath caught in her throat and she shook her head. 'Never. We will never hold back saying that ever again.'

'Good,' Wilder replied. 'Because I love you, so deeply, Thea. And if I tell you I love you a thousand times a day for the rest of our lives, it will not have been enough.'

Thea blinked back the tears that stung her eyes. 'I love you, too.'

The blast of an Aveum battle horn filled the air. The two Warswords tore their gazes from one another and looked to the head of the army once more.

'The time has come,' Talemir shouted, raising his swords above his head, the blades glinting in the dawn's rays. 'In the past, it has been the duty of Warswords to slay the monsters of the midrealms. But now, in the face of evil and darkening days, it is up to all of us. Let's break their lines. Let's shatter them from within. Let's slay some fucking monsters.' His

248

stallion reared up as he urged the horse to face the incoming forces. 'For the midrealms!' His voice projected to the far corners of their ranks. *'Charge!'*

Thea raised her own Naarvian steel, a warrior cry leaving her lips as she leant forward in the saddle and charged.

CHAPTER TWENTY-NINE

WILDER

There may have been no glory awaiting them on the battlefield, but Wilder charged headlong into the heart of the monstrous horde, with the love of his life riding at his side and uncontainable pride swelling in his chest.

Together, they were a force to be reckoned with, regardless of the odds.

Together, they were unstoppable.

The first wave of battle erupted around him with a deafening roar, a battering shudder rippling through their entire frontline as their forces collided.

Chaos. Pure chaos.

'Shadow-touched! *Shield!*' Talemir bellowed.

From their ranks darkness now spilt forth as well, and no one flinched as the shadows slid into place around the army, forming a temporary shield of protection around the perimeter. It was just enough to give them an edge, a moment to get their bearings, precious time bought.

When the shield faltered, the ground trembled under the

thunderous clash of steel and the anguished cries of howlers and men alike filled the air, as both sides warped beneath the force of the impact. Everything was a blur. Wilder slashed through the enemy while keeping his attention on their own lines. They had to hold. They had to keep formation.

The rugged, uneven terrain, marked by rocky outcroppings and steep slopes, made it difficult for troops and horses to traverse, to keep their places in the structure they had drilled over and over again. The ground itself was littered with mud and icy slush, impeding movement and hindering the effectiveness of their heavy cavalry.

'Hold!' Wilder shouted above the carnage. 'Hold the fucking lines!'

All around him, soldiers panicked as another assault tracked in a wave across the vast landscape, the screams of horses and men echoing all around, tangling with the screeches of the howlers.

Up close, Wilder could see the haze of empath magic clouding the eyes of the enemy soldiers, could feel the unease of it himself. He forced down his guilt, his pity. There was no saving these men. He could give them only one thing: a swift death. And he obliged.

'Break their lines!' Talemir was shouting from nearby. 'Smash them apart!'

Wilder steered his stallion deeper into the fray, carving a path through the enemy for their own men and women behind him.

Cut the head off the snake had been the instruction, and he scanned the battlefield for Artos to no avail. Naturally, the bastard wasn't in the thick of the fighting – but he saw a flash of gold at the rear of the enemy forces.

Wilder wrenched a spear from a corpse at Biscuit's hooves. Artos was taking cover amid the thicket on the far end of the field. *Nothing but a coward.*

Wilder raised his spear, drawing his arm back, his new armour moving with him like a second skin. He threw the spear with all his might, and watched as it hurtled across the battlefield towards the treacherous king.

A terrified horse almost trampled Artos, knocking him just out of the spear's direct path. Instead, it glanced across his golden armour, with enough force to make Artos stagger, wide-eyed in shock, but not enough to penetrate his breastplate, or take him down completely.

'Fuck.' With a frustrated growl, Wilder decapitated two howlers with one sweep of his sword, their heads tumbling to the blood-soaked snow, their bodies collapsing with the rest of the trampled dead.

Pandemonium was swallowing their forces whole.

It didn't matter how many times Wilder, Torj or Thea shouted for them to hold their lines, to smash the enemy's – their army's discipline was faltering already. Howlers, arachnes and other monstrous beasts rushed forth, eyes gleaming with malevolence as they lunged at what had become the vanguard of Warswords.

'Let's show them how it's done,' Torj called from the helm of his unit.

Wilder braced himself, rallying to the Bear Slayer, Talemir, Vernich and Thea, against Kipp's advice for them not to become a single target. Right now, they needed to give their own forces hope; they needed to demonstrate their strength and ferocity. They needed to show them the meaning of the word *Warsword.*

Together, their presence formed a near-unbreakable wall

of protection. With each swing of their swords, they slashed a swathe through the enemy lines, their blades cutting through scales and flesh with uncanny precision, allowing for the other defenders of the realm to sweep through and unleash carnage with their own orchid-imbued blades.

The agonised shrieks coming from the monsters surrounding Thea told Wilder she was handling herself just fine, and when he caught her eye across the bloodbath, her face and armour splattered with red and black, she grinned.

A fresh wave of enemy forces assaulted them, their lines faltering again, their shield wall buckling.

'Hold,' Thea's voice cut through the madness. 'Hold!'

In his peripheral vision, Wilder saw her throw a handful of silver stars, each one finding its mark in the eyes of the howlers bearing down on their frontline. Incapacitating their leaders gave the midrealms' forces a brief moment to gather themselves and reform their lines. But the reprieve was over in a second, and the swell of soldiers surged with another onslaught, a two-pronged attack this time.

Somewhere in the distance, something exploded, and Wilder was suddenly airborne, hurtling from Biscuit's back and hitting the ground hard. The impact had his teeth singing, but he rolled, leaping to his feet to avoid the trample of hooves, blades raised again.

From the ground, the battle was even more chaotic, and Wilder hoped Biscuit either found his way back to him or retreated to the outer perimeter. He slashed his way through howler after howler, their blood flowing faster than any river. He revelled in the screams of their demise. Wilder fought side by side with Talemir's shadow-touched, glad for their shadows and wings more than once.

'Cal!' Thea's voice echoed above the carnage. 'Now!'

She was still atop her mare, a vision of blood-soaked glory, motioning to her friend, who was stationed at a vantage point on the left flank.

Narrowly avoiding a collision with an arachne, Wilder looked up again to see Cal signal his unit of archers.

'Shields!' Thea shouted.

'Loose!' came Cal's cry, echoing across the clash of steel below.

The midrealms' forces took cover as arrows rained down on the enemy with needlepoint precision.

Wilder took the opportunity to fight his way to Torj, Talemir and Vernich. They coordinated their efforts, guiding their frontlines with precision, forming a relentless spearhead that drove deep into the enemy's formation.

When their lines had broken, Wilder signalled for Vernich to double back, to lead the next charge from a fresh cavalry unit. Wilder and Torj peeled away from Talemir.

'Now!' Wilder shouted. 'Shield wall!' All around him, the allied forces interlocked and pushed hard, forcing enemy lines down towards the ravine that Kipp had identified – the flood zone.

But the enemy was pushing back. Wilder scanned their unit. They needed brute force —

As though he'd just come to the same conclusion, beside Wilder, Torj broke from the shield wall and swung his hammer with ferocious strength, leaving masses of bloody pulp in his wake. It was not the first time Wilder had seen the Bear Slayer use the colossal weapon, but the devastation it caused hit him anew. With every swing, armour and bones crunched beneath its heavy iron head, blood mapping the intricate runes engraved into its surface. Torj was an artist, blending his raw power and the sheer brutality of the hammer with finesse, using the weapon's weight to create a symphony of destruction while swiftly manoeuvring to evade attacks from those stupid enough to dare fight him. Every impact of the hammer sent shockwaves through the units around them, howlers and enemy soldiers alike scrambling from Torj's path, away from the tool of annihilation he swung in his hands.

As a unit of their own, Wilder and Torj drove the enemy lines back, pushing them over the edge of the ravine into the lower-lying land, exactly where Kipp had marked —

Thunder rolled across the battlefield, the earth rumbling beneath their boots, and suddenly, the sound of rain hitting metal was upon them. Clouds gathered overhead, swallowing the gold hues of the broken dawn. A bolt of white light carved through the morning.

It felt familiar, but not quite right, like a slightly different note in a melody he knew well. Wilder marvelled at the different signature within the magic.

Wren. It was *Wren's* lightning and thunder ripping through the air, *Wren's* storm magic being unleashed around them.

The rain intensified, a downpour that echoed across shields and helms.

'She's doing it!' Torj shouted, watching as the level of water from the nearby river rose and rose, breaching its banks and surging down into the flood zone in a terrifying crescendo. A colossal torrent descended, and the enemy, entrenched and unaware of the trap, faltered as the flood barrelled towards them. Shouts of terror arose, and they lost their footing, sliding, barging into one another as the powerful wave hit.

The land beneath them gave way to the onslaught, an

enormous deluge of water and mud that swept through the entire unit, drowning the ranks completely, the current washing them away.

Hope soaring, Wilder craned his neck to see Thea and Drue leaving the flanking units to infiltrate the enemy's rear – aiming for the key commanders, and the head of the snake.

CHAPTER THIRTY

THEA

Thea used her sister's storm magic as a diversion and rallied her unit to close around the back of the forces Wren had swept away with her flood.

Still astride her mare, she rode beside Drue, the pair of them cutting down howlers and Artos' men like stalks of wheat in a field. Unable to help herself, Thea continued to scan the skies for any sign of the wraiths and reapers as she fought her way towards the rear of Artos' forces. But there was yet to be any sign of an incoming airborne attack.

Sensing Wren's magic around them, Thea's own power was dancing beneath her skin, but she kept a tight leash on it; if they needed her, she had to be at full strength.

Together, she and Drue decimated the back lines of the force, while in the distance something erupted. Likely another of Wren's alchemical concoctions. Thea looked up to see plumes of smoke rippling from the heart of the battlefield and clusters of howlers sprinting from the site.

As the smoke drifted into the sky, clearing from the ground, Thea spotted Wilder amid the turmoil, wielding those twin blades, an extension of his own strength and agility. He fought with Talemir and Torj at his sides, the three of them a formidable force carving through one monster after the next, leaving a trail of blood and guts in their wake.

Eventually, Talemir shot into the sky to return to the shadow-touched infantry, forming a skyborne phalanx that advanced steadily and methodically, shielded with shadow.

Below, Thea and Drue continued their assault of the back forces, Thea craning her neck to spot any sign of the lecherous former king responsible for all this death and darkness —

Someone shouted. Wilder.

Thea looked up just in time to see an enormous arachne coming straight for Torj.

Wilder was locked in battle with several howlers. Though he fought with all his might to get to the Bear Slayer, he was just too far. The arachnes reared up, towering over Torj.

Thea urged her mare into a gallop, surging for them, her remaining throwing stars already between her fingers. If she could just —

A glowing sphere hurtled through the air and struck the arachne square in the chest, before it exploded.

A familiar flash of gold momentarily blinded Thea, and she shielded her eyes. The screech of the arachne had her clutching her ears, the rest of the battlefield doing the same as the monster disintegrated, flecks of gold covering its writhing body.

Torj stared open-mouthed at the melting corpse, his hammer suspended in midair in shock.

Thea looked from the startled Warsword across the

battlefield, to where Wren was slinging vials of sun orchid essence at the enemy.

'You're welcome, Bear Slayer,' she shouted across the chaos, pitching another potion right into the heart of an enemy unit.

Torj shook his head in wonder, and Thea grinned at Drue.

With Wren's help, they forced the enemy back, slaying howlers and arachnes. To Thea's horror, miniature vine blights were catapulted into their forces, and for a moment she was ripped from the present. She was back at the great lake, sobbing through the pain as she cut off her own arm, the searing agony of the vine blight's grip unlike anything she'd ever felt.

'Thea!' a sharp voice sounded.

Wilder.

He was at her side, concern etched across his handsome face.

'Vine blights,' she managed.

He didn't question her, only took off towards Farissa. Thea knew he'd take care of them.

Shaking off the nightmarish memory, she spotted the gleam of gold armour at the back of the force and spurred her mare into action. She squeezed her horse's sides, picking up speed, cutting her way towards King Artos, a snarl of vengeance on her lips. He could join Sebastos Barlowe in the underworld. He would die at the tip of her blade —

A roar filled the air, the sound reverberating through the ranks with a shudder.

A gasp caught in Thea's throat.

What could only be a *frost giant* staggered towards them from the mountains. The creature was one of epic proportions, its skin as pale as the snow-covered depths from which it had emerged. With every lumbering step, and every bellowing roar, the ground trembled, and an icy shiver raked down Thea's spine as she took in not only the giant's size, but the leash of shadow around its throat, and the enormous spiked club clutched in its meaty fist.

With one sweep of that club, men went flying, some impaled on the spikes themselves. Blood rained down on the army below, and black ice crept across the battlefield.

CHAPTER THIRTY-ONE

WILDER

The enemy had a fucking frost giant. Wilder felt the blood drain from his face as he saw the enormous creature lurch towards their front line, crushing men and monsters alike beneath its great bare feet.

Panicked screams echoed through the forces. He braced himself. There was no way their lines would hold in the face of this.

'Now might be the time for storm magic,' Adrienne shouted from further afield.

Wilder was inclined to agree. Their numbers were dwindling, and of those who remained, many were frozen to the spot in terror, as black ice creeped across the gory landscape like a disease.

Slitting the throat of a nearby howler and gutting the next, Wilder sized up the frost giant with a deepening sense of dread. It was not the kind that was easily herded into the mountains with fire, as he and Talemir had once done in their younger days. Though it hadn't been cursed like the howlers and arachnes, it was controlled by darkness nonetheless. A thick leash of shadow was lashed around the poor creature's throat. Two more cords enslaved its wrists, while obsidian bled from its eyes.

It lurched towards them, its movements sluggish with resistance, as though someone in the distance were manipulating its movements, making it no more than a puppet to inflict destruction.

Which was exactly what the beast did. Its enormous spiked club cleaved through their forces in a bloody wave. Wilder knew he would remember the sight for the rest of his life – men impaled on the spikes, barrelling through their own forces.

They had to stop it before the battle was lost, before all that was left of their units was pulverised gore in the snow.

Carving his way through enemy lines and shoving his own men out of the way to close the gap between him and the giant, Wilder looked to the archers. On the ridge, Cal was leading the unit, a volley of arrows spearing through the air towards the creature. But the shadow that leashed the beast swallowed the assault in a billowing mass of darkness, protecting the giant.

There was only one thing for it.

Wilder scanned the skies. Spotting Talemir flying overhead, he whistled, loud and sharp enough to cut through the tumult. Wilder signalled to him, praying to the Furies that Tal understood.

The Shadow Prince came soaring towards him, hand outstretched, and Wilder only had a second to brace himself and hold out his own hand before Tal's wrapped around his forearm.

Suddenly he was airborne, Talemir's wings beating hard above him while his former mentor flew them straight towards the frost giant. Icy wind whipped around them and arrows soared past in terrifying proximity. Wilder only hoped Cal's aim was as good as everyone said.

As he hung onto Tal with one hand, Wilder's focus homed in on the enormous creature, searching for weak spots in its flesh as it drove its club through another entire unit of the midrealms' forces. With the way it was moving, its arms swinging across its chest, it would be near impossible to pierce its heart.

Which meant there was only one place he could strike.

The air grew even colder, and he realised they were gaining height, flying high above the madness now, closing in on the frost giant from above.

'You're up, Apprentice,' Talemir called down to him, and let him go.

Stifling a shout, Wilder fell through the air. Decades of training kept his limbs from flailing as he plummeted, not towards the blackened ice, but towards the frost giant. A thrill surged through him, blood roaring in his ears.

He landed hard on the creature's shoulder, immediately scrambling to find purchase as the beast staggered forward with a thunderous bellow. The shadows around its throat and wrists compounded in a burst of darkness, ribbons of onyx power surging straight for Wilder, already tempting his worst nightmares to the surface.

With a shout, Talemir was there, slicing through the shadows with his twin swords, his wings beating furiously to keep him aloft as he defended Wilder. Terrence soared into view, talons poised for damage. The hawk clawed at the monster's eyes with a vengeance.

Gripping the rag the giant wore, Wilder managed to get himself upright on the moving creature as it careened across the battlefield. Slashing through more tendrils of shadow that attempted to wrench him off the giant, Wilder threw himself at the beast's head, climbing up the back of its thick neck, using its lank hair as rope.

He fought back disgust and disbelief at what he was doing as he reached the crown of the giant's skull. It was flailing beneath him now, fighting the shadows at its wrists to reach up and rip him from its head. More dark power came for Wilder, digging into his memories and bringing every horror to the forefront of his mind. But the frost giant beneath him grounded him in a surreal reality, and he gripped a handful of its hair to steady himself, to hang on.

Clutching his sword with his other hand, Wilder took a deep breath, and speared his blade into the creature's shoulder. The roar that followed could have flattened the surrounding mountains.

Wilder pushed his weapon deeper into the tendons, causing the beast to twist, allowing him to direct the impact towards Artos' forces as he and the giant hurtled towards the ground.

Wrenching his blade from its flesh, Wilder aimed and, with all his might, drove the blade into the creature's brain from above.

Hot blood spewed from the wound, covering Wilder in a stream.

Suddenly, the frost giant was falling, and Wilder wrenched on its hair. At the last moment, he leapt from it, the impact as he hit the frozen earth making his teeth sing and his knees jar as he skidded across the black ice.

'Holy fucking shit,' Torj's voice sounded nearby.

Wilder could only watch; time seemed to slow as the frost giant's corpse collided with the ground, decimating two entire units of the enemy's force, crushing soldiers beneath its hulking body, sending a wave of aftershocks through the army.

Wilder felt Torj at his side. His fellow Warsword motioned to the blood coating his new armour, his face and his hair.

'Not yours?' was all the Bear Slayer said.

'Not mine.'

'Good.' Torj slammed his hammer into a howler's face with a sickening crunch, and launched himself back into the fray.

Panting, Wilder surveyed the sea of monsters and carnage. A loud mechanical groan echoed across the front line. Wiping the blood from his eyes, he shuddered as he spotted the source – a long-armed catapult being loaded on the enemy's side, ready to blow more holes in their ranks.

CHAPTER THIRTY-TWO

THEA

They were losing. Their lines had broken long ago, and even though Wilder had brought down the frost giant in a spectacular display of ingenuity and strength, despair filtered down through the ranks as the enemy loaded a catapult.

Thea had fought at the battle of Notos, had sliced through man and monster alike. But it had been nothing like this. The savage brutality, the choking nature of battle was overwhelming.

She had leapt from her mare long ago to help Drue battle back a horde of howlers. Now, she searched the field for another, desperate to clap eyes on Artos again and hunt him down through the madness. Thea was going to kill him. Twice she had saved his life. Now, she was going to end it.

Kipp's voice carried across the clash of shields and swords, and she whirled around to find him amid the fighting. Wasn't he meant to be at the back?

'Get the oil barrels! The Flaming Arrow will be ready,' he

was telling Talemir, gasping for air. 'Drench the fucking lot of them with oil and we'll light those fuckers up.'

Thea turned back to the next rush of enemy soldiers, readying herself for another attack. Kipp had been right about Artos deeming his legions disposable. Wave after wave of them hit the midrealms' forces, wave after wave of them perished, and yet the onslaught continued.

She was dying to use her magic, dying to unleash her power upon the monsters and put an end to the bloodshed. But the order hadn't come. Not from Talemir, not from Anya...

Even so, she dared to crouch amid the blur of battle and put her fingertips to the blood-soaked snow and mud. She sent a pulse of lightning across the ground, zapping a line of opponents in her path, clearing the way to their rear guard, where somewhere, Artos was lurking.

Swinging her sword, she revelled in its song as it cleaved through more howlers, severed the limbs of arachnes and beheaded anyone who stood in her way. She spotted a flash of gold armour and lunged through the throng, deflecting blows as she went.

Wind beat down on them, and Thea gasped in horror, hearing the flapping of wings.

This is it, she thought. *This is when the wraith assault begins, when we've already depleted so much of our defence.* She braced herself, anticipating the mass of darkness that was about to sweep in and swallow them all —

But it wasn't the wraiths and reapers.

It was Talemir, Dratos and a legion of shadow-touched folk.

From above, they dropped barrels of oil on the enemy, just as Kipp had planned. Shielding her eyes against the sun piercing the clouds, Thea saw Cal on the right flank, his arms expanding with his bow as he fired three flaming arrows at once into the oil-drenched unit.

Fire blazed to life. Screams of agony filled the air.

Thea fought her way to a snowy ridge and surveyed the battlefield from above. Wren had washed away much of the enemy with her flood, Wilder had crushed many more with the frost giant, and now, several of Artos' units were aflame thanks to the shadow-touched. In the near distance, she could see Kipp and Torj beating back an arachne, and further back – movement in Artos' rear guard.

He's retreating, Thea realised with a jolt.

'Now's our chance,' a gravelly voice said at Thea's side. She found Vernich there, slick with black blood, breathing hard. 'If he gets away, he'll rally an even bigger army. It's now or never. I'll cut us a path through. You clean up what I leave behind.'

There was no time to argue. The Bloodletter charged, cleaving through one enemy after another, leaving Thea to finish them off in his wake. She did exactly that as she realised Vernich was carving them a direct path to where she'd last seen Artos slinking off in the shadows.

As they fought their way through the mass of violence, Vernich taking the brunt of the attacks, Thea had a surreal moment of realisation: *war makes for unlikely allies.* She stabbed a howler through the heart and surged after the Bloodletter, wondering what he'd make of his former apprentice torn to shreds in the woods. She had the feeling he wouldn't care.

'There!' Vernich shouted, pointing towards a gap in the rear guard. 'Go!'

Thea didn't waste the opportunity. And as she sprinted

for the break in their formation, a figure leapt onto the path before her.

Wilder.

He was covered in blood and gore, but he moved like water, clearing any opponents from her route. Thea would barely have registered that she was running, were it not for the slip of ice beneath her boots and the mud that flicked up, spattering her already filthy armour.

At last, she reached the king's guard of howlers and knights, shadows roiling around them. Artos stared out at her from behind the wisps of darkness, his green eyes bright.

As the battle raged on behind her, Thea studied the ruler of Harenth, the man she thought had given her her future. The man who, in reality, had robbed her of her family. The man who had brought doom upon the midrealms.

'What a waste of a Warsword,' he called out to her, surveying the blood-soaked totem around her arm and the Naarvian steel clutched in her hand. 'There is so much we could have achieved together, Althea.'

Thea looked around at the devastation. 'You call this an achievement?'

'One of many,' Artos replied, remaining in the shadows. 'You, however, are one of my biggest failures. I thought you would have some sense of loyalty after all I did for you, but I see loyalty and honour are dead.'

'They are, when it comes to you. They have been for some time,' Thea said, adjusting her grip on her blade. 'We're here to see what we can do about that.'

She took a step forward, not caring how many howlers or Harenth knights she had to cut down to get to Artos —

'I knew what you were,' he continued, his eyes trained on her sword. '*Who* you were. I sensed your power the moment you threw that knife back in my palace, felt your lightning surging through the steel as it hit my cup.'

Thea didn't react, not even as his words sent a barrage of shock pouring through her. *She* hadn't even known her heritage back then. She'd never noticed an inkling of that power, but she felt it now... It crackled in the air.

Only it wasn't coming from her.

'I forced your hand with the Scarlet Tower,' Artos said, oblivious, jutting his chin towards Wilder, who had come to stand at her side. 'I knew putting him there would flush you out, that we'd see the heir of Delmira announce herself.'

Thea twirled her blade casually, taking a step forward. 'Well done, Artos. But you see, I'm not the heir of Delmira, not by the line of succession. I'm not the future queen.'

Artos laughed darkly. 'Oh, but you are. You are the firstborn daughter of Queen Brigh and King Soren Embervale.'

Thea met his gaze with a cold stare of her own. 'No, I'm not.'

She stepped back, pulling Wilder with her, just as darkness erupted before them, and Anya emerged from the shadows, balls of lightning crackling in her palms. 'That would be me,' she said, and hurled her magic at Artos.

Thunder roared overhead as bolts of lightning shot for the king.

Thea could no longer ignore the storm in her veins. She sheathed her blade, unleashing her own magic in a tidal wave.

Together, she and Anya blasted the king's guard into oblivion, their lightning bolts flashing, wrapping around Artos himself as he screamed and screamed.

Thea expected to feel the scrape of his empath ability

against her senses, but there was nothing, only his shrieks as the electrical current seared his flesh through his armour.

Artos' body sagged in its bonds, and he looked to Thea, his green eyes wide. 'Thank you,' he uttered cryptically, before he passed out.

All around them, the fighting ceased. The air was thick with the scent of spilt blood and the haunting cries of the wounded. Broken bodies lay strewn across the snow like discarded chess pieces on a board, their armour stained crimson.

The sounds of surrender echoed across the bloody plains. Blades being dropped in the snow, the final gasps of the fallen…

'Put him in chains,' Anya barked at a nearby soldier, thrusting her scythe at Artos' limp form. 'Take him away.'

As the power thrumming at Thea's fingertips ebbed away, she fought to fill her lungs with enough air. What little remained of Artos' forces were surrendering, if they hadn't already fled for the mountains.

'We… we won?' she said hoarsely, to no one in particular.

Wilder's stoic presence at her shoulder settled her. 'Barely,' he replied. 'But yes.'

The taste of victory was bittersweet, for their triumph had come at a great cost. Thea inhaled her first deep breath in hours. 'Artos is our prisoner…'

'He is.'

Her body sagged with relief, the aches and pains of battle slowly seeping in. 'Now what?' she asked bluntly, spotting Anya, Talemir and Vernich overseeing Artos' imprisonment.

Wilder put an arm around her, drawing her close despite the blood and guts that covered them both. 'Now, we —'

'Thea!' someone shouted, panic lacing their voice. 'Thea!'

She whirled on her heels to see Cal racing towards her, Wren not far behind him. Cal's face was covered in grime, but there was no mistaking the tear tracks down his cheeks.

Thea's blood went cold. 'What is it?'

'It's Kipp,' he panted, tugging on her arm, hauling her through the bloody slush. 'He's wounded. Badly.'

Thea's mind and body threatened to shut down as Cal dragged her to the broken heart of the battlefield, through the corpses, severed limbs and discarded weapons that littered the snow.

'How bad?' she heard herself ask, but Cal didn't answer.

She could hear the others crashing through the mess behind her, but she didn't look back to see who had followed, only forward, scanning the injured soldiers scattered across the ice, searching for a familiar head of auburn hair.

Then she saw him.

Kipp lay in the arms of the Bear Slayer, an arachne fang protruding from his chest.

CHAPTER THIRTY-THREE

THEA

A strangled sob escaped Thea as she fell to her knees in the snow beside her friend. Kipp wheezed through the pain, blood pulsing from the wound.

'What the fuck were you doing?' she muttered, noting the film of venom on the fang, the pallor of Kipp's face.

'Dancing the fucking foxtrot with a bunch of spiders —' He coughed, blood lining his teeth and spilling down his chin. 'What'd you think I was doing?'

The rise and fall of his chest was shallow and uneven, his breaths rattling as he struggled to draw air through the congealing blood.

'What's a dying man need to do to get a drink around here?' he rasped.

'You're not dying,' Cal said, kneeling on Kipp's other side, gripping his shoulder.

Kipp made a garbled sound that might have been a laugh. 'And they called *me* useless...' He choked this time, more blood spewing from his lips, his body contracting around the wound in his chest, the agony bright in his eyes. 'What I'd do for some sour mead right about now...' Tears streamed down his face, his expression contorted with pain as another wave of it seized him.

Thea's heart was pounding, harder than it had throughout the battle itself, as a realisation hit her like a blow.

She reached for the vial resting against her sternum and pulled it from the chain around her neck.

'It's not sour mead,' she said, removing the cork with her teeth. 'But it's a damn sight more useful.'

Seeing what she was about to do, Torj gave the fang a sharp pull from Kipp's chest and Kipp screamed, the wound gushing crimson, his body thrashing beneath their hold. Thea grabbed his chin and poured her Aveum springwater into his mouth.

'Don't you dare fucking die, Kristopher,' she muttered, making sure every last drop passed through his lips. 'Don't you *dare* fucking die.'

Silence fell as Kipp stopped writhing, and his eyes stopped blinking.

Thea sucked in the icy air, her heart sinking as she dropped the empty vial in the snow. Her trembling hands went numb at her sides. This couldn't be happening. She couldn't – *wouldn't* believe it. Kipp wasn't even supposed to be on the field. He was a strategist – he was supposed to send his and Esyllt's orders up through the lines.

The lifeless body before her couldn't be Kipp, because —

A gentle hand closed over her shoulder.

Somewhere close by, someone was crying.

Thea looked around to see who it was. She wanted to

shake them. No one should be crying, because the body in front of them *wasn't* Kipp —

She struggled to swallow the thick ache that pulsed in her throat as she was pulled up from the frozen ground into a strong pair of arms.

'Thea,' Wilder murmured into her hair. 'I'm so sorry.'

'It's not real,' she whispered against his breastplate. 'It can't be...'

'I know,' Wilder said, voice hoarse.

She blinked at her friend's body, his blood staining the pristine snow.

'You're with Kipp,' Esyllt had barked when she'd first joined the shieldbearers' ranks. Young and fresh-faced, Kipp had been holding his sword incorrectly, his stance all over the place, his auburn hair flopping into his eyes... But he'd offered her a sheepish grin.

'I'm Kipp. Kipp Snowden.'

Thea's shoulders slumped, shaking with silent sobs, even as she fought to stifle them. Her chest ached, each inhale dragging in the weight of loss, each exhale layered with guilt.

Another image of her friend flashed before her: Kipp swaying as he took up a tankard with both hands and bumped it against hers and Cal's. *'May you walk amid the gardens of the afterlife a whole half hour, before Enovius reads your ledger of deeds.'*

He had said that stupid toast so many times, and he always downed his entire drink, sloshing mead all down his front.

The tension in Thea's limbs yielded to a bone-deep weariness, and she let Wilder's arms envelop her as her frozen fingers rose to her cheeks. Tears had tracked down her face, carving rivulets in the grime there. She stared at the moisture on her fingertips as more of Kipp's words came back to her.

'It doesn't matter who stands against you... What matters most is who stands with you.'

No one spoke, and the silence was louder than death itself. It sank its claws into Thea, along with the horrifying truth.

She'd been too late.

'I thought... I thought it was most powerful when it was used on someone you love,' she said.

Wilder only held her more firmly in his arms.

Thea's body shuddered against him, wracked with silent sobs, her chest aching as she tried to hold them in —

A violent gasp made her jump.

She whirled around to see Kipp's eyes flutter, the wound in his chest knitting closed.

'Furies save me,' he rasped. 'Are you trying to get me killed again, Thea? Don't tell the Warsword you love me.'

Thea fell back down to her knees. With tears of relief and almost manic laughter, she smacked Kipp's arm. Gods, she almost wanted to kill the strategist herself. A tidal wave of feeling threatened to crash over her, leaving her in a trembling state of shock.

That trance-like state was broken by Cal, who knelt in the snow beside Kipp as well, shaking his head.

'You...' His voice was hoarse.

Kipp's gaze flitted to his friend as he sat up with a wince —

Only for Cal to grab him in a crushing bear hug. 'I thought you were dead, you fucking prat.'

'Technically, I was,' Kipp wheezed, rubbing his chest

beneath Cal's grip. 'And do you mind? I'd prefer to stay in the land of the living for now…'

Cal eased off him, only slightly.

With a strangled cry, Thea wrapped her arms around them both, burying her face in Kipp's shoulder.

'Not you, too,' Kipp muttered, though there was a distinct note of delight in his tone. After a beat, his long arms came around both Thea and Cal, and together, they cried and laughed in the snow.

Cal took their friend to see one of the healers, just in case, but judging by Kipp's usual dramatics, he was very much himself.

The springwater had brought Kipp back almost instantly, just as Wilder's had done to her all that time ago. Thea felt raw, as though the battle and Kipp's near-death experience had gutted her roughly and scooped out her insides. From the weary expressions around her, everyone felt much the same. But the battle was not over even when it was won, however narrowly.

Thea was glad for Anya and Talemir's orders. She set about her tasks without having to think too deeply about all that had unfolded on the blood-drenched plains. They tended to their wounded and counted their dead, the reports of casualties coming in hard and fast from the outer units.

Hours later, they found themselves in the relative warmth of the command tent, passing around a nearly empty flask of fire extract, trying to process the unimaginable loss on both sides. Artos had hurled everything he had at their forces, with no regard for the lives of his own legions, but he had eviscerated them in the process. The death toll was staggering, and rising by the hour.

Thea sat on a chest in the corner of the tent, Dax by her feet, her fingers mindlessly stroking the soft fur of his ears. His presence was a comfort to her, and a warmth over her frozen feet.

'Has anyone seen Audra?' she asked, scanning the room, trying to recall the last time she'd clapped eyes on her former warden.

'She was talking to Farissa, before the battle,' Wren offered. 'But I haven't seen her since.'

'She'll be around here somewhere,' Cal added.

Thea frowned. It was unlike Audra to miss the crucial post-battle debrief, but she shrugged it off. 'What about Anya and Talemir?' she said, finding the two leaders missing.

'Guarding Artos with Adrienne and the Bloodletter,' Drue replied from where she was draped over a chair, as though she'd melted there. 'They're not taking any chances, particularly with no wraiths or reapers taking part in this battle.'

Thea nodded. 'Good. What happens to him now?'

'We'll move him to a more secure location, then interrogate him for the whereabouts of the reapers' lairs. And anything else that might help us stop the midrealms falling to the darkness —'

Dax gave a soft bark, just as a shieldbearer made himself known in the doorway.

'What is it?' Wilder sighed from where he was seated in a wooden chair, his elbows braced on his knees.

The young man fidgeted. 'We found another body in the woods, Warsword Hawthorne.'

'Then add it to the tally.'

'We thought you should know the details about this one... It's Sebastos Barlowe, sir. He was found dead not far from the latrines. It looks like he was mauled to death by monsters.'

Thea's fingers froze in Dax's coat.

'Seb Barlowe?' Wilder asked. 'You're sure?'

'Yes, sir. He was wearing his uncle's crest.'

'And he was found by the latrines?'

'Yes, sir.'

'Very well,' Wilder told the shieldbearer, his brow furrowed. 'Add his name to the list of the dead, and Torj Elderbrock will see to it that his uncle is informed.'

'Yes, sir.' The young man sighed with relief, closing the tent flap behind him as he left.

'What a tragedy,' Thea said blandly. Wilder's gaze flicked to hers and then to the dog at her feet.

'Devastating,' he agreed.

The battle had raged from dawn until after dusk, and the post-conflict efforts had them on their feet well into the early hours of the next day. Thea had barely had a moment to process it, and truth be told, she was still reeling from nearly losing Kipp. The sight of her friend lying lifeless and unblinking in the snow would haunt her forever.

Hours later, after checking on him in the infirmary, Thea and Wilder stumbled back to their tent, exhaustion settling deep in their bones. But when they reached it, finding that someone had generously lit a torch and a small fire within, with a cauldron of water warming over the coals, Thea knew she wouldn't be able to sleep straight away.

Her fingers shook as she made to unlace her armour.

'Let me,' Wilder said, replacing her hands with his. Ever so gently, he started the task of undoing the straps and buckles, removing one piece at a time. 'Do you want to tell me what happened with Seb?' he asked quietly.

'Not really.' She released a shuddering breath, the grime coating her skin feeling even thicker, dirtier. 'He threatened to rape me.'

Wilder's hands stilled on one of her greaves.

Thea kept talking. 'He hated me so much. It blinded him so completely that he truly couldn't fathom that I'd become a Warsword, that I was better than him, that I – a woman – could kill him within seconds...'

'And did you?' His hands weren't as steady as he removed the second greave.

'Yes,' she admitted, recalling how his windpipe had crushed so easily. 'I snapped his neck. And then Dax was there. He came out of nowhere, tore Seb's throat right out of his lifeless body.'

A moment passed and Wilder stood, gathering her in his arms. 'I didn't think the howlers and arachnes had doubled back around our camp.'

Thea sagged against him, ignoring the cold press of his armour and the blood that still covered them both. 'They didn't. It was me. And Dax.'

'That piece of shit deserved to die a long time ago, Thea.' He took a deep breath. 'I only wish he was alive so I could kill him all over again with my bare hands.'

'We made it count,' Thea said hoarsely. 'But I don't want to tell anyone else – no one official, at least. If word got back to Seb's uncle, whoever he is, I have no doubt he'd want mine and Dax's heads on spikes.'

Wilder tucked a loose strand of hair behind her ear and then traced the line of her jaw, drawing her gaze up to his. 'I wouldn't let that happen, but if you want it to remain between us, it will.'

Thea covered his hand with hers. 'Thank you.'

'Are you alright?'

She hesitated. 'I will be, once I get this filth off me.'

'If you need privacy, if you need to be alone, I can leave.' Wilder spoke the words tenderly, but Thea shook her head.

'Just...' But she didn't know what she meant to say, or what she needed, only that she didn't want him to go.

Wilder seemed to understand. He nodded, and slowly, his hands went to the hem of her shirt. 'May I?'

Thea dipped her head wordlessly, lifting her arms for him.

In the soft glow of the torchlight, Wilder undressed her, peeling the battle-worn, blood-soaked fabric from her skin and gently tugging her towards the warm water on the coals. Still clad in his own filthy armour, he tore strips from the linen on their cot and dipped them into the water, foaming a bar of soap as she stood naked before him.

Pressing a soft kiss to her lips, he washed the grime from her face first, his touch so careful, so reverent, rinsing the cloth each time. The soap smelt of him, of rosewood and leather, of *home*.

Thea reached for him, but her Warsword clasped her hands in his.

'I should have done this after our first battle together,' he told her. 'Allow me the honour now. Please.'

Emotion caught in Thea's throat. She didn't trust herself

to speak, so she simply nodded, her tears nearly falling at the sight of Wilder's gratitude.

He washed her by the fire, gently scrubbing the dirt from her arms and legs, from her hands and fingernails. He dragged the warm cloth down her neck, where filth had gathered at the base of her throat where her armour stopped. As he worked, water trickled down her body, between her breasts, between her legs, stirring a pulse of conflicted desire within.

Her nipples hardened as he followed the curve of her breasts with a fresh cloth of soap, the suds sliding down her curves. His touch lit a fire across her skin, her body responding in kind.

Looking up, she noted how his gaze darkened as his ministrations dipped lower and her arousal became obvious. She didn't hide the change in her breathing, nor the parting of her legs beneath her.

A smile tugged at Wilder's lips. 'I meant to take care of you.'

'There are many ways you can do that,' Thea replied, her voice already sultry with need.

A rough laugh escaped Wilder. 'That's true enough, Princess. Then, by all means, you can help me with this.'

He gestured to his own armour, and this time he let Thea help unbuckle it and remove the pieces from his body. They fell away one by one, revealing the battle-made body beneath, desire pooling between Thea's legs at the sight. He looked like a god of war, a masterpiece of violence and power. The blood and dirt only heightened his fierceness, only accentuated the rippling muscles and unforgiving lines of his impressive frame.

His cock jutted out from between his muscular thighs,

hard and ready for her. Thea's body went molten as she imagined it sheathed inside her, filling her inch by inch.

Exhaling shakily, she reached for a clean piece of cloth and tended to Wilder as he had her. They washed one another, albeit with less patience than Wilder had started with, and when they were as clean as they could be without submerging themselves in a tub, Thea dragged Wilder to the cot in the corner.

There, they lay facing one another, almost nose to nose, Thea draping her leg over Wilder and pulling him close. A quiet gasp escaped her as she felt the silken heat of his hard cock press against her core. The pressure alone set her on fire, and she shifted her hips so that the length of him slid over her clit, her arousal slick between her legs.

'Is this bad?' she asked, bringing his hand to her breast and squeezing hard, her clit pulsing with desire as he rolled her nipple beneath his thumb. 'Are we bad people for wanting this when there are so many who didn't make it? So many in pain —'

'We've had a version of this conversation once before, Thea,' he said, pinching her nipple until she bucked beneath him. 'We can't do anything for anyone else right now. It's part of war – the waiting, the searching for something good in the in-between. It's why fighting and fucking go hand in hand.'

With a cant of his hips, his cock nudged her entrance, teasing her, and she bit back a moan of anticipation.

'So if you want this,' he said, sliding in an inch, 'then take it. It's yours.'

Thea grabbed his backside and wrenched him closer, his cock filling her to the hilt in a single slide that had her opening herself to him with complete abandon. She cried out loudly, forgetting that there was nothing soundproof about the canvas around them.

Wilder rocked against her, thrusting deep inside her and holding her close. She closed her eyes, head tipping back as the intoxicating feel of him took over her senses.

'Eyes on me, Thea,' he commanded. 'I need to watch you come apart. I need to see it.'

Her eyes flew open, and she didn't close them again. Instead, she stared into the liquid-silver depths of his gaze, watching it darken as his own desire took hold.

'Don't let go,' she whimpered as his thrusts became more vigorous, as he hit that spot inside that made her see stars.

'Never.'

He fucked her hard and slow, holding her so close that she didn't know where she ended and Wilder began. She moved with him, swallowing his carnal noises with her kisses, sinking her teeth into his lower lip before starting the kiss anew.

His hand slid between them and he pinched her clit, the sensation setting off a series of blinding ripples within.

'Fuck,' she whispered against his lips. 'Do that again.'

He did, and she half sobbed with the sensitive pleasure of it.

'Are you going to come, Thea?' he murmured, circling the spot with his thumb, knowing exactly what he was doing to her.

'Yes,' she whimpered. 'I'm going to —'

The force of it stole the rest of her words and she careened towards the edge of her climax, an unstoppable tempest hurtling over the precipice.

She didn't take her eyes off Wilder, who, with her body clenching and shuddering around him, climbed to the point of no return with her. The cadence of his hips slowed, dragging out the last of their orgasms, one deliberate stroke after the next, his moan vibrating through her whole being.

Thea clung to him, her anchor through every storm.

'Fuck, I love you,' she told him, pressing his palm to her pounding heart.

Still inside her, he kissed her deeply. 'I love you, too.'

CHAPTER THIRTY-FOUR

WILDER

Wilder could never sleep after a battle, and together, they discovered it was the same for Thea. They fucked again as the watch changed outside, and then, in the quiet early hours just before a new dawn broke, they talked.

'Do you ever wonder what the midrealms would look like with all the monsters gone?' she asked him, her fingers tracing the lines of his tattoo.

'I used to,' he told her. 'But not for a long while now... Do you?'

'Sometimes... I wonder what would happen if, after having fought so hard to be a Warsword, the meaning of it changed. What does a Warsword do when there are no more monsters to fight? No more villains to hunt down?'

Wilder drew circles on her bare back, relishing the feel of her skin beneath his touch, marvelling at the intimacy of such a small act. 'Did you come to a conclusion?'

Thea hummed with contentedness as he stroked the length of her spine. 'I figured there will always be monsters in this world. And that I'd gladly hunt them with you forever.'

'Forever is a long time.'

'Even if I had forever, it would not be enough time with you.'

Wilder stiffened at the reference to the piece of jade resting against her skin. That damn thing was always between them, always reminding them that for all the love they shared, they could not fight fate.

'Wilder?' Thea said quietly.

'Hmmm?'

'I have to talk about it...' Her hand cupped his face and forced his gaze to hers. 'I have to be able to talk about my death with you. My name day is looming, and I feel like I might burst with all the thoughts churning in my mind. Let me share this with you. Please.'

He had been trying to ignore the milestone approaching. He could feel the resistance in his very bones, the overwhelming bodily need to shove the subject far away, into the distant reaches of his mind. What he felt, he realised, was fear – fear for the pain her absence would cause. He knew it would be unbearable, all-consuming. A world without her in it? He had no interest in that.

But to anticipate the grief so intensely... It meant he loved just as hard, just as fiercely. Wilder knew he was lucky to have experienced a love so great, however quickly it would be ripped from him.

Thea's stormy eyes implored him now, and he remembered his reaction to the death notes she'd written. He'd taken that outlet from her, and so now, he needed to be that support for her.

'Alright,' he said, his voice cracking.

She sagged against him, her relief palpable. 'Thank you.'

It hurt. It hurt so deeply to speak the words, but he did it for her. 'Where do you want to be buried?' he asked.

'Burn me,' she said, without hesitation. 'Burn me and cast my ashes out to sea from the cliffs at Thezmarr.'

The image flashed before Wilder: him, standing alone on the rocky ledges beyond the fortress, the dark dust in his palm all that remained of Thea, catching in the wind, leaving him forever.

Not trusting himself to speak, he nodded, his arm around her tightening as though he alone could keep her in the world.

'I want you to keep an eye on Wren as well,' Thea murmured, like she was running through a list in her head. 'I'm glad she has Anya now, but —'

'I'll be there,' Wilder said.

'And Cal and Kipp —'

'Everyone you care for will be supported, Thea,' he told her gently.

'And you?' she asked bluntly. 'Who will support you? Who will be there through your grief? You have a tendency to shut people out...'

'Do I?' he said drily.

She slapped his chest lightly. 'I'm serious.'

Wilder sighed. 'What do you want me to say, Thea? I don't know how to navigate this any more than you do.'

'I want you to tell me that you won't close yourself off from those who love you. I want you to talk to people: Malik, Torj, Talemir, Adrienne, Drue... Whoever you need.'

'I...'

'Promise me, Wilder.' Thea's voice was firm.

He didn't think he could bear the agony of it. It was

worse than any wound he'd suffered in all his years of slaying monsters. But for her? For her he would bleed a thousand times over. For this fraction of a life with her, he'd pay the price of grief – for loving her was a privilege, and that privilege was worth any cost.

'I promise,' he said at last, the words hoarse.

Thea pressed a tender kiss to his lips. 'Thank you.'

He was grateful. It gave him the chance to gather himself, to fight back the tears that burned his eyes as her mouth roved over his. When she broke away with a happy hum, he forced a lightness into his tone. 'Anything else on your mind?'

'Only you,' she told him. 'What life might be like beyond all this. We could capture my Tverrian stallion, get me some armour to match yours, roam the midrealms together…'

'No princess life for you, then?'

Thea scoffed. 'You know I was never a princess.'

Wilder had wondered what the Embervale sisters intended for their fallen kingdom, had wondered if it would change things between him and Thea. But they hadn't had the chance to talk about it until now, and he still wasn't sure it was the right time —

'What about you?' Thea interrupted his thoughts. 'What do you want, should the future not be so bleak?'

Wilder hesitated. It had been a long time since anyone had asked him what he wanted, since anyone was willing to hear his needs and his desires, as though he deserved to have them met.

He encircled Thea's waist with his hands, pulling her on top of him before he spoke the words he hadn't dared to say aloud yet. 'I want… a life more than existence, more than survival. To experience the world to its fullest, with you at my side.'

The blanket around her shoulders slipped, revealing her round breasts, and the fate stone that rested between them. Thea rolled her hips, the soft heat of her meeting the granite hardness of him, eliciting another carnal moan from deep inside Wilder.

'Then we'd best start now,' she said.

CHAPTER THIRTY-FIVE

THEA

Their bubble had to burst eventually. As dawn broke outside, they could no longer ignore the noise of the war camp being dismantled. Thea dragged herself from the warmth of the cot and Wilder with a moan. Every muscle in her body ached savagely; the cold made matters even worse. A grunt from Wilder told her he was faring just as poorly.

'Getting too old for battles, Warsword?' she teased, watching him roll his shoulders with a wince.

'Maybe if someone hadn't kept me up all night I'd be in better shape.'

'I heard no complaints,' she quipped, smiling.

He laughed. 'And you never will.'

When they emerged from the tent, the icy air bit at Thea's nose and cheeks, but she hardly noticed as the sight before her stole the breath from her lungs. The entire camp and the battlefield beyond were carpeted in fresh snow, the glare from the sun nearly blinding.

'It's like it never happened,' she said quietly.

There was no black or red blood staining the ground, no

corpses littering the field. The only evidence from the massacre the day before was the huge mound beneath which Thea assumed the body of the frost giant lay, and the odd spear sticking up through the snow. From last night's debrief, she knew that any coherent prisoners had been put in chains and grouped in smaller units to be escorted to Vios, while any remaining wounded monsters and cursed men had been slaughtered and buried.

'Feels wrong, doesn't it?' Wilder murmured beside her, surveying the land alongside her. 'Like all those deaths, and all that suffering, was just wiped clean from the world.'

Thea scanned the plain, where just yesterday they had fought tooth and nail against the darkness, where Kipp had nearly lost his life, and so many others had… It came back to her in flashes: the feel of a throat opening beneath her blade, the shadows lashing for Wilder as he climbed atop the frost giant, that arachne fang sticking out of Kipp's heart. And Artos, bound with bolts of lightning, screaming.

Thea turned towards the command tent. 'Let's find Talemir and the rest.'

'About fucking time,' Anya said as they entered.

Torj looked up from where he was rolling several maps together. 'I advised her against interrupting.'

That brought a laugh to Thea's lips as she recalled how he, Cal and Kipp had made that mistake in Harenth. 'Where are we headed?' she asked.

'The Singing Hare, of course,' Kipp's voice sounded from behind her.

She whirled around and threw her arms around her friend. 'You're here.'

'Where else would I be?' he replied with his usual grin.

Thea held him at arm's length, surveying him. 'You're truly healed?'

Kipp bowed his head, suddenly sincere. 'Thanks to you.'

'What would the midrealms be without the Son of the Fox?' She hugged him again, hoping that the image of him lying dead in the snow would eventually fade in time, for its echo haunted her now, even as he stood whole and healthy before her.

'A dull place indeed,' Kipp declared. 'So, you're all packed?'

'We're not really going to the Singing Hare...' she said, glancing from Kipp to Torj. 'Are we?'

The Bear Slayer huffed a laugh. 'Don't ask me how he managed it, but actually, yes. We're heading there as soon as the final preparations are made.'

Thea blinked at her friend. 'How in the realms —'

'I simply pointed out the strategic benefits to our commanders,' Kipp replied, having the gall to look baffled. He counted them on his fingers. 'The town has supplies we need and medical facilities for our wounded. We need a secure location to interrogate the false king. It's on the way to Vios, where, after we're done with his questioning, Artos will be handed over to Queen Reyna to face trial for the murder of King Elkan. The good men and women of the midrealms need a morale boost... Plus, I'm not dead. We need to celebrate.'

Wilder shook his head in disbelief. 'And you managed to convince Talemir, Drue, Esyllt *and* Queen Reyna of this?'

Torj snorted. 'He did. I've never seen anything so

persuasive. Though I'm not sure his motivations are entirely altruistic.'

Kipp made a noise of shock, his hand flying to his chest. 'You wound me, Bear Slayer.'

'You'll live.'

'I almost didn't,' Kipp reminded him.

'Well, luckily Thea didn't listen to your dying wish for sour mead and gave you her springwater instead,' Wilder interjected.

Kipp bowed his head in reverence to Thea. 'For which I'll forever be in her debt.'

Wilder nudged Thea. 'Perhaps you can use that to get me out of the favour I owe him.'

Chuckling, Thea shook her head and smiled sweetly. 'Not a chance, Warsword. I want to see what sort of insanity the Son of the Fox asks of you.'

Kipp slung his arm around her shoulder. 'That's the spirit.'

Thea leant into her friend's embrace, fighting back the disbelief that he was truly here after the horrors of yesterday.

'Enough fucking around,' Anya said sharply. 'We're due to head out within the hour. Commanders, Warswords, heirs and a mismatch of other personnel will travel by shadow magic to the tavern. We're bringing the prisoner with us. He doesn't leave our sight.'

'And Queen Reyna?' Thea asked.

'On her way to a mountain residence before we meet her back in Vios for the trial. Her troops will travel with what's left of the cavalry unit and our army to the Singing Hare and the main town.'

'Shouldn't we stay and help?' Wilder cut in.

Anya ran her hands over her shaved head. 'I suggested as much, but they were united in their stance: make haste and deal with Artos.'

'And what of his forces?' Thea blurted. 'What of Tver? And the reapers?'

'We won't know until we question him. Dratos and Vernich started last night, but he wasn't entirely lucid after his encounter with you and me,' Anya replied. 'Our healers advised that we need to get him warm and fed before the real interrogation can begin.'

Thea made a face. The thought of caring for the bastard who'd wrought so much suffering on the world didn't sit right with her.

'I thought the same initially,' Anya offered. 'But it was our sweet sister who pointed out: what good is the first cut of many if he can't feel it?'

Kipp gaped. '*Elwren* said that?'

Thea patted him on the shoulder. 'You'll slowly learn that of the three Embervale sisters, *Wren* is the one to fear the most.'

She chanced a glimpse at Torj, who was busying himself with the buckles on a pack, but the Bear Slayer didn't seem surprised in the least, as though he'd known all along where the true danger lay.

Thea turned back to Anya. 'No sign of wraiths or reapers?'

'None.'

'Doesn't that —'

'Make me uneasy as fuck? Yes,' Anya replied, hoisting her heavy fur cloak around her shoulders and tying it at the base of her throat. 'But until we question Artos, we won't know any more. Talemir's got shadow-touched rangers scouting all over the midrealms, but for now… we go to the damn tavern.'

'Where is Tal?' Wilder asked.

'He went ahead with Drue and Adrienne.'

'And Wren? Farissa?' Thea added.

'Mixing tinctures and salves for the wounded in the infirmary. They're refusing to leave until it's all in hand.'

Thea nodded. 'I'd expect nothing less. What of Audra?'

Silence followed.

Thea gaped. 'No one has seen her at all?'

Anya shifted on her feet. 'I was told she was spotted riding away from camp before the battle.'

'What?' Thea blinked, looking around the tent, gobsmacked. 'Audra would never.'

'She might,' Torj said quietly. 'If there was something only she could do…'

Thea's stomach bottomed out at the Bear Slayer's suggestion. But if he was right, and Audra had intended to find them allies, she had failed. 'Do you think she's alright? She could be buried under all that snow for all we know…'

Torj raised a brow. 'Knowing Audra… do you think that's likely?'

'I don't know what to think anymore.'

The tent flap flung inward and Cal appeared, his quiver and bow draped over his shoulder, several dead hares hanging from his hand.

'If it isn't Callahan the Flaming Arrow!' Kipp said gleefully. 'What have you been up to?'

Cal shook his head, but couldn't seem to hide his joy at seeing Kipp back to his usual self. 'Figured we might offer these to Everard as payment. I doubt he'll be accepting the king's coin from Thea this time around.'

Kipp simply shrugged. 'You know what they say... Gold is gold.'

'Who says that?' Cal demanded.

Another shrug. 'People.'

Cal rolled his eyes. 'When do we leave?'

'Sylas Yarrow has command in our absence,' Anya said. 'I'll brief him and find Dratos. Then we're out of here.'

'Not again...' Wilder mumbled at Thea's side.

'What is it?' she asked.

'I...' He looked sheepish, an expression she had never seen on his handsome face. 'I fucking hate shadow magic travel,' he admitted.

A smile lifted the corner of Thea's lips. 'Oh?'

'Makes me feel queasy, alright?'

Stifling her laughter, she squeezed his hand. 'Alright.'

Anya took Thea and Kipp first, her shadows holding them in place, her wings beating loudly around them as the icy wind howled beneath them. Thea found the magic exhilarating. It felt freeing to soar through the crisp air, the landmarks below mere specks against the brilliant white snow. Chuckling under her breath, she thought of Wilder wrapped in Dratos' shadows, his eyes screwed shut in discomfort. It shouldn't make her laugh, really. But the idea that her formidable Warsword, who'd slayed countless monsters and faced the horrors of the Scarlet Tower, got queasy with a little shadow flight was a tad amusing.

She was thinking of him when her boots crunched atop fresh snow, and Anya's shadows dissipated, revealing

Everard, the owner of the Singing Hare, standing beneath the tavern's swinging wooden sign.

He wore a broad grin as he greeted them all with outstretched hands. 'Welcome back to the best tavern in the midrealms.'

Kipp strode forward, clapped him on the shoulder and laughed. 'Second best, Everard, let's not get carried away.'

CHAPTER THIRTY-SIX

WILDER

Wilder had never been more glad for a warm fire and the crisp taste of ale on his tongue. Everard had roped off an entire section for 'Kipp's party' and had piled the tables high with food and drink.

Even with the bulk of their remaining forces having made their way into the surrounding town to utilise its supplies and resources, their unlikely company of leaders seemed to sprawl across the tavern. It was a strange sight to behold. It felt like both yesterday and years ago that they had all rallied here in secret, trying to forge the first semblance of an alliance between the shadow-touched and the midrealms. Since then, shadow-touched, Warswords and Guardians had faced the true enemy on the battlefield, and now stood side by side, breaking bread. It was history in the making.

And somewhere below the raucous rooms and toasts was King Artos, chained and under guard, awaiting their interrogation, if they hadn't already started up again. He deserved every ounce of pain they inflicted on him. Wilder had seen with his own eyes the cruelty he'd inflicted upon the shadow-touched captives, the burns and welts, the haunted look in their eyes, the children in cages. Yes, Artos deserved everything he got.

The anger and resentment faded as Wilder's gaze fell to Thea across the room. She was talking to Anya and Adrienne, flicking her braid over her shoulder and using her hands to explain something. For a moment, all he did was watch her. Warmth bloomed in his chest as she smiled, her eyes bright while Anya responded to whatever she'd said. Gods, he still couldn't believe she was his. He hadn't so much as dared to dream it when they'd first met, that one day he'd be able to make such a claim. He'd denied himself and his feelings for so long, convinced that she was better off without him, that they didn't need one another.

She'd proven him wrong, time and time again.

And here they were, together.

As though sensing his gaze on her, Thea glanced across the room, finding him instantly. The smile she offered him was a private one, a smile just for him.

Wilder was so entranced by her that he almost didn't see Kipp striding towards him, a big, eager grin on his face. Apparently not even an arachne fang to the heart would stop the strategist from having a good time.

'I know you well enough now to recognise that look only means trouble,' Wilder said apprehensively.

'I disagree,' Kipp replied, his grin widening further, if that was at all possible. 'It means I've organised something you'll approve of greatly.'

'Gods, do I want to know?'

'Probably not,' Cal interjected, joining them at the table and swiping a chicken leg from the spread.

'Of course you do.' Kipp dismissed his friend with a wave. 'Head into the next room. Take your Warsword companions.'

Baffled and a little uneasy, Wilder motioned to Talemir across the room, setting his tankard down on a table.

'What is it?' Tal said, brow furrowed in concern.

Wilder didn't blame him. 'Kipp asked us to go in there.' He pointed to the doorway.

'Since when do we just do what Guardians tell us?' Talemir quipped.

'Times are changing, Tal.'

'I'll say.' But he followed Wilder into the room all the same.

'My good friends!' Marise the wine merchant exclaimed as they entered, rushing forward and embracing Wilder before he turned to Talemir, unabashed joy in his eyes. 'The famous Prince of Hearts! We meet again at long last!'

Talemir's eyes bulged. '*Marise?* What the fuck are you doing here?'

'I've been telling Wilder to come to my dead red event for years, and he's been hard to tie down —'

Wilder nearly choked on his ale.

'So I brought the occasion to him!' With a flourish, the merchant whipped a cloth from the table behind him, revealing a significant line-up of wine bottles.

Wilder suppressed a laugh of disbelief. 'How did you manage this? The world's on fucking fire and you find —'

'A dead red event? Seriously?' Talemir groaned. 'You're still doing those? I nearly died at the last one, Marise.'

Thea appeared in the doorway and, spotting Marise, waved enthusiastically. 'What exactly is a dead red event?

I've been wanting to know what it was since I met you. I thought it was something sinister...'

'Sinister?' Marise looked shocked. 'My good lady, a dead red event is —'

'A celebration!' Kipp chimed in from the doorway.

'*Precisely.*'

Thea folded her arms over her chest and waited. 'Someone explain.'

'Marise has a lot of older wine, wine that was designed for ageing,' Talemir explained. 'So every few years he hosts what he dubbed the dead red event, wherein he and his friends all sift through their cellars for the oldest wine they have and bring it to his shop. The wine has either gone completely bad – dead – or it's the most incredible wine you've ever tasted. The only thing that's certain is that you won't remember leaving.'

'If you leave at all,' Wilder mumbled.

'That's one of two certain things,' Kipp said with a wink. 'The second is that you'll have a spectacular time.'

'How would you know?' Wilder gaped.

Kipp gave a smug grin. 'The Son of the Fox never misses one.'

'I've never seen you there —'

'Haven't you?'

Wilder racked his brain for a memory of meeting Kipp long before he met Thea, for that was how many years it had been since he'd been to one of Marise's infamous events. He came up with nothing.

'What are we waiting for?' he said instead. 'Shall we start?'

'Absolutely, my dear Warsword,' Marise beamed.

Kipp removed the cork from the first bottle with a pop,

filling several glasses and handing them out. The room had filled and, bar Dratos and Vernich, the main company of rebels gathered around.

Once everyone held a glass of a richly deep red wine, Kipp raised his in tribute. 'Though the battle for Aveum was hard-won,' he said, 'we need to celebrate life —'

'Your life, you mean,' Cal muttered from the sidelines.

A few people chuckled, but kept their glasses raised, waiting.

With a fleeting scowl in Cal's direction, Kipp cleared his throat. 'Allow me to share a fitting toast to mark the occasion.' He tilted his goblet towards the gathered crowd in salute. 'May you walk amid the gardens of the afterlife —'

At the back, Talemir burst out laughing. Wilder met his gaze and chuckled as well. The Son of the Fox was something else.

There was a resounding echo of 'Cheers' all around the room, before Wren came forward. She looked fresh off the battlefield, still filthy from her time in the infirmary.

'I would like to say something as well.'

The room quietened as she took Kipp's drink from him and raised it again.

'I would like to make a toast to celebrate the name day of my formidable sister.'

Wilder's heart sank.

'Thea's name day is tomorrow, and Anya's is just two months from now. My sisters and I... We have never been able to celebrate together, so I want to mark this as the first of these occasions we'll have as a family —'

And it'll be the last. Wilder's chest ached at the thought. His hand dropped to his side and, finding Thea's, he laced his fingers through hers. It wasn't fucking fair. He hated this damper on what should have been a celebration. He hated that the past months had flown by so quickly, and that her next name day was an even crueller reminder of the fate that awaited her: a life stolen out from under her.

'To Anya and Thea!' Wren called, raising Kipp's glass to her lips and drinking deeply.

'You can't *commandeer* my party,' Kipp objected at her side, swiping an empty goblet and filling it generously.

'Watch us, Fox Boy.' Anya came forward and tapped her glass to his with a wicked grin. 'Thanks, Wren,' she added, knocking her hip against her sister's.

Dread unfurled low in Wilder's gut, his conversation with Thea the night before bleeding like a fresh wound in his mind. But when he turned to her, expecting to see anguish and sorrow, his love was smiling warmly.

Thea touched her goblet against his. 'To experiencing the world at its fullest,' she said.

CHAPTER THIRTY-SEVEN

THEA

I t was already the best name day celebration Thea had ever had. Her cheeks ached from laughing. Her drink nearly came out of her nose as she watched Kipp and Cal enthusiastically declaring that every wine they tasted from Marise's selection was the best they'd ever had, their cheeks flushing redder by the second.

Spotting Wren at the bar, Thea made a beeline for her – only to be beaten by the golden-haired Bear Slayer, who approached her sister, looking oddly bashful.

'I have something for you,' he said quietly, sliding a small, linen-wrapped parcel across the bar.

Thea was close enough to hear, too close to back away without startling the pair and too curious to look away.

Wren tilted her head. 'It's not *my* name day…'

'No, but…' Torj shifted awkwardly on his feet. 'Just open it.'

Wren's dainty hands slowly reached for the parcel. 'Some sort of weapon, I presume? Perhaps a —'

'Just open it, Elwren.'

Wren unlaced the twine and peeled the fabric back, her mouth dropping open. Thea had never seen her sister speechless before, but there she was, gaping at an odd little pair of silver scissors.

'These are what you needed?' the Warsword asked.

Wren blinked, slowly turning to lift her gaze to his. 'I…'

Torj nodded to himself. 'Good,' he said, before walking back towards Talemir and Marise.

Biting her lip to keep from grinning like a fool, Thea sidled up to her sister and jutted her chin towards the strange tool that made for an even stranger gift. 'What are those?'

Wren was staring after the Bear Slayer. 'They're secateurs,' she said, almost in a whisper.

'What?'

'Remember back in Naarva how I was saying my hand hurt from harvesting the orchids? That I do a lot of intricate work with my hands and they often ache from the repeated motions?'

'It rings a bell.' It didn't.

'In one of about ten thousand meetings, I suggested that all the harvesters be provided with secateurs, to help with the strain… They're a design from distant lands, hard to find. I didn't think anyone was listening.'

Thea couldn't help but grin then. 'Someone clearly was.'

Wren snatched up her secateurs and gave Thea a warning look. 'Not a word of this.'

Thea raised her hands in mock surrender. 'I wouldn't dare.'

Soon, Wilder came to stand at her side, chuckling softly as the debauchery unfolded around them. Cal and Kipp were making nuisances of themselves, as usual, with Kipp not-so-quietly needling Cal.

'All I'm saying is that it's nice for things to *match*, Callahan. We can't have that laughing fox on your arse cheek getting lonely —'

'Will you shut up?'

'Perhaps a dancing badger? Or a flying stag?' Kipp's eyes went wide and he grabbed Cal by the shoulders. 'No! A lightning bolt, to signify our undying friendship with the trio of Embervales!'

'I'm not falling for this a second time,' Cal muttered.

'All in good time, my friend,' Kipp said sagely. 'All in good time.'

Music drifted in from the main hall, and to Thea's surprise, it was Talemir who insisted that they dance. He swept Drue clean off her feet and carried her towards the melody.

When she glanced up at Wilder hopefully, her Warsword was already smiling at her.

'I know you don't like to dance, but…'

He took her hand in his. 'I think we've long since established that I'll always make an exception for you.'

They left the privacy of the area Everard had sectioned off for them and entered the main part of the tavern, where the air was thick with the scent of ale and roast meat, and smoke from the hearths. Drunken laughter and the hum of conversation melded with the lively tune of a minstrel's lute, creating an irresistible song that seemed to infuse life into the very walls of the Singing Hare.

Wilder led her to where the tables had been messily shoved to the walls, and the floor was slick with spilt drink. It was nothing like the grand ballrooms of Harenth or Aveum, nor was the dancing itself the stilted, formal waltz of nobles. Here, the music was fast-paced and infectious, and those on the floor threw caution to the wind and danced completely uninhibited, twirling messily, holding each other too close, laughing so hard that tears streamed down their faces.

Thea wished Ida and Samra were here, to put their Dancing Alchemist skills to the ultimate test. Across the room, Wren was trying to drag Cal onto the dance floor, much to Kipp's glee. Wren caught Thea's eye and grinned at her from across the room, any shadow of that interaction with the Bear Slayer long gone.

The Singing Hare's atmosphere had a similar crackle to Thea's lightning, filled with promise and anticipation. The entire room pulsed with the music and the rhythm of the dancers, who threw themselves head-first into the revelry. It looked delightful.

Wilder squeezed her hand. 'Shall we?'

Thea was already pulling him onto the dance floor, laughing as they were instantly swept up in the current of couples and larger groups swirling in a sea of colours and shapes. Wilder's hands encircled her waist and she leant into his touch, marvelling at how free they were here, swaying to the music, radiant with joy.

Fingers plucked the lute's strings with fervour, echoing the excited pulse of the room. Thea met Wilder's silver stare, their steps light, their bodies snug against one another. Gone was the weight of their weapons and armour. Instead they found a momentary reprieve, a glimpse of sanctuary in a world that so often seemed on the brink of destruction. And so they twirled and spun, monsters, prisons, war all fading into the background. There was only the melody, the dance and each other.

As night turned into early morning, Wilder kissed her soundly amid the revelry. 'Happy name day, Thea,' he murmured against her lips.

For the first time in years, those words sparked not dread, but joy in her heart. She had everything she'd ever wanted, and for whatever time she had left, she'd be grateful for the privilege.

They danced together, and with their friends in a huge circle, everyone swaying to the lively jig and swapping partners in a flurry of uncoordinated movements. For the first time in her life, Thea danced with her sisters, feeling the elation of their company in her bones. Sadness lingered at the edge there, for what they'd been robbed of, but this? This was a gift. This was *family*.

Stealing kisses from Wilder as they twirled around the room, Thea was so happy, so filled with joy that she could have burst.

But nothing this good lasted forever.

Which was how she knew, when Vernich appeared at the edge of the festivities, his expression grim, that their reprieve was at an end, and the war was calling them back.

CHAPTER THIRTY-EIGHT

WILDER

Wilder had known it was too good to be true, but that hadn't stopped him wishing it would never end. He could have danced with Thea forever, content to hold her in his arms and watch the smile bloom across her face.

But now, they stood in the cramped cellar of the Singing Hare along with Wren, Torj, Anya, Vernich, Drue and Talemir, looking at the bloodied prisoner. The former King of Harenth had been bound in heavy chains and fastened to an iron hook in the stone wall, but he didn't look to be attempting escape any time soon.

'He started talking?' Wilder asked with a glance at Vernich.

The Bloodletter nodded. 'Not that it made much sense.'

'I trust you weren't too heavy-handed with your questioning?'

Vernich made a noise of disgust. 'I've done enough interrogations to know when a man's about to break. This one's already broken, by the looks of things.'

'What do you mean?' Thea demanded.

Vernich's brows shot up, but he didn't berate her like he would have done in the past. Instead, he answered: 'My guess is that your little lightning trick might have been a bit much for an already addled mind.'

'Already addled?' Wilder prompted.

Artos made a garbled noise from beneath his chains, muttering something about his daughter.

'Surely he knows we'd never hurt an innocent woman?' Drue said from the shadows.

'Perhaps it's best he *doesn't* know that,' Vernich countered with a growl.

Anya stepped into the torchlight. 'He might very well mean me. The Daughter of Darkness and all…'

Artos flinched at the sight of her.

'Remember me?' Anya breathed, stalking closer to the former king, the man who had robbed her of her childhood, her family, her kingdom.

Artos squirmed, recoiling from Anya's advance, the chains rattling around him.

'I think he remembers,' she whispered, to no one in particular, her voice taunting, cruel. 'You remember forcing a scythe into a little girl's hand and throwing her to the wraiths, don't you, Majesty? You remember dividing the world in two by banishing the women warriors of Thezmarr, don't you?'

Artos rasped for air as though Anya had her hand around his throat.

She didn't.

'What's wrong with him?' Anya demanded. 'I want him to have his wits when I tear him apart.'

'Something's not right,' Thea addressed her sister. 'He

was not like this when we captured him. This wasn't us. Has he been poisoned?'

'Not a chance,' Vernich said forcefully. 'Your winged ranger and I haven't left him alone for a second. He's been given nothing but water by our own hands.'

The former king's head lolled to the side before he burst into a fit of manic laughter.

At the edge of the group, Wilder saw Wren jump at the abrupt noise, her hand flying to grip the arm of the Bear Slayer beside her. But Wilder's attention was drawn back to Artos' cackling. The sound was completely unhinged: a cacophony of high-pitched shrieks, his eyes streaming tears, wide with an utterly unsettling intensity, his face contorted in a disturbing blend of madness and ecstasy.

A shiver crept down Wilder's spine at the sinister spectacle. 'What the fuck...?'

Artos' demeanour changed again, his expression tightening into one of terror. He let out a scream, raw and ragged, trying to scramble away from something they couldn't see, his chains rattling.

'Please,' he rasped desperately; the first word he'd directly spoken to them since they'd all been down in the cellar. He screamed again, the noise sharp enough to force Wilder's hands to his ears.

And then Artos was laughing once more, deranged, garbled noises bursting from him sporadically.

'What the fuck is wrong with him?' Thea said, looking from the madman before them to the rest of the group, a crease forming between her brows.

It was Wren who approached the prisoner, crouching before him and studying his array of expressions. 'I think something is happening with his empath magic,' she muttered, more to herself than to anyone else. 'He's experiencing various emotions to the extreme... Can't you feel it?'

Artos looked right through her and keeled over as much as the chains would allow, his body seeming to crumple under the weight of all he was feeling, convulsing as uncontrollable sobs took hold. Guttural moans of anguish broke from his lips as tears tracked down his twisted face and snot dripped from his nose.

Wilder had never seen anything like it. The seamless transition between such opposing emotions was eerie, and the air around them was thick with palpable dread. Whatever this was, it wasn't good.

'Someone gag him,' came Anya's cold voice.

'No,' Wren said. 'We don't want him to choke.'

'Speak for yourself,' Vernich growled.

Wren stood, meeting the Bloodletter's gaze with a fierce stare of her own. 'We don't want him to choke, *yet*. We haven't got the information we need. Once we have that, he can choke, he can hang, you can split him in half with your sword for all I care. But first, I need to consult Farissa.'

Wilder had never seen Vernich look abashed; in fact, the expression was positively bizarre on him, but to everyone's shock, the Warsword dipped his head in agreement and moved out of Wren's way, motioning for her to pass.

'Thank you,' she said curtly before turning to Anya and Talemir. 'There might be something we can concoct to clear his mind, something to bring him back down from whatever mania this is. Only then will you get any answers from him.'

'How long?' Anya asked bluntly.

'Like I said, I'll need to consult Farissa,' Wren replied with a note of impatience.

'Go,' Talemir told her, stepping in. 'Send word down with one of the others as soon as you know more.'

Without another word, Wren climbed the stairs, the trapdoor opening and then closing behind her with a soft thud.

Cool air swept in at Wilder's side as Thea moved across the cellar to Anya. She didn't reach to touch her, but her voice was soft when she asked: 'Are you alright?'

The eldest Embervale sister stared down at their prisoner with nothing but loathing and contempt in her stormy gaze. 'I could watch him die a thousand deaths and still not be satisfied.'

'Wren will figure it out,' Thea said. 'And once we have what we need from him —'

'Then he'll be sent to Aveum for trial,' Anya cut her off.

'There was no other way,' Thea spoke gently. 'We needed Reyna's alliance.'

'Doesn't mean I have to like it,' Anya muttered.

'No, it doesn't.'

'Doesn't mean you can't rough him up along the way,' Talemir offered.

'That will be the least of it,' Anya said darkly.

Wilder ran his hands through his hair and suppressed a heavy sigh. It was hard to believe that only moments ago they had all been upstairs, swept away by the revelry of music and liquor.

'You should all go back up,' he said. 'Get some food, get some rest. It feels like it's going to be a long night. I'll guard the prisoner.'

Torj seated himself on a nearby barrel. 'As will I.'

Vernich took up a place by the king without a word, making his stance clear.

Wilder's gaze sought Talemir's. 'Well?'

The Shadow Prince nodded and made for the stairs, Drue close behind him.

Thea came to Wilder. 'I should —'

'Be with your sisters,' he finished for her. 'I know. Go.'

Thea smiled. Rising to her toes, she brushed a kiss against his lips, warm and firm, the promise of more to come, and Wilder couldn't help but draw her closer and deepen the kiss, claiming her mouth with his —

Vernich made a noise of disgust.

Reluctantly, Wilder broke away from her, and Thea went to the stairs, making an offensive gesture to the Bloodletter on the way.

When everyone but the original trio of Warswords was gone, Wilder faced Artos, who was weeping in the corner.

'What a fucking mess.' Vernich shook his head in disgust.

'For once, I agree,' Wilder replied.

Torj laughed. 'It only took a full-scale war for us to all see eye to eye.'

Scanning the room, Wilder went to one of the surrounding shelves and pulled out a bottle. 'Better late than never.'

'Don't go braiding my hair just yet,' Vernich said.

Figuring Everard wouldn't mind if they helped themselves, Wilder uncorked the wine and took a swig straight from the bottle. Desperate times called for desperate measures, after all. He handed it over to Torj, who took it gratefully.

With a jolt, Wilder realised that the last time the three Warswords had been alone together it had been at his own request, when he'd returned to Thezmarr after years of slaying monsters on his own. He said as much to the others now.

'Did you know back then?' Torj asked him.

Wilder raised a brow. 'That the midrealms were going to shit? I suspected. There were more and more wraiths coming through the Veil, no matter how many I killed. Other monsters too... There was something in the air, even then. But did I know that this would happen?' He flicked his gaze to Artos. 'Did I know that he was the puppet master behind it all? No.'

Torj passed the wine back and Wilder took another drink, letting the red cherry taste wash over his tongue and down his throat before offering it to Vernich.

The Bloodletter shook his head. 'That shit's too fancy for me,' he said, before eyeing up the cowering former king again. 'He was always a slimy bastard. Never liked him.'

'You don't like anyone,' Wilder pointed out.

Vernich snorted. 'Nor did you, until a few years ago.'

'True.'

The three of them stared at Artos for a moment, Wilder's mind taking him back to the various encounters he'd had with the King of Harenth. Jokes aside, there *had* always been something off about the monarch, something that they'd all been blind to over the years, but that nagged at them all the same.

'Thought we were done for during that battle,' Vernich said, to Wilder's surprise.

Torj made a noise of agreement. 'Several times.'

Wilder nodded. 'We were at a disadvantage from the start. Not just in numbers, but the discord throughout our own units. It never makes for a strong front.'

'The fall of Delmira was like that,' Vernich told them.

For a second, Wilder stared at him, having long forgotten that it was indeed that battle where Vernich had earnt the name *the Bloodletter*. Even in the tiny village of Kilgrave, the children had grown up hearing stories of his courage, his ruthlessness, of the rivers of blood he'd spilt in the heather.

Wilder marvelled at the fact that they'd never spoken of it before. But then, they'd rarely seen each other in Wilder's earlier Warsword years. It hadn't been until Osiris reinstated the tradition of apprentices that they'd been forced into one another's company. Then there had been the incident with Kipp, Thea and Seb, and Wilder had nearly killed the Bloodletter with his bare hands. It had hardly been the right circumstance for reminiscing about battles long past.

'What happened?' Wilder asked now.

Vernich groaned and held his hand out for the wine. 'Give me that.'

Wilder passed it over and Vernich took a long slug with a grimace. 'Where's the fucking fire extract when you need it?'

Wilder could have laughed at that. *Of course* Vernich drank fire extract —

A sudden scream from the king pierced the air, only to be abruptly silenced as a block of wood struck the back of Artos' head, knocking him unconscious.

Vernich dropped the timber and drank again before noting Wilder and Torj's stares. 'What?' he said, nonplussed. 'They didn't say we couldn't shut him up by other means.'

Wilder did laugh at that. 'True enough.'

'The battle of Delmira?' Torj prompted.

Vernich took another gulp of the wine before passing it to the Bear Slayer. 'As I said, similar in disadvantages to the one we just had... What we didn't realise at the time was that he –' Vernich jerked his thumb towards Artos. '– had been using his empath abilities to create discord among the people, long before there was any sign of trouble. When the wraiths and reapers struck, Delmira's armed forces were already sceptical of their rulers' loyalty to the midrealms. There was infighting between those who stood firmly behind Queen Brigh and King Soren, and those who were convinced that they were leading their people towards the darkness. Even the frontline wasn't united. It was bad... Friend turning on friend mid-battle... The losses were catastrophic. On that field in Aveum yesterday, it felt much the same.'

'The losses were almost as bad, though I don't think we've got the final count yet,' Torj said.

'It's too soon,' Wilder replied. 'We'll lose more to injuries... Bodies will be found, if the snow ever melts.'

Vernich grunted. 'It's fucking grim.'

A dark laugh bubbled out of Wilder. 'Isn't that what I said to you on the cliffs when I first got back? It's always grim news.'

'So you did,' Vernich huffed.

'Did anyone tell you that your apprentice is dead?' Wilder asked the Bloodletter bluntly. He wished he could have been there to see Thea snap Sebastos Barlowe's neck. Even now, when he thought of the Guardian, his blood boiled. The bastard had caused pain to so many people Wilder cared about, and he'd threatened to *rape* Thea. A quick death wasn't punishment enough for that.

'No,' Vernich said. 'And he wasn't my apprentice, not after all that shit at Notos. I got rid of him, or tried to, at least. Spineless prick if I ever did see one.'

Torj looked up from where he'd started cleaning his war hammer. 'Why'd you choose him, then?'

'Didn't. Owed his uncle a favour. He made it clear there was only one option.'

Wilder shook his head in disbelief. 'Who the fuck is this bastard's uncle? That he has so much sway?'

Vernich frowned. 'You don't know?'

'Evidently not.'

'Osiris. Osiris is – or was – his uncle.'

The revelation sent Wilder reeling. *Osiris? The Guild Master? How could they not have known?*

Torj had much the same reaction. 'You're kidding! We were always told it was someone of influence, but... Fuck, it makes a lot of sense now.'

Vernich merely grunted again.

Torj looked from him to Wilder. 'So you're saying that I'm the only one out of all of us who actually got to *choose* my apprentice.'

Vernich saluted him with the bottle. 'Congratu-fucking-lations. You lucky bastard.'

'Turned out alright for me in the end,' Wilder said with a grin.

Commotion sounded from above, and moments later, a beam of light shone down as the trapdoor opened. The stairs groaned as the usual suspects descended: Talemir, Drue, Adrienne, Cal, Kipp, Farissa, Wren, Anya and lastly, Thea, who closed the door above them and seated herself on the steps.

'What's the verdict?' Torj asked, his gaze finding Wren instantly.

The alchemist strode forward and crouched before the unconscious prisoner.

'What'd you do to him?' Anya demanded.

Vernich merely shrugged. 'Nothing permanent.'

'He was making a racket, to be fair,' Torj added.

Wren was shaking her head. 'I figured this would be the state we'd find him in,' she said, digging through her pockets and producing a small jar of smelling salts, holding them under Artos' nose. She wafted the chemical compound back and forth beneath his nostrils for a moment, before a loud gasp echoed through the cellar.

The former king looked around the room, his chin trembling, once again on the brink of an emotional breakdown.

Wren moved swiftly. She uncorked a tiny vial of something and yanked Artos' head back by his hair, pouring the concoction directly into his mouth. Bound in chains, he could do nothing but twist his head, but apparently, Wren's grip was vice-like and she held him in place until he swallowed the tonic.

'It shouldn't take more than a few minutes,' she told them, at last releasing the prisoner and placing the cork back in the vial.

'So it was as you thought?' Wilder asked, watching Artos blink slowly as he took in his chains and then the faces around him.

'He should be able to tell us himself soon,' Wren replied.

Sure enough, Artos' green eyes cleared, and he took a trembling breath. He shifted, as though despite the chains, a weight had been cast off his shoulders.

'Welcome back,' Anya taunted as she stepped forward, her eyes gleaming with vows of violence as her hand curled around the grip of her scythe. 'Overwhelmed yourself with your own magic, did you?'

Artos' lips moved, but no sound came out before he closed them again.

'You're going to have to do a lot better than that,' Anya chastised him, as though he were no more than a child who'd misbehaved, but there was no mistaking the threat lacing her words. She placed the point of her scythe just above his eye, applying enough pressure that a bead of blood soon appeared beneath the steel. 'I thought I might give you one to match mine... How does that sound, Your Majesty?'

'I – I...' he stammered.

'I didn't quite catch that,' Anya taunted.

The tension in the room was palpable. Wilder wasn't sure what would happen once Anya started carving into his flesh, if anyone would stop her —

'My daughter,' Artos croaked.

'She's safe,' Anya told him without hesitation, despite the fact that none of them knew where the princess was. 'But it's unlikely you'll ever see her again.'

'Please,' he rasped. 'I'll tell you anything.'

Anya clicked her tongue in frustration. 'Just like that? I thought we were going to have a little fun first, Majesty.' She dragged her blade ever so lightly down his face, not quite breaking the skin, but enough to leave a raised red mark in its wake. 'You like this sort of fun, from what I've heard.'

'No, no!' he begged. 'I'll tell you whatever you want to know.'

Anger flashed in Anya's gaze. It was clear she hadn't wanted this to be easy, that she wanted a reason to work him over, to spill his blood.

'Where are the *rheguld reaper* lairs?' she demanded. 'I want to know every location where they congregate, where their legions of wraiths are camped. And I want to know the main hub, the one where the king reaper resides.'

Artos recoiled from the tip of her blade as much as the chains would allow. 'They will have a new lair by now...'

Thea jumped down from the steps and came to stand beside her sister. 'What are you fucking talking about?'

The former King of Harenth looked strangely sad. 'He intended to welcome them in as soon as —'

The trapdoor banged open above them, and Dratos ran down the stairs, breathless. 'The battle for Aveum was a diversion,' he said, gripping the sword at his belt. 'Osiris has welcomed the reapers into Thezmarr. The fortress has fallen.'

CHAPTER THIRTY-NINE

THEA

As Thea looked from Dratos to their prisoner, it all fell into place. 'We showed our hand, let them destroy the bulk of our forces...'

'And now they make their ultimate move,' Kipp finished for her, his expression solemn.

Wren's cold hand closed around her arm. 'Thea... Sam and Ida... They're still at Thezmarr. So many people are. We were so worried about our numbers that we didn't – we didn't even warn them —' Her voice broke, a hand clapping over her mouth as she stared wide-eyed at Thea.

Thea's hands had gone numb. She couldn't feel them as she squeezed Wren's fingers and tried to reassure her. 'They'll be alright. They're Dancing Alchemists, remember? They'll find a way out, they're quick on their feet.'

'We just left them – cutting herbs, making tinctures...'

'That's not true. They *volunteered* to stay, you said so yourself. They made a choice, Wren.'

'But this... They had no idea this was coming,' she whispered.

'And neither did we,' Thea told her, though the words tasted bitter on her tongue.

Around them, the conversation went on, with Kipp at the helm. 'Our army is in pieces... We don't have the numbers for another battle on that scale.'

Thea's knees almost buckled. After everything they'd just been through, after winning by the skin of their teeth in Aveum, the final fight was on the horizon and they couldn't win.

Wilder's presence warmed her side as he moved close. 'But we won't be meeting them in open battle.'

'No,' Talemir agreed. 'We'll be up against a damn *fortress*. Thezmarr was built to withstand a siege, to be a rock against which the tide breaks. They'll pick us off one by one before we even breach its walls.'

Unease twisting in her stomach, Thea dropped Wren's hands, her gaze sliding back to Artos. 'What are the plans for the reapers at Thezmarr? What do they intend?'

Vernich made a noise of disbelief. 'We can't believe a fucking word he says. For all we know, he could have been fucking planted here. His capture could have been part of the enemy's plan all along.'

Anya's scythe was already tracing the curve of Artos' throat. 'Let's see what tales he tells anyway...'

The former king whimpered like a dog.

'Well?' Thea prompted. 'The more you tell us, the less you'll bleed... For now.'

Artos sucked in a breath, the words tumbling from his mouth in a frenzy of fear. 'There is a ruler among their kind, a sire to many. He has called wraiths and reapers from all over the midrealms, from beyond the Veil, to gather in a single, overwhelming force.'

'To what end?' Thea demanded, her lightning singing beneath her skin. Gods, how she'd love to unleash it now. 'What happens when they unite as one?'

Artos stared at her. If she didn't know better, she might have thought it looked like his green eyes were swimming with regret. 'From Thezmarr, they will launch their final assault on the midrealms. Every shadow, every ounce of power will come together as one. They mean to swallow every kingdom with total darkness. They mean to curse every living thing. Like a plague.'

Thea could see it: the sweep of shadows across the sky, blocking out the sun, smothering everything that was good in this world. It had been happening slowly and steadily for years, no matter how many monsters they slayed, no matter how hard they fought. Poison had crept into the lands, into the hearts of their people…

'Why did you do this?' she demanded, forcing down the urge to blast him with the lightning that crackled at her fingertips, begging for an outlet. 'Was one kingdom not enough for you?'

'I am a mere vessel.' The former king sounded distant then, as though he were drifting back towards that churning current of emotion he'd been caught in before. 'Long ago I had a feeling… and a voice told me that this was the way… A voice I trust told me that with darkness came a dawn of fire and blood… and that I should run towards it, not away from it. I felt the truth of those words with my power…'

A chill rushed through Thea, and the nervous glances exchanged around the cellar told her she wasn't the only one.

When the skies are blackened, in the end of days
The Veil will fall.

325

The tide will turn when her blade is drawn.
A dawn of fire and blood.

The prophecy had haunted the midrealms for decades, but now... now they were watching it come to pass before their very eyes. Having carried a Naarvian steel blade for years before Wilder had caught her, Thea had always doubted its validity and the way it had shaped their history, but what had once been a distant string of words was now their present, and there was no denying the power of fate.

'How long?' she heard herself say. 'How long do we have until the reapers finish rallying together and move against the midrealms?'

'A matter of days.' Then, a sob broke from Artos, and he began to cry, taking great gulps of air, the sound pitiful.

Thea nudged Wren. 'Does he need more of your potion? He's sounding like that madman again.'

But Wren shook her head. 'He's not in a thrall or anything like that. Those tears are his own.'

It was pathetic. The man before them had ended kingdoms, had created monsters in the shadows and inflicted them upon the realm, and yet here he was... a snivelling mess. With a noise of disgust, Thea turned her back on him and addressed their company.

'The way I see it, while we wait for our own scouts to return and report, we haven't got much choice but to take him at his word. If someone wants to keep him talking, then by all means do so. But whatever we do, I suggest we take our conversation elsewhere now.'

There was a murmur of agreement, and most of them started for the stairs, shoulders sagging in exhaustion and defeat. Though she wasn't ready to admit it, Thea felt much the same.

'I'll stay with His Majesty,' Anya said, twirling her blade. 'I'm sure there's a detail or two missing from his sorry story.'

Thea's heart sank. She grabbed Anya's arm. 'If you want to dabble in revenge rather than save what's left of this world, then be my fucking guest. But maybe you should think about how you wish to leave the world... Better, for having had you in it? Or a mirror of the pain you experienced? If that is what you want your legacy to be, then so be it. Just know that it doesn't make you different. It makes you the same as all the rest.'

Anya jerked out of her grip as though burnt. 'So fucking be it, then.'

Her sister's words landed like a closed fist to her gut, and Thea stood there, blinking, as Anya turned away from her and brandished her scythe at Artos.

'Where were we?'

Swallowing the lump in her throat, Thea started up the stairs. She could never know the true depths of Anya's suffering, what she'd gone through because of the man in chains before her now. She had just hoped that she and Wren would be enough to pull Anya out of her own shadows, before it was too late. Thea wasn't so sure of that now.

Just as she shut the trapdoor behind her, she heard the first harrowing scream.

CHAPTER FORTY

THEA

Leaving Anya to her torture, Thea was the last to emerge from the cellar, and did so with shock as she surveyed the tavern. What seemed like only moments before, it had been teeming with life, and now... the Singing Hare stood frozen in time, an eerie scene of abandoned chaos. Upturned chairs littered the floor; half-eaten meals, now cold and unappetising, were left scattered across the tables, while the drinks, once frothy and inviting, had congealed, the condensation on the tankards long gone. The stale scent of panic permeated the air and the tavern itself, once a haven of revelry, was now desolate.

The others were waiting, uncertainty etched on their faces.

Wilder's eyes flicked to the trapdoor in a silent question, but Thea gave him a subtle shake of her head. It was to Everard that she looked next, nervous energy flitting through her. The tavern owner was behind the bar, cleaning glasses with a rag, his cheeks drained of colour.

'Gotta keep my hands busy to keep them steady,' he told

her when he met her gaze, though the tremor in his voice betrayed his terror.

'What happened here, Everard?' she asked, approaching the counter, careful not to tread on the broken glass across the floor.

'Darkness swept through the tavern, like a mist at everyone's feet. I don't know what it was – a warning of sorts, perhaps. People panicked. They fled...' He gestured to the mess. 'The end of days is here at last. Help yourself to whatever you'd like. We're not long for this world now, however valiantly you all fought.'

Thea opened her mouth to speak, but found herself suddenly lost for words. *The end of days is here at last.* She had always known that her time in the midrealms would be fleeting, but she had never assumed the same for the people she loved. Wilder, Wren... Cal and Kipp, Anya... All of them deserved their futures. They all —

'No liquor for anyone.' Kipp's voice cut through her thoughts, his command surprising. 'Water and tea only. We need clear heads. Where can we work, Everard?'

'Wherever the fuck you'd like, lad. The Singing Hare is all yours.'

'Wrong,' Kipp said sharply. 'It's yours. The Laughing Fox is mine, or will be one day. And I don't mean to see it overrun by shadow any time soon. I will not go quietly into the fucking darkness... Will you?'

Kipp's words seemed to spur everyone else into action, and soon they were dragging tables across the room, shoving them together to make a larger one they could all sit around.

The air hung heavy with the pungent scent of spilt ale and damp wood, the quiet punctuated every now and then by a particularly loud scream from the cellar. Thea took her seat, wishing Anya would join them, but knowing it wasn't her place to do or say more. Anya had to make her decisions for herself.

It was Vernich who spoke first. 'We don't have the numbers. It's that simple. Even if we did, our resources are depleted. Our remaining men are exhausted and wounded.'

'Then there's the small question of how we'd even get everyone to Thezmarr without draining what little energy our shadow-touched have left,' Dratos added.

'All fair points,' Kipp said. 'But let's talk about what we *do* have and what we *can* do. First, we gather what we can – weapons, supplies and any willing soldiers —'

'They won't come,' Cal said glumly. 'You saw what they were like on those fields. They were almost as likely to kill one another as they were the enemy. And once we tell them it's basically a death sentence? Well, I can guarantee they won't be lining up.'

'Then perhaps it's not about survival,' Wilder countered, sinking into the chair beside Thea and taking her hand in his. 'Perhaps it's about making a final stand...'

'And what? Dying before we even touch the outer walls?' Dratos scoffed. 'You mean to attack Thezmarr, the most impenetrable stronghold in the midrealms, with a handful of men?'

Thea felt her Warsword's grip tighten around her fingers as he spoke. 'I mean to take as many fucking shadow wraiths with me as I can. I'd have thought we all shared that sentiment.'

Dratos considered him for a moment before he shrugged. 'I guess I can get on board with that.'

'Yes, yes,' Esyllt said. 'Everyone's a fucking hero. Furies save me, can we *please* talk tactics?'

'Usually for an assault like this, you might start with using starvation as a siege tactic and cut off supply lines to the fortress,' Wilder replied. 'But... we're not up against ordinary men. I mean, do we even know what reapers and wraiths *eat*, besides power and people's souls?'

Talemir gave a snort. 'It hardly matters at this point. The monsters will outlast us in that regard. With the enemy's talons in Thezmarr, I don't see how we can penetrate the stronghold. As I said before, it was literally built to withstand an attack like this one.'

The nape of Thea's neck prickled and she saw Kipp's eyes brighten as they met hers across the table. 'They don't know Thezmarr like we do...' she ventured.

'Osiris does,' Torj pointed out.

'Unlikely,' Thea said. 'Else you'd think he'd have done something about the fact that Kipp had been sneaking off to the Laughing Fox for sour mead every other week.'

Torj blinked for a second before facing Kipp. 'I fucking knew it.'

Kipp merely answered with a grin.

'So, if we do indeed have a few days, we could potentially use the network of tunnels beneath the kingdoms?' Drue said, bringing them back on course.

'It's a big *if*, but yes,' Esyllt replied.

Thea poured herself a glass of water and drank deeply before she spoke again. 'We've got no choice but to trust Artos' word... We'll all be dead or worse by the end of the week anyway. So we have to try.'

Beside her, Wilder nodded. 'We should send a scout to the Bloodwoods, see what reinforcements they've added to Thezmarr's existing defences. Once we know what we're dealing with, we can move our remaining forces into place.'

Kipp cleared his throat. 'I suggest a multi-pronged attack. If we can take the walls, we'll have Cal and his archers rain sun-orchid arrows down on them from above. If their ranks are organised, we'll use Wren's explosive devices – so long as we avoid our own shadow-touched. If we have a force at the gates with a battering ram as a diversion, I can lead another through the tunnels and attack from within once the gates are breached...'

Cal gave a sarcastic laugh. 'Is that all?'

'No, actually,' Kipp said. 'I think we should blow up the Great Hall.'

'*What?*' Esyllt barked, gripping the sides of his chair. 'You're mad.'

Kipp grinned. 'Often that goes hand in hand with genius.'

'I'd beg to differ,' Esyllt replied.

'If we destroy the hall, we decimate the heart of their operation. It might give us a chance —'

'You're forgetting one thing.'

It was Anya's voice that sounded from the edge of the room. She stood leaning against the wall, her scythe bloody but sheathed at her belt, and she caught Thea's eye before she addressed the company.

'You have three storm wielders to unleash upon the enemy. And the might of Delmirian fury.'

'I was getting to that,' Kipp said, turning to Thea and Wren with a grin. 'I think it's about time the Embervale sisters united on the battlefield, don't you?'

CHAPTER FORTY-ONE

WILDER

T he first thing Wilder noticed at Kipp's declaration was how Torj stiffened in his seat. He looked around as though they were all mad – the near-manic grins the Embervale sisters were sharing hardly dissuaded the notion.

'Wren's not trained,' he objected. 'She can't —'

'Can't *what*, Bear Slayer?' Wren challenged. 'If memory serves, I was the one saving your arse on the battlefield at Aveum.'

'This is different,' Torj argued. 'This is an attack on a *wraith-infested fortress* —'

Wilder already pitied his fellow Warsword. Arguing with an Embervale sister was like arguing with a brick wall. Torj would be better off saving himself the hassle and admitting swift defeat.

'A fortress *I* grew up in,' Wren countered. 'A fortress I know just as well, *if not better* than you —'

'I'm a fucking *Warsword* —'

'And I'm a fucking *storm wielder*.' Forks of lightning shot out across the tabletop, causing several people to leap back in shock, but Wren's eyes, bright with power, were fixed on the Bear Slayer in challenge.

'If you're so concerned about her lack of battle experience, perhaps you should be her guard,' Thea offered.

Torj's mouth fell open. 'That's not what I meant.'

Wilder had to bite a knuckle to keep from laughing.

Kipp's voice commanded their attention once again. 'Wren? What do you want to do? It's your choice.'

'I want to fight,' she said firmly. 'Alongside my sisters and friends. There is nowhere else I'd rather be.'

Wilder could practically feel the pride radiating off Thea beside him, and for a brief moment he marvelled at how far they had come. From squabbling siblings to a united front, facing the end of the world together. He met Talemir's gaze across the table, similarly awed that after all this time, after all his anger, he and his mentor were fighting together again as well.

'Good,' Kipp said.

Vernich cleared his throat and looked at the strategist. 'It was smart,' he said with difficulty. 'To keep their powers in reserve...'

Kipp blinked slowly, clearly in shock, as was the rest of the company. His eyes narrowed as he replied, 'I'm a smart person. You might have known that sooner, had you not had me beaten to within an inch of my life and sent to the infirmary.'

Silence fell across the table. Not everyone there knew of what Vernich had ordered Seb to do when he and the others were shieldbearers, but Wilder remembered well enough. He'd found Thea bleeding to death in a broom closet. She still had the scar along her ribs to prove it. By her account, Kipp had suffered worse.

'It was poor judgement,' Vernich said quietly, his lined face flushing. 'I meant to harden you up for battle. I meant to make the shieldbearers unbreakable. But that's no excuse.'

Wilder remembered the brawl he'd had with Vernich after finding Thea. He'd broken the Bloodletter's nose, and that had been the least of it.

'What are you trying to say, Vernich?' he prompted now, a small, cruel part of him enjoying his fellow Warsword's discomfort.

A muscle twitched in Vernich's jaw. 'I'm sorry,' he said. 'I'm saying I'm sorry.'

A lesser man might have made him squirm a little more, might have humiliated him further. But Kipp, Wilder was coming to learn, for all his jokes and teasing, was no lesser man.

The Guardian offered Vernich his outstretched hand, which the Warsword grasped in his own, shaking it firmly. 'Apology accepted,' Kipp said, before motioning to Esyllt. 'The maps, weapons master?'

With reports of their casualties and remaining supplies coming in from Aveum, the allies talked long into the night. The dancing and drinking from earlier felt like it had happened a decade ago, to other people. Now there were only the cold, hard facts of war, and the impending doom of the world as they knew it.

Someone cleared their throat at the tavern's main door. Wilder looked up to find Commander Sylas Yarrow in their midst, flushing deeply.

'What is it?' Wilder said coldly. He wished he'd pummelled the bastard even harder after the way he'd spoken about Thea in the war camp. Yarrow was lucky he was still able to stand.

But it was to Thea that the commander looked, regret shining in his eyes as he approached and slowly unsheathed his sword. He knelt before her, offering the blade. 'The Warsword was right.' His voice was stripped of all contempt. 'You are owed my apologies, and my allegiance. It was an honour to fight on the same field as you, Warsword Embervale. And I would do so again in a heartbeat. My sword is yours.'

A smug sense of satisfaction washed over Wilder. Commander Yarrow was not the first to be taught a lesson or put in his place by Althea Embervale, and nor would he be the last.

Wilder noted the subtle flush creeping up Thea's neck as all eyes in the room latched onto her. 'Perhaps you can share that sentiment with the rest of the camp,' she said.

'I have,' Yarrow answered, his head still bowed. 'I don't have many men left, but they are ready and yours to command.'

Thea blinked at him, and Wilder squeezed her tensed thigh under the table.

'Thank you,' she managed, with a glance to Esyllt. 'Our weapons master can give you the details. All weapons will need to be treated again with what's left of the sun orchid essence.'

Flushing, Commander Yarrow scrambled to his feet, lifting three fingers to his left shoulder in a Warsword salute before Esyllt ushered him away.

Thea's leg bounced beneath Wilder's grip and she wriggled in her seat, scanning the faces before them. 'Still no word from Audra?'

Wilder knew Thea had been asking after her former

warden to no avail. Even now, Farissa shook her head in response.

'Not that I know of.'

Thea made a noise of frustration. 'Something is wrong. She wouldn't miss this – not a chance to defend the midrealms, to fight for Thezmarr.'

'There is nothing we can do,' Wilder told her gently, squeezing her leg again. 'We have no spare units to send to look for her. We can only focus on the battle ahead. Audra thought she was doing the right thing in Aveum, but none of us can change that now.'

Thea merely grimaced, toying with her fate stone.

They kept talking, until at last Talemir sat back in his chair, looking as exhausted as Wilder felt. 'So it's settled?' he said. 'We'll send Artos to Vios' dungeons, and then make our final stand tomorrow at sundown?'

Murmurs of agreement sounded around the table.

'There's no point in delaying any longer than that,' Wilder said. 'We only risk giving the reapers more time to rally, or having them move on the midrealms early.'

'Two hundred men...' Vernich muttered with a shake of his head.

'And women,' Thea corrected him.

Vernich dipped his head in apology. 'And women.'

'I don't know about you, Bloodletter,' Thea said. 'But I've always relished beating the odds.'

Wilder pressed a kiss to her temple. 'That you have.'

He had no notion of the hour when the company retired and Thea led him to the same room they'd shared last time.

Memories came flooding back as the door opened. Someone had left the fire burning in the hearth, illuminating the modest space beyond. During their previous stay, they'd fucked on nearly every surface, and Thea's magic, which had been dormant for a year, had come surging back.

Now, his storm wielder looked longingly at the empty tub in the corner. 'I think it'll be a long while until we enjoy such luxuries again…'

'I think you might be right.'

She sighed. 'Nothing has ever beaten those hot springs in Tver, anyway.'

'Not the bath aboard the *Furies' Will*?'

'Not even that. Those hot springs were something else.'

Wilder smiled. 'One day I'll take you back there.'

'Wouldn't that be something…'

Though she'd spoken of defeating the odds only moments before, there was no missing the note of grief in her voice, and the subtle wistfulness that told Wilder she didn't think she would live to see the hot springs again.

'I'll take you back there,' he said more firmly this time, drawing her into his arms. 'One way or another.'

'I'd like that.' She sagged against his chest, her arms wrapping around his waist and locking together at the base of his spine. 'We should get some sleep.'

'We should.'

They peeled their clothes off and stumbled to the bed. Exhausted as he was, Wilder's mind whirred with battle tactics and visions of Thezmarr, and with thoughts of the woman who lay next to him.

They lay on their sides and faced one another, the sheets rumpled around their waists. Thea's hands were tucked under her cheek, the soft glow of the fire gilding her beautiful face and the curves and hollows of her body.

'This could be the last time we...' She trailed off, her voice trembling, tears lining her eyes.

Remembering her words to him in their tent at Aveum, Wilder stroked her jaw with his knuckle and kissed her tenderly. He wouldn't deny that horrors awaited them at Thezmarr, nor the fate that had been chasing Thea her whole life. Instead, he broke from their kiss and cupped her face, memorising her features.

'Then we'd best make it count,' he said.

Wilder slid his hands down beneath the sheets and gently rolled Thea onto her back, spreading her legs apart. He shifted so that he was on top of her, bare chest to chest, before he slid down, leaving a trail of soft kisses from the crook of her neck past her collarbone, mapping the curves of her breasts and waist.

His cock grew heavy between his legs as it hardened with his arousal, each pass of his lips over her causing it to pulse with need. The sheet came down with him as he moved, and soon, he was on his knees between her thighs. He gently bit the tender flesh there, coaxing a small cry from Thea, before putting his mouth to her core.

She moaned loudly then, the sound vibrating along his bones and stirring the ripples of desire within. Gods, he could listen to that sound forever.

Thea's hands shot into his hair, gripping hard while he lavished her with his tongue as though he had all the time in the world. He spread her open, gaining better access to suck on her clit and slowly sliding a finger inside her.

Thea writhed beneath him, her hips rising to his face,

demanding more. He loved how wet and ready for him she was, the tip of his cock damp with his own need for her.

'Wilder,' she panted. 'Please.'

He moved up her body, relishing the heady sensation of his hard length sliding through the wetness he'd created between her legs.

Thea reached for his cock, and he moaned as her hand wrapped around it, guiding him to her. He moaned louder still as his tip breached her entrance and he covered her body with his, needing that closeness, needing to kiss her, to breathe her in for as long as he could.

Wilder burned for her, his mouth finding hers desperately. He traced the luscious curve of her lips and she opened for him, allowing his tongue to brush against hers. As he kissed her deeply, thoroughly, he pushed further inside her.

They panted in unison, their desire heightening with every slow thrust, their hips arching to meet one another.

It was different this time. Slower, gentler; as though they were savouring every second of each other. Wilder did exactly that. He relished every point of contact, every silken touch of her skin, the way she clenched around him, her ankles crossed at his lower back.

Their usual rough, frenzied fucking was replaced with something more aligned with the moment: a slow and decadent worshipping of one another. He moved inside her with luxurious strokes, building their pleasure together, the drawn-out sensations utterly intoxicating.

Blazing-hot need coursed through Wilder as Thea reached between them and circled her clit. He could feel the brush of her knuckles against his abdomen as she played with herself and he moaned as his balls tightened, threatening to spill his climax deep inside her. Gods, he couldn't hold on much longer.

His love for her hit him anew, a force not even the Furies could contend with.

He sank even deeper, hitting that spot inside that had her crying out, his name a plea on her lips.

As they both reached the precipice, their eyes locked onto one another's, wide with longing and desperation. He slowed his movements, dragging out those final building moments.

'You asked me what I wanted?' he rasped, thrusting into her slowly, deeply. 'I want more than war stories and bloodshed. I want to build a life with you, Thea.'

At his words, a sob broke from her, her legs tightening around him.

And together, they came undone.

CHAPTER FORTY-TWO

THEA

T he following day, Thea and Wilder dressed for war.
Donning their armour and their weapons, they met
the others outside the Singing Hare, ready to fight. Thea
could feel the lightning at her fingertips, vying for her
attention, demanding to be unleashed upon their enemies.

Soon, she told herself. Soon she'd light up the sky with
her storms. She could almost taste the vengeance on her lips.
They'd taken the only home she'd ever known and turned it
into a cesspit for the vilest of monsters. They'd taken her
sister from her and changed her against her will. No matter
what happened on that battleground, she'd make sure they
paid dearly for it.

For the first time in her brief experience of battle, there
was no waiting. The time for strategy and plans was long
past, and the song of violence beckoned.

With their company assembled, it was Drue who
addressed them, clad in armour of Naarvian colours.

'Dratos, Talemir and Anya spent the morning moving our

forces from Aveum to the outer borders of Thezmarr. They're ready to fight,' she told them, her blue eyes fierce, her red-streaked hair braided down the side, just like Thea's. In fact…

Thea looked at all of them: Drue, Adrienne, Wren, Farissa… They all wore their hair in a side braid, just as she did – a nod to the women warriors beyond the Veil, and a nod to her, the woman Warsword among them. The gesture made her throat ache. She had dreamt of something like this, long ago.

'The braids look good,' she ventured.

'I had less to work with,' Anya said at her side, running a hand over her closely shaved scalp. 'Maybe I'll grow it out after this.'

'Don't,' Thea replied. 'It suits you.'

Anya gave a hoarse laugh. 'I always thought so… Are you ready?' she asked.

'As I'll ever be,' Thea admitted. 'Are you?'

Anya scanned the snow-covered woodlands beyond the tavern and breathed in the crisp air. 'I've been ready for a long time.' Her wings materialised at her back, her shadows unfurling from her. 'Shall I take you and Wren?'

Thea nodded, motioning for her sister to link hands with them.

'To Thezmarr?' Anya said.

'To Thezmarr,' Thea echoed.

The sisters landed close to the coast, just beyond the reach of the Bloodwoods, the briny sea air enveloping them, chasing away the remnants of Anya's shadows. In the distance, Thea could just make out the harsh lines of the fortress stretching into the grey sky.

'I've wanted to come back here for so long,' Anya murmured, her eyes locked on the spires. 'I never thought it would be like this...'

Thea didn't say anything, only moved a little closer to their eldest sister. She would never know the pain of being ripped away from family as Anya did, of never having a sense of home, but that didn't stop the sadness blooming in her chest. For Anya and all that she'd lost and suffered, and for the three of them, having been robbed of each other for so long. The Furies had a poor sense of humour, to unite them as the midrealms fell to pieces.

'Come. We should saddle up,' Anya said, already moving towards the treeline. There hadn't been enough shadow-touched left to move proper cavalry units from Aveum, but the frontlines, at least, had horses.

Quickly and quietly, their modest force gathered as dusk fell around the Bloodwoods. It was a fitting spot to prepare for war, surrounded by gnarled trees that bled the blood of warriors long dead, and whispered secrets with the rustle of their leaves.

'If the Warswords have a moment...?' Wren's request was quiet but firm.

Thea motioned to Wilder, who brought Torj, Vernich and Talemir to them beneath the low branches of a dying willow.

'I didn't have enough supplies to make these for everyone, but after what Wilder told us about the Scarlet Tower, I thought we'd best take precautions...'

Wren handed each of them a strange-looking pellet the

size of a thimble. Thea held it between her thumb and forefinger, studying it.

'Should you be captured,' Wren told them, 'bite down on it. It will release a lethal dose of Naarvian nightshade... The enemy will not have the opportunity to add you to their ranks.'

Thea stared at her sister, unsure whether to be impressed or terrified by her cool and calculated instructions.

'I suggest tucking it into the neck or shoulder piece of your armour. Warsword armour in particular has a specific place for such a thing.' Wren pointed it out on Talemir. 'If your hands are bound, you'll be able to free it from the patch with your mouth and still access it.' She turned to Thea. 'I know your armour isn't the same, so I made this...'

It was a patch of leather, which, with quick fingers, Wren loosely sewed into place where Thea could reach it with her teeth if need be.

As Thea slipped the poison pellet inside, she wondered if this would be how she left this world – by her own hand.

With the means to end their lives tucked away safely, the Warswords were the first to mount their horses, taking the lead and starting the march through the main Bloodwoods. They were to ride the Mourner's Trail for the last time, drawing the reapers' attention outwards, so that Kipp might utilise the lesser-known entrances to the fortress from within.

But as the trees closed in around them, Thea saw just how much poison had seeped into her former home. As they drew nearer, they saw vine blights strangling the ancient trees. The sight alone triggered a deep lance of pain in Thea's wrist. Her breath whistled between her teeth as she winced, the agony following the line of her scar.

Wilder's horse came up alongside hers. 'You alright?' he murmured, low enough for only her to hear.

Rubbing her wrist, she nodded. 'We've got bigger things to worry about.'

As they rode deeper into the Bloodwoods, the monsters' scent became pungent enough to make Thea gag, the smell of fresh earth long gone. The forest was a far cry from the one she remembered. The dark glades had been beautiful and mysterious once, the canopy lush, the leaf litter damp and sliding beneath her boots. But like everything else in the midrealms, the Bloodwoods were dying. No leaves peppered the trees' branches; no birds called from above. It was silent in a way it had never been before: the intake of breath before the last exhale.

It wasn't long before they came upon the Mourner's Trail – the only true way in and out of the fortress, the trees either side reaching over the road and joining in the middle, creating what was once a leafy tunnel, now just an archway of skeletal branches. There were no shadows, not yet, leaving the route clear for them to approach – a trap, or a tactic to cause unease and suspicion. But they had no choice, not with Kipp relying on them to draw the enemy's focus away from the fortress, and certainly not with the weight of the few catapults they'd managed to transport from Aveum.

The narrow, rocky path seemed smaller to Thea somehow. Two years ago she had followed the trail out of Thezmarr with Wilder at her side, heading for Delmira. She had never imagined returning here with an armed force at her back. She had fought to become a Warsword for so long, only to come to this point – to use her Furies-given abilities against the fortress that had raised her.

Now, the trail seemed to hum in Thea's presence, welcoming her home.

But it didn't feel or smell like home, not anymore.

The wind rustled the brittle branches of the trail, sweeping up any debris in its path and pulling them towards Thezmarr. Thea shifted in her saddle, glancing back at the force behind her.

Two hundred.

Two hundred men and women, a combination of shadow-touched, Guardians and common folk, all marched along the Mourner's Trail in her wake, and Thea knew without a doubt that soon enough, they would come to understand the road's name intimately.

As the fortress walls came into sight, Esyllt signalled for the catapults to be taken off-road. His expression was all hard lines and determination. 'They'll cause significant damage,' he said to Thea as he directed two soldiers and their cargo into the woods. 'But I'd sooner see it in ruins than in the talons of those monsters. Thezmarr has stood against them from the start.'

'We'll raze it to the ground before they can hold it another day, sir,' Thea told him.

The weapons master sat up straighter in his saddle. 'I always liked you, Zoltaire. Fucking terrible at cleaning armour, though,' he added as he found his place in the ranks once more.

The laugh that formed on Thea's lips died as a rider appeared ahead.

A lone figure atop a black mare – the leader of Harenth's royal guard, Captain Barker. Thea had only dealt with him once before, in Aveum, where he'd ushered Princess Jasira to safety after their trouble on the road. He drew the reins up short a few yards ahead, scanning those who stood before him.

'Some familiar faces,' he said, his eyes tracking across Thea, Cal, Kipp, Wilder, Torj and Vernich, widening as they landed on Talemir. Thea saw a flicker of fear in the captain's gaze before he gathered himself and spoke again, loudly enough for the back lines to hear. 'It does not have to end this way. You do not have to die today. Join me, and there is no need for you to perish at the foot of those walls. Join me and the ones you love need not be swallowed by the shadows.'

Thea urged her mare forward a few steps. 'And who are you to offer such clemency? We have your king in chains. Do you expect us to believe that you hold any sway over the monsters inside Thezmarr's gates?'

'I have influence —'

'We're done with people who have influence,' Talemir cut him off, giving Thea a subtle nod.

In a flurry of movement, she was at the captain's side, her blade a blur of silver sweeping through the air before it sliced through flesh, tendon and bone.

Captain Barker's head hit the road and rolled from the Mourner's Trail.

'One less monster to deal with,' Wilder commented, with a note of satisfaction.

Thea let her ruthless smile show as she pushed the man's still-twitching body from the saddle, watching it fall to the side and hit the ground with a thud. 'Looks like we've got another horse. Who needs one?'

With one enemy leader now dead, they marched across the final stretch of the Mourner's Trail until the thick stone walls and fortress gates were in full view. Tattered banners clung desperately to the towers, bearing the insignia of a guild that once protected the midrealms from darkness, now gripped in its shadows. All around the parapets, shadow wraiths were poised like watchful statues. The air was thick with their choking scent.

Somewhere behind Thea, she heard the battering ram being prepared, but no volley of enemy arrows came for them, no lashes of onyx power... Whoever was leading the defence from within Thezmarr's walls was allowing them this attack.

The battering ram collided with the gates, the impact shuddering through the ramparts and the ground below.

The long, heavy pole swung back and forth again, striking for a second time.

Stomach churning with unease, Thea looked down the frontlines, waiting for someone to speak, to rally the courage or foolhardy recklessness of those who were already doomed —

'Now's your chance, Princess,' Wilder murmured at her side. 'Told you that you might make a speech of your own one day...'

With the battering ram as her war drum, Thea surveyed their ranks. Sure enough, the eyes of the allied forces did not fall to Talemir Starling, nor to Anya, the Daughter of Darkness, and not to Wilder Hawthorne either. They looked to *her*.

A former child of Thezmarr, a girl turned warrior, Althea Nine Lives, the Shadow of Death, the wraith slayer. The storm-wielding Warsword. Althea Embervale.

Thea took a deep breath and lifted her chin, urging her mare forward so she could address the final fighting souls of the midrealms.

Unsheathing her sword, she projected her voice across their ranks. 'Today, we face a reckoning,' she called. 'I do not need to tell you that we are outnumbered, that our forces are outmatched, and that the shadows of annihilation loom large.'

The battering ram collided with the gates again, shaking the very foundations of the fortress.

'With the odds stacked against us in every way, this battle will test the very heart of us. But it is in these moments of dire peril that legends are born. It is battles like these that forge warriors with blood and steel. I stand before you now not as a Warsword, nor an heir of a kingdom, but as a sister of the sword. You may not know me well. You may not know me at all... But I know you.'

Thea braced herself.

'You are the true warriors of the midrealms – those who have been knocked down time and time again, only to rise up stronger than before. What those bastards behind these walls fail to comprehend, what they can never grasp, is the indomitable spirit that resides within each and every one of you. Together, we are a tempest that will rage. A storm that gathers must break, and by the Furies will we break upon them.'

The battering ram broke through the gates, splintering the iron-bound timber. It caved in with a roar.

Thea raised her blade and shouted her final words for all the world to hear. 'If this is to be our final stand, let us make it worthy of legend!'

CHAPTER FORTY-THREE

WILDER

The gates of Thezmarr had splintered apart, a sight Wilder had never thought he'd live to see. As Thea led the charge into the fortress, their horses' hooves thundering over the fallen gates, Malik's fighting words came back to him, as they always did: *Glory in death, immortality in legend.* It seemed a fitting motto, today of all days.

As they burst into the fortress, horror sank its claws into him. Around them, vine blights strangled the ivy across the walls, seeking out new hosts, creeping across the ground.

Thezmarr had been made into a lair: a deep, despairing lair, home to everything it had been created to fight against. Darkness had their home in its clutches, and the proof was harrowing.

Night had well and truly fallen and the moon hung low, shrouded in dark clouds and shadows, casting an ominous glow upon the battlefield and the masses of monsters before them. The ear-piercing wails of the howlers echoed as they banded together and hit the midrealms' unit in a wave. In seconds, Wilder was assaulted by the cacophony of battle – the clash of steel, the screams of their fighters, the haunting shrieks of the shadow wraiths that lay in wait within the walls. The creatures' acrid scent tangled with the sickly-sweet perfume of fear that clung to their own forces.

Wilder steered his stallion into the fray, the bitter taste of desperation coating his tongue. It was pandemonium. Shadows lashed out at them from the wraiths on the parapets above, while the howlers took advantage of the distraction, cleaving into their men with gut-wrenching screams.

Gripping his saddle with his thighs, Wilder unsheathed both swords and let his steel sing. He cut through the howlers like butter, one by one, not even deigning to watch as they fell onto the blood-slicked cobbles; he was already onto the next. As he fought, he could feel the pulse of evil in the fortress, an otherworldly malevolence echoing through the very fabric of the place – and yet he could see no reaper at the heart of the fray, no sire of darkness watching on from the turrets; only chaos and carnage.

In the centre of the courtyard, Thea, Vernich, Talemir and Drue were fighting back an onslaught of howlers, defending against those curling whips of power dredging nightmares to the surface. Their forces were splintered already, a great many dead, a great many more injured. By the entrance to the Great Hall, Anya, Dratos and Adrienne battled three wraiths who'd deigned to partake. Terrence flew overhead, aiming his talons at the monsters' eyes.

The fortress was overrun. And there was still no sign of the reapers.

'Where's Cal?' Wilder shouted at Torj, who was wielding

his war hammer to great effect, leaving a trail of bloodied pulp in his wake.

'Should be in position by now,' Torj said, slamming his hammer into the face of a howler with a sickening crack, blood spraying.

But when Wilder looked to the walls, where their archers were meant to be in place, there were only wraiths and their shadows.

'Fuck,' he muttered, scanning the raging turmoil. 'We need to get up there!'

Torj motioned towards one of the watchtowers. 'That way.'

As the battle raged on, the Bear Slayer and the Hand of Death carved a path through the enemy, their Naarvian steel creating a symphony of destruction and pain. Wilder relished the feeling of throats opening beneath his blade, the sound of the screams that pierced the air at his will. It was brutal and bloody, but also a rallying cry to their forces. Both he and Torj knew well enough that a show of strength could harden the resolve of broken warriors, and they needed all the resolve they could get.

At the foot of the tower, Wilder leapt from the saddle and started for the stone steps, Torj close behind. They should have seen the first volley of arrows by now, which meant that something was terribly wrong atop the walls.

Heart pounding, Wilder sprinted up the stairs, thrusting his swords into the soft bellies of the howlers in his path, cutting off a head, then a second one. They had to get to Cal, and fast.

The steps became slippery with blood, but determination grounded Wilder as he reached the door at the top. The fortress trembled, and he wondered what Thea and Anya were unleashing below. They'd agreed not to use storm magic until the reapers made themselves known, for they would come in force, and the storm wielders would need every ounce of lightning and thunder to fight back.

Throwing himself out onto the parapet, Wilder saw the problem.

Darkness billowed, and at the centre of the wall, Cal was strung up like an animal, shadows binding his wrists and ankles, another tendril curling around his throat. He was held in midair, his body fighting the onslaught of whatever nightmares the wraiths were forcing upon him. His mouth was wide open, screaming, but no sound came out.

With a shout, both Wilder and Torj surged for him.

Together, the Warswords cleaved through the shadows with their steel. A dozen images swarmed Wilder's mind – Malik, Talemir, Thea, all at the mercy of the reapers, all suffering. But he gritted his teeth and fought the visions back, just as he battled the lashing tendrils of obsidian, severing them and freeing Cal from their clutches.

The young Guardian fell, knees crunching on stone as he landed on all fours, gasping for air, tears streaming down his face.

Wilder whirled around, anticipating the wraiths descending at any second.

They didn't.

Instead, the shadows dissipated around them, revealing the remains of Cal's archery unit. Many were lifeless on the stones, their eyes frozen wide in shock, their mouths agape with silent screams. But there were a few in similar states to Cal, dry heaving, hands around their bruised throats.

'Everyone up,' Wilder ordered, twirling his blades. 'Cal,' he barked. 'On your feet.'

'Yes, sir,' he rasped. Eyes still streaming, Cal staggered upright, reaching for his bow. 'Archers!' he wheezed, his voice hoarse, broken. He shot Wilder an apologetic look. 'You may have to give the order.'

'That I can do,' Wilder said, turning to the handful of archers. 'Your men and women are dying down there! Nock!' he bellowed.

The men struggled to their feet, but did as ordered.

'Draw!'

Wilder scanned the parapet, horror dawning as he did. For as the shadows fell back, they revealed long spikes lining the walls, and impaled there...

Bile rose up the back of his throat, but he forced it down, forced his attention back to the trembling archers.

'Loose!' Wilder shouted.

The first volley of arrows rained down on the monsters below, their tips treated with sun orchid essence, bursts of gold exploding in the courtyard. Wilder prayed to the Furies that Cal and his comrades aimed true.

He lifted his sword, motioning to the new wave of howlers breaking into the courtyard. 'Again!' he roared. 'Nock... Draw... Loose!'

Screams echoed from below, and the metallic tang of blood drifted in the air.

Torj was moving towards the stairs. 'I'm going to see about the catapults. They should be raining fire upon this shithole by now.'

Wilder merely nodded and returned his attention to the archers. He desperately wanted to be down amid the fighting, but from the look on Cal's pale face and his lack of voice, they needed someone to rally them. Wilder only hoped they hadn't yet spotted the spikes... He made sure not to look himself, so that he didn't draw their attention that way. There were enough horrors below, let alone those that surrounded them.

'Nock!' he called again. 'Draw!'

He watched the archers do as he bid, their bowstrings pulled taut, their chests expanding.

'Loose!'

This time, when the arrows rained, so did rocks and flaming balls of twine, courtesy of the catapults beyond the walls. It seemed Torj had found them and taken them under his command, wreaking havoc upon the fortress that had once been their home. Glass shattered, and the thunderous roar of a turret crumbling echoed across the parapet.

'Take cover!' Wilder shouted to their own forces.

Fire and stone pummelled the fortress, and Wilder could take it no longer.

'Callahan.' He gripped the Guardian's shoulder, forcing Cal to meet his gaze. 'You're the Flaming fucking Arrow. These men are yours to command. Command them.'

Cal's expression hardened. 'Yes, sir.'

Wilder didn't wait. He sprinted once more for the stairs, hearing the echo of Cal's firm orders as he rushed to rejoin the fray.

The courtyard was a bloodbath.

And Thea was at the helm.

Wilder fought his way towards her, needing to be at her side amid so much death and destruction. He was assaulted from all directions, barely registering as a blow found its mark. With singular focus, he sliced through one howler after the next, parrying and stepping over the dead, both monster and human alike. Arrows littered the ground, and in the near distance, great plumes of smoke billowed from a blazing watchtower. From the courtyard perimeter, Wren and Farissa were throwing vials of weaponised powders and potions, glass shattering upon the enemy and dousing them with all manner of alchemical horrors.

When he reached Thea, she glanced at him, eyes wild as she swung her blade and beheaded a howler in one fell swoop.

'We need to find the reapers. We need to end this,' she shouted, thrusting her sword into the gut of another monster, splitting the creature from navel to nose, showering herself in black blood.

She didn't so much as flinch.

Back to back, they fought together, bodies of howlers piling up around them as they went. Wilder scanned the courtyard, looking for any sign of the reapers manipulating this whole bloodbath, but there was nothing. Only howlers and wraiths, vine blights and the odd arachne, hitting the midrealms' forces in brutal waves.

But with Thea at his side, hope began to bloom. Together, they were unstoppable, and they became a beacon for the others. He felt the change in the air, felt it as their unbroken resolve lifted their forces. All around them, the midrealms' soldiers rallied. Talemir, Anya, Drue and Dratos all moved with a resurgence of energy. They would not rest until the fortress was reclaimed, until the last howler, the last reaper was vanquished, until the wraiths were nothing but forgotten whispers in the wind —

Darkness erupted, threatening to send Wilder and Thea flying across the cobbles. Screams echoed from every direction, and the hope that had bloomed so fleetingly in

Wilder's chest was snuffed out. A barrage of emotions hit him, so hard that he staggered with the force of them, blinking back burning tears.

'What the fuck...?' Thea murmured beside him as the shadows receded, just enough to reveal the figure wielding them.

At the heart of all that darkness was Princess Jasira.

CHAPTER FORTY-FOUR

THEA

T hea stared at Princess Jasira, at the shadows pouring from her fingertips, at the wraiths standing guard either side, and at the enormous *rheguld reaper* looming at her back.

A daughter of darkness.

A strange tingling warmth spread through Thea's chest, unnatural, uneasy…

And then, she blinked as each piece of the puzzle clicked into place. She understood.

'Your father isn't the most powerful empath in history,' she said. 'You are.'

Jasira looked pleased. 'It's about time someone understood my worth. I always thought it would be you, storm wielder.'

Thea loosed a trembling breath, shadows pulsing everywhere. The battle around them slowed, and then ceased completely as Jasira reached out with black tendrils. The dark power danced around Thea, attempting to coax her magic to the surface.

Thea didn't take the bait, not yet. For there was only one reaper behind Jasira, and they needed all of them together for lightning to strike in the same place —

'Don't you like what I've done with the place?' Jasira asked lightly, her shadows directing Thea's gaze to the fortress walls.

With a flick of her wrist, the shadows up there receded, and Thea gasped as all around the perimeter, cruel spikes were revealed...

Adorned with the heads of those who worked in the fortress.

Thea could hardly breathe as she recognised the contorted face of Thezmarr's cook, the head healer, the groundskeeper.

She wanted to look away, to unsee it all: the missing eyes, the tears of blood staining sallow cheeks, the gaping mouths, the torn-out tongues.

From above, a flaming arrow flew for Jasira, but she deflected it with a shadow as though it were some slight inconvenience.

Thea couldn't believe it, *wouldn't* – even as she stared at the faces she'd grown up with. Madden, the stable master, and his apprentice Evander were there, their faces frozen in horror, iron spikes visible through their open mouths.

The strangled noise that escaped Thea was more animal than human as her gaze fell upon two more familiar faces.

'It wasn't hard to find out who mattered to you... Osiris was more than willing to question anyone and everyone,' Jasira said slowly. 'The Dancing Alchemists dance no more – they don't have bodies for that.'

Thea's stomach bottomed out, but it wasn't until she heard the broken cry from Wren that she knew it was true.

'Samra... Ida...' her sister whimpered at the gruesome sight of their friends' heads impaled on iron spikes.

'Why?' Thea croaked, tearing her eyes away from Sam and Ida, focusing on Jasira instead.

But Anya came forward, staring at the weapon in her hand and then at the princess in a daze. 'It was you...' she said, voice faint. 'It was you wielding this scythe all those years ago. You brought the darkness down on Thezmarr. Artos framed me... to save *you*.'

'I was stronger than him, even then,' Jasira told them, her shadows flickering. 'He developed a taste for power before I was born, of course... Delmira, Naarva, all succumbing to his magic, turning on one another from within. But my father lacked imagination, and he didn't understand... For years he has been trying to break free of my control, but my power eclipsed his early on. This is my destiny. I am the Daughter of Darkness that was prophesied. I will bring the dawn of fire and blood.'

The wraiths leashed to Jasira grew restless and Thea's magic crackled beneath her skin, surging through her veins. She smelt rain in the air, and took a step closer to both her sisters, feeling their magic rolling off them as well.

Jasira smiled at the show of unity. 'I have been waiting for this for a long time...'

The princess was no warrior, but she didn't need to be – she was the most powerful empath in history, and with one flick of her hand, she had the midrealms' forces in her thrall. Thea gaped at the horrific scene before her as shieldbearers and Guardians started to scream.

There was no need for Jasira to unleash the wraiths. She only needed to unleash herself.

Heart racing, Thea scanned their battered units, their

faces etched in terror, some even turning their own blades on themselves —

'No!' she shouted, surging for a Guardian who did exactly that. She was too late. His dagger pierced flesh and bone, blood flowing freely from the wound. He was dead in seconds.

Jasira flooded their allies with a tidal wave of unbearable emotion. Thea felt it herself, a bursting sensation in her chest, as though it were all too much and she couldn't stand the pressure of it.

With a cry, lightning shot from her fingertips, shedding Jasira's hold on her.

Thea looked to her sisters – only for the reaper at the princess' back to lunge for her. Talons ravaged her arm and she fell back, slipping in the blood on the cobbles. But with a kick of her legs, she was up on her feet again, sword raised.

'Come on then, you piece of filth,' she hissed, twirling her blade in invitation. 'Your heart can join all the rest I've carved out.'

She threw herself at the monster, the rest of the world fading away as she parried and sidestepped its slashing claws, as she cut through the shadows surging for her. She looked at the vile thing in disgust, the stench of it filling her nostrils. Its horns curled over its head like a ram's, its leathery skin no more than a grotesque barrier between her blade and its heart.

The creature hissed, sending a wave of onyx power for her. For a moment, she was back in the Great Rite, fighting the possessed version of Wilder, cutting through her own wrist with Malik's dagger. She was watching Wren and Cal and Kipp choke on shadow. Each assault was like a knife to the gut, threatening to take her legs out from under her.

But Thea's lightning answered her call, surging forth in brilliant white bolts, slashing through the darkness. As her magic hit the monster, she felt Jasira's magic within it – for the Daughter of Darkness was controlling the creatures with her empath abilities, feeding into their more primal emotions, but leashing them to her will all the same.

Thea blasted the reaper back, watching as Wilder leapt into the air and plunged his swords into the creature's sinewy chest, black blood spurting. With a roar, he ripped out its heart and threw it at Jasira's feet.

Around them, several wraiths disintegrated where they stood, clearly the sired kin to the reaper.

But Jasira just laughed. 'There are plenty more where he came from, Warsword.'

'And they'll all meet the same fate,' Thea said, squaring her shoulders.

Jasira gave a dark smile and raised her hands.

Wraiths burst from the fortress, hissing and swiping their talons at the few remaining midrealms units.

'To me!' Thea cried. 'Form the lines!'

Those who heard rallied to her, but Jasira turned her gaze upon Talemir Starling, her shadows coiling and ready to strike.

'Shadow Prince,' she said, her icy tone cutting through the mayhem. 'You've been a problem. When I'm through with you, you won't even recognise that little son of yours.'

Talemir's expression transformed into one of savage rage – and Thea watched in pure terror as he lunged for the Daughter of Darkness, leaving his side exposed.

CHAPTER FORTY-FIVE

WILDER

Wilder didn't think; he simply moved. One moment he was standing atop the reaper's corpse, and the next he was throwing himself in front of those tendrils of power, blocking their path to Talemir with his own body.

The pain lanced through him like a white-hot blade from the forge, singular and agonising. He hit the cobblestones and rolled. But Wilder had suffered enough shadow magic to force himself back up, brandishing his swords at the true master of darkness.

He didn't glance back to see if Talemir was alright. He only stared the princess down, bracing himself.

When darkness came for him, he was ready.

Lash after lash he deflected, cleaving through the power and closing the gap between him and Jasira.

'Did you like the tower, Warsword?' she taunted from the safety of her shadows, pummelling him with more of the same nightmares and visions he always saw. 'My father put you there at my behest. I wanted to see what it took to break a warrior like you.'

'There's no breaking a warrior like me,' he said. 'And all you did by putting me in that prison was make me stronger.'

In his peripheral vision, he saw a flash of lightning. The sight of Thea's magic fuelled him. He cut through Jasira's next lash of shadow with so much force that she was sent reeling back with a cry.

He made to run her through with his blade, but more wraiths flooded the fortress, a force of flapping wings blocking out the moon.

The tumult of battle ensued and Wilder was nearly overcome with the jostling bodies and swinging blades. But suddenly Talemir was at his side.

'You know I had her,' the Shadow Prince growled.

'Sure you did,' Wilder replied, signalling to Cal and his handful of men on the wall as Wilder himself made for a swarm of wraiths surrounding the Embervale sisters.

Fire arrows lit up the sky, and the shrieks of wraiths filled the air once more.

There was a deafening cry, and a fresh force of midrealms men and women burst from the fortress, and from the cellar grate that flung open amid the cobbles. They charged into the fray, blades raised and shouts of vengeance on their lips, with Kipp in the lead. It wasn't just warriors, but tavern patrons too, plus Albert, Marise and Everard, all brandishing swords of their own, throwing themselves at the enemy, their grit just about making up for their lack of finesse —

Thunder rolled overhead, and the scent of rain filled the air.

Anya and Thea were at the heart of the chaos, each of them calling to their storms, lightning and wind whipping through the night around them. But where was Wren?

Panting, Wilder spotted the youngest Embervale on the steps of the fortress, Farissa at her side. Both women launched small round bottles filled with alchemical concoctions and sun orchid essence, immobilising entire units with bursts of gold. He remembered Wren suggesting that they thicken the substances to an oil-like consistency so that it stuck to the enemy and wasn't easily washed off – it was working.

With Talemir at his side, Wilder slayed wraith after wraith, howler after howler, his Furies-given stamina holding strong.

'We need to find the reapers,' he shouted to Tal. 'Otherwise it's all for nothing.'

'And Jasira —' Talemir pointed with his sword to where the princess had fallen, but there was no sign of her.

'Fuck,' Wilder muttered, his heart sinking as he spotted the clouded blue eyes pinning them from the surrounding walls. 'I think we found the reapers.'

There were more of them than Wilder could count, and even with the sun orchid essence coating the regular steel weaponry of their forces, he knew it wasn't enough.

'Thea!' he shouted over the pandemonium.

Her head whipped around, eyes latching onto him instantly. Then her gaze landed on the reapers, her jaw clenching at the sight.

'Furies fucking save us,' Talemir breathed beside him, wiping the perspiration from his brow.

'The Furies won't do a fucking thing,' Wilder told him. 'But the Embervale sisters might.'

He motioned to where Thea and Anya had reached Wren across the battlefield, the three of them standing shoulder to shoulder as they surveyed the host of reapers now at their door.

Together, they summoned the storm.

CHAPTER FORTY-SIX

THEA

At long last, Thea wielded her ultimate weapon. Amid the howling darkness, she stood tall with her sisters. Fate had robbed them of a shared history, of the chance to know one another as Delmirian heirs, but it had not stopped them uniting. It had not stopped them forging their bonds anew.

She was struck by an image of the three Furies: Iseldra, Morwynn and Valdara, standing side by side as the Embervales did now.

As Thea's lightning sang within, ready to be unleashed upon the world of shadow, so too did Wren's and Anya's. In a blinding flash, their magic linked together. It was like different notes from the same song intertwining, each sister's magic subtly different but forging together in harmony.

Thunder cracked through the sky, echoing off the stone, causing the ground beneath Thea's boots to tremble, loose rock coming away from the fortress walls. Magic flowed through her veins, and she felt its likeness thrumming from her sisters either side of her as they conjured tempests from within, and summoned those beyond the borders of Thezmarr. Above, the clouds opened up and a downpour began, rain pelting the world in hard, sideways sheets. Around them, the wind picked up, tearing at their hair and clothes, gaining momentum as each sister dug deep for that well of power.

'Now,' Anya murmured, just loud enough for Thea and Wren to hear.

Their hands shot out, and the tempest broke.

More thunder erupted as lightning crackled at their fingertips.

To Thea, the rest of the battle had faded away – there were only the reapers, who seemed to lick their lips at the taste of the Delmirians' power. But they did not scare Thea, not with her sisters at her sides and her lightning blasting through the air towards the monsters, illuminating the darkness with blinding brilliance. The rain pelted her skin, but she revelled in its song, its scent, washing away the creatures' acrid stench as she flung her hands out, directing her lightning straight at the host of reapers.

Their screams filled the air.

Thea and her sisters summoned a vortex of wind, the gale sweeping away an onslaught of shadows that came for them.

With a determined shout, Thea filled the rain with a current of energy and blasted the first line of reapers. Their bodies went flying from the wall, hitting the stone below with a crack, the Warswords lunging for them to finish them off.

Anya was drawing all three storm wielders' power together, and it was unlike anything Thea had ever experienced. The storm roiled in her chest, joining forces with her sisters', the chaos intensifying as more clouds rolled in and thunder roared above them.

Together, they shot bolts of lightning straight for the next line of reapers, the crackling energy searing their shadows and making them writhe in agony. The force of it was intoxicating; the raw power of nature combined with the magic surging through her entire being. Thea felt it in every fingertip, every toe, deep in her bones. Rain came down in a torrent and she tasted it on her lips before she unleashed another colossal fork of lightning, bringing it down from the black sky above and striking another reaper with her unrelenting fury. Sparks flew, and even in the downpour, Thezmarr caught alight, fire blazing to life on the walls.

Enraptured, she watched as the storm swallowed lashes of shadow, as the reapers on the perimeter retreated —

A clouded blue gaze bored into hers and she didn't have time to cry out, to take so much as a breath before the monster lunged for her.

Caught up in the frenzy of their joint storm, Thea faltered.

Not even all the Furies-given strength in the midrealms could have stopped the blow. A punch of obsidian, straight to the chest, sent her flying. Thea was ripped from the link between her and her sisters, the abrupt, searing pain of it stealing the air from her lungs, her eyes streaming tears. Limbs flailing, she was brutally thrown skyward, up onto a parapet. She hit the stones hard, the back of her head colliding with the rubble of the ruined fortress wall. She felt the trickle of blood almost instantly, at the nape of her neck and down her spine beneath her armour.

With pain blooming all over, her magic seemed to choke. She reached for it, hoping she might cauterise her wounds as she'd done in the Great Rite, but something forced her power down.

Dazed, she tried to get to her feet, but something pinned her back into the rubble —

A reaper.

The jagged tips of its talons hovered across the skin just over her heart.

And time slowed.

This is it, Thea realised. *This is how I die.*

She had waited twenty-seven years for this moment, and as promised, Fate had come for her. There was no Aveum springwater to save her this time, no tricks up her sleeve. Only storms and darkness.

Thea tasted blood on her tongue. She fought to get enough air into her lungs, the reaper's talons piercing deeper —

And then the pressure was gone.

The monster was thrown back from her, cords of lightning wrapping around its throat and dragging it across the ruined courtyard.

The scent of rosewood and leather enveloped Thea, and suddenly Wilder was at her side.

She met his silver gaze sadly, hating the devastation she found there. 'If this is it...' she croaked, blood leaking from the corner of her mouth. 'Then know that I loved you fiercely. Every second was worth it. You were worth it —'

Thea choked on a sob as all that she would miss flashed before her. Her life with Wilder: chasing after her Tverrian stallion with him through the rolling hills, passionate nights by the campfire, *I love you* whispered in the quiet breaths between the rest. She would never see Wren become a master alchemist, nor Cal become a Warsword. She wouldn't have another sour mead with Kipp, nor a —

'Don't you dare.' Wilder pulled her to his armoured chest. 'Don't you dare give up.' The words were an echo of ones he'd said before, in the Bloodwoods after her shieldbearer initiation test. 'I won't let you,' he told her. 'I won't let you go.'

Thea wanted to touch his face, to trace his jaw one last time, to bring his mouth to hers. But her hands were clumsy.

Wilder's arms trembled around her. 'We said after you went to Aveum that we'd never part again. I mean to uphold that vow.'

Thea felt cold. She didn't know if it was the wound at the back of her head, or the dark marks that bled over her heart.

Wilder rested his forehead against hers, tears spilling down his handsome face, creating tracks through the blood and grit. 'Please.'

'I'm sorry —' Her voice broke. 'I didn't want to leave you. I didn't want to die, not yet.'

A shadow cast over them both, a figure emerging on the parapet. 'You're not the one who's going to die,' Anya said, crouching at Thea's side. 'Chew this.'

She shoved something into Thea's mouth. When Thea bit down, she recognised the bitter taste.

Dried iruseed. The same herb Wilder had given her when she'd nearly bled to death in the broom closet courtesy of Sebastos Barlowe. It worked the same as it had then, her senses prickling back to life. The pain was still there, but she was conscious, alert, her hands able to move as she directed.

Beside her, Wilder's breathing was ragged. 'Fuck,' he

muttered, pressing a hard kiss to her temple. 'Don't ever do that to me again.'

But Thea's gaze drifted to Anya, something about her words niggling at Thea. 'Who's going to die?' she rasped. 'You said I'm not the one who's dying... So who is?'

Anya grimaced, her hand reaching for something.

She pulled Thea's fate stone from beneath her armour, snapping the knotted leather cord as she took it between her fingers. 'This was never yours.'

Thea could only stare.

'You had it in your hands when we arrived here. It used to stop you crying. But it was mine. It was always mine. When I came back to Thezmarr to see you and Wren, and I said I didn't speak to you? I lied. I begged you to remember me. And then I gave you the stone for good.'

Remember me.

The words from the seer came back to her, along with the press of the fate stone in her palm as a child.

Remember me.

A flash of flower necklaces in tiny hands.

Remember me.

Throwing the cursed thing out to sea, only to find it on Wilder's side table hours later.

Remember me.

Her blood running cold as she scanned the forest floor in Notos for the piece of jade she'd torn from her neck and cast aside.

'Here,' Cal had said, offering an outstretched hand. And there it had been: the pale green stone that had haunted Thea her whole life.

Remember me.

'You gonna ask me about it?' she had prompted Anya in the

Singing Hare, taking the piece of jade between her fingers and rubbing her thumb along its edges.

'I don't think I want to... Those things never did anyone any good.'

Remember me.

Thea watched as Anya's fingers wrapped around the fate stone now. A seer hadn't whispered those words to her.

Her sister had.

Her older sister, by ten months.

Twenty-seven wasn't just her age. It was Anya's as well.

As Thea's senses came back to her, she gaped at the piece of jade in her sister's hands. For years she had worn that stone around her neck like a curse. For her whole life she'd flung herself into danger, believing that she wouldn't die.

And she wouldn't. Not by fate's hand. Not today.

For the stone wasn't hers.

It was Anya's.

The reality of that realisation hit her harder than any blow.

'Anya,' she croaked, reaching for her sister. But Anya's attention snagged on something – *someone* – else, on the battlefield below.

Fastening the fate stone around her neck, Anya's eyes were trained on the frenzy beneath them, tracking a hooded man scurrying across the ruins. He clutched a sword to his chest but did not use it, did not assist any of their warriors in need.

Fury blazed over Anya's expression as she too realised what Thea had mere seconds ago. Whoever it was was fleeing the fortress, making for the shattered gates —

A feral smile broke across Anya's scarred face as darkness

unfurled from her palms and her membranous wings flared open at her back.

With the iruseed flowing through Thea, her wound was forgotten. She scrambled to her feet, just as Anya dived from the parapet.

She was a vision of onyx glory, of formidable power. And at her command, a great gust of wind swept through the fortress, tangling in the wraiths' shadows, lightning sparking off the stones.

Anya's wings beat furiously, and she landed before the figure below, stopping him in his tracks.

Thea and Wilder darted from the parapet, leaping over the rubble and racing to reach Anya's side. For this was no ordinary deserter.

Anya stared at him, blood dripping from her scythe. 'Do you recognise me, *Guild Master?*'

Thea gaped. Though she'd listened to the reports of Osiris' part in the fall of Thezmarr, it was another thing to watch it unfold before her, another thing entirely to see the man who had run the guild fleeing from its burning shell.

Osiris' eyes narrowed as he took in Anya's shaved head and scar. 'Should I?'

Anya gave a dark laugh. 'I suppose all little girls look the same to you when they're disposable... Just as you are now.'

Osiris scrambled backward, only to hit the wall of Wilder's chest, blocking him in to face his fate.

Amusement laced with malice lined Anya's features.

'I have waited for this for a long time, Guild Master. Do not think it will be over quickly.'

With a flick of her wrist, her scythe slashed across Osiris' cheek, leaving a line of blood in its wake. He cried out, his hand flying to the cut.

'Save your strength,' Anya said. 'There will be many more...'

Thea watched on in horror as her sister painted her vengeance upon the former Guild Master. A slice down his face that mirrored her own scar. Then another.

Osiris screamed, falling to his knees, holding his hands out. 'Please. I beg for mercy!'

'What mercy did you show me all those years ago? What mercy did you show the poor souls that you and Artos turned into monsters?' Anya gave a broken laugh. 'Mercy? You'll find none here —'

But just as Anya raised her scythe again, a reaper's lash of power struck her from behind, hard and fast as a blade.

Blood sprayed. Lightning shot from her fingertips, searing her attacker in a blaze of brilliant white light, but she staggered.

Not believing her eyes, Thea lurched forward, panic clawing at her insides.

Osiris bolted away as Anya collapsed. Thea scrambled for her, Wilder's hand on her shoulder. All around them, Thezmarr was burning in the wake of her sister's lightning.

With a sob, Thea pulled Anya into her lap, cradling her there as blood trickled from the corner of her mouth and pulsed at a deep open wound in her side.

'I will leave this world worse than I found it,' Anya rasped, a tear tracking down her face.

'No —'

'You can't lie to a dying woman,' Anya said weakly. 'Perhaps the gods will see fit that this dawn of fire and blood will wipe the slate clean. They will start anew when I'm gone...' She wheezed, her breath rattling in her chest as she gave a dark laugh. 'If I were them, I wouldn't have the stomach for it. Not after what we've done to this place...'

'Just hold on,' Thea begged, rocking her sister and looking around for someone, anyone, who could help.

'Thea,' Anya murmured. 'It's over. Finally, it's over.'

Thea's own face was wet with tears as she watched Anya's face drain of colour. 'I don't want you to go.'

'I'd stay if I could.'

The reality of her sister's wounds hit her hard. It was Kipp all over again, only this time, there was no vial of Aveum springwater to save her. Thea could feel Death's shadow creeping nearer. She struggled to swallow.

'Don't leave like this, without any hope for the world.'

'I wanted to scorch the earth with my fury,' Anya croaked, trying to shake her head. 'But there's hope... Just not with me.' Anya's tired eyes stared at Thea meaningfully, and then flicked to Wren, who was surging towards them.

Anya breathed out, the sound ragged and pained.

She did not inhale.

With a cry, Wren fell to her knees beside Thea, just as the light left their sister's eyes.

'No,' she pleaded. 'Anya, wake up.' Wren shook her by the shoulders, but her body was limp, her gaze blank.

'She's gone, Wren,' Thea told her, passing a hand over her sister's face to close her eyes and gently removing the fate stone from Anya's grasp. 'It was hers,' she said. 'This never belonged to me.'

Wren didn't seem to register her words, and Thea wasn't sure she had either. She knew distantly that Anya had lied to her by omission. For twenty-seven years Thea had thought that the stone was her burden to bear, that death was lying in wait for her, and she'd acted accordingly.

HELEN SCHEUERER

'All those risks,' she whimpered, horrified at her own behaviour. 'All that recklessness…'

'You truly were Althea Nine Lives, then,' Wren said quietly, clutching their sister's lifeless hands.

For a moment, unimaginable anger coursed through Thea, all directed at their dead sister. Anya had let Thea believe she was not long for this world, she had —

But the anger morphed into something deeper, something far more painful than rage.

Grief.

Thea's chest was too tight. A vice-like grip squeezed her heart and wouldn't loosen. She couldn't judge Anya for how she'd chosen to live her life, not when she was still here and Anya was not.

Thea didn't bother to wipe the tears as they rolled down her cheeks, as she placed Anya's scythe in her hand and across her chest, like the warrior she was.

'I will etch your name upon the stone swords of the Furies,' she vowed. 'You were just as much a hero as any Thezmarrian. You defended the midrealms until your last breath.'

Wren placed her own hand over Thea's.

They both gasped —

For Anya's magic was leaving her body.

And surging directly into them.

Storm magic filled Thea's whole body. There was not an inch of her that wasn't humming with lightning. From the blazing look in Wren's eyes, she felt the same.

Audra had been wrong. Transferring power *was* possible.

Anya had left them one last gift.

CHAPTER FORTY-SEVEN

THEA

Thea's whole body trembled with the force of the raw power as she stood. Wren did the same beside her, the pair of them standing over Anya's body as her magic wove its way into the very fabric of their own.

Something unseen tugged at the corner of Thea's senses, and she moved on instinct, conjuring a vibrant bolt of lightning at her fingertips and hurling it into the dark —

A scream echoed off the walls and a reaper staggered forward, only to be hit with another bolt, this time by Wren's hand.

The monster lurched towards them, and Thea was *glad*. Her magic surged: lightning, wind and rain swirling into a fiery vortex that she sent hurtling towards the reaper, right for its heart. The air around her and Wren crackled, and they speared the creature with bolt after bolt of pure energy.

They burned out its dark heart, but it wasn't enough – not for Thea, and by the look in Wren's eyes, not for her either. With lightning and thunder they would avenge Anya, and they would bring the fucking reapers and their ilk to their knees.

As though Thea had voiced the challenge aloud, a fresh wave of howlers, wraiths and arachnes swarmed the broken gates and scaled the walls of Thezmarr.

'Gods,' Wren muttered in disbelief. 'Even with storm magic, we...'

'We won't last,' Thea finished for her, looking to where Wilder, Talemir, Torj, Vernich, Drue, Adrienne and Dratos all fought at the heart of the courtyard. They were exhausted, even those with Furies-given strength.

Thea scanned the grounds, looking for something – anything – that might help. Cal was on the wall with his archers, but there were only a handful of them now, and judging by the intervals between arrows, they didn't have many left.

'Wren.' Thea turned to her sister. 'Gather as many arrows from the fallen as you can. Take them up to Cal. Blast any enemy with lightning as you go.'

'Shouldn't we stay together?'

'I'll find you again, but right now, we need Cal guarding us from above, and if he doesn't have —'

'Find me,' Wren cut her off, and started wrenching arrows from the corpses around them.

Beyond the fortress walls, by Thezmarr's cliffs, darkness gathered. It loomed low in the sky, an otherworldly presence that made Thea's skin crawl. There had been no sign of Jasira since her declarations, nor had they faced all the *rheguld reapers* at the princess' disposal. Tearing her eyes away from the shadows on the cliffs, Thea was willing to bet that was where they were. That desolate place at the edge of the world was where all these fucking monsters were pouring from.

She fought her way to Wilder and the others, throwing bolts of lightning as she moved. When she reached them, she realised there was someone missing.

'Where's Kipp?' she shouted above the chaos, driving her blade into a howler's gut and kicking it away to free her sword. Her limbs were heavy with exhaustion, and her chest ached for Anya, whose body lay amid the wreckage. It didn't feel real.

'Haven't seen him,' Vernich replied as he slit the throat of a wraith and left Drue to cut out its heart.

Panting, Thea turned to Torj, but the Bear Slayer shook his head.

'I can't remember the last time —'

But he was cut off as an arachne leapt from the walls, its fangs aimed right for him. He ducked and rolled just in time, as Thea threw a ball of lightning at its face.

The monster didn't even shriek. Its body simply spasmed as the lightning burned it from the inside out and it collapsed in a heap atop the rest of the carnage.

Thea twirled her blade and fell into the dance of death. Slice, thrust, parry, slice, thrust, parry. But it didn't matter how many monsters she slayed – more spilt across the walls and through the gates, as though their numbers were endless, as though their units were being replenished by the second. Wraiths blocked out the sliver of moonlight, charging from that billowing cloud of black on the cliffs.

Wilder's gaze met hers, and she saw the sadness there. As more and more monsters swept into the courtyard and the allies' strength flagged, she heard the unified intake of breath from her friends. This was it; it truly was to be their final stand.

Had they made it worthy of legend? She didn't know, not anymore.

No amount of lightning could save them from this assault. They had done all they could.

And they had failed.

The scent of burnt hair was nearly choking, and the hissing of the attacking creatures set Thea's teeth on edge, even as she raised her blade again, her arms aching. Darkness swept across the fortress in a heavy fog —

A horn blasted through it, echoing off the remaining walls and rubble, followed by the thundering sound of hundreds of hooves.

'What the fuck...' Thea craned her neck, blood roaring in her ears.

The riders bore no sigil she recognised, their armour foreign and strange to her. More of Jasira's forces from beyond the Veil? Her throat constricted as she saw their flag dancing in the savage winds. She didn't know it.

Clutching her sword so hard her knuckles threatened to split, Thea dug deep. She could rally her power once more, enough to give the allies a fighting chance against the fresh wave of enemy forces spilling into Thezmarr. Storm magic gathered beneath her skin, surging to her fingertips, ready to be weaponised once more —

Horses flooded the courtyard, breaking through the deluge of shadow, their riders wearing full armour, their swords gleaming in the flickering light of the moon.

Thea whirled around, trying once again to find a banner she could recognise, a marker of some kind as the warriors stormed towards the monsters, shouts of triumph and determination on their lips as they cleaved through the enemy.

And then, Thea saw her at the helm.

Audra.

With a warrior's cry, the older woman raised her blade and split a howler in two, blood spattering across her pristine armour and shield.

A strangled sound escaped Thea. Audra was here, and she had brought the former women warriors of Thezmarr with her. They moved as one unified, disciplined unit, a force to be reckoned with. Thea gaped as Audra led her army in an assault on the first line of monsters, beating them back, slicing them open, trampling them beneath warhorses.

A fresh burst of lightning coursed through Thea as she witnessed history in the making. Here, in the face of unending darkness, the laws of old men meant nothing. Their words and rulings held no weight.

At the sight of their new allies, the remaining Warswords, the shadow-touched and their comrades rallied, gathering together. With another bone-chilling battle cry, Audra raised her sword and led the charge from the perimeter, the army of women warriors at her back.

Thea joined the fray, and from above, Cal rained arrows down on the enemy charging at them, fire bursting to life before them. Thea became one with the force of women, charging their steel with her lightning, blasting monsters from their path —

Vines shot out from the ground and the surrounding rubble.

Screams of agony pierced the air.

The vine blight roared to life, its arms surging forward for new hosts. Thea's heart leapt into her throat. Another wraith advanced on Audra. Without thinking, Thea let the jewelled hilt of her *ceremonial* dagger leave her fingertips in a blur of silver. She watched as it soared through the air, spiralling towards Audra —

It embedded in the monster's face, mere inches from the former librarian, who didn't hesitate. She wrenched the weapon from the wound and grinned wildly as the creature disintegrated before their very eyes.

Audra's warriors had seen it too, and looked from their fearless leader to Thea, understanding something that she herself did not.

Audra fought her way to Thea's side and handed the jewelled dagger back. 'You're not done with this,' she said.

Bewildered, Thea took it and sheathed it at her belt, just as a swell of howlers came forth.

The women warriors rallied, not to Audra, but to Thea.

'Shield wall!' she bellowed over the mayhem, praying to the Furies that the women would —

Metal flashed in Thea's peripheral vision, followed by countless rhythmic thuds and the scrape of steel.

Dozens of shields slid into place around her, one after the other.

And across the blood-soaked battlefield, an impenetrable wall of steel formed.

'Brace,' Thea cried, lightning surging at her fingertips as she charged the metal with her power. 'On my count, raise and bring them down *hard.*'

No one questioned her. No one flinched at the magic pouring from her and into those shields.

'Raise!' she shouted.

The wall lifted as one.

'Down!' she cried.

As the shield wall hit the bloody ground, lightning rushed across it in a wave, and obliterated the row of monsters in its path.

A triumphant cheer echoed down the line of women warriors, someone even clapping Thea on the back.

'Someone's learnt a thing or two,' Audra said, leaping down from her horse and surveying the piles of monster corpses.

'Anya's dead,' Thea blurted, the words sounding foreign on her tongue. 'The true Daughter of Darkness was Jasira, Audra. It was Jasira all along —'

Thea didn't realise how much she was shaking, not until Audra gripped her shoulder and steadied her. 'We are all daughters of darkness, Thea. We were born into a world of it, a place that would dictate the way in which we defend ourselves, the way we live our lives. No more. That world is no longer. And the next one will be what we make it.'

Audra's words washed over Thea like a wave, and her former warden gave her a nod before throwing herself back into the fighting.

Thea took a breath, and found her magic waiting, a new surge of energy, a new purpose coursing through her.

And then, with bolts of lightning like spears in her hands, she unleashed herself upon the monsters.

CHAPTER FORTY-EIGHT

WILDER

Lightning blazed across the battleground, and Thea brought wraiths and howlers to their knees. In his peripheral vision, Wilder watched her. She was power incarnate, a tempest personified, a Warsword of the highest calibre, and gods, he loved her.

When all this was over, he would tell her. He would tell her a thousand times over and then a thousand times more. He'd ask her to be his wife, traditions be damned.

But there was no time for that now. He thrust his blade into another howler, fighting the fatigue that had long ago latched onto his bones. They had been fighting for hours. Were it not for the billowing darkness in the sky, he might have wondered if dawn had come and gone.

He faltered. The darkness was amassing at the cliffs beyond the fortress, rising into the sky, seeming to flourish from a point near Thezmarr's border...

'Tal!' Wilder shouted, fighting his way towards his former mentor. 'Tal!'

Talemir looked around madly before he clapped eyes on Wilder motioning to the gathering shadows on the horizon.

'Can you and Dratos scout it?' Wilder called out, ramming the pommel of his sword into a howler's nose before slicing his second blade across its gut, rotten intestines spilling out.

With a whistle, Talemir signalled to Dratos across the battlefield.

'Feel free to take out as many wraiths as possible on the way,' Wilder added, as the two shadow-touched warriors spread their wings and launched themselves skyward.

Not wasting another moment, Wilder forged a path through the fighting to the entrance of the fortress. Monsters were still spilling from within, and he meant to put a stop to it. He left a trail of corpses in his wake as he headed to the Great Hall, before stopping in his tracks.

It was a husk.

At the head of the hall stood the Three Furies – imposing stone carvings of the three mighty weapons brandished by the original Warswords. Anchored to the ground, the sculptures reached up to the ceiling, where the hilts pierced through the rafters and into the night sky. Only now, they were wrapped in slithering shadows. And where crackling fires had once blazed in the hearths of the hall and tables had seated great warriors, there was a raging whirlpool of darkness. With shadows rippling from the thick stone pavers, a portal yawned wide, monsters pouring forth from its depths.

What had Kipp called the hall? The heart of their operation?

'Fuck,' Wilder muttered.

'Hawthorne!'

He whirled around to see the strategist in question at the doorway.

'Get out of here,' Kipp panted. 'I've got it covered!'

Wilder was already moving towards him. 'What do you mean?'

'Wren gave me something – we're going to blow up the chambers below.'

'Esyllt said —'

'Our dear weapons master had a change of heart,' Kipp replied.

Wilder nodded. 'Bring it down. Like you said. Bring the whole thing down,' he rasped, shaking his head in disbelief at the sight. The darkness was already desecrating the stone swords and everything they stood for.

'Exactly!' Kipp said. 'As soon as you get the fuck out of the way.'

Wilder gripped the strategist's shoulder. 'Don't die again.'

'Trying not to,' Kipp muttered, practically shoving him from the hall.

Wilder left Kipp to his explosions, and sprinted back to the courtyard – only to skid to a stop in shock.

A vortex of dark magic had opened up in the heart of the fray, sucking in monsters, men and women alike, their screams silenced as they disappeared into the gaping black hole.

It was an even larger portal than the one Wilder had just seen. Audra and her army were battling the wraiths that poured from the abyss, but nothing prepared Wilder for what he saw next. A *rheguld reaper* – the largest he had ever seen, its sinewy flesh covered in miniature wraiths that crawled across him like spiders.

A wave of nausea hit Wilder at the sight, but he forced

himself forward, swords raised, ready to slash and carve until he could no more —

But the reaper lashed out with talons and shadow, raining smaller wraiths down on the field below, a sickening wave of darkness and violence taking hold.

Panic seized Wilder's chest in a cruel fist as he was overcome, swarmed by dozens and dozens of wraiths, their talons scraping over his armour, cutting into his exposed flesh. He barely felt it. Not as the *rheguld reaper* stalked towards Thea, who was similarly overcome, fighting back an onslaught of wraiths and reapers, blood dripping down her face.

'Thea!' Wilder shouted, but he was too far away, too overwhelmed —

A deep warrior cry filled the air. Wilder's gaze snapped up to see Torj leap from the surrounding wall, his war hammer raised over his head.

Wilder's heart shot into his throat.

There was no way a strike from that hammer could kill the reaper, only momentarily divert its attention from Thea... But Torj was airborne, hurtling towards the monster, and the portal of darkness behind it.

'*Torj, no!*' someone in the distance screamed, realising at the same time as Wilder that he was buying Thea time with his life, that he would be swallowed by the black vortex.

All Wilder could do was watch as the Bear Slayer's mighty form soared through the air, his hammer poised for impact. It was as though time had stagnated in the final moments before his death —

A formidable crack cleaved through what little remained of the fortress, and a blaze of light blinded Wilder. Staggering back, the wraiths falling away from his body, he shielded his eyes, blinking through spotted vision to see a bolt of lightning collide with Torj's hammer.

It hadn't come from Thea, who was still overrun with monsters on the ground herself. It had come from the parapet.

Where Wren was holding out a trembling hand.

The iron seemed to absorb the shock, the power of her storm magic, sparks racing through the runes on the weapon as Torj soared through the air and brought his hammer down on the reaper's head.

Its horns shattered upon impact. With lightning still crackling from his hammer, Torj drove the creature down into the ground, the mass of darkness, the swirling vortex surging for them both. Shadow erupted as the Warsword hit the cobbles and tendrils of obsidian obscured everything from view, swallowing the reaper and the Bear Slayer whole.

Wilder loosed a shaky breath, his whole body tense as he took a step forward, towards the dissipating coils of night.

Shouts sounded from those on the parapets as they saw first what the vanishing shadows revealed.

Solid ground; strange, scorched patterns extending out across the cracked cobbles.

Torj Elderbrock had sealed the portal, banishing the reaper and the monsters closest to it back to the festering pit from which they'd come.

The Warsword hadn't succumbed to the pull of the darkness. He knelt on one knee in the rubble, braced over his hammer, sparks still flitting along the iron. Torj lifted his head slowly, and Wilder froze.

The golden-haired warrior was no more. He had been kissed by lightning and thunder, and scorch marks blackened the ground where he knelt. Thrumming with renewed Furies-given power, he stood. His hair, now silver, caught in the wind as he squared his shoulders. His gaze, now as dark as the shadows he'd vanquished, went to the young storm wielder on the parapet.

'Holy shit...' Wilder muttered, words Torj himself would usually say.

He felt Thea at his side, following his stare from the Bear Slayer to Wren. 'Incredible,' she whispered. 'She let him wield her power.'

And then the moment was gone, swallowed up by the rest of the battle still raging on. Talemir and Dratos chose that moment to land before them. The determination blazing in their eyes was all the confirmation Wilder needed.

Facing Thea, he grasped her hands in his. 'We have to go to the cliffs now. There, you can end it.'

Thea gave a single nod. 'Yes,' she said simply.

'What about Wren?' Talemir motioned to the flashes of light atop the walls.

Wilder shook his head. 'Her magic is needed here. She needs to defend what's left of our forces.' He turned back to Thea and cupped her jaw, forcing her eyes to meet his. 'You can do this. You were forged with blood and steel, with lightning and thunder... You were made for this war, made to end it, and you will, for all of us. When I first saw you spying on the Warsword meeting atop the cliffs, I sensed it in you even then.'

Tears lined Thea's eyes. 'What?'

'Greatness,' he told her.

CHAPTER FORTY-NINE

THEA

Wrapped in shadow, Talemir and Dratos took Thea and Wilder to the edge of the world. A red dawn bled into the horizon, illuminating the cold, hard lines of Thezmarr's black cliffs, hemmed in by jagged mountains and savage seas. Below, giant waves barrelled through the clouds. Thea could taste the storm on her tongue as her boots hit the rocky terrain.

Darkness rippled from the ledges above, and Thea didn't hesitate to start towards it. She was ready to unleash her wrath upon the monsters who'd taken her sister from her, who'd all but ripped the world in two. She was ready to end this madness once and for all.

Thea recognised where she was instantly. The caves where Cal and Kipp had almost died, where a storm had raged and brought her to her knees, the weight of her power nearly overcoming her. It was where Wilder had first witnessed her magic, too, and asked, *Who are you?*

Now, she knew. She was Althea Embervale, Warsword,

storm wielder, heir of Delmira, enemy to Jasira Fairmoore and the reapers... And she would be the end of them.

At the mouth of the cave, shadows lashed out, but Thea was ready. She seared them with her lightning and called upon the storm. Rain came down in a torrent, lashing back at the darkness, beating it into submission, revealing Princess Jasira beyond.

The stench was overwhelming, as was the hissing of reapers and wraiths behind her. 'It's the reaper lair,' Thea told Wilder and the others. 'The one Anya was searching for. Destroy the monsters within. Her Highness is mine to finish.'

Jasira didn't even try to stop the warriors as they pushed past her into the cave at Thea's orders. Instead, she licked her lips and studied Thea, as though she were a hunter and Thea her prey.

'You truly think you can best the Daughter of Darkness? I was prophesied to end this world.'

'Perhaps you were...' Thea said, taking a step towards the princess, her hand brushing against the hilt of her sword. 'And perhaps I was prophesied to start it anew.'

We are all daughters of darkness. Audra's words came back to her as an echo, and there, atop the jagged cliffs, Thea summoned her magic, that kernel within blooming into something savage, something fierce. She had brought lightning and thunder down on the fortress and its monsters, but here... here was the truest monster of all.

Ignoring the lash of Jasira's shadows, and the screams of the reapers within the cave, Thea tipped her head to the sky, and conjured her storm. It roiled within her, and answered her call from beyond the cliffs, dark clouds rolling in, rain pelting down.

She met Jasira's gaze and her storm eclipsed the darkness, fracturing the sky into a thousand pieces with brilliant bolts of lightning. Their heat cracked stone, shearing through rock and earth and shadow. Waves gathered in the violent seas below, breaking against the cliffs in giant deluges of white foam.

Thea mastered it all.

The prophecy hummed in her mind, a reminder, a promise.

In the shadow of a fallen kingdom, in the eye of the storm...

Her storm raged, a war song of vengeance for the midrealms. This tempest was like no other; it was her masterpiece – a rich tapestry of wind, rain, lightning and thunder, all of it surging not only with her power, but with Anya's too. And when she could hold it in her body no longer, when it was on the brink of bursting from her chest, her hand gripped her sword.

A daughter of darkness will wield a blade in one hand...

Thea channelled her power through her entire being and unsheathed her Furies-given Naarvian steel, sending the lightning right down the blade.

And rule death with the other...

Thea had ruled death time and time again, so many times she had become its shadow. Bolts of blinding white danced along the steel as she closed the gap between herself and Jasira in three quick steps.

When the skies are blackened, in the end of days...

The princess' eyes widened, her shadows faltering.

'It ends here, Jasira,' Thea said quietly.

'It never ends, Thea. You think it matters that you might take the fortress? My darkness is everywhere. In the air around us, in the land, in the hearts of monsters and men. In *you*.'

Thea struck out with her lightning —

Jasira's shadows swallowed it whole.

Gripping her sword, Thea lunged, but an invisible force hit her hard in the chest and her knees buckled beneath her, her blade clattering to the ground. She suddenly couldn't take in enough air, and she gasped raggedly, her lungs burning as empath magic assaulted her.

Jasira faded from her vision, and in her place was Wren, a vine blight wrapping itself around her as she screamed in agony. It drew her into its tangled, poisonous nest as her limbs flailed and she sobbed.

Thea shouted, but no sound came out.

Sam and Ida's heads on spikes came next, their expressions frozen in horror, their faces lined with evidence of their horrific torment.

Bile hit the back of Thea's throat.

A flash of shadow momentarily blinded her before revealing Anya's broken corpse on the cobblestones of the fortress. And Kipp's. And Cal's. All dead.

'No!' The word came out as a whisper.

Thea was on the blood-slick cobbles with them, and Wilder was dying in her arms, the light leaving his silver eyes.

'It never ends,' Jasira said again, her voice distant and eerie.

A vicious onslaught of images attacked Thea – memories, fears, futures that threatened to come to pass, all encompassing her in a whirlwind of pain and sorrow that had her choking on her sobs.

This was what the most powerful empath in history could do backed by shadow magic, backed by an army of monsters.

On her knees, tears streaming down her face, breath shuddering out of her, Thea reached for the one thing she had left. Her fingertips brushed the jewelled dagger at her belt.

'You were not born to wield steel and steel alone.'

Lightning crackled in her veins once more and she felt an otherworldly presence surround her – not one of darkness and malice, but one of fury.

Iseldra. Morwynn. Valdara.

They were here.

The Furies were with her.

'There are few who can face themselves as well as their nightmares and emerge whole on the other side,' they whispered.

Shadows dispersed, revealing the former Princess of Harenth, her eyes wide.

Unsheathing the fine blade, Thea staggered to her feet, charging the steel with her storm magic, her Warsword vows coming back to her in a rush of power.

'I swore to cast the evil from these lands. I swore to hunt, punish and kill any and all who threaten these kingdoms. It *does* end, Jasira. And it ends with you.'

'No, I —'

Thea thrust her dagger between the princess' ribs, through flesh and bone, just like she'd done to all the monsters who'd come before.

Jasira let out a gasp as the blade penetrated her heart. Her hands shot out, gripping Thea as her legs gave way beneath her.

Thea let her slide to the ground, her dagger still protruding from Jasira's chest. Behind them, Wilder, Talemir and Dratos emerged, covered in black blood, gaping at the storm raging around the cliffs.

The Veil will fall.

A rumbling noise sounded in the distance.

Beyond the churning seas, beyond the forks of lightning and roiling clouds, the impenetrable wall of mist, which had guarded and then haunted the midrealms for as long as anyone could remember, shuddered.

The impact reverberated in the earth beneath their boots, in the mountains past the cliffs, and in whatever realms existed outside their own.

In one cascading wave, the Veil fell.

And beyond it was golden light.

Thea slid her dagger from Jasira's heart, wiping the blood on the dead princess' cloak and turning to face the receding tempest.

The tide will turn when her blade is drawn.

Her storm took the remaining tendrils of darkness with it, revealing the sun's watery morning rays, the blood-stained cliffs, and the plumes of smoke drifting from the rubble that was once the fortress of Thezmarr.

Thea slid her hand into Wilder's as they surveyed the scorched world before them.

'A dawn of fire and blood,' Wilder murmured.

CHAPTER FIFTY

THEA

In the light of day, the devastation across Thezmarr was brutal. The once formidable stone walls that had stood tall for centuries had been reduced to piles of rubble and debris, some parts still on fire.

As Talemir set Thea down in the ruined courtyard, her knees threatened to give way. Once, it had been a hub of bustling activity, where warriors readied their horses, where shieldbearers were given their orders for the day. Now it was a sea of broken weapons, scorched earth and lifeless bodies. The cobblestones – or what remained of them – were stained with black and red blood, marking where defenders of the midrealms had fallen against their monstrous enemy.

Thea's storm had swept away the scent of burnt hair, but in its place, the air was thick with the metallic tang of blood and the heavy odour of burning wood. Beyond the courtyard, the fortress itself was in ruins too. Heart sinking, Thea approached the edge of a crater in the building. The mighty stone Furies, the monuments Thea had vowed to carve Anya's name upon, had toppled, taking half of the Great Hall with them.

'What happened here?' Her voice was raw, and she wasn't speaking to anyone in particular, just staring in a daze at the mass of rubble.

'Kipp blew it up from below,' Wilder said at her side. 'There was a portal... The hall was overrun with wraiths...'

'And the wraiths, the howlers...?' Her eyes roamed the splintered timber, the dust drifting through the air, the broken bodies among the wreckage.

'Those who were sired by the reapers we killed on the cliffs perished,' Talemir answered, approaching the pit of debris, his arms folded over his chest.

Drue came to his side, nodding. 'They turned to ash right before our eyes. Your and Wren's storms swept them away in the wind.'

'And the rest?' Thea pressed.

'We killed all the remaining howlers. We took no prisoners —'

'But the wraiths? The reapers? Those who weren't linked to the ones killed in the caves?'

Drue sighed. 'We did what we could. Cal and his men shot them out of the sky. But we didn't get them all. Without an aerial force of our own, we couldn't run them down. Some escaped.'

Thea's stomach roiled with unease.

'It was the best we could hope for,' Audra's voice sounded.

Thea looked up at her former warden, the former librarian of Thezmarr, her armour slick with blood, her weapons still unsheathed at her sides.

399

Following Thea's gaze to the blades, she shrugged. 'We've been finishing off any wounded monsters on the grounds.'

'Good.' Thea tore her eyes away from the remnants of the Great Hall, her gaze instead drifting to where she and Wren had left Anya's body. 'We need to...' She trailed off, suddenly unable to form the words.

Wilder's hand found the small of her back, his sturdy presence offering a small measure of comfort. 'Without being sure of the fortress' structural stability, we've got no choice but to assemble in the open. Gather any commanders and people of influence left standing in the courtyard.'

As exhausted and bereft as everyone was, they did as he bid, putting the call out to the far reaches of the battlefield.

In a daze, Thea surveyed the familiar faces that convened in the dust and blood, amid the bodies and the ruins. Wilder, Talemir, Drue and Audra were already there, but Thea breathed a sigh of relief as she spotted Cal and Kipp. The Guardians were covered in cuts and scrapes and dirt, but seemed otherwise unharmed. She spied Farissa sitting on an upturned barrel, her head in her stained hands.

Adrienne and Esyllt staggered forth from the ruined building, both coated in dust and Furies knew what else, the weapons master leaning on Adrienne for support. Thea couldn't see where he was wounded, but his face was contorted with pain.

'We can't find Osiris,' Esyllt said. 'The spineless coward must have run off after —'

'We'll find him,' Audra cut him off. 'He will answer for his crimes, one way or another.'

Panic rose in Thea's throat as she scanned the limping women warriors, the handful of shadow-touched soldiers, and the group of midrealms folk who were scattered around the courtyard, all bearing signs of injury.

'Where's Wren?' she demanded. 'Where's —'

'She's right here,' Torj Elderbrock answered, striding into the courtyard with Wren a few steps behind him.

Thea stared at the Warsword for a moment, at the changes the battle had wrought upon him. Against the blood and dirt covering his powerful frame, his now-silver hair seemed more prominent, and the sea-deep blue of his eyes brimmed with an emotion Thea couldn't pinpoint.

No one addressed the change in his appearance. They simply stared at the lightning-kissed Warsword in their midst, until Wren pushed past him, holding a bandage to her neck.

'What happened to you?' Thea asked, noting the blood staining the linen.

'She got cocky with her lightning,' Torj replied with a shake of his head. 'Missed the reaper that was —'

'That's not what happened,' Wren said. 'I —'

A shout cut through Wren's words, and everyone's eyes snapped to where Dratos had fallen to his knees in the wreckage. There, he lifted Anya's lifeless body to his chest with a broken cry.

Thea's heart fractured all over again, watching the shadow-touched ranger cling to her dead sister. She made to move towards him, to comfort him, but Adrienne and Drue were already halfway there.

The Naarvians crouched at their friend's side, but he shot to his feet, his wings flaring at his back. 'I can't do this —' His voice cracked, and without another word, he launched himself skyward.

A heavy silence fell across the courtyard. Thea felt Anya's

absence keenly, like a piece of herself had been ripped away, leaving a gaping hole in its wake. She should be there with them. Though hard-won, the victory was just as much Anya's as anyone else's. Thea hated the injustice of it all.

Anguish and loss hung thick in the air, wrapping around those left standing like a shroud. All Thea wanted to do was find somewhere quiet to curl up in a ball, away from the heaviness of everyone else's sorrow. But in the midst of the profound sadness, she felt a flicker of something else: lightning. Not her own, not Wren's, but Anya's, gifted to them, a power to strengthen their resolve. And that was exactly what they needed in that moment – *resolve*.

She took a deep breath and straightened, pushing her shoulders back as she surveyed the group. 'There will come a time to mourn our dead,' she said, fighting to keep her voice steady. 'But there is work to be done here.' Her eyes were tired and gritty, burning with unshed tears as they sought Kipp and Esyllt in the small crowd. 'I take it there are practicalities that need to be carried out? Logistics of the aftermath of all this?'

Kipp nodded. 'We need to assess the casualties, and categorise them: wounded, missing and dead...' He faltered at the last word.

Esyllt took over. 'With the fortress' foundations in question, I suggest we set up a temporary infirmary in the training arena for those who need more extensive treatment. It's not ideal, given its openness and its distance from here, but we don't want anything collapsing on top of our wounded while we tend to them.'

A murmur of agreement followed.

'We can burn our dead on the Plains of Orax, as is tradition,' the weapons master continued. 'When those

things are done, we can look to the future. But for now…
For now we do what we can.'

Completely numb, Thea helped carry the wounded to the
training arena on stretchers until she was unsteady on her
own feet. It wasn't until a gentle hand guided her to a seat
that she realised she'd stopped in her tracks and was staring
into nothingness.

'Let's take a look at that head wound.' Wilder's voice
brought her back from the darkness, as it always did.

'It's fine.'

'I wasn't asking,' he said.

Thea closed her eyes as his fingers parted the hair at the
back of her skull, the sensation distant, as though it were
happening to someone else. She hardly registered the sting
of matted hair being prised from the wound, nor the burn of
the rubbing alcohol Wilder used to clean it.

'It needs to be stitched,' he told her.

She didn't have the energy to reply. She simply sat there
with her eyes closed against the throb of pain behind her lids
as he worked. Thea barely felt the pinch and pull of the
needle and thread.

'Did someone check Wren?' she asked, remembering the
bloodied bandage her sister had been clutching.

'Farissa is with her now,' Wilder answered quietly.

'Is anyone else hurt?' She realised how stupid the words
sounded as they left her lips. Everyone was hurt, the pain far
deeper than any delivered by the slash of a blade.

When Wilder was done with her sutures, she forced him
down onto the seat she'd occupied and surveyed him

critically. She had seen him go down beneath the onslaught of those wraiths in the courtyard when the portal had opened up like the maw of a great beast. Both of them had taken the brunt force of those monsters, and unsurprisingly, her Warsword looked worse for wear. He was covered in slashes and scrapes, which she tended to with the fresh linen and rubbing alcohol. Wilder didn't so much as flinch at her ministrations. He was clearly in shock as well, and it was enough to coax her from her own mind.

Thea knelt before him and waited until his silver eyes met hers. 'We survived,' she told him. 'You and me… We're here. We're still standing.'

Slowly, Wilder nodded. 'We are.'

Thea cupped his face and brought her mouth to his in a soft, tender kiss. 'I love you,' she whispered against his lips.

He took a deep breath, as though he were savouring the moment, savouring her; as though the fact that he was able to do so surprised him. 'I love you, too.'

As much as Thea wished they could stay in that moment, the realities of the aftermath of war were far from over. Ignoring the protests in her muscles, she got to her feet and offered Wilder her hand. 'They'll be lighting the pyres soon,' she said. 'Will you come with me to say goodbye?'

His roughened palm slid against hers and he stood with her. 'Always.'

The Plains of Orax had somehow emerged from the battle largely unscathed, the grassy stretch of land unblemished by the violence that had stained the fortress. It was a surreal

sight. The only evidence of the conflict here were the pyres
that littered the fields.

Thea had only seen the funeral rites once before, when
they'd burned Lachin and five other Thezmarrians after the
reaper battle amid the ruins of Delmira. She was worlds
apart from the girl who had stood there that day, watching
the flames climb higher, until they kissed the sky.

Now, the pyres were countless, and larger, holding more
dead than Thea dared to imagine. It had been one thing to
witness the fall of so many in the chaos of battle, but to see
their lifeless bodies lining the timber structures, to watch
Audra's warriors pack bundles of wood around each base,
ready to be lit... Thea struggled to swallow the lump in her
throat as she spotted Wren by a pyre closer to the cliff's
edge: Anya's.

Wilder squeezed her hand, but even he couldn't quell the
wave of grief and regret that rushed through her as they
approached Wren. They had lost Samra and Ida. And they
had lost Anya twice: once as small children, when she'd been
ripped away from them, and now, after they'd just found
each other once again. Thea felt the injustice bitterly, along
with a tangle of other emotions. Anya had been her sister,
but they hadn't known each other long. The grief she felt at
her loss was also the loss of what they could have had, had
fate been kinder, had they been able to cherish that bond of
sisterhood into later life. The pain was so raw, and so deep
that Thea felt it in the marrow of her bones. All the while, a
little voice in her head told her: *it should have been you.*

Trying to gather herself, Thea released Wilder's hand and
went to the edge of the plains, looking out onto the Chained
Islands off the coast of Thezmarr. It was where she, Cal and
Kipp had completed their initiation tests as shieldbearers,

where she'd taken the first official step to becoming a Warsword of the midrealms. The small archipelago remained unchanged, its islands linked by thick chains, towering high above the crashing waves below. Something else had changed, though... Beyond the jagged rock faces, where a wall of mist had once stood, was a vast expanse of sea and light.

'Thea?' Wren called.

She started, having lost herself to whatever lay beyond the horizon. Turning back, she saw that not only Wren and Wilder were waiting for her, but Cal, Kipp, Talemir, Drue, Torj, Adrienne, Audra, Esyllt and Farissa as well.

'Dratos?' she asked, only for Talemir to shake his head.

'I think Dratos will say his own farewell elsewhere,' the Shadow Prince told her sadly.

Thea hurt for Anya, that one of her oldest, closest friends wasn't here for her funeral. But she understood, as best she could, that people had to grieve in their own way, and that Dratos' grief had taken him far away from this place. She only hoped he'd gone somewhere with happier memories of Anya.

Thea peered over the arrangement of sticks to look upon her sister one last time. In death, the hard lines of her face had softened; even the brutal scar down her eye seemed less vicious. Thea hoped it meant she had found some semblance of peace in whatever came after this life. Her scythe rested across her chest, along with her fate stone...

Thea couldn't stop herself from reaching for it, turning the jade over against the worn fabric of Anya's clothes, only to find the stone completely smooth.

The number that had been engraved there was gone.

'I didn't think you'd want to keep it,' Wren said quietly at her side.

'You were right.' Thea placed the piece of jade back with Anya and stepped away.

All around the Plains of Orax, torches were being touched to the kindling beneath the pyres, flames blooming to life and licking up the timber frames.

'Does anyone wish to say something?' Adrienne asked as one of Audra's warriors came forth with a torch for them.

Thea's words got stuck in her throat, and tears stung her eyes as Wren fidgeted at her side. Even at a glance, her younger sister seemed different: harder somehow, older.

Wren lifted her chin, revealing a jagged cut down the column of her throat, and addressed their friends.

'It feels strange to be the one to speak of Anya, when many of you knew her for so much longer,' she began. 'But she was our sister. It was a rocky start at first... but by the end, she was a part of us. We gather here now to remember her. Anya was complicated, but steadfastly loyal to her cause and her companions... She was a mosaic of contradictions, a blend of darkness and light, and as such, she mirrored the very heart of humanity.'

Wren sniffed. Still not able to find the words herself, Thea put a comforting arm around her as she continued.

'Anya faced every challenge in her life with an unmatched ferocity, and yet, behind her steel exterior, there was a heart that beat with loyalty and love for those she held dear. When the dust has settled and we break bread together again, I hope we can celebrate her bravery on the battlefield, her resilience outside of it, and her unbreakable spirit.'

Wren's words sank into Thea, and at long last, she let the tears spill down her face, a soft cry escaping her lips.

It should have been me. It should have been me.

With a nod to Wren, Talemir took the offered torch and stepped towards the pyre. 'I wish it were Dratos doing this honour. He knew Anya the longest...' Talemir hesitated, but with a nod of encouragement from Drue, he cleared his throat. 'Rest in peace, dear friend. You will be remembered and cherished as long as tales of valour are told.'

Tears flowed freely down Thea's face as Talemir touched the torch to the tinder beneath the pyre, and the fire roared to life. Flames engulfed the timber structure, swallowing Anya with it. Thea watched the blaze intensify, plumes of smoke drifting up into the sky to gather with the rest.

She was still holding Wren when her sister's head came to rest on her shoulder, her tears wetting Thea's shirt, her body shuddering with silent cries.

'She gave us her power,' Wren murmured, staring into the flames. 'What in the realms do we do with it?'

'Use it well, I guess...' Thea closed her eyes against the heat of the fire, allowing it to warm her face. 'But not now.'

'What now, then?' Wren asked.

Thea opened her eyes, watching the flames climb higher, watching the smoke drift towards that bright horizon. 'Now, we say farewell.'

CHAPTER FIFTY-ONE

WILDER

T he days that followed were a blur. Wilder spent much of them assessing the damage to the fortress with Torj and Vernich. To the naked eye, Thezmarr's mighty stronghold was in pieces – the Great Hall was gone and the outer walls were no more than piles of rubble. But the fortress had good bones, and there was much that could yet be saved. The residences, the teaching quarters and the war room, of all things, were salvageable with the right reinforcements.

As they worked, there was no missing the change in Torj, not to mention his new look, which took some getting used to. Wilder found himself startled more than once by his friend's silver hair and dark eyes, and the glimpse of lightning-shaped scars across his tattooed chest peeking through the fabric of his shirt.

'Quit the fucking staring,' the Bear Slayer finally snapped, and Wilder could hardly blame him.

'Sorry,' he muttered, busying his hands with the weapons inventory before glancing up at his friend again. His fellow

Warsword had been distant since his brush with lightning, distant and deep in thought. 'Torj?' he asked.

'What?'

Wilder braced himself for anger. 'Are you alright?'

Torj looked up from his task, his eyes stormy as they fell upon Wren, who was grinding herbs in a mortar across the hall. 'When did you know?' he said, voice low.

Wilder's brow furrowed. 'Know what?'

'That Thea was the one for you?'

Rubbing the back of his neck, Wilder felt a pang of sympathy for the Bear Slayer, whose dark gaze hadn't left the beautiful alchemist. 'I always knew,' Wilder told him honestly.

Torj nodded with a sigh of resignation. 'Figured as much.'

The clean-up efforts were intense, so much so that Wilder hadn't yet had the chance to return to his cabin with Thea. As much as he longed to sink into his own bed and wrap his arms around her, most nights they simply slept where they collapsed from exhaustion.

Adrienne was overseeing the clearing of the courtyard. Her face was grief-stricken, but she gave out orders with her usual efficiency. Masses of rubble were removed, catapults dismantled and discarded weaponry gathered. The Naarvian general did what she could, but it would be months, maybe even years until Thezmarr was in any semblance of a working state again. Her efforts, however, did yield another result: the discovery of Osiris' hiding place. The former Guild Master was discovered in a partially ruined chamber, cowering as he had through the entire battle. Adrienne saw him put in chains and under guard to await Thezmarr's judgement, though Wilder knew he wasn't alone in secretly wishing she'd simply cut his throat.

Thea was caught up in talks with Wren, Audra, Kipp and Esyllt. Wilder saw the ravens come and go from the armoury, which they'd commandeered as their meeting house, though he didn't give much thought to whom these messages were sent. No one had seen King Leiko since before the battle at Aveum; Queen Reyna was still licking her wounds from said battle, while King Artos awaited trial in her ice dungeons. It left two of the three kingdoms without rulers, and the third hanging on by a mere thread. With Anya gone, Thea was now heir apparent to Delmira, but no one had broached the subject yet, which was wise. They had enough to deal with as it was. Plans for long-fallen kingdoms could wait.

With Farissa at the helm, Audra's warriors helped tend to the wounded, and the makeshift infirmary at the training arena was less full by the day. People from all walks of life who'd taken part in the battle returned to the fortress, injuries healed, ready to assist in whatever way they could.

No one had heard from Dratos since he'd found Anya's body, and Wilder didn't expect they would for some time. He didn't know if the nature of their relationship went beyond friends, but he had glimpsed that grief when he'd thought Thea lay dying in his arms... If Dratos needed to take to the skies to find reprieve from something similar, then Wilder would never begrudge him that.

～

As they slowly started to put the broken pieces of Thezmarr back together, Wilder sensed another farewell on the horizon. Sure enough, late one afternoon, Talemir approached him in the stables.

'It's time we returned to Naarva,' the Shadow Prince said, a note of regret in his voice.

Though it felt like a punch to the gut, Wilder dipped his head. 'I understand. You need to get back to Ry.'

'We've already been gone too long.'

Wilder cleared his throat and offered his hand. 'It's been an honour to fight alongside you again.'

Talemir glanced down at his hand before knocking it away abruptly and pulling him into a hard embrace. 'The honour has been mine, brother.'

Wilder gripped his former mentor's shoulders. 'Thank you... For all that you've done. Now, then... and in the years between. Without you, we wouldn't have won this war.'

'We all had our part to play.' Talemir smiled, releasing him. 'I almost called you "Apprentice" then... But —'

'You realised I haven't been your apprentice in over a decade?'

'I can't be that old.'

Wilder scoffed. 'I assure you, you are.'

'Matured like a fine wine then, eh?' Talemir said with a grin.

'If that's what you need to believe.'

A pointed cough sounded from the door. 'About time you two kissed and made up,' Drue said with a note of amusement. She gave Wilder a wink before she addressed Talemir. 'I miss our son and his menacing ways. Take me home, husband.'

Talemir beamed at her, as though hearing the word

husband from her lips still gave him joy after all these years. 'I was just saying goodbye.'

Drue came forward and wrapped her arms around Wilder. 'Don't be a stranger, Hawthorne,' she said. 'Naarva is no secret now, and we'd love to have you and Thea any time.'

'Thank you,' Wilder replied. 'I hope it's not long before we see you again.'

Terrence soared into the stables then, landing on Drue's shoulder with an impatient squawk. Apparently the hawk was ready for the kingdom of gardens as well.

Wilder walked them out to the corral, where Talemir's wings materialised and his shadows swirled as he pulled his wife into his arms.

Wilder raised a hand in farewell. 'Be seeing you,' he said.

When Talemir and Drue had gone, Wilder found Thea alone in the armoury, poring over a spread of maps and scrolls. She was rubbing her temples with a grimace.

Wilder leant against the doorframe. 'Long day?'

Thea's gaze snapped up to his, her frustration instantly softening at the sight of him. 'The longest.'

'I was going to go back to the cabin. Come with me?'

She pushed off from her workstation and came to him, wrapping her arms around his waist and locking them at the small of his back. 'Gods, yes,' she muttered, resting her forehead against his chest.

He huffed a laugh and kissed the top of her head. 'Come on, then.'

With their arms around each other, they walked through the woods, towards the western foot of the mountains. The further they got from the fortress, the less evidence of the battle there was. Soon they were surrounded by trees, and it was as though the scorched ruins of Thezmarr were a distant dream.

'We haven't talked about it,' Wilder ventured, with a tentative glance at the beautiful woman at his side.

Thea gave a rough laugh. 'There hasn't been much time for talking yet... And you'll have to be more specific.'

After a moment, Wilder said, 'It wasn't your fate stone.'

'No, it wasn't.' Thea chewed on her lower lip, deep in thought. 'It doesn't feel right to celebrate it – that my life isn't over... Not when it cost Anya hers.'

'I understand.'

'Truthfully, I don't know how I feel about any of it yet. That for all those years, I let a fate stone that wasn't mine influence how I behaved, the choices I made...' She looked up at him. 'But how can I regret anything? How can I be sorry when everything led me to you?'

Wilder saw the conflict in her eyes, the unbroken swell of a summer storm. He wished he could take that pain, that guilt away, but he knew better than anyone that it was her burden to bear, that only she could free herself from its confines.

'But I'm grateful,' she said suddenly. 'Grateful that it's not the end, grateful that I get this time with you. That we have our lives together ahead of us.'

He stroked his thumb down the back of her hand. 'As am I.'

Thea smiled at him then, and for a moment, it was as though the war had never happened, as though shadows had never ruled. She shone brighter for him than the sun.

'Gods, I love you,' he told her. He had promised himself

he'd never hold back from saying it again, that when the words rose in his chest he would say them to her, wherever they were, whatever they were doing.

'I love you, too,' she said.

But her smile froze as his cabin came into view, and she stopped them in their tracks.

Wilder followed her gaze to his home.

Scorch marks scored the once-quaint porch. What had not been burned away was splintered and broken, including the front door.

'Wilder...' Thea breathed. 'I'm so sorry...'

Shocked, he said nothing, but approached the cabin, dread turning his stomach leaden. Inside, the place was no better. Parts of it had been set alight. The roof of the bedroom had caved in. His belongings were scattered across the floor in pieces, his potted plants either missing or ruined.

Wilder ran his fingers through his hair and sighed. 'I don't think this was done by wraiths and reapers...'

'What then? Howlers?'

He shook his head. 'I think this was done long before Thezmarr was taken by the enemy. It must have been after Notos, when I was declared a fallen Warsword.'

Thea seemed shocked. 'You think Thezmarrians did this?'

Wilder huffed a laugh. 'You're forgetting your own anger so easily. Remember how you felt? Imagine that in the birthplace of Warswords...' He crouched by a bit of missing floor, where dirt and ash met splintered timber. 'This isn't recent. The embers here haven't been hot for a long time.'

Thea made a noise of despair, hugging her arms to her stomach as though she felt physical pain at the broken sight before them. 'Your beautiful home...'

'It's just a building, Thea,' he told her. 'You're my true home.'

'But...'

Shaking his head, he went not to her, but to the untouched cupboard against the wall. There, he rummaged through the shelves until he found what he was looking for.

He held out the arrow to her, and when she took it from him with a look of disbelief, he smiled.

She turned it over in her hands, eyes wide. 'You kept it?'

It was the arrow he'd shot at her when he'd found her spying on the shieldbearers in the Bloodwoods. The arrow that she'd gripped in the tree above her as he'd fucked her for the first time.

'Of course I kept it,' he told her. 'It's always been you, Thea. And as long as I'm with you, you're the only home I'll ever need.'

Wilder took her in his arms then, his gaze drifting back to that broken patch of floor, noting a speck of colour for the first time.

'Look,' he murmured, pointing it out to Thea.

For amid the ashes, something bloomed.

Leaning down, he kissed Thea, long and slow. Despite the wreckage of his cabin, hope awakened in his chest. For the first time in a long time, he realised that beneath the festering darkness, the world had been beautiful, and it would be again.

CHAPTER FIFTY-TWO

THEA

The weeks after the battle for Thezmarr were long and gruelling, but there was nothing Thea was dreading more than the meeting due to start at any moment. She'd already put it off for as long as she could.

Ironically, the war council chamber was one of the largely untouched remnants of the fortress, the room unchanged but for the boarded-up window behind the thick curtains that were now in tatters. It had always been dimly lit, though someone had recently added more candles so it wasn't as dark. Their flickering light illuminated the mahogany table running down the room's centre. Six high-backed chairs surrounded it, along with several other mismatched seats that had been crammed in at the last minute. With the nearby shelf overflowing with books and the trolley of decanters in the far corner, Thea wasn't sure how they would all fit, but to her dismay, they managed.

Soon, she found herself seated at the head of the table, with Wilder to her right and Audra to her left. Something was different about her former warden. She wore her spectacles again, and her usual stern expression, but...

'Your daggers,' Thea blurted. She had returned the one in her possession only days before. 'Where are your daggers?' The jewelled weapons had been a part of Audra for as long as Thea could remember. She was never seen without them strapped to her belt.

'I had to give them back sometime,' Audra replied, with a note of amusement.

'Back to who?' Thea blinked. 'Weren't they yours?'

'More of a long-term loan...' Audra's eyes twinkled. 'From Iseldra, Morwynn and Valdara.'

'The daggers belong to the *Furies?*'

'What did I tell you, Thea? The smallest blade can make the biggest difference.'

Gobsmacked, Thea opened her mouth – to say what, she didn't know – but the rest of the room had now filled with familiar faces: Wren, Cal and Kipp, Torj, Vernich, Adrienne, Esyllt and Farissa. It felt strange to be there without Talemir and Drue, and even more surreal when Thea sought out Anya at the other end of the table, and she wasn't there. As the others settled into their seats, she kept waiting for Anya's patience to wear thin, for her to silence them with a snappy remark or sarcastic comment. Neither ever came, and it made her chest ache.

'Still no word from Dratos?' Adrienne asked, glancing around the room.

Thea shook her head. 'Not yet... but give him time.'

Adrienne merely nodded and sat back in her chair.

'Well.' Vernich's gravelly voice cut across the table. 'Who called this damn meeting?'

Thea suppressed the urge to groan and pinch the bridge of her nose. Instead, she thrust her chin at Esyllt. 'He did.'

Esyllt threw her a sharp look before addressing the company. 'It was high time we discussed the state of the midrealms and the plans we've put in motion to get the kingdoms back on their feet. First… the original fallen kingdoms.'

Thea steeled herself. 'It was agreed that we'll leave Talemir and Drue to decide how Naarva moves forward now that the shadows have receded from its lands. They'll advise us in due course what their intentions are for the kingdom and its capital.'

'And Delmira?' Torj asked.

Thea swallowed. 'I have never had any interest in being a princess or queen. That has not changed. Wren?'

Wren looked up, the movement revealing the fresh scar down her throat. 'I see no reason to raise Delmira from its ruins any time soon. It can house no displaced people, its lands are barren, and its restoration is not paramount to the tasks we find ourselves facing with the rest of the midrealms. We go where we are needed first. We do what we can. With so many of Thezmarr's great alchemists gone, that is where I mean to start.'

Thea's heart ached, both for Wren and for the loss of Sam and Ida. Wren's voice hadn't faltered, her shoulders hadn't caved, but Thea could see the tapestry of sorrow in her eyes.

'And what of Tver, Aveum and Harenth?' Adrienne asked. 'There have already been reports of riots in Hailford, and —'

'We've taken care of it,' Audra cut in. 'The beloved sister of King Artos' wife, the late Queen Maelyn, has been temporarily granted regency. The people of Harenth loved

Maelyn, so the appointment has been welcomed warmly, particularly by the common folk.'

Esyllt spoke next. 'Thankfully Queen Reyna is much recovered since the battle for Aveum. It was with the help of her visions that we were able to track down King Leiko of Tver. He was under the empath control of Princess Jasira, forced to do her bidding. Upon the princess' death, that fugue state seems to have lifted, and though he is weak, with the help of Thezmarr, he will be able to rule Tver once more.'

'Is Thezmarr in a position to offer help?' Wilder asked bluntly. 'I don't mean to detract from the good work we've done here, but —'

'It's a shithole,' Torj finished for him. 'And we have no Guild Master. Our resources are limited.'

'Then let's talk about the Guild Master,' Esyllt said, turning to Thea, determination blazing in his eyes in a way that made the hair on her nape stand up.

'What?' she blurted.

'It's yours,' Esyllt said. 'The Guild Master title.'

Thea couldn't help herself; she laughed. 'You're joking?'

'I wasn't, no...' Esyllt replied, frowning.

'All I ever wanted was to be a Warsword. Not a princess, not a Guild Master: a Warsword.'

Esyllt blinked at her as though she'd just spoken in the ancient tongue of the Furies.

'There is a person far more suited to such a role,' she countered, swinging her gaze to Audra. 'You, Audra. I can think of no one better. Take Thezmarr. You and the women it belonged to long ago. Take it back and make it your own.'

Something sparked in the librarian's eyes. 'Oh?'

'Forget the part about it being a shithole,' Thea forged on.

'Rebuild it. Forge it into what it was meant to be. The next world is what we make it, right?' She echoed Audra's own words back to her.

The corner of Audra's mouth twitched as she turned her attention to the other Warswords. 'And no one would have an issue with this?'

Wilder and Torj both shook their heads, while Vernich snorted. 'I'm retiring. Do whatever the fuck you want.'

Thea grinned at her former warden. 'Congratulations, Guild Master.'

Audra didn't quite return her grin, but the glint in her eye said just as much.

'What of our prisoner?' Adrienne asked, refocusing them on the task at hand, ever the general. 'What is to become of the former Guild Master?'

'Death,' Thea replied. 'We agreed that for his crimes, he is to be sentenced to death.'

They had laboured long and hard over that decision, debating as to how it reflected the new world they wanted to create. But in the end, it was the only justice for someone of his station who'd sold them out to monsters, who'd assisted Artos in framing a child for the evils that cursed Thezmarr long ago.

'Where is he now?' Wren asked.

'He's being held in one of the old alchemy workshops, guarded by several of Audra's best warriors,' Esyllt said.

Wren nodded. 'Good.'

Audra cleared her throat, looking to the Warswords and Adrienne. 'What news of the Veil? What consequences have arisen in the wake of its fall?'

'None,' Wilder said at Thea's side. 'By all accounts so far, it was not the barrier of protection we were told it was. It doesn't – nor did it ever – harness a world of darkness beyond... But you already know that.'

'Many suspected,' Audra admitted. 'A secret kept for millennia, its origins unknown. I always knew there were realms and kingdoms beyond it.'

'That's where your warriors were all this time?' Thea asked.

Audra looked amused. 'That's not my tale to tell.'

'What happens now that the Veil is no more?' Cal asked. 'Do we send scouts?'

'We might have to,' Esyllt replied. 'While we destroyed a great many wraiths and reapers, a handful escaped. They're our responsibility to hunt down, before they wreak this kind of horror on another realm.'

Thea's gaze flicked to Wilder. The hint of his dimple showed beneath his beard, but his eyes were trained on Esyllt.

The weapons master brought his hands together on top of the table. 'Now, onto the matter of —'

'Where's Wren?' Torj asked suddenly.

Frowning, Thea looked to the seat Wren had occupied only moments ago.

It was empty.

'Shit,' Torj said, already on his feet. '*Osiris.*'

He bolted from the room, and Thea found herself sprinting after him through the fortress, Wilder close behind. She wasn't sure she understood what the Bear Slayer was so panicked about, but it was enough to spike fear in her own chest.

They skidded to a stop before one of the old alchemy workshops, the door guarded by two of Audra's warriors.

'Is someone in there with him?' Torj demanded. 'Is someone in there with Osiris?'

The women eyed him suspiciously. 'Four of our sisters keep watch inside.'

'And?' Thea pressed, her heart racing.

'And the alchemist. She came just moments ago.'

'Did you search her?' Wilder asked. 'Did she have any weapons?'

'Wren needs no weapons,' Torj muttered, forcing his way between the guards and using his shoulder to cave the door in.

They barged inside, startling the guards stationed around the perimeter of the room, to find Wren seated at a workbench with the former Guild Master of Thezmarr, a pot of tea between them.

Thea heard the others from the meeting fill the room behind her while Wren sipped daintily from her cup, not in the least surprised by their dramatic entrance.

'W-What's going on?' Osiris stammered, placing his own cup back down on the bench. His face still bore the scabbed-over cuts from Anya's scythe, but he hadn't been harmed further in their custody.

'You left our meeting to have tea with our prisoner?' Esyllt barked from the door.

Tea. The word reverberated through Thea as her gaze dropped to the seemingly innocent pot.

But there was nothing innocent about it. It was Wren's own invention.

The Ladies' Luncheon.

Esyllt's harsh tone didn't faze Wren. Instead, she took another sip and looked to Osiris, who was growing paler by the second.

He covered his mouth to cough. Once, then twice, before he drank from his teacup again.

Suddenly, his eyes bulged, and his hands flew to his throat as he gasped for air. The ceramic cup shattered into a hundred pieces as it hit the ground.

'Good gods,' someone muttered behind Thea, but she was transfixed by the purpling of Osiris' face. Coughing and spluttering violently, the former Guild Master fell from his stool onto his knees, his hands clawing at his throat.

White spittle foamed at the corners of his mouth as he wheezed, crawling to Wren, tugging on the hem of her skirt. The alchemist drank her tea as she watched on.

Crimson lined his teeth.

Blood clotted in the corners of his eyes.

'Help me,' he choked, dribble running down his chin.

When Osiris had rasped his final breath, Wren pushed him from her skirts with the tip of her boot in disgust.

He fell back, slumping to the floor, dead.

'Elwren...' Farissa murmured, pushing to the front of the crowd, her mouth agape at her apprentice.

'We sentenced him to death,' Wren said calmly. 'I wanted to be the one to do it. The man who helped seal Anya's fate, the man who took so much from Thezmarr and the midrealms...' She surveyed the shocked expressions around the room, including Thea's. 'Did you think I'd have no stomach for what needs to be done? When it's deserved, it's an easy choice.'

Thea stared at her sister. 'Is it always so... brutal?'

'Only if you make it so.'

It was Kipp who came forward and marvelled at the Ladies' Luncheon teapot. 'I think I love you,' he told the alchemist.

Adrienne shook her head in disbelief as she approached Wren, clapping her on the shoulder. 'Killed by a teapot... I'll have to tell Drue and Tal about this.'

Hours later, when the shock of Wren's actions had worn off, Thea slipped away to the Bloodwoods. She needed silence, she needed space, she needed the comfort of the bleeding trunks and the crisp air. Only when the forest enveloped her and the canopy blocked out the afternoon sun did she breathe more easily.

She hadn't ventured through the glades since they'd marched on the fortress. Now, the shadows and vine blights had gone, leaving the forest to recover, the scent of damp earth filling Thea's nostrils once more. She inhaled it, grateful that the trees still stood, that the midrealms remained. It was surreal to think of what the world had been like only weeks before.

Thea wove through the dense trunks as she had years ago, staying off the main trail out of habit. The memory of Esyllt's voice rang out through the trees.

'A month ago you were mere students, boys whose purpose did not extend beyond the ordinary... Today, you are shieldbearers of Thezmarr and you have come here to the Bloodwoods hoping to be something far greater.'

Goosebumps rushed across Thea's skin as she reached the familiar clearing. It seemed smaller somehow. Rolling her shoulders, she reached for the throwing stars in her boot and widened her stance.

Slowly, Thea lost herself to the rhythm of old training drills and target practice. As she flicked her wrist and aimed her silver stars at a distant tree trunk, she paid tribute to Sam and Ida, who would never again play Dancing Alchemists. And Anya, who had lost and given so much. The thoughts awakened the dull ache that so often kept her company.

Next, she twirled Malik's dagger of Naarvian steel between her fingers and threw it with flawless precision, embedding it right in the centre of the stars in the tree. The sight pleased her, making her glad she hadn't lost her touch in the weeks of negotiating and planning rather than training.

Finally, she unsheathed her Warsword blade, revelling in the comfort of its perfectly balanced weight. She closed her eyes for a moment, listening to her breathing, channelling that kernel of magic to the surface, letting it dance with her Furies-given strength and agility. Then, she launched herself into a series of manoeuvres, feeling the tension ease from her body as she practised each slice, each parry, every twirl of her blade.

Princess of Delmira. Guild Master... She wanted none of it. All she'd ever wanted was this. The song of steel in her hand, the wind on her face —

A twig snapped close by, and Thea whirled around, scanning the forest.

Her gaze fell upon the tree, her silver stars gleaming there, only... her dagger was missing from the centre of the target.

'Looking for this?' came a deep, familiar voice.

Thea's heart stuttered at the sight of him.

Leaning against a tree, clad in his black armour, was the love of her life, twirling her dagger between his long, tattooed fingers. 'I know a Warsword who still needs a Tverrian stallion...'

CHAPTER FIFTY-THREE

WILDER

Watching Thea ride across the gilded hills of Tver in pursuit of her stallion was a thing of beauty. With her braid dancing in the wind behind her, she urged her mare into a gallop across the rugged landscape, lassoing her rope over her head as she rode, the mountains framing her in sage and gold.

Wilder only wished Malik and Talemir were there to see her as well. She was doing far better than he had, having spotted her stallion in the herd within moments of their arrival. He sat atop Biscuit, lifting a flask of fire extract to his lips as his brother and mentor had done, watching on in pride.

Wilder let out a cheer as Thea's rope looped around the stallion's neck and she slowed their pace, bringing the majestic creature to an angry halt, its back legs kicking out. His chest swelled as she leapt down from her mare, her cheeks flushed with exertion. She approached the rearing stallion with her hands raised, murmuring soft words Wilder couldn't hear.

Her dark brows furrowed in concentration, Thea soothed the horse, inching closer and closer until the flat of her hand rested against its gleaming black coat. The stallion huffed, but Thea continued to talk, stroking its neck gently. As the beast calmed, it stared at her, as though recognising her.

Wilder let out a breath as he witnessed it for the first time from afar: the piece of the puzzle clicking into place for the legendary beast. *Warsword. Rider.*

As though that piece had slid into place for Thea as well, she ever so slowly reached for the lead rope around the stallion's neck and removed it, the horse bowing his head as she did.

Her gaze instantly found Wilder's, a wide smile breaking across her face.

The sight nearly floored him, and for a brief moment, he was taken back to the image he'd seen when he'd been a prisoner of the Scarlet Tower – of Thea in his cabin, a simple band of silver around her fourth finger. *One day,* he vowed. *One day I'll ask her to be my wife.*

But for now, Wilder steered Biscuit towards Thea as she turned her mare loose and saddled her new stallion. 'You did it,' he said, beaming.

'Was I faster than you?' she asked, rubbing the flat of her palm against the horse's forehead as it nickered softly, nuzzling into her touch.

'Maybe,' Wilder replied with a teasing grin. 'But you know what this means? It's time to name the mighty creature. I was thinking —'

Thea threw a hand up. 'Don't you *dare.*'

Wilder laughed. 'I wouldn't dream of it.'

~

The midday sun shone in golden rays as together, they rode through the sweeping, richly textured valleys of Tver. With Thea at his side, Wilder felt more at home than he ever had in his cabin back at Thezmarr. Here, beside the crystal-blue rivers topped with white foam as they coursed through the gorges, he felt content. He felt free.

Eventually, he brought them to a beautiful woodland area and jumped down from the saddle, offering Thea his hand, though she didn't need it.

'This way,' he told her.

'Where are we going?' Brow furrowed, Thea followed him, her stallion falling into step behind her. Wilder was glad she didn't recognise the spot yet. He'd discovered that surprising Thea was one of the truest joys in his life.

'You'll see.' When they reached a small grassy glade, Wilder took her reins from her and looped them over the saddle horn. 'They can graze here,' he said.

'But Pancake —'

She stopped herself, her eyes wide. She hadn't uttered the warhorse's name aloud yet, but Wilder knew it had been on the tip of her tongue for hours. He'd planted the seed himself.

A deep laugh burst from him, and Thea put her head in her hands.

'Gods,' she muttered, cheeks flushing. 'And I thought Biscuit was a terrible name for a Warsword's horse.'

Still chuckling, Wilder laced his fingers through hers and tugged her towards the treeline. 'Biscuit and Pancake... They make quite the pair.'

'Malik's going to love it,' she said, laughing at herself. 'Are you going to tell me where we're going yet?'

Smiling to himself, Wilder said nothing as he led her through the trees, until they came upon the spot he was looking for. 'I promised I'd take you back here...'

He watched Thea's mouth fall open at the sight of the ribbons of steam drifting up from the surface of the hot springs.

With a lazy grin, Wilder removed his breastplate and shirt, letting Thea's gaze roam over the planes of his chest and the bolt of lightning he'd had inked over his heart. She bit her lip as her eyes raked lower, to the muscles along his abdomen.

'What are you waiting for, Princess?'

A soft whimper escaped Thea, which only emboldened Wilder further. Keeping his eyes locked on her, he pushed his boots off at the heel and undid his belt, and then his buttons, sliding his pants and undershorts down his thighs.

When he was completely naked before her, he took his hard cock in his hand and stroked it up and down, the tip already damp with need. 'Well?' he said.

Thea licked her lips, her hands drifting to the buttons of her shirt. 'Two can play at that game, Warsword.'

Still stroking himself, Wilder watched Thea undress, each layer that fell to the ground sending a bolt of desire straight to his balls. When she freed her breasts from the band she wore, he couldn't stand the distance any longer. He closed the gap between them in a single step and crushed her naked body to his, moaning as her nipples hardened against his chest, as his cock pressed against the soft skin of her stomach. He gripped her hair at the back of her head and forced her gaze up to his.

Silver eyes met celadon, and for a moment he simply swam in the tempest of feeling he saw there.

But he'd never known Thea for her patience. She broke eye contact, her lids fluttering closed as she kissed him, hard.

In a tangle of limbs, they claimed one another with mouths, tongues and teeth, white-hot need surging through Wilder at the feel of her. She was perfect, she was everything, and he had to bury his cock inside her, *now*.

Scooping her up in his arms, he carried Thea to the steaming water. Hissing at the heat, he walked them into the hot spring, eliciting a soft gasp from Thea.

He released her, only to back her up against the ledge, his hands tracing her curves with a quiet moan, coaxing her nipples into even harder points.

Bracing herself and gripping the edge of the spring, Thea wrapped her legs around him, drawing him close, so that his cock brushed against her core. Her head tipped back at the contact, giving him access to her breasts above the waterline. Wilder trailed kisses across her soft skin, biting softly before taking her nipple into his mouth and sucking gently.

Thea moaned, and the sound made his cock jerk against her, sending a frisson of longing through his entire body.

'I want you,' she whimpered, rolling her hips, guiding his cock down the centre of her.

He shifted beneath her and notched himself to her entrance, sucking in a breath as the overwhelming urge to drive into her took hold.

'Wilder...' she warned.

His blood heated at the needy note in her voice, and she arced against him, her thighs widening around him, demanding more. He reached between them and toyed with her clit, and with a loud cry, she writhed under his touch, water sluicing over her breasts as she panted.

'Wilder.' A demand this time.

Satisfaction bloomed at that, and he was more than happy to oblige. He took her mouth with his in a searing kiss, and he slid home.

Inch by inch by inch, he took her, and the moan that escaped him was pure carnal need.

'Fuck...' he groaned as she tightened around him and he savoured the wet heat. Gods, he would never tire of this, of the feel of her.

Wilder slid out, only to thrust back inside her, hard, sinking even deeper this time, to the point where his vision blurred from the force of it. He fell into an uninhibited, unapologetic and relentless rhythm, Thea's nails digging into his back with every thrust, unleashing something feral within him. He wanted to mark her. He wanted to possess every part of her.

'You're mine,' he told her, teasing her nipples, slamming into her to the hilt. 'You always have been.'

'Yes,' Thea cried, clawing at his back. 'More —'

He gave it to her; he gave everything to her. With every rough cant of his hips he built that pressure from within, hitting that spot deep inside of her.

'Wilder, I'm going to —'

Just the words pushed him past the point of no return, and he increased his pressure on her clit and thrust into her with a moan, feeling the first waves of his climax edge closer as she clenched around his pulsing cock.

And as they came apart in a final rush, they did so together.

Panting, Wilder rested his brow against hers and for a

moment, simply breathed her in. Even in the hot springs she smelt like sea salt and bergamot, like home. 'I love you,' he whispered against her lips.

Thea kissed him, slowly, luxuriously, as though she were memorising the taste of him before she broke away. 'I love you, too,' she said, shifting her hips.

Wilder felt himself grow hard again almost instantly, always ready for her, always wanting her. He felt Thea not only against his body, but in his bones, in his blood. She was a part of him now and forever.

Wilder slid inside her again, this time in a torturous, gradual glide, relishing how she opened for him.

He looked into her eyes, loving every flicker of that untamed storm within. 'I always said you'd be the end of me,' he told her, throat bobbing. 'But I was wrong. You're the beginning.'

EPILOGUE

THEA

Three months later

The Laughing Fox tavern was just as full as it had been before the war, and just as raucous, if not more so. A musician played the lute on the small stage at the far end, filling the room with an array of slightly off-key melodies, accompanied by the bawdy singing of patrons. The rich scent of the tavern's famous roast boar wafted from the kitchens, along with the malty aroma of spilt ale.

The dartboard and billiards table were occupied, as were all the booths and tables Thea could see. The bar at the centre of the vast room had a line three people deep all around it.

'Good to know some things don't change,' Wilder murmured in her ear with a note of amusement.

Thea smiled at that as she watched a trio of friends dance arm in arm, nearly knocking over a tray of drinks with their enthusiasm. The warm, inviting atmosphere of the Fox wrapped around her like a blanket, and she realised why

Kipp came back time and time again. Even when she was on official guild business, there was a comfort here. Not to mention the place was home to some of her fondest memories.

But as the door swung closed behind Thea and Wilder, the hair on the nape of her neck stood up, her skin prickling as the room fell silent. Her hand drifted to the pommel of her sword and Wilder tensed beside her, poised for a fight.

The letter had come from Audra, so Thea didn't know who to look out for in the crowd – perhaps Esyllt, or one of the women commanders —

Suddenly, a warm hand clapped her on the back. 'Albert! A round for the returning Warswords!' a familiar voice shouted, the tavern roaring back to life around them.

Tears pricked Thea's eyes as she took in the floppy auburn hair and the long arm waving about as orders were doled out.

'And who's paying for it this time, lad?' Albert grunted.

Thea's face split into a wide grin as Kipp had the gall to look offended, before he turned to a nearby group of patrons. 'Who wants the honour of buying these heroes a drink?'

Thea caught Wilder's eye across the group of men who spilt forth to do exactly that, offering them the three-fingered salute to their shoulders. Her Warsword simply shook his head and muttered something that sounded a lot like, 'Son of the fucking Fox...'

Kipp enveloped her in a bone-crushing hug, nearly lifting her clean off her feet. 'Ah, it's good to see you,' he said. 'Both of you.'

Thea's chest felt fit to burst and she squeezed her friend back, hard. 'I can't believe you're here. I've missed you.'

Kipp offered Wilder a grin before swiping their tray of foaming tankards from the bar and making his way towards the booths at the back. While his lanky frame had filled out a little over the last few months, Thea's heart warmed to realise that the rest of him hadn't changed a bit, evident in the wink he aimed at a nearby serving girl.

'What is this mission from Thezmarr, then?' Wilder asked.

But Kipp waved a finger in reprimand. 'All work and no play makes Warswords incredibly dull, Hawthorne.'

When they reached the booth, Thea let out a cry of surprise, her hand flying to her mouth. For there was Cal, with a broad smile, and as he stood to hug her, a jolt of shock shot through her. She grabbed him, holding him at arm's length to survey him. His hair was shorter, his shoulders were broader, but that wasn't it...

Iron gleamed at his right bicep. Thea gaped.

'*You did the Great Rite?*' she all but yelled. 'You're a fucking *Warsword?*'

Cal beamed and wrestled her into a hug. 'Couldn't let you have all the glory forever, could I?'

Thea could hardly contain her excitement. 'When did this happen? Where? How? Where's your sword?'

'At least pass the drinks around before I have to listen to that saga again,' said another familiar voice.

Torj Elderbrock strode up to their booth, fresh tankards of ale in hand. He seemed larger than life all of a sudden, his silver hair tied back in a knot, his dark blue eyes sparkling.

Queen Reyna's words came back to her then: *I have seen that gold will turn to silver in a blaze of iron and embers...*

The winter queen had foreseen the Bear Slayer's fate.

The man himself gave Thea a smile. 'Glad you're back.' Then he looked to Wilder and offered his large hand.

To Thea's – and apparently Torj's – surprise, Wilder laughed and batted it away, embracing his fellow Warsword like a long-lost brother. 'Good to see you're still keeping such entertaining company.'

'We're not all bad.'

A head of bronze hair and a pair of celadon eyes appeared at the booth's edge, and a gasp escaped Thea as Wren smiled back at her.

'If it isn't Althea Nine Lives,' her sister said, hauling her into a hug.

It had been a long three months since they'd seen one another, and Wren was more beautiful than she'd ever been. Thea had always deemed her younger sister the prettier of the pair, but now... Something about her had changed, had amplified her beauty in a way that Thea couldn't quite pinpoint —

'For Furies' sake,' Kipp whined. 'Can we *please* have a drink? You can do just as much gushing over one another sitting down with a tankard of mead in your hand.'

Still reeling from the shock of the reunion, Thea couldn't help but laugh as she slid into the booth after Wilder, Wren taking the place on her other side. Kipp, Cal and Torj took the opposite bench, looking a tad ridiculous all crammed in together, particularly with the enormous silver-haired Bear Slayer on the end. But Kipp's joy was infectious, as always. Eagerly handing out the tankards, he pulled the fullest one in front of himself and looked around.

'How about a toast?'

A collective groan sounded around the table as Kipp got to his feet and cleared his throat.

'May you walk amid the gardens of the afterlife a whole half hour —'

'Before Enovius reads your ledger of deeds,' Thea and Cal finished, knocking their tankards against their friend's, laughing.

It wasn't long before Kipp ordered another round of drinks, and another, and another, each time somehow managing to find some unsuspecting patron to foot the bill. Thea sat back against the cushion, her cheeks aching from smiling so hard. Cal was a Warsword. Kipp was as brazen and ridiculous as ever. Wren had left her poisons and potions, and was joking with the others as though she were one of them. Torj was in one piece, the corner of his mouth twitching as he not-so-subtly watched Wren.

And Wilder... Wilder's hand covered Thea's beneath the table, his dimple deep in his cheek as he laughed with the others.

There was much to catch up on, and Thea drank in the news of Thezmarr like a parched vagabond. Audra and Esyllt had overseen the rebuilding of the fortress and had opened its gates to shieldbearers once more – all were welcome. Malik had helped them rebuild the library, and when Torj had left Thezmarr just a few days ago, he'd been happily braiding belts before the hearth with Dax at his feet. True to his word, Vernich had indeed retired and now lived in a fishing village no one had ever heard of, catching trout by day, drinking fire extract by night.

No one had heard from Dratos since the final battle, and Adrienne had returned to Naarva to search for him.

Wren was in the middle of telling Thea how Farissa had sent her to retrieve some rare plants for a new experiment when Kipp gave a dramatic gasp and grabbed Wilder's arm.

439

HELEN SCHEUERER

'Remember that favour you owe me?' he asked, his gaze locked on something across the room.

'Yes...' Wilder replied tentatively.

'I'm calling it in.'

'Now?'

'*Now*,' Kipp said urgently. 'See that golden-haired beauty over there? She's been eyeing you up all night. Introduce me.'

Wilder groaned. '*That's* what you want to use a Warsword favour on?'

'I know a lot of Warswords now.' Kipp shrugged before puffing out his chest. 'And a little less judgement would be appreciated.'

Wilder barked a laugh. 'Very well, then.'

Thea and Wren had to get out of the booth to let Wilder pass, Thea appreciating his powerful form as he moved across the room to the blonde. She felt a brief stab of pity for the woman as her gaze grew hopeful at the Warsword's approach, Kipp close on his heels.

'You're Wilder Hawthorne,' she said in awe.

Wilder scraped the loose hair back from his forehead and pushed Kipp forward. 'And this is my friend, Kristopher Snowden.'

'Good friend.' The strategist sidled up to her. 'But you can call me Kipp,' he added with a charming grin.

The woman seemed confused. 'Are you a Warsword as well?'

'Furies save me, no,' Kipp replied. 'I *am*, however, the mastermind behind everything they do. Isn't that right, Hawthorne?'

Wilder rolled his eyes at Thea before turning back to Kipp and his new companion with a nod. 'Would have lost the war without him.'

The woman put a hand to her chest in shock. 'Truly?'

'Truly,' Kipp replied solemnly. 'Now tell me, have you had the sour mead here?'

Thea had to bite her fist to keep from laughing as Wilder returned to the table with a look of utter bafflement.

'I'd say you get used to it,' Cal offered with a grimace, 'but you never do.'

Chuckling, Wilder picked up his tankard of ale. 'Easiest favour I've ever given.'

'I'd watch out. He racks them up quicker than you think...'

But Thea's attention was pulled elsewhere. To the empty seat beside her. And the empty seat opposite it.

'Where's Wren?' she said suddenly. 'And Torj?'

Both Wilder and Cal looked stunned, their eyes falling to the empty spaces in the booth.

'No idea...' Cal replied at last, though his gaze flicked towards a door at the far end of the tavern.

After a moment, Thea refilled their tankards and rested her elbows on the table. 'Tell us, how are you finding Warsword life, Callahan the Flaming Arrow?'

They talked late into the night, Cal regaling them with stories of his work for the guild since earning his Naarvian steel.

'That reminds me,' he said, pulling a scrap of parchment from his pocket. 'Audra asked me to give this to you – both of you.'

Wilder took it as Cal stood – or tried to, several times, before actually managing it.

'Goodnight, friends,' he slurred happily before giving a Kipp-like bow and tottering off into the crowd.

'What is it?' Thea asked, nodding to the letter.

Wilder scanned it, his brow furrowing in concentration. 'Audra's given us a suspected location for a small group of wraiths...'

A smile tugged at Thea's lips. 'Is that so?'

'It is.' Wilder's silver gaze was bright.

'And?' she asked.

He hummed, wrapping his hand around the back of her neck and lifting her face to his. The rest of the tavern faded away as he kissed her deeply, thoroughly, as though they had all the time in the world. Now, after everything they had been through, perhaps they did.

As Thea's toes curled in her boots, he broke away abruptly.

'That depends on your answer to my question,' he teased.

'What question might that be?'

'Althea Embervale,' Wilder said, cupping her hands in his, staring deep into her eyes with nothing but love.

She drew a trembling breath, unsure of what would come next.

Wilder's answering smile was wicked. 'Will you hunt shadow wraiths with me?'

A laugh burst from Thea's lips, a broad grin spreading across her face as her heart soared. 'I thought you'd never ask.'

ACKNOWLEDGEMENTS

Imagine how dazed I am to find myself at the end of not only another book, but the finale of my third series. It's surreal to say the least, and I want to pause for a moment to tell you just how much *The Legends of Thezmarr* and your support of it has meant to me...

The truth is, this series changed my life. What started out as a 'risky' move into a romance subgenre turned out to be the gateway to one of my greatest passions, and I'm so grateful for that. These past few years of writing Thea and Wilder's story have brought me so much joy and opportunity, and many incredible new friends. Thank you for being a part of that.

As I say in every acknowledgement, the creation of these stories is by no means a solo effort, and as such, there are quite a few wonderful people I need to officially thank.

First, to the love of my life, Gary: thank you for your unending support and for your invaluable feedback. By the time this book comes out, I hope we're drinking pinot noir in front of the fireplace, brainstorming what comes next.

Thank you to Sacha Black for the pep talks, the voice memos and for beta reading this series from the very beginning.

To Anne Sengstock, I don't know how I managed without you. Thank you for being the best cheerleader, PA and friend an author could ask for. No one manages a street team like you.

Speaking of street teams, a massive thank you to every member, past and present. Your love for *The Legends of Thezmarr* has meant the world to me, and has helped the series find its readers all around the globe.

To my mum, Bronwyn, thank you for proofing these final pages, and for your support. And of course, all my love and thanks to the rest of the Scheuerer clan back in Sydney as well.

As always, thank you to my friend and editor, Claire Bradshaw. Not long until we see your incredible book on the shelves now!

Thank you to my wonderful friends who continue to show their support in numerous ways: Angelina, Meg, Eva, Lisy, Aleesha, Ben, Hannah, Natalia, Fay, Erin, Danielle, Phoebe, Maria, Podge, Joe, Bethany, Annie, Chloe and Nattie.

And of course, last, but never least... Thank you, dear reader. Having you here for this adventure has been a privilege and I hope you stick around for what's next.

Much love,

Helen

ABOUT THE AUTHOR

Helen Scheuerer is the bestselling fantasy author of the series: *The Oremere Chronicles, Curse of the Cyren Queen* and *The Legends of Thezmarr*. Her work has been highly praised for its strong, flawed female characters and its action-packed plots.

Helen's love of writing and books led her to pursue a creative writing degree and a Masters of Publishing. She has been a full-time author since 2018 and now lives amidst the mountains in New Zealand where she is constantly dreaming up new stories.

www.helenscheuerer.com

ALSO BY HELEN SCHEUERER

The Oremere Chronicles:

Heart of Mist

Reign of Mist

War of Mist

Dawn of Mist

Curse of the Cyren Queen:

A Lair of Bones

With Dagger and Song

The Fabric of Chaos

To Wield a Crown

The Legends of Thezmarr:

Blood & Steel

Vows & Ruins

Fate & Furies

Shadow & Storms

Standalones:

Slaying the Shadow Prince

Made in the USA
Monee, IL
31 October 2024

69061927R00266